Scars and Songs

Mad World Book 3
Shane's Point of View

A novel by
Christine Zolendz

Scars and Songs

Copyright Christine Zolendz © 2013

1

This is a work of fiction. Names, characters, places, and incidents are the products of the author's imagination or are used fictitiously. Any resemblance to actual events, locales, or persons, living or dead, is entirely coincidental.

Cover Design by okaycreations.net

Editor extraordinaire: Frankie Sutton http://frankiesfreelanceediting.blogspot.com/

Dedication

This book is dedicated to all of you that asked to hear Shane's side of the story.
To my lovely Porn Fairy Crystal Faulkner.
To the BEST BOOK CLUB EVER...The Triple M Bookclub - for all your support and just for being as obsessed with reading as I am.
To Tracy Thurlow Lebo for the title – it was all her idea!
To my mom – I could not have done this without you.
And to Dan (my rock star) and my little monsters – Hailey and Emmy.

And to Hurricane Sandy who destroyed Shane on October 29, 2012 – Eff you!
To all the effing amazing readers and authors that came out and helped me raise money to rebuild especially Rebekah Gardiner Covay – I seriously love you.

Table of Contents

Prologue

A warm breeze fell on my skin and I could smell the lush fragrance of the wildflowers that she always twisted into her dark midnight hair. Anticipation of seeing her for the *very last* time pulled and gnarled at my insides. Gabriel and I would walk the pathway to the human's home every evening. I could not help myself; her soul *intoxicated* and called out to me in low whispers. As we arrived, a low roll of deep thunder resonated through the thick glades and lush forests that surrounded us. *Was that my only ominous symbol of what was to come?*

In a time when we didn't yet know what love *truly meant*, a day when her fingers traced my lips...how had she captured my immortal heart *so completely?*

The truth was that I had not been touched by the gentleness of human hands and my heart ached at the thought of my loneliness and want for it; for *her*. Only her. My thoughts were consumed by *only her*.

I knew what my brothers and I, the Grigori, the Angelic Watchers were brought into this world for; to guard over the humans. Simple. Yet, I could not stop myself from thinking of the utter pain of *not knowing her*. I could not just watch over and protect her without *loving* her. I needed to *know her*, to be *near her*...And I was. For years, she and I had a special friendship, a tight bond that coiled deep around my heart. The archangels said this would be the last day we were on Earth, the last that I would *ever* see of her because of what the *others had done*. The *other* Grigori, in all their lust and glory, took the human women for themselves and created chaos. Now the world needed to be purged and cleansed of their crimes. *The floods were coming.*

For so long, Selah and I sought out each other's companionship, each other's *innocence, while the world churned in its maelstrom of evil*. Sitting with our toes dipping into the river…composing music together…my heart was captured one piece at a time with each day she let me hold her hand…until that last night when her beauty in the moonlight overwhelmed me. She was the only *good* and *pure* thing left in the world. *Untouched.*

How do you say goodbye to *your heart*? Your *soul*? The one thing that you *loved more than yourself.* I could still feel her arms slide around me as we gathered each other closely, her face nestling into the crook of my neck; fitting into me *perfectly.* She felt *made for me,* as if I was standing there for the first time, a *whole being. How could this be wrong?*

Am I supposed to forget *this*? Forget *her*? Just turn a blind eye to the mountains of emotions and pretend I never lived *this*? This is where the great love story of my existence *ends*? At its *beginning*?

The most bitterness of sorrows is made out of the hardest goodbyes. I held her until her tremors stilled and her tears slowed, and there seemed no more left in her to cry. I held her until her cheek pressed against mine, and her heather colored eyes looked up into my soul. I held her until a slow heat began to build between us. Until a pure innocent moment of madness overwhelmed us; where our bodies overruled our minds, and that rising heat between us turned to fire that roared over our reason and senses.

My hands glided over her back slowly, and barely touching, with the heaviness of feathers, they slid into the silky cool waves of her raven hair. Trembling, I lightly brushed my lips over her cheek, breathing her in. A gentle graze of the lips like a soft caress from a butterfly's wings; a shy hesitation as they touched, as if we both were taking the time to memorize the feeling before our lips met for the first time. Hovering in that moment, just before our lips touched, we whispered words that bound us forever. *Love.*

Softly, tentatively, with our lips barely touching, as if we were lovers looking for each other in the dark. Her lips as soft as rose petals drew me in, and I kissed them slowly and sensually. My desire; my love. It completely stole my breath away. *How could this be wrong?* Our lips moved together, opening to each other, melting into each other. Heart. Soul. Body. Mind. Twisting like a musical symphony pulsing through the night. Clinging to each other in our beginning and our ending. Her lips were aching with sweetness, the pure black silken cascade of her hair gliding across my skin. Twisting and grasping it in my fingers, I pulled her in deeper. I kissed her slowly, reverently, and I knew without any loss in faith that nothing would ever compare to that single moment when I first kissed my Selah, and knew that my love for her would last beyond *what forever was*. My lips smiled against hers, and when I pulled away from her lips, I gazed into her beautiful silvery gray eyes. I whispered my last words to her, "You have my heart, *forever.*"

Beneath my hands, her lush body, just barely brushing against my chest, hummed with her wildly beating heart. The last sound I would ever feel or hear from her.

I hadn't counted on Gabriel bearing witness to my transgression. *Gabriel*, my Grigori brother, my best friend, and *my betrayer*.

Therefore, for just a few moments, we believed the illusion of belonging to our own precious world; our own paradise. As I locked my eyes with Gabriel, who was watching us, hidden, I knew that there was no such thing as *us*. Love had smiled on us for the briefest of time, but it did not welcome us; its brilliant face had turned away from us, leaving us to say our goodbyes.

In the place where Gabriel hid, tears rimming his eyes red, the forests and green slopes turned black. The sweet orchards and splashing waterfalls rotted and ran dry. As Gabriel stood over me, watching, the stars began to rain down from the sky, as great tears do when paradise is lost. His expression changed frighteningly fast—it was anger and hatred, greed and jealously, envy and despair. My personal apocalypse felt to me, both one of the most beautiful and most heartbreaking events of my existence. It's where my beloved was torn from my arms, and Gabriel, my brother, dragged me to hell; all for the innocence of one *kiss*.

This is where I thought my story ended, but it was truly only the beginning.

Then the darkness came.

When I opened my eyes, I felt for the very first time in my existence, what it truly was to experience fear. I knew exactly where I stood from the smell of utter despair rising from the cold stones of my cell, and the complete lack of light. I knew that standing there, not in my human form, but in my angel form, that my wings were *gone*.

I once heard Michael and Gabriel call that type of prison a Renounce or Tergiverse. The only cell in Hell that can break an angel from their faith, from their soul, from anything that meant anything to them, *if they didn't fight hard enough*. It strips you of your being and breaks your spirit; a human would be brought to dust.

It was so narrow that my back and shoulders touched the icy cold stones of the two walls on the side of me and the one my back leaned against. I only had room to lift my fingers to brush them against the smooth metal of the prison door that stood in front of me. If I could, I would have fallen to my knees. I remained there days, months, years, decades. Time was no longer *there*.

After an eternity of imprisonment, the harsh light assaulting my eyes blinded me when my cell door opened. I could see nothing of the creature that bound my hands with thick cord, only heard the bristling of its feathers to know it was one of my own.

He pulled me through a long tunnel that held nothing but

door after door of the small standing prisons. The sounds of angels weeping filled my ears until I thought they would bleed. *Horror. Terror. Maddening Desperation.*

The creature pulled me through a small entryway and into a cavernous room. Above us, I could hear the sounds of choirs singing and the laughter of paradise. I knew what I would see if I looked up, and my body *ached* to be home.

Beneath my feet, blood red cobblestones stretched into a narrow walkway that would guide me across the great expanse of the pure darkness that lay below. I've heard many times that somewhere there was a doorway to the opening of hell. Little did I know that it was so wide, so empty and silent, and so *easy* to fall into.

The creature pushed me across the stone scaffold until I stood before four golden thrones. The four archangels, Michael, Gabriel, Raphael, and Phanuel occupied each throne.

Before I could utter a sound, Gabriel's voice echoed throughout the room, thunderously vibrating the stones underneath my feet. "The corruption brought on by the Grigori degrades the human race. We saw much blood being shed upon the earth and all lawlessness being wrought upon the earth. The souls of men have called their suit against the Grigori, who said to bring our cause before the Most High. Thou seest what hath been done, who hath taught all unrighteousness on earth and revealed the eternal secrets which were in heaven, which men were striving to learn. For your involvement, Shamsiel, you will be condemned."

I looked straight toward Gabriel, "Where is Selah?" I knew I did nothing wrong.

Gabriel turned his head from my stare. He rose up from his throne and stormed off into the background. "That pathetic human is worth more to you than your wings, than your eternity, so be it. You should have never fallen in love with the girl. It would have been better to fall from the top of Mount Sinai though. It would have hurt a hell of a lot less," he whispered.

Michael's expression softened as he listened to our brother's rant. "The child will be brought straight to paradise. She will be *spared*," he promised me.

Instantly, Gabriel's wings engulfed me. *Devoured me.* I stood at no trial; I was NOT given a chance to plead my case. I was condemned; exiled. *Fallen.*

Then came the darkness again, illuminated only by the burning fires of Hell. Fiery. Fury. Breaking. Shattering my soul.

Lifetimes.

Ions.

Eternities.

Hell.

Until the low whispers of hope blew across my soul on a slight cool breeze. I fell to earth; set free.

Free?

As my eyes opened for the first time in centuries, the soft light of a dying sun streaming through a tarnished dirty bar window met me. My body, now completely human, was splayed across a cold wet tiled floor. Somewhere above me was a lone dripping sound, which joined with the incessant buzzing of an insect trying to fly to its death against the filthy window. Now here, everything is a dimmed, lackluster and dulled vision of the world I once knew. My surroundings left a bitter taste in my mouth filled with despair and numbed each of my senses. I felt this air was not worth the breath, yet my heart continued to pump its blood, the dirty oxygen running rampant through me. The body I was in trembled, shook and racked with convulsions. A silver tipped needle lay beneath the sickly ashen skin of one of my arms; a small trickle of rusty red blood rolled away from the brightly bruised puncture. Then my new body purged itself of its contents; heaving foul toxic wretchedness all over myself.

A pale-faced girl sat next to me with deep purple moons beneath her wide dilated eyes and giggled. Then the memories of this life I now have to live, introduced themselves to me. This is me now, a miserable waste of life, *Shane Maxton*. Heroin addict. Junkie. Sexual deviant. Thief. Liar. Filth. Human scum.

It took three weeks for this disgusting human body to go through withdrawals from whatever God-awful substance it shoved in its veins or up its nose. Twenty-one nights of vomiting, convulsing, craving, sweating, and trying to tear the skin off my new shell as I accustomed myself to living someone else's life. Three long weeks shivering and sweating under thick blankets, alone and confused.

Actually, living in this man's body, *being human*, with all the irrational emotions that came with it, was worse than hell itself. This world was less of a shadow of what it once was. It owned its own darkness, chaos, and evil. It was impossible to describe how different the sunlight shone on Paradise compared to here now. Everything once radiated with warmth and a glow, and you could see, feel, and taste each and everything living thing...where now it was a dull worn down substitute of a world that was long ago left to its own anguish. Earth was a deeper, richer place then, where everything from a speck of dust to a blade of grass to a mountain peak had its own life and story; everything was just made of *More*.

Now, Selah was gone. I am nothing more than a bag of flesh and bones, Shane Maxton, when I was once a god among men.

Months passed as I stayed in Shane's body and became *him*. There was nothing else for me to do, but to *be Shane*.

I had been Shane for nine months. Nine excruciating months in this human body that is roughly nothing more than a highly advanced mass of nerves. Emotions, hormones, wants, and needs rule it. Walking, talking monkeys. With their own minds, their own reasons, and their very own *freedom*.

Since I was no longer an angel, since my wings and *my everything* was taken from me, *I fit right fucking in*.

The only thing to do was try to forget who I was. Forget whom I loved. Just. Fucking. Forget.

Chapter 1

I was so drunk, the room spun and tilted around me. Music was playing in the background, some upbeat pop song that made me want to smash the speakers with the *almost* empty bottle of whiskey I was holding onto. *Jack Fucking Daniels* and I were hoping he could cure me of this life. The thumping of the bass was vibrating whatever it was I was sitting on. Thump. Thump. Thump. It pulsated through my bones. Thump. Thump. Thump. My head pounded to the music, the rest of my body was comfortably numb. Thump. Thump. Thump. The whiskey thumped through my veins; I sincerely thought they were fuller of alcohol than my own blood. I had kept the poison swimming in my veins for the last nine months trying to block out this sad, pathetic life I had been thrown into.

I felt a slight tug on my bottle. A strange pair of hands was wrapping themselves around it. Peeling my eyes open slowly, I saw they were attached to a girl who was sitting with her head between my legs. For a second, I wondered how I got there and I looked around. It was Tucker's apartment, the one he shared with two of my band mates, and it seemed as if there were a few girls here too. Must be another party. Tucker was sitting next to me eyeing the girl at my crotch. "Hey, sweetheart. When you're done with him, you should come over here with those hot little lips," he said.

Squeezing my eyes shut tight, I tried desperately to crush the sharp sense of panic that started building beneath my skin. I'm still Shane. I'm still in Shane Maxton's body. Stuck. Human. Forever.

My body felt as if it were caught in a violent riptide, pulling me, yanking me under. Drowning me. I had no more strength, or *want*, to try to break free; I just needed to sink to the bottom. Lose myself to some sort of oblivion; let myself be consumed by the darkness.

"Oh, beautiful, for spacious skies! For amber waves of grain, for purple mountain majesties above the fruited plain! America! America! Blah, blah, la, la, la, laaaaa..." Tucker's voice drunkenly sang off key.

"What the hell are you doing?" The question was mumbled, garbled so that I could barely understand it. Opening my eyes to watch the conversation, the girl was kneeling between my legs, lips over my dick; talking to Tucker. "Well?" She asked. "Why in the world are you singing the National Anthem while I do this?" I'm sort of surprised that my dick found its way into a willing mouth while I was unconscious, but not *too* surprised. It wasn't the first time; not even the fifth time. *Yeah, I seemed to live a charmed life.* Although it seemed sort of surreal having her suck me off *and* talk with Tucker at the same time. *That should disturb me more, shouldn't it?*

Tucker barked out a laugh and nudged me with his elbow. "That's not the National Anthem," he slurred. "It's just a patriotic song. The fucking National Anthem is The Star Spangled Banner, you twit. And I'm singing the shit so his dick will go limp and you can start sucking off mine!"

My head felt so heavy it slammed down against the back of the fake leather couch I was sprawled out on. I struggled to get words past my lips. The room spun faster and I was just starting to feel the warmth of the mouth that was wrapped around me, taking me deep into her throat.

"Shut up, Tuck," I murmured as I grabbed the back of the girl's neck, threaded my fingers through her hair and started pushing and pulling her faster against me. I didn't even know the chick's name. Hell, I didn't even remember how I got here. Last thing I remembered was being on stage. And all I could clearly think about was how some *Taco Bell* burritos would be awesome right about now.

The girl slid her mouth all the way off me, poured the bottle of whiskey over my dick and sucked it up so damn fast that not one drop fell to the floor. The liquid was cool and her mouth was hot, but that's about the only sensation I felt. Hot. Cold. Hot. Cold. I'm too drunk. Drunkity-drunk-drunk.

"Now, *that* is fucking talent! She didn't spill any of it. Can I call you Hoover? Dyson? No, no…Dirt Devil. The Vacuum Vixen," Tucker slurred.

It took all my strength to turn my head to look at Tucker. He was grabbing the crotch of his jeans *and hell*; I don't even want to know what it was he was freaking doing right now. *Creeper.* There's no way in hell I could cum in this chick's mouth with Tucker that close to me, and I just knew he was looking at my junk and *he was in fucking awe.* I still wanted a burrito. I mushed the girl's face off me and stumbled around trying to stand. The girl who was just blowing me crossed her arms over her chest and pouted. I couldn't even focus on what she looked like. I thought her hair might be red…

"Come on, Shane, let's go to your apartment," she whined.

"No way, uh…*whateverthefuckyournameis.* Tuck here needs a blowjob more than I do. *I'mgoingtosleep.*" I turned to Tucker and shook my head; the movement almost made me fall flat on my face, but I stood my ground. Okay, I freaking slumped against the wall, but whatever. "Tucker, that was the creepiest shit ever. If you ever get that close to my junk again while it's getting sucked, I swear I will rip your eyes out and microwave them."

Blowjob chick jumped up in front of me and I flinched back. The room spun even more. It was like a demented out of control merry-go-round. Immediately, I feared she'd grow a pair of fangs and try to suck the life out of me. I slid down the wall awkwardly. *Why the hell was the floor so close to me?* Damn, being this drunk made walking anywhere so…impossible. "Dude…where the hell are my feet?"

"No, Shane don't go! And I already told you at the bar,

like fifty thousand *brazilian* times, my name is Jolie…Come on, let me take you to your apartment. I'll take care of you and then we could both sleep and…"

Fifty *Brazilian* times? This chick is as smart as a brick. I grabbed my bottle of whiskey out of her hands. "Hell. No. I don't   sleep   with   girls   at   my   place. *Whatthehell?Gosucksomeoneelse'sdick.*"

"But YOU'RE the lead singer! Not him."

"*Twat*ever,   I'm   leaving.   And   the *whiskeyiscomingwithme.*" That *is* all I am; lead freaking singer and worthless guitarist. There's nothing else to me. Empty. Hollow. Not even a glimmer of the walking god I once was. *I'm the lead singer.* What the hell does that even mean? Who cares? I didn't cure fucking cancer with my voice, did I? Nope. I sure didn't cure cancer with my dick, so why the hell does she want to jump on it. It's not like I'm ever going to have a *thing* with her.

"You suck, Shane Maxton!" The girl yelled after me.

"Yeah, but I'm not as good as you, sweetheart."

By the time I stumbled to the hallway and looked back, the chick was sucking on Tucker's bottom lip. With the same lips that were just on my cock. I vomited all over the rug. Then I laughed, because there was no way in hell I was cleaning that neon green puke up and I doubted anyone saw me do it. It would be yet another stain on Tucker's rug that everyone would wonder about, like the deep red one under the table. *I swear I thought that's where he might have killed a hooker.*

Stepping right over it, I staggered to the door, waved goodbye to whoever *could* see me and practically crawled down the hall to my apartment. Every night was the same. Every. Night. Another show tomorrow night, another party. Each one ended with me trying to…forget…

Hearing my front door slam shut behind me startled me, drowned all the voices into the outside world, and relieved me of some of my stress and anxiety.   Sounds of the music and the party were gone, and finally I was by myself, where I could just *be* me, and not the piece of shit jackass they knew me to be. I toppled into my bedroom, reached for my guitar and poured out my soul.

Walking that long winding road
It's dark and I'm all alone
Here I am, somewhere in here
But where the hell is home
I sing these words of sorrow for who I am inside
A boy with a tarnished halo, damaged dreams
And brothers who have lied
I pray for my grace and redemption
With hope in this human shell
Through all the smoke and ashes,
And the fires I've called home in hell
But, I will never regret my deed
For her, my heart still longs
Taken, she was what I was made for
All I have now are my scars and songs
And here I am
All alone again
With all my scars and songs
Strung out from this world
Where angels don't belong
-Shane Maxton Mad World
Dear God, I fucking miss her.

I passed out, wrapped around my guitar with my zipper still open and my junk laying out on my thigh. Ready to relive the same mindless, worthless and pathetic existence tomorrow night.

Chapter 2

Of course, the party was still going strong when I woke up at six o'clock the next morning. However, by then, it had spread into my apartment and I was no longer in my room. I was in the Bone Room and I was not alone. There was a long tan body almost naked lying next to me. *Huh?*

She was squeezed into a tiny black skirt that was made with such little material, the soft curves of her ass peeked out of the bottom, and they were fucking smiling at me. *Hellllooo.*

I stood up slowly and reached for my boxer shorts that were draped over the back of the armchair in the corner of the room. After grabbing them and pulling them up quickly, I stood in the soft glow of the rising sun through the window, and gazed down at the figure in the bed I had just left. Her back was facing me, her head resting on her arm, and her long, golden blonde hair fell around the pillows that surrounded her.

What the hell did I do last night? I looked down at the girl, vomit rising in my throat, and tried to remember what happened after I played my guitar. In my room. Alone.

I remembered the knock on my door. The blonde was topless, and fuck, I *am* only human.

Then we were in the Bone Room and were walking clumsily, kissing and sucking at each other, tongues and mouths and fingers touching each other as we stumbled onto the bed. She pulled my boxers down and her lips were immediately wrapped around my cock so tightly, it almost hurt.

I remembered opening the slut drawer and throwing a wad of condoms at her and using them all. I took a deep, pained breath and ran my hands over my face. Guilt flooded through me, causing a thickness in my throat. It had been nine months, and the guilt was still so damn overwhelming. I did all this shit to punish myself, to forget myself, to forget Selah. I drank to forget her, to forget being what I was, and I slept with the trash that threw themselves at me, trying to pretend they were all her and trying to forget I would never see her again.

The body on the bed shifted. "Are you leaving me already, Shane?"

My muscles tensed, and I swallowed the guilt back. "Yep."

The girl sat up and the sheets fell from her, giving me a full view of a pair of perky little tits. She tilted her head and batted her eyes. "So that's it? Or you want me to come back around later tonight after the next show?" Her hands slowly started caressing her own skin, cupping herself and trying too damn hard to keep my attention. She reeked of desperation and all I wanted was to take a shower to clean her scent off me.

The mattress on the bed creaked loudly as she kicked the rest of the sheets off and slid her hand suggestively down her stomach and under her little skirt. She lifted up the material so I could see her fingers as she ran them through her wet skin. She spread her legs real wide as I watched the show.

I shook my head and gave her my sexiest smile, "Nah, thanks though. It's been...fun." Turning, I walked to the door and then gave her one last glance. "You need a cab or anything, just let one of us know."

"Are you kidding me? After everything we did last night, *that's it?*" She shrieked. "I-I thought that we were fucking amazing together. I-I thought..."

I spun on my heels and cocked my head at her. "You knew the deal when you knocked on my door."

She bolted up, grabbed her shirt off the floor, yanked it over her head, and glared at me. "Do you have any respect for women? Do you give a shit about me at all?" Her shirt was on backward, so I laughed. She threw a pillow at me.

I crossed my arms over my chest, "When a stranger walks herself into my fucking private bedroom, tits all out, begging me to use her for a night, I fucking will. Why the hell not? You didn't care much about yourself or your safety last night when you crawled on a stranger's lap and bounced up and down on his cock. Why should that stranger give a shit about you after? I don't even know your name. A guy is only going to treat a chick the way she treats herself, and if you don't respect yourself, then why the hell should I?"

Storming out of the room and into my bedroom, I slammed my door shut and locked it. Fuck everyone. I didn't understand any of these humans or there crazy-ass emotions that I was now terrorized with. Collapsing on my bed, I slept until my alarm woke me to get ready for our next gig.

As I mindlessly got ready, my stomach clenched, knowing that I would repeat the same shit as the night before.

The night started the way it always did, with the guys and me meeting up at the bar before a gig. A crowd of girls sat at the table next to us as we horribly tried pick up line after pick up line on them. We all made a game out of it, because really, after a show, *every* girl that said no to us would be on her knees in front of us later, mouthing how great we were. *Every girl. Any girl. No problem.* I had yet to meet a girl who knew the word no. Not when the guys from my band, Mad World, was around anyway.

Tucker, who wasn't even in the band, was the best at the game, but that's because he had the worst pick up lines in the world. I believe he had a book somewhere where he wrote them all down.

"Great legs, what time do they open?" Tucker called out to the girls, laughing as he did so.

Chuckling, I chimed in. "If I flip a coin, what are the chances of me getting head?" The girls made disgusted faces in our direction, shaking their heads in disbelief.

Alex, my rhythm guitarist and keyboardist, elbowed me in the gut to listen to his line. "Hey, how about you sit on my face and let me eat my way to your heart?" He shoved his tongue between two of his fingers and wiggled it towards the girls sexually. I laughed harder.

Brayden, my bassist, snorted like a pig and beer shot right out of his nose. Howls of laughter rang out from our table. Then he called over, "I got the F-C-K. All I need is U!"

Ethan, my drummer just laughed along with us. He never participated in our immature games. He'd be the first one of us divorced with 2.5 kids and a dog. *Probably a freaking cat too.*

Tucker rolled another out. "If this bar is a meat market, you must be the prime rib!" That caused the girls to stand up and move to another table farther away from us idiots. All except one light haired girl who flipped me her middle finger, but stayed firmly planted to her seat, crooking her lips into a sexy little smile. *Easy.*

I got up from my seat and leaned over her table, right in front of her face. "I would love to," I whispered. I held my hand out for her, and just as I thought she would, she grabbed it with sweaty palms.

I took her into one of the back rooms. It was as good a place as any to get laid. Most of the time, I was too uninspired by the easy women that opened up their legs for me even to bother to take them home. And they were *all* easy. I didn't even have to look anymore. They just jumped in my arms after a show. Let's be honest, they jumped right on our dicks right after a show, no need to sugar coat it. It is what it is. *Easy.*

The girl walked right into the storage closet, lifted her skirt to her waist and bent over, *ready.* She wasn't even wearing any fucking underwear. *Holy shit. Maybe I should use two condoms with this one if she's that fucking easy.* She leaned over a shelf full of cases of beer, stretched her chin over her shoulder and smiled, "My name's Crystal." *Now she tells me?*

"Hey, hi. Nice to, uh, meet you," I laughed. *What the hell did I care what her name was? I was never going to use it.*

She turned her head around, spreading her legs wider. "God, I can't wait to tell all my girlfriends I hooked up with the lead singer from Mad World. Those girls I was sitting with just now, I just work with them. They don't know how famous you are." *And there it was, the reason my cock got so much action. I was Shane Maxton, lead singer of Mad World.* Famous. Yeah. No one knew who the hell I really was.

I was happy when she turned her head back around, because I wasn't particularly in the mood to look at her face anymore, and her damn voice was threatening to make my poor dick go limp.

"But don't think I do this sort of stuff often," she said looking back over her shoulder as I slid on a condom. "I don't want you to think I'm easy," she said huskily.

"Yeah, we wouldn't want anyone to think you're easy," I chuckled. I grasped her bare hips and slid inside her so easily I knew damn well she was probably the easiest girl I'd ever met.

She moaned loud like a porn star, which just made me laugh. I watched her buck up against me with detached interest and checked my watch. I had about ten minutes until I needed to be on stage.

Crystal shrieked, hollered, moaned, talked dirty, and at one point, which scared the freaking hell out of me, she neighed like a horse. *I'm not lying.* When I felt her tighten around me, I let myself release, taking only a small amount of the knotted sexual tension from my body. It would have been better jacking myself off. I wouldn't have gotten such a freaking headache, and I was alone either way, anyway. I smacked her on the ass and pulled myself out. "Thanks, babe. See you around." By the time I reached the door, I completely forgot what she said her name was.

I walked out of the closet and sauntered onto the stage. My body should have been satisfied; relaxed, but it never was after I was with a girl. It twisted in knots and made me want to go to confession. *Now that's the most ironic thought ever.*

As usual, someone's black lacy bra flew into my hands. I should open a lingerie shop with all the crap these chicks threw at me, I'd make a mint.

And, just like I did every night before I played, I searched the audience, looking for something I had no idea of, just knowing that something was out there somewhere and that one day, if I found it, I could go back home. Back home to see *her*.

I grabbed the microphone. The vision of Selah clouded my mind, the way she always did before I sung. Although, it had been so long since I'd laid my eyes on her, her image thinned and blurred, and I feared one day soon, I wouldn't be able to remember how beautiful she was.

I started the set with a slow song that always made me think of her. My body trembled, just remembering how her hand felt in mine, but that was long ago, and I knew I'd never see her again. She was dead. All I had was now, and the dozens of empty girls I could stick my dick in to try to forget about her. I slept with any damn girl that I could, just to erase her. Any kind of girl, tall, short, blonde hair, red hair, any girl that didn't look like my Selah; all they had to do was smile at me and I was in.

The rest of the songs blurred by, the audience radiated, echoed my energy; making me feel like I still had wings and could soar above them.

The music took over and I shoved all thoughts of her in my head away. I hid them deep, so I wouldn't think about them for the rest of the night. I would never be going home. I would never get my wings back, and I would certainly never see her again. That time was gone, over, done. There was no love or hope for me in this world.

Just then, slapping me from my thoughts, an awesome brawl erupted in the middle of the dance floor. From where we stood on stage, we saw the entire thing, fists flew; some great roundhouse kicks and an unbelievable back flip. Finally, something that made me *feel* again. My body grew raw and itched to feel the violence. *God, did I miss the sweet violent madness of dishing out the wrath of God.*

24

That's when I noticed her.

The stage lights glimmered on a whirl of long, shiny, jet-black hair, bringing out its hidden midnight blue highlights. She balanced two drinks in her hands, which were made of the milkiest ivory skin I had ever seen. Her face peeked out from behind the veil of her dark hair and I would have given a limb to see the rest of her features, that's how much her essence intrigued me. The waves of rage that had come over me from watching the fight turned into a slow burning carnal hunger. My heart thundered in my chest erratically.

One of the brawlers hit his elbow right into some little blonde wispy chick that bounced right off the raven-haired girl. Her drinks splashed up and spilled down the front of her white tee shirt. She threw down the empty cups and yelled a string of profanities.

Without thinking, I jumped down in front of her. Her head lifted to reveal flawless ivory skin, her jet black hair cascading around a face that would haunt me forever. Her eyes shot up to meet mine and I had trouble breathing. They were the most unnerving color of light grey, more silver than anything, framed by thick, long, black lashes. No one should have eyes that color, with a touch of lavender that swam deep in their depths. I could bury myself in them and never resurface again. *My God, she looked just like Selah.*

"*Wow*," I breathed. It was the only freaking coherent thought that I had in my brain at that moment. My breaths were deep and uneven. *Damn*, I wanted *her*.

She rolled her beautiful eyes and backed away a step when she got slammed from behind and vaulted into my arms. The sheer electric shock of touching her made me realize what it must feel like to be struck by lightning. She pushed off me as if I was the plague.

The poor girl stepped right into the path of the fight and I had to grab her away from them before she was trampled.

She looked behind her towards the fists and feet flying through the air, but didn't seem the least bit scared or even affected by it. She just looked back into my eyes and covered her wet shirt with her arms. A rush of the most exquisite color of crimson flushed her cheeks. I wanted to reach my hand out and touch them; feel how soft they were; how warm her skin would be under mine. I wanted to taste her; sink myself deep inside that milky white flesh. *Holy crap, I must be losing my mind*.

Maybe it wasn't my mind. Maybe it was just me being stuck in this messed up body. Or, maybe it was those beautiful, plump, pink lips or the soft curve of her chin against the darkness of her hair.

Ethan grabbed me by the shoulders and brought me back down to earth. "Come on, Shane!" He called, pulling me towards the fight.

I couldn't tear my eyes away from hers. "Yeah, one sec, bro," I called to him. She was mortified, standing there wrapping her arms around herself. I *had* to help her. I took off my shirt and pushed it into her hands. For the first time, standing in front of her, I noticed, and I mean *really* noticed, how very wet her shirt was. My eyes slowly traveled down the milky white skin of her neck to the tight wet material of her shirt. It was completely see through, and *holy shit*, did she have on the hottest red bra that made the curves of her breasts look, well, let me put it this way; whoever I *was* taking home that night wouldn't be who I was thinking of; she'd be the one on my mind.

Shit, I could see myself taking her from the back and her beautiful face slamming into my mattress, her hair wildly covering the sheets. I gave her a wink before I joined in to break up the fight. I wondered how hard it would be to get her to come home with me. Probably not too hard, I was Shane Maxton after all. I had a liquid effect on *all* women's panties. *But she was too hot to just take in the back room*. Yeah, I wanted to spend some time on her. Some time *in her*.

26

Through the whole fight, I couldn't shake those eyes from my thoughts. Getting an uppercut to my jaw rattled my head a bit, but even that didn't divert my mind from her. I tried to look back in the direction she walked in, but all I could see were fists flying at me. Then the damn fight stopped. Marty, the bouncer at the front door, knocked the two opposing guy's heads together and that was it. It was kind of comical in a way, how they just crumpled to the floor after they bounced off each other.

Ethan gave me a high five, but I couldn't have cared any less about the fight. I needed to find where the girl with the silver eyes went. "Bro, did you see where that girl went?" I craned my head around, looking all over for her.

Ethan smiled wide and nodded. "The insanely hot one you were talking to when I pulled you into the fight?" *Yeah, he certainly noticed her too.* "Nah, I didn't see which way she went."

I patted him on the back. "I gotta find her. Come on, walk around the bar with me, and help me look for her."

He laughed loudly. "Why, you want your shirt back? She'd definitely win any wet tee shirt contest, that's for sure."

"No, dude, did you see her eyes? Holy crap," I said.

Ethan stopped walking and gawked at me as if I just kicked a puppy. "Her eyes? *Really, Shane?* Did you get knocked in the head hard or something? Shane Maxton noticing a girl's eyes?"

I shrugged and couldn't get rid of the stupid grin I knew I was wearing on my face. I must have looked like a complete ass. I knew he never saw me smile like that before. "Dude, you didn't see those eyes. Please, help me find her!" I laughed.

We ran through the bar like two horny fourteen year olds. I turned around every dark haired girl I saw (a few guys too) to look into their faces, but I *couldn't* find her. I even tried to beg one of the waitresses to go in the back to the bathrooms to see if a silver-eyed girl was in there, but she just laughed at me. *Janie.* She was probably still pissed at me about not calling her back. I told her I wouldn't. I even told her not to give me her number. I told her I wasn't one for more than a one night thing. *Every girl thought they could change my mind. It cracked me up, really.*

I swear, I think we looked for at least thirty minutes. I even ran outside and down the block. I was a man obsessed.

Alex was the one that got me to stop looking for her. He smacked me in the back of the head and introduced me to some blonde girl with a huge rack. Alex was hooking up with what had to be the girl's sister, because they looked almost like twins.

She started talking to me about how great I played and how hot I was on stage. *Blah, blah, blah, what-the-hell-ever.* Her voice was irritating and I was quickly getting pissed off that I couldn't spend the rest of the night looking for the silver-eyed girl. She just went on and on trying to have this serious conversation with me, and all I could think about were all the sexual positions I wanted to bend the silver-eyed girl in.

I told Alex I was going home. The blonde chick begged me to stay, said it would be worth my while. I highly doubted it; there wasn't anything she could do that some other girl couldn't. *They all felt the same on the inside.*

That's when I saw her.

Waves of black silky hair crashed down around the most perfect face I'd ever seen. My stomach tied itself in knots. Dressed in my huge tee shirt, she sat next to my friend Lea. My best friend Conner sat behind Lea, his hands wrapped around his girl's waist, practically holding her up. Tucker sat on the other side of the silver-eyed beauty, ogling her as if she was the last girl on earth. I couldn't blame him, she put every other girl in the bar to shame; everyone looked plain compared to her. Coughing and sputtering into my hands I had raised to cover my face, I had trouble swallowing the huge freaking lump in my throat.

Clearing my throat, I pulled up a chair and placed it right between her and Lea. "Hey, how'd you like the brawl?" I asked everyone. I only looked at her though.

Unfortunately, the blonde chick was still following me as if she was my lost little puppy. I ignored her. The only thing I saw were those silver eyes, the waves of her dark hair and that perfect creamy skin that I needed to sweep with my tongue.

I was freaking myself out. I never got crazy like this over anyone. I couldn't even tell you the last time I actually looked into a girl's eyes and noticed their color. I wasn't one for looking in anybody's eyes.

Some people say you could see right into a person's soul through their eyes. Being stuck here in this world, surrounded by humans and their ignorant blind emotional flesh was one thing. Looking into their souls and seeing the depth of faith and hope was another thing. A thing I *couldn't* do. The eyes before me were demanding and strong, and I was drowning in them. I couldn't look away. *Shit.*

Sitting down, I continued to stare right at her. I must have looked like a starving man, because that's how I felt. My palms started sweating. Damn, *that* never happened before either.

Then, of everything that could possibly freaking happen, the blonde Barbie doll who was following me, plopped her ass right on my lap and started sucking on my neck and biting my ear. *Like a fucking blood sucking vampire.* My first impulse was to stand up and dump the bitch on the floor, but I didn't want everyone to think I was *that* much of a douche.

The whole time, the gorgeous girl that I'd been looking all over the bar for was just looking at me with an unaffected look on her face. *This was insane. Yeah, she was hot, beyond hot. Okay, hotter than the hottest freaking girl I'd ever seen. Shit - I had to stop. The real Shane would never be doing this.*

She was just a piece of ass, just like all the others. She'd be easy to score. So why the hell were my palms sweating, and my heart thudding in my chest? Because I wasn't really Shane, and she looked so damn much like Selah.

I groaned inwardly, trying to think of some way to get this

other girl off me, so I could talk to silver eyes. Before I could say anything, Lea drunkenly belted out, "Ugh, Shane, get a kennel for your lapdog, the sounds of her slopping your ear is making me wanna hurl again!" *Ha, I loved Lea when she was drunk, she was hysterical!*

That did the trick and the blonde chick stopped molesting me. "Jealous much?" Blondie said back to Lea. *Eh, she had balls.*

I watched those silver eyes roll and her lips turned up into a smile that made sweat break out on my forehead. *What the fuck? I must have been losing it.*

Lea continued to mouth off at the blonde, which didn't bother me a bit; it made her keep her mouth off me. "Yeah, I'm always jealous of Shane's conquests. They are the equivalent of a blow up doll. With the brains to match." *Ha, that was a good one, Lea.* Although, I wouldn't call any of these girls *conquests*, it wasn't a conquest if they were giving themselves freely. I hadn't won *anything*. They weren't a *prize*, they were just a distraction.

True to form, the blonde came back with, "What the hell does that mean?" Silver eyes seemed to be enjoying the bantering. Her smile widened and she laughed along with Lea. It sounded like music. *Yeah, I was fucking losing it. I had to stay away from her. She would bring a man to his knees.*

"See, you just proved my point." Lea slurred and looked at the silver-eyed girl and smiled. "Maybe if we use big words, it will leave?"

I was just about to get up and leave. I just wanted to walk away and never lay my eyes on her again. One night would never be enough for me with a girl who looked like that. I'd been to hell *and back*, and *she* scared me more.

When I leaned forward to get up, that's when I saw it. The mischievous way those eyes sparkled and the devil may care smile that lit up her face. *I couldn't fucking move.*

"Lea, you should never have a battle of wits with an unarmed opponent." Her voice pierced me to my seat. *I needed to leave.* Yeah, but I just sat there like an ass, staring at her.

"Shut up, skanks! You're both just jealous." The vampire who was just sucking on my neck couldn't think of anything better to say. She just stuck out her tits, like *that* was her ace of spades in the game.

"Slut," Lea smiled drunkenly.

Then silver eyes got serious and leaned in closer to us. "Yeah, listen, you should really stop now, because I'm betting that the smartest thing that could ever come out of your mouth would be a penis. And, that's not going to make you winner of this war of words, sweetie." *Damn, I had never been more turned on by someone in my life. Lives. Whatever. Maybe someone slipped something in my drink? I was definitely losing it. Crap, I had to adjust myself in my pants.*

Lea laughed so hard at what her friend said that she spit water all over the place. That made the blonde get off my lap, scream and dance around. I had no freaking clue what she was screaming. My eyes were locked on those silver ones, and they were looking right back at me. My breath left me. *Who the hell was this girl?* And why did the blood in my veins slam through my body like that? Pulsing. Pounding. Surging.

I smiled. I thought it was one of the best smiles I ever gave too. *It did shit.* She just sat there laughing along with Lea and ignored my smile *completely*.

I tensed my muscles and grabbed the bottom of my chair to keep myself seated. The sane part of me wanted to walk away, the rest of me wanted to jump on her and taste her lips. She rolled her fucking gorgeous eyes at me as if she could read my mind.

"Hey, thanks for the shirt before. Would have been cold walking home like that. You didn't have to do that," she laughed sweetly.

Oh, hell yes I did. I had to do anything to talk to her. Her eyes were piercing me to my seat, and I had to kill the urge to drag my hands through that dark, ink-black hair and touch her until she moaned my name in a sexy whisper.

The blonde chick continued to freakin' dance around and yell.

The silver-eyed girl broke our stare *as if it didn't just freaking kill me.* She motioned to Lea and they started getting their stuff together to leave. *Holy crap! I needed her to stay. No, no. I needed her to go.*

That wicked smile teased at the corner of her lips again. She stepped closer to the blonde. "Just think of it like this. I got him half naked for you already. Try to enjoy yourself. He looks like someone who has a land mine in his pants."

"Huh?" The blonde asked.

"You know a land mine; small, hidden, and explodes on contact." That was the best insult I'd ever heard. *And I'd make it this life's goal to prove her wrong.*

I jumped up and practically killed myself trying to block her from moving any further. Her hair brushed over me and the smell of wildflowers filled my senses. *Holy shit.* She bit her lower lip between her teeth and it took all the restraint I had in me not to reach out and touch her skin, or grab a handful of that thick black hair and pull her towards me, crushing her lips to mine.

"So, you must be Lea's best friend, the one she grew up with and talks about all the time, huh?" *Okay, so that wasn't the most intelligent thing I could have said. But, really at that moment, I was surprised I was capable of more than me want you now, grrr.'*

"Must be," she teased.

Shit. I was so screwed. I gave her another one of my charming smiles. "Do you have a name?"

"Yes, I do," she said; she just didn't bother telling it to me.

She looked me in the eyes, biting her lip again and slid past me. The way she did, not breaking eye contact with me, was *so freaking erotic,* the damn land mine in my pants almost did go off.

Lea whispered in the background to Conner loud enough for everyone in the bar to hear, "Conner, watch her outwit him, just watch."

I glanced at Lea and rolled my eyes. When I locked my eyes back to those silver ones, they smiled right back at me. My dumb mouth just started talking before my brain did any of the thinking. "I'll just call you *Red* then, since I can't get my mind off that sexy little bra I saw you in before." *AH HELL! WHY DID I JUST SAY THAT?* I just wanted to say anything to make her stay, even if she got pissed off at me. *Crap, I was Shane at fourteen again.*

She leaned in so close to me that my heart skipped a few beats. She looked down at my lips and back up to my eyes. My heart hammered in my chest erratically. I thought she was just about to kiss me and that I was going to have a heart attack at the same freaking time.

"Why not, Lacy? Or, did you miss out on the soft silk and lace material it was made from? Too bad you'll only get to see the color." She fluttered her gorgeous eyes at me and continued, "You know, if you're going to be a smart ass, you should start with being smart. Otherwise, you're really just an ass. Enjoy the rest of your night."

My heart stopped. I opened my mouth to say some smart-ass flirty remark back, but she held up a creamy delicate hand to my face. All I could do was think about where I'd like to feel that hand on me.

"Please, save your breath, you might need it to blow up your date later." She walked past me and out the front door.

Yeah, I was screwed. I met my match. She'd brought me to my knees already.

My heart sank when I watched Tucker scramble after them with Conner taking up the rear. Tucker was all fucking smiles and opening doors; jealously streaked through me. *He better not put his fucking hands on her.*

I looked down and saw how tight my fists were clenched. *What the hell was this about? I seriously need to go throw myself off a bridge right now; I didn't even know who I was. She was just another human girl!*

Ethan sauntered up beside me with a beer in hand. "Did I just witness a girl flat out not even notice you?"

I nodded. "Dude, I can't even breathe right now. I need a drink before I do something stupid, like run after her."

A giant grin plastered itself over Ethan's face as he shook his head and handed me his beer.

I chugged the whole thing down. That just made it worse. *I just have to get her face out of my head.* "Hey, where's Alex with those blondes?"

Ethan silently grimaced at the empty bottle I handed back to him.

I turned around to the table and there they were, except for now, they doubled and there were four blondes sitting at the table. All were patiently waiting for the band's attention. Alex sat in the middle of them smiling. Thankfully, the one who had just been yelling and screaming was calmer. Sitting down, pouting and moaning, but calmer.

I sat down hard on the chair opposite the table from them, "Ladies," I smiled.

Alex slid a cold beer across the table to me and nodded in the direction of the front door. "Who was the goddess wearing your shirt?"

I shrugged as if she didn't matter. "I think that's Lea's roommate. She's hot." All the girls at the table moaned in annoyance. That just cracked me up.

Ethan sat in the chair next to me, and chuckled low. "The word hot does not do that girl justice."

One of the girls at the table pouted. "You know, there are four very hot girls sitting right here and you are talking about

34

some other girl who already left!"

Alex grabbed the girl and just started kissing her. It was like the beginning of a really bad porno film. I had to look away. But, I was happy he shut her up. I didn't want her to start talking shit about the silver-eyed girl. There would be no way I'd let her say anything bad about her. *Yeah, then I'd look like a real sappy knight in shining armor's ass.*

Brayden sat down on the other side of me and grunted at the table. One of the girls got up off her chair and sat down on his lap. "Uh, do I know you?" he asked.

She started whispering in his ear. His expression was classic, complete mortification. "Please go sit back over there," he said. "Why don't we talk first before you try to do all that stuff you just said? Besides. I think most of that crap is illegal."

When she grudgingly left his lap and sat back down on her chair, he jabbed me playfully in the arm. "Shane, did you see Lea's friend, Grace? Man, she was smoking hot."

Everybody noticed her. *Grace. Even her name alluded to her beauty.*

I leaned back against my chair and inhaled a long breath. "Yeah, I sort of met her. I had to give her my shirt because she spilled her drink all over herself during the fight."

My band mates looked at me as if I had grown another head in front of them.

Alex leaned forward. "And here I thought you bagged her in the back and that's why she wore your shirt! Okay, okay, lemme get this straight. She *spilled* her drink on her shirt and you gave her *yours*. What color shirt was she wearing? I'm just *wondering.*"

I just smiled wide, remembering.

Ethan cleared his throat and answered for me. "She had on a very white little shirt on, and the sexiest red bra I have ever seen under it when it was soaking wet."

My band mates raised their beers to me.

Alex laughed, "Well here's to chivalry, and to douchebag friends who don't share in the good fortune of finding a good wet tee shirt contestant!"

"Cheers!" We all called out together.

The girls around the table remained silent. Then Alex resumed kissing his girl, which led to everyone starting to talk and introduce themselves.

I just sat back and watched my band; my best friends; my roommates, my brothers. They had no idea who I really was, who *I'd been*. Yet, they were more trustworthy and honorable to me than the angels who I was truly brothers with, the ones who condemned me to this hellish eternity. *What I would have given to be born human.* I would have been with Selah, end of story; perfect life. We could have loved each other without it being a crime, lived a long life together and died together.

These guys in front of me had no idea of heaven, intense bliss, or how close to hell, being on earth truly was. In my own way, I envied them.

Ethan was snapping his fingers in front of my face, "Hellooo! Shane? You still with us? We're going to play pool, are you coming?"

I looked around the table. Everybody was standing and walking toward the game room. *Huh? Where the hell was my head at?*

I looked up to Ethan whose face was creased with concern, "Nah, dude. I'm just gonna finish my beer and call it a night. I'll see you at home."

Ethan sat back down and leveled his eyes to mine. "What's up? You okay?"

I hesitated. Then I just laughed, "Yeah, man. I'm just wiped out." His eyebrows pulled together, but he just nodded and stood up. "Sure, man. See you at home." I watched him walk away. Walking casually into the game room, as all the girls in the bar turned their heads when he walked by. The majority turned around and looked back at me too, probably assessing their luck at going home with me tonight. Little did they know that not one of them would have a chance. I had absolutely no desire to be with anyone that night, unless it was Grace. *That fucking scared the hell out of me.* I've been here on earth in Shane's body for months trying to forget about Selah, now this girl who looks exactly like her is going to be here reminding me of her every time I see her. This was *bad.* I would be at Lea's apartment practically every single day!

I downed the rest of my beer and headed for the stage. I climbed up, grabbed my guitar, and packed it away in its case. I slung it over my shoulders and jumped back off the stage. A group of girls sighed loudly and ran over to me, but I just excused myself and said I had a prior commitment to get to. I just wanted to go to bed, *alone.*

I walked past the game room and stood in the doorway watching my friends play pool. Alex was loud and obnoxious as always. His mother would always thank God for his good looks, because his personality was quite abrasive. He was intensely outgoing and had been born without a brain to mouth filter. Brayden was the quiet, thoughtful one, who was artistic and poetic. Ethan was the romantic, comical, blond haired teddy bear, the size of a quarterback. I waved goodnight to them and walked to the door. They would know something was up. I was always the last one home and the first one to dive into bed with a girl. Thank God, each of them would know me well enough to have the sense not to say anything.

The icy February air hit me like a sledgehammer to the face when I stepped outside. I didn't give a crap though. I took the long way home and passed Lea's apartment. I knew Conner would be staying there tonight, he always did. I toyed with the idea of ringing the bell when I passed by, but all the lights were off. I stood on the bottom of the steps and wondered if Tucker stayed too.

My gut retched. Tucker was a good buddy, but he wasn't good enough for Grace. He was a slob, he was beyond arrogant, and he was a *lawyer*. He could lie through his teeth *and* believe himself.

Not to beat around the bush here, but I didn't want Tucker with Grace because I didn't want anyone else to be with her. She was too much like Selah. I would cringe every time he would hold her hand, every time I knew he lied to her about being with other girls. Shit, I would probably kill him in his sleep if I knew they...

I ran my hands through my hair. These thoughts were going to kill me. *She was just another girl. I would prove it to myself. She was just like the rest of them. She just was the prettiest one. No big deal. I would get to know her and I bet within a day, I would be done with her. She wasn't Selah. Selah has been long gone. Dead for over 2,000 years. Grace was just a regular girl.*

I would give her my smile. She'd talk about getting her nails done. She probably was still in college, making a career out of it, until she meets Mr. Money, the guy who would take care of her. She probably tweets about each time she uses the bathroom and posts a Facebook status of her location for each hour. Never felt heartache, never lost anyone, and sure as hell doesn't know what it's like in hell. She would end the night with her legs wrapped around me, telling me what a great singer I was, and how many children she would like to have with me. She would have already picked out their names. I would tell her I didn't do relationships, I didn't do love, flowers or Hallmark cards. I wouldn't even sit through a chick flick. I was deathly allergic to them. She would have tears in her eyes, but they wouldn't fall. Because she would have known, because I would have told her before I slept with her, that I didn't do any of that shit and she wouldn't be the one to change me. Nobody can. And she would pretend to care, but all along, she would get what she wanted. To sleep with the singer and lead guitarist of Mad World. She would have bragging rights to tell all her friends. That was all that beautiful package would be made up of. Fuck, I'm ranting in my own head.

What if she was more?

I stopped myself right before I rang Lea's doorbell. I worked myself up so much I was panting. I wanted to tell Grace off. I wanted to walk right into her room and...I stopped. I turned around and walked back down the front steps. I pushed myself over to the pavement of the sidewalk and down the street.

I walked the two blocks between our apartment buildings like a madman. I couldn't understand what was happening to me. Why was this girl getting under my skin? I couldn't even complete a full thought.

I jogged up my front steps and opened the lobby door to my place. The warm stale air made me feel heavy and slow.

I lumbered down the hallway to my apartment and unlocked the door. I went straight to the bar and poured myself a whiskey. I slammed it back and stared at the empty glass in my hands. I refilled the little fucker and left it on the counter.

Making my way to the bathroom, I ran the shower, needing to clear my head. After stripping off my clothes, I stepped into the hot stream and let the water run over my face, closing my eyes tight. But the shower did shit to clear my mind, because the minute I closed my eyes, those stunning silver eyes were searing into my conscious, refusing to be forgotten or pushed aside.

I slammed my hands flat against the slick wet tiles of the shower and roared like a caged animal. The grief threatened to choke me; it welled in my chest and tore at my heart. Jumping out of the shower, I slid over the wet tiles of the floor and crashed my body up against the wall. I needed another drink.

Still dripping wet, I stormed into the kitchen, gulped down the other shot of whiskey and tossed the glass in the sink.

Then I went back, grabbed the rest of the bottle of whiskey, and carried it into my bedroom.

With the full bottle, I played my guitar until the sun rose. I drifted off to sleep sometime after.

I dreamt of silver eyes, soft lips, and silky black hair that smelled of wildflowers after the rain.

I woke up with a haunting melody in my head that curled its notes around every inch of her soft naked body that had haunted my dreams. *Great. Now she was my muse.*

Chapter 3

I showered and dressed faster than I ever thought was humanly possible. I put on running clothes, hoping that Conner would be up for a workout. We jogged together every morning, even if he had stayed at Lea's.

When I thought about it, for the past few months I walked over to Lea's apartment almost every morning to meet up with Conner to run and have coffee. I hadn't realized how serious Conner must have been getting with Lea. *Then again, I hadn't thought about anything other than my music and my dick. Anything else hurt too damn much.* I couldn't even begin to comprehend why the hell I was let go from my prison in hell and placed on earth again. And I sure as hell didn't understand why I was stuck in Shane Maxton's body.

I snatched a handful of aspirin to help kill the dull throbbing in my head and heard voices. I walked into the kitchen and found Ethan sitting at the table with Tucker, eating sandwiches.

Ethan, Conner, and I were roommates, so it wasn't odd that Ethan was sitting at the table. Tucker sitting there was strange. He lived down the hallway in the apartment next door, with Alex and Brayden. His old man owned our building. That's why we got away with all the crap we did. Tucker usually never came over though; he was such a slob that we never invited him. Last time he was here, he burnt an enormous hole in our leather couch when he lit a Cuban cigar. We were cleaning ashes up for days after. The jackass didn't even smoke; he just wanted to flaunt the cigar, and how expensive it was in everyone's face.

I nodded to the two of them and grabbed a bottle of water from the refrigerator.

Tucker was going on and on about some hottie he met last night, "I'm totally serious. I think I found my first wife!"

Ethan was shaking his head while laughing with his mouth

full of food.

Tucker took another bite of his sandwich, and started talking and chewing at the same time. "I mean it. She is so beautiful...and she's nice; really nice. She's not anything like the gang of blonde bedbugs Alex brought home last night!"

I popped the aspirin in my mouth, cracked open the water bottle, and gulped some down half listening to Tucker's story.

Ethan swallowed what was in his mouth and nudged his head at Tucker, looking at me. "Hey, Shane. Tuck here says Grace is going to be his first wife. Got anything to say about that?"

The water caught in my throat and I choked it down. I gasped and coughed, almost hurling the pills back up.

Ethan sat at the table with a knowing grin glued to his face. "Yeah, I thought that would be your reaction," he murmured.

I cleared my throat and croaked, "Tucker, are you talking about Lea's friend? Long black hair, beautiful eyes?"

Tucker offered me a smile full of sandwich. "Oh yeah. And instead of calling her Grace, I'm gonna call that hottie, *Google*, cause she has *everything* that I'm looking for in a woman." Tucker raised his asinine hands to high five us but we both ignored him.

Ethan guffawed. His eyes danced between Tucker and me. I didn't understand what he was playing at. Maybe he wanted me to knock the crap out of Tucker, or maybe he just wanted to see my reaction to Tuck liking Grace?

Ethan held up an index finger, giggling. "Tucker here is confessing to meeting the woman of his dreams last night, *the girl he is going to marry*," he looked at Tucker and laughed more. "Tuck, why don't you tell Shane about those bedbugs from last night? You know the girls you met up with after you left Lea and Grace's apartment."

Tucker slammed his hands down on the table. Pieces of

his sandwich flopped onto the floor, but he didn't even notice. *Jackhat.*

"Oh man, Alex and Brayden came home with four girls last night. I bagged two of them at the same time. Man, it was AWESOME!"

I clenched my fists, "What about Grace? Tuck? Did you do anything with Grace?"

Ethan laughed so hard that tears were falling down his cheeks.

Tucker jumped up, more of his sandwich dropped to the floor. "No, she's going to take some time to bang. I gotta take a leak."

I glared at Ethan when Tucker was out of the room. "What are you trying to do? I don't want to hear about him and Grace, or him having a threesome. What's your problem?"

Ethan stood up and pushed his chair out. He grabbed his empty plate and walked over to the sink, placing it in. He turned around and leaned against the counter. "Just watching your reaction, Shane."

I knew it.

He folded his arms across his chest. If anyone else was standing there looking at the features of my giant friend, they would have called them menacing.

"Shane, you had me running all over the bar last night because you wanted to meet a girl when you saw the color of *her* eyes. You looked like a lost little boy until you saw her sitting there with Lea." He dropped his hands dramatically to his sides. "You said nothing was up last night, but left before everyone else did to go home. *Alone.*"

I sat down on one of the chairs and started lacing up my sneakers tight, being as nonchalant as I could about the topic of his conversation. "Yeah, so. What's the big deal? She's beautiful. I didn't hide that fact from you last night, I wanted you to help me find her." I stood up to leave.

"Shane, I didn't say these things to see if you liked her. That's obvious. I said them because I wanted you to see your reaction to someone like Tucker, who wanted to just sleep with her." He stepped forward and pointed his finger at me. "This is one of Lea's best friends. And Conner is one of ours. Grace isn't the sort of girl you could just sleep with without consequences. Everyone will get hurt in the process. But, the way you acted last night and now, dude, I'm your best friend...you *like* this girl. Don't screw it up by trying to sleep with her immediately."

I chuckled. "Yeah, well I'm hoping when I get to know her I can shake whatever illness I've caught and shake her from my mind."

"What if you can't, Shane?"

"You know I don't get into relationships. You know I don't ever lie about it. I don't need to lie to any of them. It'll be her choice."

He put his hands up in the air as if I was robbing him at gunpoint. "Shane, your fists are clenched, your face is red and you're planning on running over there right now, and it isn't to workout with Conner. All because you *don't* want Tucker to do what *you want* to do with her? Shane Maxton never gets jealous, *ever*."

"Yeah, I got you, thanks." I left before Tucker came back and before Ethan could say anything else.

I grabbed my keys, phone and wallet off the bar, stuffed them into the pockets of my sweats and ran out the door. On the way there, I thought about every word Ethan said to me. He was right; I just couldn't tell him anything. I certainly couldn't tell him I once wore wings and because of the one relationship I did have in my life, I'd spend the rest of my existence in hell and *this* wonderful place again. I couldn't tell him that I never had relationships because no one in this world could ever replace Selah. Ever.

There was no way I could tell any of them. They would all

have to assume I was just a player, because before I got here and my soul got slammed into Shane's body, that's who Shane *was*.

When I got to their apartment, Conner and Lea were both awake watching cartoons. Lea jumped up to make coffee when I came in. Conner and I helped her in the kitchen with the cups, our normal routine.

"So, Shane...how was your *friend* last night? Sorry if I was being rude, I guess I drank way too much." Lea's cheeks were bright red; the rest of her was a bit green.

"Eh, I thought you were pretty funny. I think that chick ended up at Alex's," I shrugged and pretended I didn't know.

Conner slapped me on the back, "Dude, coffee first, or a run?"

I looked around the apartment for signs of Grace. *Maybe she was out already. Maybe she spent the night somewhere else. With someone else.* The thought bothered me more than it should have.

"I'm ready to run, coffee when we get back," I answered.

Conner agreed and ran off in search of his running shoes. Lea walked back into the living room and curled up on the couch.

"Are you feeling okay?" I asked. "Maybe we shouldn't leave you alone here?" *Loaded question.*

"I just drank too much last night. I got some bad news and I couldn't handle it," she sighed. "I'll be fine. Grace is home with me so I won't be alone. Thanks though."

She picked up her eReader that rested on the edge of the couch and opened it, ending our conversation. I was going to ask her about the bad news, but I guess she assumed that I wouldn't and she started reading. *Wow, how callous and cold does she think I am?*

Conner came into the room ready to go, so we just took off. I was pretty bummed that I didn't get to see Grace. She was probably a real high maintenance snob anyway and I needed to erase her completely from my mind. I couldn't be pining after some stupid human girl. That's what got me in trouble in the first place. Not that I would ever think that Selah was a stupid human, she wasn't. She was the most perfect soul I ever met, perfect for me anyway. I was just so sick and worn out from this punishment.

We started a slow-paced jog and headed toward Central Park.

The park was filled with crowds of people. Some were jogging, some practicing Tai Chi on the grass, some were tourists pointing and smiling; and it was just the beginning of an icy cold February. That's one of the things I loved so much about living in New York City; you can walk right out your front door and the world was laid out in front of you. So many different people. In a backwards way, it reminded me of heaven.

It didn't take me long to lose my train of thought and start thinking about those silver eyes again. *Damn.* "So, that girl from last night is Lea's old roommate?"

Conner tilted his head towards me while he ran. "Yeah, the girl you gave your shirt to. That's Grace."

I didn't say anything else for a few minutes. Then, I couldn't help myself, "She got a boyfriend or anything?"

He gave me a smirk, "Why? Are you interested in becoming one?"

"No. I was just wondering about her having one. Tucker seems to want to marry her. Is she interested in him?"

"No," he said.

"No what?" I asked.

"No, she doesn't have a boyfriend," he answered.

"And...what about Tucker?" I pried.

Conner laughed. "I don't think he has a boyfriend either, but it would explain a lot if he did."

I laughed along with him. *It would explain a lot.* "Yeah, man. I bet he's got a crush on Alex."

"Hey, now," he continued laughing. "Don't knock it. Alex

is hot!" We stopped jogging, because we were laughing so much. We parked ourselves on a bench and just watched the rest of the runners pass us by.

"So, do you think she might like Tucker?" I had suddenly come down today with chronic verbal vomit of the mouth.

"Is this your ass backwards way of asking about her? What the hell, are you twelve again?"

I ran my hands through my hair, yanking hard at the ends. "I can't get her out of my mind, bro."

He watched me carefully. "Look, Shane, Grace is really great. She's smart, nice, pretty...all that stuff and more. But I don't think you are her type. Besides, she's got a lot of family problems she's going through right now, so I doubt dating Tucker or *anyone* is on her mind at the moment."

Shoving me in the shoulder he asked, "Hey, how was that blonde last night? I was hoping that she and Lea were going to get into a cat fight and start ripping each other's clothes off." *I guess I did a good job at making sure all my friends thought I was just a regular human jerk all this time.*

We laughed and raced each other back to the apartment. Lea was still on the couch reading and Grace still wasn't around. Ripping off our sweaty sweatshirts, we threw them at Lea, and then we fought each other into the kitchen, trying to get through the door at the same time.

"Immature idiots," Lea called us sweetly from the other room. "Hey, Conner, get me a cup too. I waited for you boys!"

I watched Conner make two cups of coffee and traipse out to Lea like a man in love. I pulled my sweaty undershirt over my head and hung it around my neck. Pouring myself some coffee, I wondered if Conner knew how lucky he was. I leaned against the counter and looked up to the ceiling. The sounds of Conner and Lea giggling echoed softly to my ears.

That's when she walked in.

A wild tangle mess of sexy black hair blocked her view of

me. She padded in barefoot, toes painted dark red. Her legs were long and bare. My eyes inched all the way up them. She wore a tiny pair of boy shorts that made me want to cry. My tee shirt from last night hung loosely over one beautiful bare shoulder.

She almost dropped her coffee when she turned and saw me standing there.

For the briefest time, we stood there with our eyes locked onto each other, both of us half dressed. I could have sworn I saw something behind those eyes, some sort of shared loneliness that I knew all too well.

Conner came in and broke through the heavy silence in the room. His voice seemed canny and high-pitched; it reminded me of the real Shane scraping his nails down a chalkboard when he was a kid. He rambled on about us going jogging.

She just stared at me. I watched as her eyes flickered over me, yet she showed no emotion, no want, no need, and no interest. *Nothing.*

I was standing across from her, forcing myself not to lessen the distance between us and devour her. My gaze shifted from her eyes to her lips, her throat, her collarbone, her smooth curvy legs...

Conner rambled on. He could have been telling us that the apartment was on fire and I wouldn't have heard him.

"You still have my shirt on," I croaked. I wanted her to know how much that meant, how much I would have given to be the one to be wrapped around her all night keeping her warm. My cheeks burned with heat and I smiled at how young and alive I felt standing there in front of her. For the first time in this body, I actually felt really *human.*

"Would you like it back right now?" she whispered.

Conner shut his mouth. I leaned forward toward her. I didn't want her to take it off in front of Conner. She took my advance as a yes.

"Sure thing," she sang and hopped out of the kitchen,

leaving her coffee behind. I exhaled like a man who had been holding his breath for years. She came back in with oversized sweats on and threw my shirt at me, smacking me right in the face with it. It plopped down into my hands.

"Thanks again," she said as she walked away. I looked at Conner.

Conner shook his head, eyes wide. "Um, that was a tense moment. Seriously, I feel like I just watched you guys have sex with each other right in front of me. I feel dirty, and a bit horny now, thanks." He poured more coffee into his cup and shook his head.

I gave him a serious look. "You think she's interested?"

He frowned and sipped his coffee. "Shane, I think you should leave her alone. She knows you don't have a serious bone in your body. We warned her about you. She's not some skank you pick up in a bar because you're in a band, she's my girl's best friend."

"But, it would be okay if she and Tucker hooked up?"

"Dude, Tucker wants to get married and be normal one day. You, on the other hand..." he trailed off and offered me an embarrassed look.

"Go ahead, finish your sentence," I said.

"*Don't.*" Conner walked into the living room and I followed. Lea and Grace seemed to be in the middle of a serious conversation, but it stopped as soon as we entered. Grace walked out of the room when she saw us; her eyes were red and welling with tears. *Shit, I wanted to grab her and take her pain away. If only I was still an angel.*

"Everything okay?" Conner asked.

I felt like a jerk; this had to be about me. "Did I piss her off? Shit, I didn't make her cry or anything did I?" I had to say something with more of Shane's real personality, "She just asked if I wanted my shirt back. Thought maybe I could get to see her almost naked again!" Most of the time I hated the person Shane

49

had been. When he was here, he was a self-serving, pathetic drug addict, the complete opposite of who I'd been. Being in his body was just like being in hell. No, actually, right now I would take the burning fires of hell over *this*.

Lea jumped off the couch, her eReader dropping heavily to the carpet. "Shane, you are the biggest, egotistical, self-centered, man I have ever met. If you think for one minute someone like Grace would spend more than a second with you on her mind, you're more than stupid." Her voice got louder. "Her brother died yesterday. Ass hat!"

She ran out of the room and Conner went right after her.

Ass hat? Her brother died yesterday?

I was standing by her side in the kitchen before I even knew I moved. I balled my hands into fists so I could stop myself from reaching out to touch her. "I'm sorry...Grace, I didn't mean to be a smart ass. I didn't know about your brother, I didn't mean to..."

She shook her head and sighed. *She didn't even look at me.*

"I'm being serious, Grace, I know how much it sucks to lose someone you care about." I leaned in closer to her, it made me dizzy, but I wanted so badly to take away her sadness. *If I was still an angel, I could have.* "Look at me."

She turned her head and those breathtaking silver eyes were bright red and full of tears. My eyes diverted to her lips; I couldn't look at her tears, *they were killing me*. The most disgusted expression appeared on her face. Without knowing it, I must have done something else to offend her. Maybe it was for the best. Let her think I'm a self-serving pig, let her go out with Tucker or some other guy who could offer her the world, not a fallen angel without a heart to offer her.

"It is what it is. You said nothing that affected me, Shane. Thanks for the condolences for my brother. Do yourself a favor. Don't bother trying to mess with my head; it'll be a waste of your time. I won't sleep with you. Just treat me like one of the guys and we'll get along fine and then you won't have to stand over me in a kitchen pretending you give a shit about anyone other than yourself."

A thousand thoughts slammed through my head. I wanted her. I needed her. This wasn't me. I wanted to drop to my knees and let her know I was once a god. I wanted to touch her lips to mine and take away all her pain. God, I just wanted to kiss her, feel her warm tongue against mine. Looking down at the floor, I let it all go. This life was another one of my punishments. There was no way I'd be allowed to have any comfort; any happiness, any hope. *She must have been put here to punish me more.* "Who said I wanted to sleep with you? You're just one of the guys. I don't *do* guys."

Surprisingly, she cracked a beautiful smile and started laughing.

I slid my hands off the countertop, dropped them to my sides and backed away from her. "Although, I have to admit. You are the sexist guy I've ever met."

Then I walked out of the room before I threw myself on her and kissed her.

I collapsed onto the couch and hung my head in my hands. My body shivered and I wasn't cold. It just wanted to be near her. *So this would be my second visit to hell, huh?* They couldn't contain me in my prison any longer and brought me back to earth. Made me think there was a chance at forgiveness, but there was only a reminder of what I could never have, a reminder of everything I'd lost and more.

Conner and Lea made their way out into the living room again. Lea and I apologized to each other. They curled up on one of the chairs and cuddled. I watched them in awe.

Grace came in a few minutes after and sat on the couch with me. Lea flipped through the channels on the television. *Nope, no giant elephant in this room.*

My phone started going off immediately. A dozen text messages from Ethan telling me more about Tucker and his exploits from the night before.

After a while, Grace stood up and went to the door, bent down and picked up sneakers.

Lea sat up. "Where are you going? We were going to go to the bar again tonight around ten." She gave a nod towards me. "His band is playing again. Want to hang out again? I'll let you get drunk this time and hold your hair back," she pleaded.

"I'm getting antsy. I thought I'd go for a run," Grace answered, not looking up from putting on her sneakers.

I gave up texting Ethan and tossed my phone onto the table. *She likes to jog, huh?*

"Well, what about hanging with me tonight? We haven't seen each other in six months, and I missed you!" Lea whined.

"I don't know. I'll see how I feel after my run. If you're not here when I get back, I'll text you." She hurried out of the room and out of the front door.

Conner and Lea looked at each other and then to me.

Lea stood up, "I really don't think she should be alone with everything that just happened with her brother, Jake. Shoot, I hate going running with her."

"I'll go with her," I offered. "It'll give you guys a chance to be alone. Conner told me he was horny in the kitchen." I didn't wait for Lea to disagree with me or even laugh at my audacity. I just leapt to my feet and dashed to the door, picking my sweatshirt up off the floor on the way.

Grace was stretching on the front steps when I walked out. Her perfect body bending and twisting; even in sweats, the girl was making my mouth water. I moved beside her and stretched along with her.

She froze when she noticed me there. "What are you doing?" she asked with narrowed eyes.

I didn't want her to think this was a weak move to get her

to sleep with me, so I challenged her. "I thought I'd run with you," I chuckled. "I figured you wouldn't care; you know since you're just one of the guys, and this is what I do with the guys. Unless you don't think you could handle it."

Her eyes narrowed more and that gorgeous sly smile appeared on her lips. "I'll try my best." Then she bolted into a dead run.

Not a jog, not a fast walk. *A balls to the wall dead run.*

She headed towards Fifth Avenue; hooked a right and sped past the Metropolitan Museum of Art. She crossed into Central Park and started on the Reservoir Loop around the Jacqueline Kennedy Onassis Reservoir. I tried to keep up the pace, silently. Who was I kidding, there was no way I could run that fast and talk at the same time; *that's* why I stayed silent.

She ran the park loops twice. *Holy shit, I completely understood why Lea hated to run with her; this was inhumane.* We must have done twenty miles; running at full speed. My lungs ached and the stitch in my side was like a knife plunging in my gut continuously. But Grace, she looked like she had been relaxing on a freakin' beach the whole time. For the last fifteen minutes of the run, I choked back the vomit that was threatening to splatter itself all over the path through Central Park I was running on.

Dusk had settled over the city when she slowed down and jogged slowly to her building. She stretched her legs on the steps again. I watched as she moved her body fluidly, gracefully. I was filled with awe. I was also filled with pain from head to toe. I cleared my throat to make sure she knew I was still there.

She spun around and regarded me what looked like a hint of respect.

"You're a runner, huh?" I said, trying my hardest not to pant or show how completely out of breath I was. It didn't work, I stuttered and stammered, panting like a slobbering Saint Bernard all over myself.

She squished up her face and gave me the most adorable exasperated expression I'd ever seen anyone give. "I said I was going for a run. You assumed that I wasn't *man* enough?" she asked.

"Not many people surprise me, Grace, you just surprised the shit out of me." She completely ignored me and unlocked the front door. I sighed to myself. I hated having to watch her walk away from me. "Did my heart love till now? Forswear it sight, for I never saw true beauty till this night," I whispered.

"Shakespeare," she whispered back.

I hadn't realized I quoted him out loud. Her expression was beautiful and haunted. I knew I needed to stay away from her; she would make me want to have a human life that I know I would never be allowed to have. I turned to walk away, but couldn't help myself and I turned back, but continued walking backwards. "Hey, you coming to the bar tonight?" I called to her.

She stopped and turned around, "Maybe, I don't know, I have to see how I feel after a shower."

I felt the smile burst across my face. How could I *not* say something back to *that*? "Do you need help with that? I'd like to see how you feel after a shower too..."

She slammed the door on me, but before she did, I saw her smile. *Damn, she was beautiful.*

Chapter 4

I walked home slowly. My body was screaming at me to shut down. I dragged myself into a hot shower and stayed under the stream for at least an hour. I gulped down more aspirin to try to numb my throbbing muscles.

Hauling myself onto the couch, I sat with just a pair of jeans on, waiting until I had to leave for the show. My eyes blurred and my head swam, darkness engulfing me. The warmth of Selah's soft hands in mine filled my dreams.

However, it was Ethan's huge hands that shook me awake.

It took me a minute to figure out where I was and what I was supposed to be doing. Realizing I had only a few minutes to get my stuff together before the gig, I jumped up and was surprised that my body felt rested and just a bit sore.

Ethan and I made our way to the bar and commandeered our favorite table. I leaned back comfortably with a beer in hand. Alex, Brayden, Tucker, and Conner, showed up a few minutes later and joined us. I almost bit my teeth clear through my tongue, trying not to ask Conner if the girls were going to show up.

The place just started to get crowded when I notice an insanely pair of sexy black leather boots walk through the front door. Her tight jeans showed off her curves and the way she walked through the crowd made every man in the room notice her. Grace was simply perfect.

Tucker jumped up when he saw her. A stupid smile lit up his face; I wanted to punch it the fuck off.

Conner grabbed their coats, hung them on the back of two chairs, and acted the part of gentlemen. She wore a flattering sweater that hung off one shoulder and her hair fell in thick wavy curls to her waist.

Lea stood in front of the table and waved a hand towards

us. "Grace, you didn't get to meet the rest of the guys last night. Of course, you know Tucker and Conner," she said. "This is Ethan the drummer, and this is Brayden, the bass player; you know Shane already."

Alex came up to the table with a huge bucket of icy cold beers for everyone. "And that's Alex," Lea continued. "He plays rhythm guitar and keyboard." Alex gave her a smile and raised his eyebrows. Lea grabbed Grace away from Alex and moved her into the seat next to Tucker. Tucker handed her a beer and leaned into her ear to whisper something to her. She gave him a smile that never reached her eyes and she whispered something back to him. *Shit.* Rage burned in my stomach. Tucker was looking at her with his beady little greedy eyes. He was practically eye fucking her in front of everyone and she was *smiling* back at him. I almost asked him how his threesome was from the other night, just so Grace would know what kind of a guy she was smiling at, but I decided not to be a douchebag. *Yet.*

Tucker flicked his eyes towards me and he smirked. *What the fuck?* It felt like he was staking a claim, calling dibs on the new toy. I wanted to rip his heart out and hand it back to him. I couldn't even explain the feelings that rocked my body at that very moment. I held my beer so tight that I felt like I could smash it with just a little more pressure. *Is this what jealousy was? How pathetically human of me.* If he touched her in front of me one time, I was going to kick him hard under the table and say it was an accident. I swear I wanted to bust his nuts right there. Realizing I was glaring at Tucker hard, I ripped my gaze off him and chanced a small glance at her.

Her eyes were on mine. We held a private glance together for just a moment, but a strange calmness rolled in slow waves over my body. I didn't know what the hell was happening. I didn't know what control this human had over my body, but I knew I couldn't give her any more.

Ethan tapped me on the head with his drumsticks to get

my attention. I could barely move. I didn't want to leave her here with Tucker. I didn't want his hands on her perfect skin. But what could I possibly say or do? I desperately wanted to tell her she reminded me of the love of my existence, and that I needed to be with her, even if it was just for one night. *Yeah, how crazy would I look then?* I nosily pushed my seat back and stormed toward the stage.

"What the hell was that look?" Lea asked Grace when she thought I was out of earshot. I didn't wait to hear Grace's answer. *I had to get this girl out of my mind.*

I jumped on the stage and felt the pulse of the crowd. This was my own way of getting high now, my only way to remember how it felt to be invincible.

I started the set with a nod to Ethan. A tornado of rage burst through my hands as I danced them over the strings of my guitar. The crowd hummed and echoed back the intensity of the melody I threw at them.

I blasted through each song. Every note I played, every breath I took was a small piece of my soul breaking and smashing beneath the feet of the dancing crowd. Grace's silver eyes, and the thought of her in the audience watching me from somewhere below me, was a constant thought in the back of my mind. I played like there was a fire ripping through my body, and there was, *its name was Grace.*

At the end of one song, Alex motioned to my harp guitar and smiled. I nodded to him and agreed. Lea and Grace appeared near the front of the stage. I gave Lea a wink, because I knew this was her favorite song.

I ran to the back of the small stage and picked my twelve string up. My fingers moved along the strings before I could even strap it on. I walked to the front of the stage and twisted an intricate melody painlessly from my fingertips.

I sung the words as if they were they first ever to be whispered into being. I watched Grace's face as the emotions bore on her features. *Shock, awe, desire, elation, and longing.* A surge of pure adrenaline tore through my body, knowing that I put those expressions on her face. *Me.*

I locked eyes with her and *sang.* Sang my heart out. The heat of the spotlights above me burned through my clothes and sweat beaded across my skin. I kneeled down on stage to close the distance between us, my fingers playing my twelve strings like I wanted to play her body.

Tucker walked up behind her and spun her around to dance with her. His features were so human, terrified of rejection, *yet longing, lustful, and greedy.* My heart ached; it burned. She was born into this world and I hated that, just like Selah, and I wasn't the right one for *her* either. She was forbidden to me; and her prize in this shitty world would be someone like Tucker.

We ended the set and were immediately assaulted with bras and panties. I made sure Grace watched me as I grabbed a sexy little bra and held it to my nose. I was done. I've done my time in hell desperate to be with someone I was forbidden from, I couldn't let myself spend my eternity here desperate for someone who reminded me of her. *To hell with this, I was **going** to erase her from my mind.*

Jumping off the stage, we were surrounded by a crowd of beautiful women. Two of them piqued my interest. I told them I couldn't tell which one was hotter, so I would be taking them both home, *if they were good.* They giggled. I rolled my eyes in my mind. Of course, they wouldn't care, any self-respecting woman would have told me to go home by myself. *I guessed these weren't self-respecting women.* These were the kind of chicks I had to stick with, those I knew would *never* touch my soul.

The guys and I sat around our table with a girl on each of our laps. I had my two. *Yes, erasing the thought of Grace was what I was going to do. Easy.* I was nice and comfortable with the two hotties on my lap, no problem. *Then why the hell did I feel like I wanted to run the fuck out of there?*

Conner and Tucker sat down with us, bringing a bucket of ice-cold beers with them.

Grace sashayed over to our table with a whole bottle of Tequila in her hand. Standing behind her was Lea armed with a handful of shot glasses.

Her eyes glanced at mine and she gave me a beautiful smile that threatened to melt my heart. I held my two girls tighter and she just shook her head at me, as if I was being a silly boy. Maybe I was, but I wanted to lose interest in her, I wanted to forget her.

Grace held the tequila over her head. "Okay, ladies and gentlemen here is the first drinking game of the night: Fuzzy Duck!" she announced. "Here are the rules. Everyone starts off taking one shot. Then we pour another. We go around the table and each person has to say Fuzzy Duck. The first person to mess up, takes a shot and around and around we go!"

Lea held the glasses as Grace poured shot after shot and slid each glass to a person without spilling a drop. *She's done this before, damn that's kind of hot.*

We played game after game and in a short time, all the blondes were trashed and everyone was feeling happy.

I tried not to watch Grace, but my eyes kept grazing her lips as she laughed, or noticing how her hair fell over her bare shoulder. How could any man not notice? She was by far the most beautiful at the table, *in the whole fucking bar.* I was finding it hard to pretend she wasn't there. I definitely couldn't fathom how I could forget her.

The girls on my lap seemed to be the drunkest, or were at least pretending to be the drunkest. Maybe chicks thought if they got drunk that would justify all the nasty slutty stuff they would be doing later. *Whatever.* I hated sleeping with drunken girls and I never did. Who the hell wants to be with someone who could puke on you at any moment?

One of the girls elbowed the other one off my lap and started doing this little dance for me. It might have been sexy if she wasn't acting so slobbering drunk and just trying to show off. The dance wasn't for me. It was for everyone else.

"Holy Strippers, Batman! Are you *that* desperate to make sure he goes home with you?" Lea called to the girl. I didn't even know her name. I just grabbed her legs to try to make her stop.

The crazy bitch started moaning.

I looked past the blonde and watched Grace's reaction. God forgive me, but I wanted her to care. I wanted her to be pissed off. *Nothing.* How the hell can this shit *NOT* affect her?

"Maybe she just needs a few dollar bills?" Grace said laughing.

"Ah! Change the porn channel! You're gonna give me an STD over here!" Lea shouted.

The blonde stood up and shouted back at Lea. "Why don't you mind your own business, skank!"

"Skank? Me? I'm not the one giving a lap dance in public to a guy I just met." Lea jumped to her feet. *Maybe Conner would get to see a cat fight after all.*

The blonde must have gotten scared because she backed up into me.

Lea continued to yell at her, "Don't even try, you might find me smacking the slut out of you in a minute!"

I heard all of it, but all I saw was Grace. She effortlessly jumped in front of Lea, blocking her from fighting. "Let's dance, who cares what she's doing." She gave me a strange sad expression and pushed Lea towards the dance floor as Lea yelled, "Well, I care. My boyfriend is watching it!"

Tucker and Conner followed them into the crowd laughing.

The two blondes tried to sit back on my lap, but I got up. "No thanks, ladies. You're both very beautiful, but you're both a little too drunk for my taste."

The lap dancer giggled, "I was just pretending. I don't get drunk, I just get more awesomer, so it's all good!"

More Awesomer?

I stared at her in disbelief, "That just makes it worse." I walked away from her and grabbed my coat and my guitar. I passed Grace dancing with Lea and I sat down at the bar and watched her. Tucker and Conner danced around them, Grace and Lea laughing carefree in the middle. I could have watched her body move all night. *I did.* I watched the way her hips moved to the rhythm; the way she lifted her hands and ran them through her hair and the way she sang the songs to her best friend. I watched her until she left with Lea and Conner. Tucker followed them out.

If I believed my prayers would have been heard, I would have prayed that Tucker didn't touch her. I knew I had no right to want that, but I did.

I went home alone. I paced my room; I paced the apartment. Then I decided I was going to go over there and kill Tucker. Okay, I probably wouldn't really kill him, but I was insane with jealousy and I needed to see what was happening. How in the world did humans deal with this asinine emotion every day? This jealously crap was going to kill me. I didn't even know this girl; she just resembled someone. *I'm insane, that's it.* I didn't care. I had absolutely no logical thoughts in my brain. I changed into a pair of black running pants and a dark sweatshirt. I couldn't even think straight as I ran through the lobby of my building; all I saw was red.

As I reached the front doors, Tucker walked through them. He was alone. "Hey, Tuck. Thought you'd still be at Lea and Grace's. What are you doing home so early?"

He gave me a dejected face and laughed. "I guess she must be one of those nice girls I keep hearing my mother talk about."

Relief blanketed my body as I chuckled. "Wow, I thought those girls were just a myth."

Tucker looked around me and shrugged. "What the fuck are *you* doing home already?"

I shrugged back. "Too much peroxide with that group."

Tucker laughed. "Are they all still at the bar? Maybe I could jump in your grave. You mind? You didn't do those two chicks yet, did you?"

"Uh, no. I didn't *do* anybody."

"Hell, even after that lap dance? Shit, that got me so horny!" He ran out the door and I watched him walk briskly down the street back towards the bar. *I hope Grace doesn't fall for him, he'll just hurt her and then I'd really have to kill him.*

Still antsy and full of energy, I left. I walked along the city streets walking in and out of the stores that stayed open all night for the tourists. I sat in a small diner, drank coffee, and chatted with the waiters. When the sun rose, I found myself sitting on Grace's stoop wondering if it was too early to ring the bell and ask her to go running with me. Then I decided I was a complete ass and needed to walk away before anyone saw me. *Wasn't I supposed to be trying to get her out of my mind?*

Just as I was about to leave, she came running out and stumbled right over me. "What the hell are you doing here?" she asked giggling. She didn't look angry; she actually looked happy to see me. Her smile made my freakin' knees weaken.

"I was going for a run. Thought you or Conner would be up for one," I croaked breathlessly, just from the sight of her. It was as if I was looking at a ghost. *Like it was Selah standing right in front of me.*

She laughed with a smile that shamed the sun. "Conner won't be up for a while. Shane, did you even sleep? I only got like three hours."

A warm rush of heat ran across my cheeks and forehead. I hoped she never finds out I stayed in the bar and watched her, stayed up all night thinking about her, or waited all morning outside her front door just to be with her. "Nah, I'll sleep later. I have too much energy."

She smiled wider, "Wow, that must have been a really great lap dance, huh?"

"Shut up!" I nudged her with my elbow and laughed. I ran, heading for Central Park and started on the same loop as the day before.

Thankfully, she ran slower and we talked about all the people we passed on our path. We quickly made a game out of it, creating a life for the person, each story funnier than the next. She had a sense of humor like no one I had ever met before. A few times, she had me almost stumbling into trees because I was laughing so hard.

I ran with her for three hours and I didn't want to stop. I followed her up her front steps. Her beautiful sweaty hands held the door open for me and I went right in. We sat together on the couch and laughed while watching the television.

All along, I thought about how I shouldn't be there. I shouldn't be next to her, but I was in love with looking at her.

"Oh, my, God! Did you two just have sex out here? Ewww. Grace! Come on, Shane, really?" Lea yelled when she and Conner walked into the room. They both had the most horrible bed hair. Grace and I laughed.

Grace placed her hands over her chest and in a sweet southern accent asked, "What? Y'all seriously think we just had sex? Here on the couch?"

The way her voice sounded and the beautiful innocent expression she gave made me lose complete control of my laughter and I couldn't stop. "If you guys look like this after you guys get freaky, that's awesome. But, no, we just came back from a run. I wouldn't touch Grace if you paid me. She's really a man," I explained to them, choking on my laughter.

Grace's smile lit up the room, her eyes dancing with

secrets and whispers I desperately wanted to be part of. I softly nudged my hand against her knee to get her attention. Her eyes widened as my fingers brushed against the soft material of her pants, and I heard a low gasp escape through her lips. "I'm starving. Grace, you hungry, *bro*? I'll make you breakfast."

Her wide eyes narrowed playfully as the look of disbelief shadowed her face. "Are you even capable of pouring cereal into a bowl?" she asked. *I can cook almost as great as I am in bed.*

"Are you insulting me?" I laughed.

"Um. No not really. It was an honest question," she smiled.

I walked toward the kitchen and waved her to follow. "C'mon. You have to be just as hungry as I am after all that sex, I mean all that running."

"Oh, so now you're saying you *do* have sex with guys?" she laughed as she threw a couch pillow at me. I couldn't stop myself from smiling as she followed me in. We left Lea and Conner in the living room gawking openly at our flirting.

I rummaged through the refrigerator and all the cabinets, knowing exactly where everything was. There were way too many times I had crashed over at Lea's and made it up to her by cooking Conner and her a meal. Usually, it was to get away from the other guys partying and their crazy antics. I would just tell the guys I spent the night over at some girl's place; they always believed me.

"So, honestly, why did you think I wouldn't be able to cook?" I asked as I settled on making an omelet. I stripped off my sweaty shirt without a thought and started to make her breakfast. I hadn't realized that I even took my shirt off until I turned my head around to look at her because she hadn't answered me yet. Her eyes were slowly following the flowing designs of my tattoos. I watched them, drinking me in, roaming from the dragon on my elbow to the tribal bands along my arms and traveling across to the dove wrapped in its own broken wings on my shoulder. I never felt more bare in front of a woman before. Completely and utterly naked, down to my soul. It was as if she could read between the inked lines and know my story, my soul out in the open, my fall from heaven. And I wanted it, I wanted this beautiful creature to know my story. To know *me*. It made a chill run up my spine.

Her eyes slowly moved further along my skin, inching their way across my chest and down my stomach, and even in this human body filled with my cold dead angel's heart, I couldn't help but feel *hope*.

I placed a plate of food in front of her as a splash of crimson colored her cheeks. "Spinach, mushroom, green pepper and cheese omelet ala Shane," I said. "You haven't answered me. What is it about me that makes you think I can't cook?"

Grace picked through the omelet inspecting it carefully, tentatively putting a small forkful to her lips. Her shoulders relaxed as she chewed. I guess she thought I was going to poison us both.

Tilting her head up at me, she said, "You just strike me as a shallow person who gets everything they want from other people. I would have bet you've had a different blonde make you breakfast every morning of your life." Those beautiful lips of hers turned downward as she talked, but not from disgust, from pity. *That* intrigued me. I never saw anyone look at me in Shane's perfect body and *pity* it.

Trying to keep the conversation light, I laughed. "Well, you are half right. I am shallow. But, I can cook, and honestly, I like chicks with jet black hair better than blondes. Well? Is it good?"

"Yeah, sure. Thanks. I didn't realize how hungry I was," she mumbled. I was betting that it was the best omelet she'd ever had, but she'd never own up to feeling that way. At least never to me.

"So, what's the deal with you? What's with the intense

Shane revulsion? I've never had a girl not jump at the chance with me. Or, wait, are you into chicks?" I teased.

She graciously played along with my teasing and laughed along with me. "So you think because I'm not falling for your crap that I *must be* a lesbian?"

"Bi? Maybe just playing hard to get?" *I hoped I wasn't pushing this too far.*

Some sort of flicker of emotion danced behind those eyes. "You really are full of yourself. Brace yourself, Shane, this might be hard to hear," she teased, "but you just don't do it for me. Sorry."

That made me want her even more. My soul ached to tell her who I really was. The hairs on the back of my neck prickled with the thought of telling her my secrets, just to see if the real me who was hidden from those soulful eyes, would do it for her. "So, who *does it* for you then?"

Her eyebrows burrowed together and she stood up and walked to the counter. Turning her back to me so I couldn't read her expression, she opened the dishwasher and loaded her plate in noisily. Turning around, she straightened up and leaned her elbows against the counter with a thoughtful look on her face. She looked incredibly sexy. "Someone who doesn't think of me as a walking vagina," she blurted out.

I laughed so hard my sides ached. I laughed, not because what she said was funny, but because I felt like the complete opposite toward her. Yes, I wanted to be with her, but in so many more ways than just the one way, she thought.

A slow, hesitant, tight smile appeared on her face, and my stomach dropped. "And what's your deal? What happened to you that makes you think that women were put here to serve you? Maybe something happened that makes you so insecure that you would be incapable of having a relationship or normal friendship with a girl?" Shit. *I guess I went too far.*

"There's no deep dark reason, no insecurity, nothing to

read into. I just don't want anything more from someone. Ever. There is no need for it. Every girl I sleep with knows my intentions clearly. They want to fuck the lead singer of Mad World. I give them what they want and get what I want from them. There's no need for more. None of *them* are worth more than that." I was done with the conversation. She needed to know that those chicks meant nothing to someone like me. "So, what do you do? Where were you living all this time?"

She flinched as if I had asked her a painful question. "Jobless at the moment. I've been living with my brother in a hospice for the last few months, so my job was just to try to make him comfortable."

Wow. How many women in their twenties would be able to put their lives on hold to take care of a sick brother? I had never met a human with compassion for another like that. The conversation was getting worse. I wanted to find something about her that would make me NOT want her anymore, not information that would make me fall in love with her.

"That's heavy. What about your parents? Did everybody in your family just move there to be with him?" I asked. *Maybe they forced her to go?*

"Nope. My parents are both dead. It was just Jake and me. How about you? What's your family like? Where are you from, what do you do?"

Damn. She was a beautiful person inside and out. I hated myself for wanting her so much. I hated myself for wanting to be more human than I was. I hated myself for wanting her to be Selah.

"Normal family. They all live in Florida now. Nothing dysfunctional. My parents are still married, no one had dependency problems, and no one ever hit me. And being the lead singer for Mad World really pays all my bills," I sneered. The tone came out all wrong and the words sounded so harsh, but I could barely contain the rage I was feeling inside myself, *for myself*, at that moment. I wanted this hell to be over. I didn't want this beautiful creature to be shoved in my face by mocking angels somewhere above me. It was beyond cruel and evil to dangle this need in front of me just to punish me for falling in love so long ago.

The coarse pitch of her voice snapped me from my own rage. "Hm. Sounds like you're put together all nicely. Even though you're standing here having a difficult time having an innocently normal conversation with someone of the opposite sex, knowing that there is no way in hell I'd ever sleep with you. No, Shane, you are not *dysfunctional* in any way." She stormed out of the room as if her ass was on fire.

I bolted up out of my chair and stumbled over the table to try to get her. "Wait, Grace..."

"Save it for someone who would actually care about what you had to say, Shane," she yelled back to me. Then she practically ran down the hall and slammed her bedroom door. I even heard the lock click in place.

With soft steps, I walked to her door and stood staring at it. I leaned my arms against either side of it, and fought against the idea of knocking. *It would only get worse.* She would only hate me more. I needed to leave her alone and just live as Shane, not as *Shamsiel, the fallen angel.* I wasn't an angel anymore. And there was no way someone like Shane Maxton was good enough for Grace. *Please, God, let me get her out of my thoughts. No matter what she looks like, she's not Selah.*

I left without saying goodbye to Conner and Lea. They weren't in the living room when I passed to leave. Hopefully, they had enough sense to know I'd left and lock the door behind me. I slammed it behind me loudly to emphasize my departure.

When I got home, my apartment was empty. It was only 10:30 in the morning, and way too early to start drinking for a Sunday. I walked to my bedroom to get my guitar. I figured I'd spend the day with the love of my life, an inanimate object whose existence wouldn't send me straight to hell.

Chapter 5

A small yellow sticky note hung squarely in the middle of my bedroom door.

Your phone is off. Emergency. Call me - Ethan

I took my phone out of my pocket and turned it on. The screen blew up with voice messages and texts. Without reading or listening to any of them, I called Ethan. He picked up on the first ring. "Shane? I've been trying to reach you all day..."

"All day? Dude. It's only like 10:30, what's up?" I laughed.

"You didn't get any of our messages?" he huffed.

"No, I just got your sticky note on my door. Why? What's going on?"

"We're at the hospital. Alex got jumped last night by that chick's boyfriend. He's banged up pretty bad," Ethan explained.

"What? I'm coming now. Where are you?"

"Lennox...Dude, I think both his arms are broken...oh...I'm going in with him now to get x-rays. He is such a wuss. We're all still in the waiting room," he said.

"I'll be right there."

I jumped in the shower and washed as fast as I could. I threw on whatever clothes I could find and ran out the door. I shivered when the outside frigid air hit my wet hair. My head would probably form icicles if I walked, so I waved for a cab and jumped into the first one that stopped for me.

When I got to Lennox Hill Hospital, I walked through the emergency room and right into the triage unit until I found three idiots sitting on a gurney behind a closed curtain, asking one of the nurses if she wanted to give each of them a sponge bath. Of course, the nurse was giggling at them.

I pulled the curtain open to see Brayden and Ethan sitting on opposite sides of a *very* messed up Alex. He looked *horrible*. His lip was busted open. There was an open bloody gash over one of his eyes and he couldn't move without whimpering. Yet, he smiled when I walked in and cracked jokes about the reasons I might have stayed out all night and why no one was able to find me until 10:30 that morning. His lip bled when he laughed and dripped a long strip of dark red blood down his chin, "Damn, Shane. She must be something special if you left the bar early and stayed with her until now. Who is she?"

"I think that guy didn't hit you hard enough if you believe *that*. What happened?" I asked.

"Ah, the girl's boyfriend was hiding in the closet, and as you can see...he handed my ass to me. Anyway, who is the girl you've been with all night? Wait, if you're hiding it, maybe it's a guy. Because, I always wondered about you, you're way too pretty," he laughed and then squinted his eyes in pain.

I cracked up. "You're the only one for me, Alex," I batted my eyelashes at him. "So, really, what happened?"

Alex's face turned serious. *Well, as serious as Alex could get.* "I took that girl home, and I didn't even sleep with her." His cheeks turned bright red, "Okay, I didn't sleep with her *last night*. Her boyfriend jumped out of the closet with a wooden bat. I put both my hands up to block the swing. Then he just pummeled me and ran like a girl when I got up to go after him."

"Yeah, then I get this crazy call from Alex's cell phone. But it's not Alex, it's the girl screaming at me that she thinks Alex is dying in her living room," Ethan said laughing.

"She thought I was dying, but didn't call 911. She hit my phone history and called the last person that *I* had called. Thank God, I hadn't just called my mom," Alex chuckled.

The doctor walked in then and explained the results of the x-rays to Alex. Both his arms were broken, one arm in three different places, and they would need to be in casts for at least six weeks. He just about cried when the doctor said he wouldn't be able to play guitar or piano until they healed.

Brayden, Ethan, and I, had to hold him down when the

doctor set his arms so they could put the casts on. Then someone else came in, cleaned, and stitched his lip up. I asked them if it was possible for them to stitch his lips together, but no one except my friends found the question amusing.

We left the hospital around 3:30 that afternoon and stood like four fools in front of the entrance trying to figure out what we were going to do. *Without Alex, we wouldn't be able to play any gigs for at least six weeks.* We walked straight to Lea and Grace's apartment, knowing that's where we would find Conner, who had taken the role of our manager and promoter long ago.

Conner is the one who introduced us to Boozer's Bar while we were still in high school, when his older brother snuck us in on a busy Friday night. We hung out quietly sipping beers at a back table listening to a punk band until their set was over. Not being able to help ourselves, we started playing the instruments that had been left alone on stage. The guys who owned the instruments drunkenly laughed at us, but Boozer, the owner, admired our confidence. Conner talked him into letting us play a gig and the crowd that packed the bar for us was insane. Boozer hired us every weekend after, and we'd been there ever since. He used to let us have two beers max a night when we were underage and half the cover charge at the door. We lived like kings. *We still do.* Especially now that the band bought the bar from Boozer, and we just kept the name. Boozer was now our manager, and ran the bar for us. It was a very lucrative business, and we still got to play our music any time we wanted to.

When Lea opened the door, the first thing she saw was Alex's messed up face, and the first thing she did was scream. And it was one of those earsplitting screams that chicks do that make your insides curl and make you want to vomit and tear your freaking ears off. She pulled him by the front of his shirt and yanked him through the doorway, "Oh my God, Conner!

Conner!"

Conner came running, stopping dead in his tracks at the sight of Alex. "What the hell happened to you?" Conner demanded as Lea dragged Alex through the living room and shoved him onto the couch. Everybody started talking all at once, trying to relay the story. Alex made himself sound more and more like a hero each time he repeated it, his casts comically waving dramatically as he retold the story he dubbed, *The Adventure with the Bitch and Baseball Bat*. I leaned against the front door and watched the mayhem.

I was looking down at my cell to check the time when all the voices stopped at once.

"Are you seriously wearing teddy bear pajamas?" Alex asked someone. I snapped my head up to look at Alex, as he arched one eyebrow, "That is incredibly adorable and sexy." I followed his stare. Grace had come into the room. She wore a cute pair of pink flannel pajama bottoms that had fluffy teddy bears all over them, and a tight pink, almost sheer tee shirt for a top, without a bra underneath. *Yeah, without a bra*. I wanted to wrap my coat around her so everybody would stop staring at her. I didn't want anyone's eyes on her but mine.

Grace pointed down and lifted her foot up to show Alex her slipper. "Complete with my comfy teddy bear slippers. What in the world is going on in here? Why are both your arms in casts?"

Brayden was the first one to exhale. "This loser spent the morning in the hospital after getting his ass kicked last night."

Everyone else still had their eyes glued to Grace's skin tight shirt. Alex's fucking tongue was hanging out of his damn mouth as he gawked at her. You could seriously see everything through the freaking shirt, *EVERYTHING!* Shit, the curves of her body made me so aroused; I could barely think straight. *Were my friends feeling the same way looking at her right now? I quickly looked at each one of the guys. Shit, hell yeah they were thinking the same fucking dirty things as me!*

Grace stepped closer to Alex and pushed some hair off his forehead to inspect the cuts and bruises. *Ahh, please don't fucking touch him like that, go back in your room, change your fucking clothes!*

Oblivious to her effects on the opposite sex, she remained there. Perfect. Sexy. Forbidden. "Holy Crap," she murmured. "What the hell happened?" Alex just stood there with his mouth open, drooling, staring at her chest. His face was bright red.

Lea answered her for him. He was probably incapable of speaking to her right then, most likely because all the blood in his entire body was pooling in his dick, "Seems that one of the bimbos from last night had a boyfriend. That said boyfriend introduced himself to Alex by way of his fists and a baseball bat." Lea then started handing out bottles of water and bowls of chips to everyone.

"A baseball bat?" Grace gasped. *Even her gasp sounded sexual! Stop it, Shane!*

"Yeah. The dude jumped out on me from the closet with the bat. I threw my hands up to block it. Broke both my arms and did some other stuff that I can't remember now because you're standing in front of me wearing all that innocent sexiness and my head is all fuzzy," Alex explained. His face turned even redder.

"Please tell me the boyfriend looks worse," she pleaded.

Ethan roared with laughter, "I think maybe Alex hit him with some splatters of blood, but that's about it!"

Ethan moved closer to Grace. *Shit, Ethan please don't touch her. I can't control these human emotions, I don't know what I'll say or do.*

Fuck, I felt like I was about to burst. My skin tingled all over my body as if it was electrically charged. Sweat broke out all over my face. I wanted Alex and Ethan to get the fuck away from her. I wanted her to put a damn shirt on that wasn't freakin' *fucking invisible*! "Yeah, well, that's all really funny. But who is gonna play rhythm guitar this weekend, or next? Or, how about the week after that? Who the hell are we gonna find who could play as good as Alex, and play his keyboard, and sing, and learn all the fucking songs before Friday night?" *Damn, I just made myself sound like an inconsiderate tool, all because I'm so freaking jealous I can't think straight.*

Ethan stopped moving towards Grace, which is exactly what I had wanted to do. Unfortunately, now everybody in the whole room was eyeballing me. Not until I saw the scowl on Grace's face did I think I had said it with too much fury. Little did these people know what really was burning my insides. Hell, I could probably play rhythm, keyboard and lead guitar; all I wanted was Grace to want me and it was tearing me up inside that she was so out of my reach. So close to everybody else.

I looked at Conner for help. He must have seen the confusion and craziness in my eyes, because he took over. He waved his hand at me like he was saying, *"I got your back, bro,"* and calmly captured the room. "Listen, it's only Sunday. We have until Friday night. You know there is a shitload of guitar players in New York City that have your CDs and know your music by heart. Let's ask around, make some fliers and have a small audition on Thursday. You guys can pick the best player. You definitely won't find anyone who could play the piano and the guitar like Alex, but just don't do the songs that call for both. Alex, how long do you have to have the casts on?"

"Six weeks or so," Alex muttered looking down at his casts.

"Okay, so it's only for a few weeks. Just *think* of the exposure it'll get you with having auditions. But if that's not good for you guys, cancel the next six weekends. Take a break," Conner advised the band, but he was just looking at me. In his own way, telling me to take a break and calm down.

I nodded my head at him and mumbled so no one else but him could hear, "Thanks, Con, I owe you one."

He offered me a salute in acknowledgment while the rest of the room discussed his advice.

"We can always get Tucker to do it. It's been a while, but I bet he remembers how to play," Ethan offered. *Yeah, that would be the worst idea ever. Being on stage would add to his enormous ego. He was in the band with us before and he never took playing seriously. He just reveled in all the attention it got him.*

Lea left the room and Grace jumped up to follow her. I waited maybe a minute or two, listening to the guys talk and then went in after them. Yes, I was definitely demonstrating signs of stalker-ish psychopathic behavior. *Wonderful.* Crown me the king of Douchedom.

Lea was in the kitchen sitting at the table. She was giving Grace a pouty face. "They may be jerks sometimes, but they are really great guys, even Shane."

Okay, this was probably an awkward conversation to be walking in on. I should just leave. But my feet just rooted to the spot like a freakin' tree. I cleared my throat and asked, "Even Shane what?"

Both girls jumped and stared at me with giant open eyes. Deer caught in headlights.

Lea tilted her head, looked at Grace's expression, and gave me a sly smile. I didn't get what it meant, but I knew she just had some special thought that had to do with me and Grace. "We were just wondering what we could do to help, that's all? Um, how long were you standing there?" Lea smiled.

I looked right into Grace's wide silver eyes; there was something she didn't want me to know, something she was afraid of because I saw *raw fear*. "Long enough to know that we are jerks, but really great guys, even me," I said still locking my eyes with Grace's.

Lea giggled at Grace and me standing there, "Yep, that's how I feel about you guys in a nutshell. So what can I do to help?" She asked, jumping out of the chair she was sitting in. Grace didn't move at all.

"Do you have markers and paper? We could make some posters and put them up in all the local bars," I said, not breaking eye contact at all with Grace as I answered Lea. That was what I had heard the guys discussing before I left them. I didn't know if they really needed the crap. I was kind of just grasping at straws so I could see what the hell was going on with Grace.

Lea busied herself getting whatever she needed, yanking open drawers and slamming closets, hooting whenever she found things we could use.

Grace still sat at the table as if she was waiting for me to tell her I knew whatever it was I almost walked in on. She looked like a frightened little girl and all I wanted to do was wrap my arms around her and take her fear away. *Shit, this was getting worse.*

I leaned back against the counter and folded my arms. "You look like you are terrified. I really didn't hear anything else you and Lea were talking about, so please take that sad horrified look off that beautiful face," I said.

Grace didn't move and didn't even acknowledge my comment. I only walked out because Lea came back in asking us what we wanted on our pizza, because she was going to order a few pies. If Lea hadn't come in, I could have just stayed there all night looking at those soulful eyes as they looked right back into mine. I had no idea what Grace saw in mine, but I couldn't help but hope she looked past Shane and saw the real me.

We ended up lying around the living room designing posters to hang in the bars in the area explaining our predicament. We had a large following in the New York City area, so I was betting that Conner's idea was going to be a great one.

Each of us sat around a giant poster board and colored in

letters while eating pizza on paper plates. A comfortable silence hung in the air and just the soft sounds of markers on paper could be heard. The strong stench of permanent ink stained the air.

I repeatedly snuck glances at Grace as she lay on her stomach and colored her poster. Her legs bent at the knee and she lifted her teddy bear slipper clad feet into the air. She caught me watching her once and her cheeks burned crimson; I could only wonder what her thoughts were of me that she blushed so deeply. Whatever it was, just the thought of her mind on me made my heart sputter in my chest.

She scanned the rest of the room and giggled. "Does anyone else feel like a five year old on a play date?"

Alex chuckled and yelled, "We always act like we're five years old, I mean Brayden even picks his nose and eats it."

Choking on a mouthful of pizza, Brayden shouted, "Yeah, well, Alex has the cooties!"

"So we look like five years old, huh?" Ethan barreled over to Grace. He wrapped his arm around her and held her in a headlock, giving her nuggies on the top of her head.

Grace screamed when he grabbed her. She dropped to the floor on one knee and easily got out of his hold, which surprised the crap out of me. It was ninja quick like she was skillfully trained in the art of self-defense; even Ethan's facial features expressed surprise at her escape. She bolted out of his reach and grabbed her open water bottle. Her lips curled up in that sexy devilish way and she ran back at Ethan. The look of complete shock was on his face as she dumped the entire bottle over his head.

Conner and Lea went after each other with their water bottles. Brayden jumped up on the table, pulled his jeans down and mooned everyone. I really could have done without seeing his skinny white ass shaking in my face.

I held my open water bottle and watched Grace until she

noticed me looking at her. She noticed my bottle first, and then looked at my eyes, back to my open water bottle and to my eyes again. She bit her bottom lip. I could swear to hide a bigger smile from coming out. Then she ran.

Alex saw the exchange between us and he jumped, broken arms up, right in Grace's path so I'd be able to catch her. "Get her, Shane, get her!" he cheered me on.

She slammed right into Alex's chest and bounced off of him. She stumbled backward and fell on me, both of us tumbling to the floor. For the briefest moment of complete rapture, she straddled my body. Her hands on both sides of my head, our eyes locked. *Holy shit*, I never wanted to grab someone's face and kiss them as much as I did then.

I felt her body shift to leave me, and hell, I didn't want her to. I leaned up on my elbows, bringing our faces closer. *Holy crap, she bit her lower lip when I did*. I easily rolled her body over, so I was on top of her. I pinned her down and offered her an evil laugh.

Alex kicked over a bottle of water, since mine flew out of my hands when her body collided into me.

I tried to open the damn thing with my teeth. I didn't want to use both hands to open it, because that would mean I'd be putting all my weight on her or she'd have a chance to escape. I didn't want to chance either.

She jerked her body up underneath me. The thrust of it almost sent me flying, but I held my position. *Damn, it felt good to have her under me.*

She still held her lip between her teeth, a coy smile teasing the edges. A slow rosy glow traveled across her cheeks and down her neck, like the most exquisite sunrise.

I leaned down closer to her; her eyes widened and her pupils dilated. Her lips parted and her body tensed. If we were the only two people in the room, I would have kissed her. I chose not to. I wanted to but I couldn't, she'd probably try to kill me if I did. Instead, I lowered my face even more, touching her ear with my lips and breathed out slowly. "She is a mortal danger to all men. She is beautiful without knowing it, and possesses charms that she's not even aware of. She is like a trap set by nature - a sweet perfumed rose in whose petals Cupid lurks in ambush. Anyone who has seen her smile has known perfection. She instills grace in every common thing and divinity in every careless gesture. Venus in her shell was never so lovely, and Diana in the forest never so graceful as you," I whispered. Lifting my head up, I looked deep into her eyes. She stopped trying to wiggle away from me and seemed to arch her body deeper into mine.

"Cyrano De Bergerac, Shane? For a self-serving man-whore, you know way too many romantic quotes," she whispered. *How the hell does she know my quotes?* She tried to squirm underneath me again, which just aroused me more. I wanted to kiss those beautiful lips so bad it physically hurt me not to. The thought snapped out of my mind when one of her hands got free and she slapped me in the face with her pizza. Then she smashed it in; I rolled off her laughing.

I laughed even harder when Grace launched another slice of pizza and it landed right in the middle of Alex's forehead, sticking there for a few brief moments before falling. What made it even funnier was the ass was trying to whack at the pizza with his hands, but because of his casts, he couldn't bend his arms to reach his face. So his arms were just flailing in the air like he was trying to land a plane. *Fucking epic.*

The food fight ended when Lea started screaming about pizza on the ceiling. Without complaint, we cleaned everything; even Alex with his broken arms and pizza smeared forehead. He probably just cleaned up to impress Grace, because he *never* cleaned. Alex and Tucker's apartment was unbearable to hang out in because of the disgusting mess in it. Brayden complained about it all the time, since he lived there too-but he never did anything to change it. Alex's mom once even paid a cleaning service to go there twice a week as a surprise for them. The poor girl quit after a few weeks because of Tucker and Alex's over the top flirting with her. She slept with them both though. Girls always do when they find out about the band.

When the apartment sparkled with cleanliness, we split ourselves up in groups to hang the posters we created in a few bars around the neighborhood. I took control of the situation because I wanted to spend some more time with Grace. Not to make any moves, but just to hang out with her and talk. I figured that the Cyrano De Bergerac quote today and the Shakespeare from the other day was a bit too much. I was also feeling desperate to find something to take her out of my mind, *anything. There had to be something that I could learn about her that would make me shake the feelings.* "Conner and Lea, you guys hit the Bowery Ballroom and the bars around there. Brayden and Ethan, you guys hit the Highline and wherever else you can think of on the West Side. Alex, you go home. Both your arms are broken and you look like an idiot. Grace and I will hit the East side."

I smiled at her shocked expression. "Ready?" I asked her.

"Uh...yeah...sure," she answered arching her eyebrows up to the middle of her forehead.

Laughing at her reaction, I grabbed her coat and tried to put it on her like a gentleman. She yanked it out of my hands before I could even try to put it on her and shoved her arms in the sleeves.

"Don't worry, I won't try anything, unless you've change your mind..." I joked.

If looks could kill, she would have shot me at close-range, bullet right between my eyes. I flung my hands over my head in surrender. I stepped closer to her. "Yeah, Grace, I got it. You'll never have sex with me. Right. I know. Maybe I'll make up a few tee shirts so there'll be no confusion for anyone who thinks my dysfunctional ass can't just innocently flirt."

She continued putting her coat on, stuck her tongue out at me and walked out the front door. *Damn, what I would do with that tongue.*

I followed her down the street to the corner of the block and we stood there watching for the light to change so we could cross the avenue.

"Thank you for helping," I said quietly. I looked ahead into the distance not wanting to see how much of a disgusted expression she wore from being with me.

From the corner of my eye, I saw her head turn up to look at me. She seemed to watch me for a moment, probably measuring my sincerity. "No problem. Conner and his friends are very special to Lea, and I'd do anything for her," she looked back away from me. "Besides, it's just handing out a few fliers. I'm not playing a guitar for him, just helping you guys find someone who can."

The thought of her playing guitar like Alex made me laugh inside. God, that would be the worst thing ever. I'd never get her out of my mind if she could make music with me. *Selah and I made music together.* I decided she couldn't, I didn't even want to know if she could. I was crazy about her too much already. "Yeah, that would be a hoot. Those delicate little hands of yours playing Alex's heavy riffs, now that would be hysterical to see."

She gave me a little glance, but said nothing. We continued our walk and placed posters up in about half a dozen bars. Everywhere we went people came up to me and patted me on the back saying they'd spread the word about the auditions. Everyone was sorry to hear that Alex wouldn't be able to play for a few weeks, but each person was visibly excited about who would possibly become a new member of Mad World, at least for a little while.

Grace was outgoing and friendly to everyone that stopped to talk to me. Each guy that came to talk to me only had eyes for her, and each girl gave her a jealous once over and walked away angry. She captivated every person she met, from the old guy who swept the floors in Tramp's Bar and Grill, to the ten-year-old kid who helped his father bus the tables at Mac's Pub.

She even fell into a relaxed conversation with me as we walked along the busy city streets. Anybody passing us by would have thought we were a couple. Maybe from the way I looked at her, or maybe the way I put my hand on the small of her back and the comfortable way she leaned into my touch. Whatever it was, it was like a small sliver of heaven to me.

"Hey," I tugged on her coat softly as we stood in front of the bar we posted the last flier in. "I was going to head over to Boozer's, maybe grab a beer, want to come?"

"Yeah, that sounds great," she replied. A smile swept over her lips, illuminating her eyes. *My God, she is the most beautiful woman I have ever seen in this life.*

"Well, damn, Grace," I whispered. "When you smile, it certainly does some serious damage to a man's insides."

Blinking quickly, she looked away and started walking, shoving her hands deep into her coat pockets. I had to run to catch up to her and we walked the rest of the way to the bar in silence. However, there was a huge smile plastered on her face and I knew it was what I said that put it there.

Chapter 6

Alex was sitting alone at our regular table when we got to Boozer's. We ordered a bucket full of beer and a basket of cheese fries as soon as we joined him. Lea and Conner met us there, after I texted Conner. Brayden, Ethan, and Tucker came in a few minutes after.

When Tucker saw Grace, he shoved my chair over, *with me still sitting on it*, and pulled over another chair in its spot, to sit in between us. "Hey, Shane, you don't mind, right?" *Oh, hell yes I mind.* I didn't say anything though. Tucker would act like a jerk within an hour and Grace would hate him. He'd screw it up himself and I needed to have her witness for herself how much of a jerk he was. I wasn't going to be a douchebag friend and tell her.

Alex burst out laughing at Tucker's efforts to get Grace to notice him. "Wow, Tucker. What are you, like twelve?" Alex teased.

Tucker lifted his shoulders and let them drop dramatically. He tilted his head adoringly at Grace, "Dude, I just want to sit next to the prettiest girl in the bar, that's all." *Oh, he was so slick, wasn't he?*

Alex laughed at him and slapped the table. "Tuck, you think she looks pretty now? God, you should have seen her in her little pink teddy bear pajamas before. It made me start thinking of *very* indecent things," Alex whistled and winked at Grace.

Tucker looked down at her and raised an eyebrow. "Hmmm. Damn, I miss all the good stuff."

"Oh yeah," Alex continued. "She looked all sweet and innocent. I just wanted to corrupt her." Alex was egging Tucker on.

"Corrupt her? What were you thinking of doing? Show her the smallest penis in the world? Make her dislike men forever?" Lea asked him, laughing.

"Yeah, dude. One night with you and she'll run screaming to a convent," I offered.

Alex nodded agreeing with me. "Ah. You're probably right. But, sorry, Grace, watching you in those little pink pajamas, put pictures in my mind of how freaky I'd get with you."

Grace didn't seem to be bothered about anything they were saying, she just laughed along with everyone. *She didn't even blush.*

"So, Alex, what kind of freaky things go on in your place? Hmm? What's the freakiest thing you've ever done?" Lea asked. *Holy crap, can I tell a few freaky tales about Alex.*

"I love bondage. I'd love to spank you, Lea," he said. *Man, is that true. I've seen him tie a few girls up.* "But what I'd really love to know is what freaky things you get up to, Lea," Alex continued. "And you too, Grace." He gave her one of his predatory smiles and leaned in closer to her; it made my stomach drop.

Grace beamed. She doubled over, bursts of breathy laughter escaping from her lips. She looked up and winked at him, "I bet you would, Alex."

Conner threw a handful of cheese fries at Alex causing him to lean away from Grace. "Leave my girl's freakiness outta your thoughts," he laughed.

I leaned across the table closer to Grace, leaning my face so close to hers our noses almost touched. "Okay, Lea's off limits because she's Conner's girl. I'd like to hear about Grace though."

Tucker shoved me so hard that he almost pushed me off the chair. "Real nice, ass!" He screamed at me. Grace flinched. A frown etched itself across her beautiful face. Confusion clouded my brain. Why was it okay when everyone else flirted and teased her, but I got the look of death when I did it? I gave her a confused, unblinking stare.

"Some of my close friends have called me Black Widow, because after I sleep with someone, I kill them," she joked. The laughter just didn't reach her eyes, and I knew what I had said bothered her. I wished I understood why.

"I have no doubt in my mind that you have had that effect on men, since I feel like I've died every time you've smiled at me." I spoke the words so softly I didn't even know if they reached her ears.

She narrowed her eyes and looked away quickly. She couldn't even meet my stare. While the rest of the table kept on laughing and talking nonsense, Grace got up and walked away with some empty bottles. She walked over to the trashcan and threw them in. Then she walked up to the bar, sat by herself on one of the stools, and threw down a fistful of twenties.

I watched her talk to Ryan, the bartender, who gave her a deep throaty laugh and a wink. He pulled down a bottle of Jack Daniel's black label and poured her a shot. She put the glass to her lips and gulped it down like a champ. Ryan watched her as she drank, wringing his bar towel in his hands, and then adjusting himself in his pants. *Fuck, even Ryan wanted her.*

I got up to talk to her. I wanted to apologize, tell her how fucking beautiful she was and how she made me a mess inside. But, Tucker put his hand out to stop me, "Let me talk to her, Shane. I'm the one that's in a relationship with her, not you."

His words made me stumble back into my chair. *Relationship? With Grace? What the hell did I miss?* "Wait...what?"

Tucker ignored me and sauntered up next to Grace at the bar. He gestured to Ryan to pour two more shots. His hand slid down to the small of her back as he leaned down close to talk to her. My blood started to boil.

She tried to move away from his hand nonchalantly by turning to face him and clinking her shot glass up against his.

They sat together and talked closely. Every time Tucker tried to touch her, she would move away. She looked uncomfortable and agitated. I watched her down about four shots and then Tucker made his move. He brought his hand up to her face and caressed her beautiful pale cheek with his greedy fucking fingers. He lowered his face and said some line to her and my head almost exploded with rage.

She took another shot and turned away from him and her eyes collided with mine. Her jaw tightened and her posture stiffened. Her fingers flexed at her sides and she slowly released a deep breath. She turned on her heels, away from me, and grabbed Tucker and whispered something in his ear.

Whatever she said made Tucker jump and run towards our table. She walked to the door as he grabbed their coats off chairs. His feet shuffled as his cheeks reddened looking at the table. "G-Grace wants to be alone with me!" he stuttered. Then he ran out. My freaking heart went with him.

Ethan smacked me in the arm. "What's up with Tucker and Grace?"

I shrugged. He gave me a deep laugh, "Shane, you look a little green, are you okay? I sort of feel bad for Grace, poor kid. You know he's going to do something stupid like he always does and she's going to think he's a jerk."

"Damn, Ethan. What's wrong with me? I wanted to go after her and stop her," I whispered.

A thoughtful expression shadowed his face. "Shane, I'll admit it. Grace is the prettiest girl I have ever seen. But, you have to ask yourself, what do you want from her? Nobody is going to let you hurt her, so don't go after her just to sleep with her."

"But, I don't just want *that*, that's the fucking problem," I said.

Lea's head snapped in my direction and her eyes almost bulged out of her pretty little head. *Damn, that's all I need, Lea to know how freaking crazy I am about her best friend. She probably won't let me in her apartment anymore after this to try to keep me away from Grace.*

I shook my head at her, "Don't say anything, Lea. Please."

She just gave me a tight smile and looked away. We stayed at the bar for another hour. I didn't join in any conversation, or listen to any of them talk. I sat and wondered what it was that was happening to me. I kept looking at the door to see if the archangels Michael or Gabriel were going to show up and yell, *"Surprise, this is your punishment phase two, hell on earth!"* Complete with angelic bells and whistles sounding.

When Lea and Conner stood up to leave, she gave me a small nudge. "Hey. Do you want to come back with us? I'm sure you'll feel better when you see how quickly Grace will come back from being with Tucker." She nodded at me and took my hand.

I wanted to tell her everything.

Ethan came back with us and we watched television. Conner and Lea snuggled on the couch with Ethan and me on the chairs on either side.

Exactly as Lea said, Grace came home five minutes after us. I sat up and almost ran to her, but Lea hissed at me under her breath, *"Don't* Shane. You'll scare the shit out of her."

"Hey," she said walking through the room, only flicking a small glance at me.

"Hey, yourself. Where did you and Tucker go?" Lea called after her.

She got as far as the opening to the hallway and took off her coat; her back to us, "He took me for a ride in his car." She turned and looked at Lea with a guarded expression, "Can I talk to you for a minute?"

With a concerned face, Lea followed her quickly down the hallway.

I had a sinking feeling in the pit of my stomach that Tucker did something. In a way, I hoped that he showed her what an inconsiderate selfish prick he could be, but on the other hand, I didn't want to see Grace get hurt.

Ethan tapped me on the knee, "You don't think Tucker did anything to hurt her or anything, right?"

"Dude, I was just thinking the same thing. I swear I'll kill him, Ethan."

Ethan shook his head at me, "Then you *do* understand why I don't want you putting the moves on her either!"

"Shut up." I said as I stepped over the coffee table to get past Conner's stretched out legs and walked quietly down the hallway.

Lea was just coming out of her room. "Is she okay?" I whispered.

"She's better than anybody I know, she just wants to be alone, literally," Lea answered. She grabbed my arm in hers and walked me back to the living room. "Shane, you don't have to worry about Tucker. Just try to be a friend to her. She's not ready for anything more from anyone right now. She'll just push you away. Trust me on this."

Ethan and I left a minute later. *At least, I knew she was okay and away from Tucker.* But how the hell was I just going to be a friend to her, like Lea said?

A friend. A person attached to another by feelings of affection or personal regard. At least that's the definition of it on dictionary.com. *A confidant, companion, ally, associate, comrade, partner, mate, pal*; I wanted to be it all and *so* much more. *I was so screwed.*

Early that next morning, I left my apartment dressed in my running gear. I knocked on Lea's door and waited for her to let me in as she did every morning, with a bright smile on her face and a cup of coffee in her hands. Today, her hair was disheveled and she still wore her pajamas, and there was no coffee in sight. *Scary.* Not the way Lea looked, just the fact that there was *no freakin' coffee made.* In my opinion, not having your morning coffee could be used as a great defense in a murder case. *That's just my opinion though.*

"We slept late! Come in and help me get Conner up and make some coffee!" she said.

Conner was still asleep, covers over his head, moaning that he needed just five more minutes and then he called me Mom. *He's such a jackhat.* I had to help Lea yank his body off the bed. We ended up spraying water on his face to get him to sit up and open his eyes. Torturing him like that, I have to say, was quite enjoyable.

Lea, in her usual adorable way, knew exactly what she needed to do to *keep* him awake. She invited him to shower with her. I had to make the damn coffee.

"Stay for coffee, Shane, but let's skip the run today, okay?" Conner laughed as Lea yanked him into the bathroom.

I chuckled from the kitchen, "Enjoy yourself, Conner!" I waited for the coffee pot to fill up (it felt like a freaking hour), poured myself a cup of coffee, and listened to the two of them singing in the shower.

When my ears were just about to start bleeding from their awful singing, the most beautiful creature quietly slipped into my sight. She wore a tiny little black tank top and a pair of boy shorts. I gripped the table with my hands and forced my eyes to stay on hers and not leer at every other inch of her bare skin I could find. Trust me, I wanted to look at those gorgeous creamy legs and the way those tiny shorts wrapped themselves around her hips; but I didn't. *I deserved some sort of a freakin' medal for it, that's how damn hard it was.* That's how damn hard *I* was.

"Morning, Sunshine!" I said; voice screeching as if I was just hitting puberty. *Not embarrassing at all.*

She poured a cup of coffee and stirred in some sweetener. I watched her hands as she made it, burning the memory of how she took her coffee in my mind. Tilting her head shyly at me, she smiled. "Good morning. Um, do you come here for coffee every day?" she asked.

My legs started nervously tapping against the legs of the table so I stood up and pushed my hands through my hair, trying to straighten my cloudy brain. "We were going on a run, but he slept late. I'll be out of your way in a minute," I explained. Her beautiful eyes sparkled at me and of course, I couldn't control my mouth, "Unless you feel up for running with me?"

The horrible singing echoed in the background and she gave me a questioning look in the direction of the bathroom. It made me wonder how she would sound singing in the bathroom, *or really how she'd look.*

She smirked as if she could read my damn mind.

I laughed, "Why the hell are you looking at me like that? No strings attached. I'm seriously just asking if you want to go running with me. Nothing else."

She pointed to herself, running her fingers quickly across her body. "And you're not going to start joking about me standing in front of you with this on," she asked. *Damn, girl. Do you understand how hard it is not to freakin' look at your body right now?*

God, I wanted to look at where she pointed. I wanted to see all the details I was missing, but I just focused on her eyes. "Well, I'm sure you'll change if you want to go running." Voice. Cracking. *AGAIN.*

Bubbles of laughter burst out of her, "Who are you and what have you done with that male chauvinist pig called Shane?"

I rolled my eyes at her. "Har, har, har. You coming or not?"

"Sure. Let me just change." She turned and walked away.

I froze and my heart thudded in my throat. *Never, never was I ever this aroused before.* She walked away, and my eyes dropped to the creamy skin of the perfect roundness of her ass peeking out from the bottom of her shorts. Her long, dark, silky hair fell in a sexy mess that draped over her shoulders and back. My mouth went dry, and a soft muffled sigh escaped my lips.

When she was fully out of my sight, I ran to the kitchen sink and splashed icy cold water over my face. Conner and Lea continued their screeching melodies in the shower. I thought about garbage, dead people, hell; anything to erase the most perfect backside I just witnessed. I needed to get this girl out of my system before she killed me.

Grace met me in the living room, dressed for running. *I still saw her half naked.* I opened the door for her and started stretching without a glance in her direction.

We ran for two hours in beautiful silence. Just the sound of her breath next to me was all I needed.

We ended the run by her apartment and she held the door open for me, walked straight to the refrigerator and threw me a bottle of water.

There was a subtle shimmer in her eye. "I'm going to take a shower," she said and left me standing alone in the kitchen. I stood there like an idiot for a minute trying to decide what I should do. *Do I just leave? Jump in the shower with her? Maybe stay and make her something to eat?* We left to run without having anything but coffee this morning.

I leaned heavily on the counter, trying not to imagine her with a soapy lather all over her body. I busied myself making a lunch for us. I made turkey wraps with an olive salad. Then I sat and waited.

Twenty minutes. *Chicks and their long showers, I don't get it.*

Thirty minutes. *Isn't she going to be all pruney by now?*

One hour. The shower still ran. *What. The. Hell.*

An hour and thirty minutes. *There's no way there was warm water for that long in a building this old.* I walked into the hallway to knock on the door to see if she was okay.

Before my knuckles could rap on the door, I heard the pipes squeal and the water shut off. I leaned against the wall by the kitchen, waiting to see if she was okay. She came out wrapped in a towel, shaking; water dripping from her hair. Her skin looked almost blue, but her eyes were red from crying. She looked lost. Haunted. I couldn't hide the look of surprise on my face even if I tried. There was so much more to Grace than I knew about, and the more I got to know, the more I opened my heart for her.

"I made lunch, if you're hungry," I whispered. *I wish I could take away your pain.*

Her cheeks colored, making her look alive again. "Yeah, sure. I'll be right there." *If only I was still an angel. Then I would have the power to take away her pain.* I would never regret loving Selah, but I would always regret not fighting my punishment harder and not being able to be an angel any longer.

Five minutes later, she came into the kitchen. Her hair was still wet and she wore a purple shirt that made her eyes turn lavender. *Selah's used to do the same.* I cringed at the thought that I could ever compare someone to her. Selah was gone, and I would never have the honor of feasting my eyes on hers again.

"Sorry, I took so long. I really didn't think you were going to stay," she said hunching her shoulders. She looked like a little girl that got caught doing something wrong.

I laughed, but the sound had an edge to it that I couldn't hide. "Is that why you took so long, so I'd leave? All you have to do is ask me to, Grace. I just thought after a two hour run on an empty stomach, you would like some food." *This poor girl must think so little of me.* Why did I have to end up in a worthless piece of shit's body?

She rolled her purple eyes at me. "No, ass. I didn't stay in there because of you. Not everything in this world revolves around you, you know. And thanks, I am starving," she said sitting down.

I was confused by her quick change of character. She was hiding stuff from me and I didn't understand what or why. But, hell, I wanted to figure her out.

"Will you be joining me or are you just here to watch me eat? It's pretty good, by the way," she smiled warmly.

I just stood there frozen and watched her eyes. I wanted

to say so many things at that moment. I wanted to tell her everything I could about me, about my punishment, about hell. I wanted her to know exactly how much she looked like someone I gave up everything for, and how, without a doubt in my soul, I would do it all again.

Then she started choking on the food. I ran over to her. "Are you okay? Is it that bad?" *What the hell? I didn't know what the first thing to do to help someone if they were choking.*

She burst out laughing, and wiped her eyes. "Oh God, Shane. It's delicious. I'm choking because you're sitting there, staring at me like the taste of your turkey wrap depends on your life."

I tried my best to muster up a laugh and sat down to eat. *I'm freakin' losing it. This girl is just too much like...*

"Man, you made my eyes tear up," she sighed.

"Those are such gorgeous eyes, there should never be tears in them," I whispered. *Shit, shit, shit! I shouldn't have said that.* "Your purple shirt is reflecting into them, and it's making them look lavender."

She threw her head back and laughed. "No wonder you were staring at me like that. Yeah, I can change my eye color if I wear certain colors, but most of the time, they are dull gray."

It was my turn to choke on my food. *Was she kidding me?* "Grace, there is nothing dull about those eyes. And you're right, this shit is delicious. You're welcome." We ate the rest of our lunch in silence. When we finished, she helped me clean as if we were a well oiled machine. I got my coat and my bag with all my running gear inside and I started for the door. I didn't want to leave though; I wanted to spend more time with her. "Have anything planned today?" I asked.

"No, not really," she said looking everywhere but in my eyes.

"I was just going to play around at the studio, wanna come?" *Come on, Grace, say yes. I need to play you the song that you, without even knowing, inspired me to write. It's the only damn way I can possibly tell you what is going on in my mind right now.*

"Studio?" She looked curious.

"Yeah, we have a sound proof studio apartment. That's where we practice every day," I explained.

Her pupils dilated and the biggest smile I'd ever seen fell across her face. *Shit, she was breathtaking.* "How many apartments do you guys have?"

"Tucker's father owns the building. We get them for low rent and all of us chip in anyway. So, do you want to hang out?" I asked again.

Grabbing her coat, she nodded to me. "Tucker and his family seem like they have it all, huh?"

Tucker was an assbag, why the hell was she asking about him? I hated him right then. The thought of her with him made my skin crawl. I knew something had to have happened between them last night, I just hoped it wasn't anything serious. "Yeah, Tucker has it all," I said flatly.

We started our walk to my apartment with her hair still a little wet from her shower. She didn't seem to be bothered by the coldness of the icy air; she seemed to welcome the shivers it brought. Or maybe they were being caused by her thoughts of Tucker. *Holy crap, this girl is making me want to murder one of my best friends in his sleep. Man up, Shane, and get a grip.* She's just another hot chick. Spend some time with her. Try to be her friend. Then bag her. Easy.

"Did you have a good time with Tucker last night? I saw you left the bar with him," I asked her softly pulling on her coat sleeve.

She looked up to me, but didn't look me in the eyes, "Yeah, he took me for a drive." *Shit, he has a jaguar. Did she like him for all his flashy toys and money? A gold digger? Yeah, that's it. I nailed it.*

"So, do you like him?"

She clenched her teeth and cringed. Then she hesitated for a few seconds before asking me, "What? Why are you asking me these questions?"

"I was just wondering. That's all. You just didn't look too happy with him sitting at the bar last night. I was surprised when you left with him." *Why the hell can't I shut up?*

She stopped walking, looked up at me, and stared straight into my eyes. *Holy crap, did that make my pulse race.*

"What do you mean?" Her voice was soft and wondering. *Damn, I wanted that voice to call out my name because I was deep inside her making her feel things she never felt before.*

"It was the way you responded to him," I stammered.

"Shane, what the hell are you talking about? How did I respond to him?" Her eyebrows gently pulled together as she waited for my answer.

I tried to feign indifference by looking away. I looked up at the sky, swept my gaze along the street and then looked back to her. *Ah, might as well tell her.* "He put his hand on the small of your back and you squirmed away from him each time he did. It looked like you were going to drink the whole bottle of Jack when he started rubbing his thumb on your back. The worst was when he touched your face, you cringed, yet you left with him." I sighed and looked down at my feet, "I just didn't understand it at all." *WHAT THE HELL AM I DOING? Just write WUSS across my forehead in permanent marker. Smack a sign on my ass that says WHIPPED.* I needed to staple my mouth closed.

"Strikes me as strange that you would notice all those things that you say I did. But, really who I go home with isn't any of your business. I don't ask you about all the girls you take home."

"You can. I don't hide anything." *I would tell you that I haven't been with anyone since the night I met you. I'd tell you that I don't want anyone but you.* Then I would probably toss myself into the East River.

"Shane, I would probably get pregnant from you just telling me the things you did," she laughed.

Shit. This is not how I wanted this conversation to pan out.

She started walking again. No more words passed between us. I pulled her arm towards my front door when we reached my building. I held the door open for her and led her to our basement studio with my hand gently on her back.

Thankfully, Ethan was there, sitting behind his drums twirling his sticks between his fingers. I had no idea how to talk to this girl, how to be alone with her. Even though I shared Shane's memory, I didn't share in his outgoing comfortable way with women. Shane never had a serious relationship memory, he was shallow and when his soul was here, he was far worse than Tucker. I was surprised that his friends never asked about the huge difference in his personality change when he left and I came in. Maybe they chalked it up to him quitting his drug habit cold turkey. Little did they know that he didn't. They'd never know how he overdosed in one of the bathroom stalls in Boozer's with some girl he'd gotten high with. They would definitely never know how he did it on purpose, swallowing an entire bottle of Oxycontin before shooting up heroin, as the drunken girl lying next to him giggled. He killed himself by overdosing *on purpose*, when he could have been someone amazing. He didn't deserve to be on this earth, there was no way anyone could save that soul. Lucky me though, my soul got thrown into his body, yea me...wooowhooo. This human life sucks.

Ethan took one look at us and bellowed a throaty laugh. "Hey, Grace. Here to listen to us?"

She gave him a small nod and a beautiful smile.

He winked at me and smiled wider, "That's great. Shane never lets chicks come down here." *There he goes, throwing me under a bus.*

I walked ahead of Grace as she took her coat off and made herself comfortable. I grabbed one of my acoustic guitars and sat myself on the floor. I strummed a chord, debating if I should play the melody that has been haunting my dreams since the first night I met her. "Girls shouldn't be allowed down here. I can't find my muse if some chick is trying to suck on my neck," I laughed. "Besides, it's Grace. She's just one of the guys."

I wanted to say more. I wanted to tell her the fucked up crazy feelings that she was creating in my head. Instead, I decided I would play her the haunting melody. There was no way she'd understand the notes and the emotions from it, but at least I could get my feelings out to her the only way I could. I closed my eyes and let the notes breathe their sounds, filling the room with my sadness.

Slow, melancholy notes twirled through the air. So sad and haunting, it almost hurt to play them.

When I opened my eyes, Grace was kneeling in front of me hugging her arms around her stomach, fists clenched tight. Her features held an anguished expression, her eyes shining and feverish.

I held her gaze and sang the words, just to her.

Never thought love would speak my name
Calling me out from the shadows
So long I have been hidden
Beneath the surface, where the darkness flows
You breathed life into me
The minute my eyes found yours
Waking me from my lonely grave
Leaving footprints along my deserted shores
I know you'll never know
How it feels to me when you say my name
Or the inferno you create in me

With your simple flame

Our eyes held each other's long after I stopped playing and the air between us was thick with feeling. I knew then, she had to feel something for me, something was just stopping her from taking a chance on me.

"That was the most intense song I have ever heard, dude! That was crazy! Play that again and lemme find a good beat," Ethan said.

"Yea, sure, Ethan," I answered. I didn't look at Grace for the rest of the time. *I couldn't.* I just bared my soul to her and she'd never know it was really her I was singing about, never know she was the one who brought me back from being too much like Shane, to give me *hope.* To want to be a better man.

Brayden and Alex showed up to practice and soon my mind was fully on my music, my muse sitting in front of me unaware of her spell over me.

Some time later that day, Grace quietly said goodbye to everyone and headed for the studio door. I offered her a low, "Night, Grace."

I watched as she walked away and my chest emptied. *I couldn't let her go.* I jumped after her and caught up with her by the stairs. "Sorry, Grace, I get really involved in there," I explained.

"Why would you be sorry? Listening to you guys play was epic. You guys sound even better without all the screaming half-naked girls," she grinned and bit down on her bottom lip. *Holy hell, was she flirting with me?*

My heart leapt at her words and her smile. "I'll walk you home," I offered as I walked with her up the stairs and toward the front door.

"That's not necessary, go back to practice," she said touching my arm lightly.

I was about to take her hand in mine when an icy chill

blew in from the open door.

"I'll walk her home for you," Tucker's voice called from the door.

Grace and I both jerked our heads up at the sound of his voice. He was dressed in his work clothes. His briefcase dangled from his shoulder like a woman's pocketbook.

"That's okay, it's only a few blocks," Grace said.

"Well, it's dark out and a beautiful girl like you should have someone to protect her," Tucker replied with a slick grin. *Fucking Lawyer.* "I'll get her home, Shane, you can go back to practice."

She moved forward and I took that as her way of ending my disagreeing with Tucker. "Great. Thanks Tuck. Night, Grace," I said walking back down the stairs.

When I got to the basement, I leaned against the wall of the hallway and bent down; I could barely breathe without her. "Michael? Gabriel? Please, tell me what the hell is going on!" I growled under my breath. "I don't belong here, this is worse than hell." Silence answered my prayers. *No surprise there.* There was no way that I would be able to watch anyone start a relationship with Grace. It would be torture for me to watch Grace fall for anyone. Why was this part of my punishment? *Hadn't I paid my dues in Hell?*

I heard footsteps coming down the stairs quickly. I stood straight up, waiting for one of the archangels to appear in the doorway, ready to explain everything.

Tucker walked in, all serious. His eyes widened in surprise when he saw me, "What's wrong with you, dillweed? You just scared the crap out of me. Why are you standing in the hallway?"

"Where's Grace? I thought you were going to walk her home!" I snapped.

"Yeah, look, she's fine. I have to practice for the show. I want to blow her away, you know, so I can get her to *blow me*," he laughed. I didn't. "No, Shane, really; I want to impress her with my playing on Friday night. C'mon, teach me one of those cool riffs that get you laid every night," he said opening the studio door.

Asshole.

There was no shutting him up for the rest of the night. All he talked about was Grace and how he was taking her on some big extravagant date that Wednesday.

"What did you say?" I demanded when I finally decided to listen to him.

Tucker smirked at me. "I am taking Grace on a date Wednesday night, to the hottest, most expensive restaurant in Manhattan."

I stood up quick, knocking over my guitar in my haste. "No fucking way."

"Yeah. I told you we hooked up. I was supposed to go take her out on Friday, but she couldn't wait to go out with me so she moved our date to Wednesday night. Which is cool, because now I can take Alex's place on Friday." He turned and gave Alex a high five. Alex yelped in pain as Tucker whacked his casts with his palm. But, Tucker didn't even notice that he hurt Alex, he just kept running his mouth off. "Hey, Alex, how soon do you think I'll be scoring the amount of girls you do after I take your spot in the band?"

Alex tried to cross his casts in front of his chest, "You'll never score as many girls as me, you're *not me*. You're just the WINGMAN, Tucker. You're such an ass, that you make all of us look like princes." He got up in Tucker's face, "And what the fuck man? You're taking out *Grace*, why the fuck are you talking about bagging other chicks? Damn man, if I had even a slight chance with that girl, I'd leave all the others behind."

Alex walked away and stood beside me. The rest of us just glared at Tucker, probably all agreeing with what Alex had just said.

"How much did you pay her to go out with you?" Ethan muttered.

"Shut up, dick," Tucker replied. He looked at me deadpan, "Shit, man. Her fucking lips were amazing."

Her LIPS were amazing? He KISSED her? I can't breathe.

I glowered at him. "I'm done practicing. I'm out of here." I walked to the door and looked back at Tucker who was fumbling with Alex's guitar. "Oh, and Tuck, if you hurt her in any way, I swear I will fucking kill you." I slammed the door behind me.

I stayed away from everyone for the rest of the night. I seriously thought that if I saw Tucker or heard anything else about him touching Grace's lips, I might actually kill him. I continued the routine Tuesday too. I spent the day at the Metropolitan Museum of Art staring at the painting *The Angel Gabriel Appearing to Zacharias* by William Blake, wishing Gabriel would come to me. *What the hell was I supposed to do?* She chose the ass-rag instead of me. *What the hell could she see in him besides his money? Fuck, I could play the money card too, if I needed. Fuck, what difference did it make? I needed to get her out of my mind and someone else in there.* I had to keep reminding myself that the only reason I was so obsessed with her was because she looked so much like Selah. *But she wasn't Selah.* The dead don't come back.

Ethan sent me a text Tuesday night when I didn't come home. Another wonderful attribute of living in Manhattan; you can stay up all night and always have a place to be.

Ethan: You okay?

Shane: Wonderful

Ethan: Where the hell r u?

Shane: In Hell

Ethan: ????

Shane: I'm fine. Just need 2 clear my head.

Ethan: Does this have to do with Tuck and Grace? Or are you with a girl?

Shane: Just got to be alone for a while.
Ethan: You're not using again, right?
Shane: NO! I promise you I am not using ANYTHING
Ethan: You really like her
Shane: Yeah

I visited Saint Patrick's Cathedral and called on my long ago brothers, but none of the archangels came. Knelt down in a pew, still no one came. I sat down on a bench in Central Park and prayed, none of the archangels came. I went inside each church or temple I could find; still no one came. I hopped from club to club; bar to bar, getting drunker and drunker, nobody showed up then either. I toyed with the idea of jumping in front of a train, you know, just to see if someone came then. I didn't have the guts.

Stumbling into my apartment at four o'clock Wednesday morning, I passed out on my bed. I dreamt about her.

Ethan knocked on my door at four o'clock Wednesday afternoon. "Shane, can I come in?"

I growled at him. "Leave me the hell alone."

I felt the bed move when he kicked it. "Damn, Shane! You smell like an open whiskey bottle! Take a shower. Where the fuck have you been?"

"In every piece of holy ground this island has, looking for God," I mumbled from under the covers.

He laughed, thinking I was joking. "Did you find him?"

"No, I think he quit his day job. Why are you bothering me?"

Ethan sighed. "Just worried about you, bro. C'mon, get up, shower and let's go out." He kicked the bed again before he left.

I was showered and dressed twenty minutes later, coffee in hand. Grace was a small thought pushed safely in the back of my mind. Ethan and I grabbed something to eat and met up with Conner, Lea and Brayden at Boozer's a little after six o'clock. The absence of Tucker and Grace made me think of every reason in the world why I should be someplace else. What if they ended up coming back here, so he could parade her around like his trophy? The thought of how she might look in the afterglow of having sex with that fuckard made my skin crawl. I needed to wet my dick in someone else and forget about her. *Fucking Tucker.* And it didn't help that every time I looked at Lea, she offered me these knowing eyes full of pity.

Conner's phone rang at seven. Even over the people around the table talking, I could hear Alex yelling on the other end of the phone. Conner motioned for everyone to be quiet as he stood up to continue the conversation. A serious expression crossed his face that made the hair on the back of my neck stand up. He paced back and forth, eyes wide. "What? Okay, okay. Where are you? No. I don't have a clue where he is. Yeah, yeah I'll find him. Hang tight."

Lea looked curiously at him, "Who was that?"

"Holy shit! We gotta get Tucker. Alex is in Manhattan Central Booking, he was arrested!"

You have to be kidding me.

Of course, Tucker's phone was off. *Probably didn't want to be bothered while he was plowing Grace.* Spikes of heat ran across my face and I clenched my fists tight.

We grabbed a cab and raced down to where Alex was, and sure enough, he was pathetically sitting behinds bars in a cell, surrounded by other people in the same dumbass predicament.

Alex laughed when he saw us. The officers were kind and let him lean his head on the bars and talk to me, while Conner continued trying to reach Tucker.

I smiled at him, "What the hell did you do now?"

"I went to see that chick Cara again tonight. That asshole beat the crap out of her for bringing me home the other night. So I made sure he knew he couldn't mess with her anymore. Shane,

I couldn't let him get away with hitting her, it just wasn't right. I just kicked some of his windows in. I couldn't do much, I don't have working arms," he smiled proudly. "Just get Tucker, he'll get me out of this mess."

I nodded and walked to where the rest of my friends were standing.

"Brayden, Ethan, you guys stay here with Alex until we find Tucker, or his father." I looked at Lea, "Give me your cell phone. I'm calling Grace."

"Don't you have a cell phone?" Ethan asked.

"Yeah, well...since she's on a *hot date* with Tucker and he's not answering his phone. I'm thinking that maybe she wouldn't be answering any calls from anyone but Lea."

Once outside, Lea and I called Grace. Her phone rang once and she answered.

"Helllllooo," she sang into the phone. *Uh oh, she sounds like she's been drinking.*

"Grace?" I asked as calmly as I could while rage surged through my veins at her.

"Shane?" She whispered.

"Where's Tucker? He's not answering his phone? Where are you?" I demanded. Lea yanked her phone out of my hands and she immediately started yelling at Grace. I grabbed the phone back and I could clearly hear the conversation on the other side of the phone between Tucker and Grace.

"What is wrong with you, Tucker? Give me my phone back!" she screamed.

"You are embarrassing me!" he snapped.

"Give me my phone or I'll give you something to really be embarrassed about," she threatened.

"Hello," Grace's voice calmly echoed in the phone.

"Grace, are you okay?" I asked. If I heard Tucker say one disrespectful thing to her, I was going to scare the shit out of him with my hands.

"What's going on, Shane?" Her voice was soft, no anger in it at all. Shit, my insides turned because she was with another guy.

"We need Tucker. Alex needs a lawyer. He's in Manhattan Central Booking," I answered.

"Oh no, what happened? Oh, forget it, you can tell me later. But, I don't think it's a good idea that Tucker drives, and you might need to call his father if you want a lawyer who isn't drunk," she said.

"You have got to be kidding me. Where are you? I'll come and get you," I whispered into the phone.

"We're eating sushi," she sighed.

"Ew," I groaned.

"Tell me about it," she laughed.

"So where would you be eating this sushi, exactly?" I asked.

"Just meet us at The Time Warner Center in Columbus Circle."

I clicked the phone off. I wanted to get her away from Tucker as quickly as I could; Tucker was a real jackass when he was drunk. I looked over to Conner. "Let's get a cab back to Lea's. I'll take Grace's Jeep and go get them. Grace says Tucker's drunk and shouldn't drive. Conner, call his dad, because Tucker is going to need help if he's as drunk as I think he sounded."

We jumped in a taxi and drove back to Lea's apartment, all talking over each other and at the same time. When we got to Lea's, we ran into the house and we rummaged through Grace's room for the keys to her Jeep. The rumpled unmade sheets covering her bed made me insane with jealousy at the thought of any other man that was ever in there with her. *Right now, I just needed to get her away from Tucker.*

"Hey, do you think Grace will be pissed at me for driving her Jeep?" I asked Lea.

"Shane, I think she'll be happy that someone is making

sure she got home safely," she said. Tilting her head and walking over to me, she touched my shoulder, "Hey, Shane. Someone like Tucker really isn't her type. She's got a lot of...issues with guys, and she doesn't really date anybody unless I talk her into it. She's been...hurt before. I can see the way her going out with Tucker is affecting you...I'm surprised really."

"Doesn't matter. Grace would never go for someone like me, right?" I moved away from her and she held onto my shoulders tighter looking me straight in the eyes.

"Shane. You want someone like Grace interested in you? Use your words and your actions. Most guys don't know this, but a woman's G-spot is in her eyes and ears. If you look in her pants, you're never going to find it."

"You're pretty awesome, Lea."

She moved away from me and continued the search for the keys, "Oh, but Shane, if you make my best friend cry, I will tie your pretty little rock star ass up naked and let the homeless men in Central Park have their way with you."

Finding the keys, after a fifteen-minute search, I ran down the street to where the Jeep was parked and opened the door. The sweet wildflower fragrance of her shampoo made my stomach do weird shit. Either I had to go to the bathroom, or I was a grown man with butterflies in my stomach. Let me spell it out, W.U.S.S.

I started the Jeep, pulled out and turned down Lexington Avenue. I squealed a right turn onto West 57th Street and barreled down until I reached 8th Avenue. I headed toward Columbus circle, rounded the corner and saw Tucker and Grace standing far apart from each other on the sidewalk. I took that as a good sign.

I pulled the car up onto the curb and slammed in into park. Grace was shivering on the sidewalk, while Tucker was yapping into his cell phone. The one that had been so conveniently shut off the whole entire time we were trying to call him.

I pushed open the door, pulled back the backseat and literally threw his dumbass into the back. He didn't even stop talking on his phone. I slammed the front seat in his face. "Dude!" he yelled at me.

I held my hand out for Grace and she took it. I gently helped her into the Jeep and closed the door for her. I drove back across town and down the East side toward Centre Street. Grace's eyes were on me as I drove. I only flicked a glance at her once and I found no anger in them. I would have given my right arm to know what she was thinking when she looked at me that way, though.

"What happened?" she whispered, while Tucker made drunken lawyer-ish phone calls from behind me.

"Alex was out with that chick whose boyfriend jumped him. The boyfriend had roughed her up after the incident with Alex, and well, I think Alex went to the guy's house and I guess stood up to him. He kicked through some windows or something."

She leaned her head against the window and sighed.

I pulled up to Manhattan Central Booking and Tucker's father was already standing out front waiting for him, hands across his chest, looking every bit like the pissed off high and mighty ambulance chaser he was.

I opened my side of the car door to let Tucker get out. When I got back in and closed the door, Tucker gestured for me to open the window to talk. He leaned his dumbass head in and talked across me to Grace, "Grace, I'm sorry. I know that this was one of the best nights of your life. I'll take you back to Masa whenever you'd like."

Fury flickered across her eyes. "Oh, we'll have to talk about that, Tucker," she bristled. I couldn't help but smile.

Tucker didn't hear her; he just gave her a wide drunk grin, "I know, it was amazing. Grace, you're amazing." He looked at me, saw how close his face was to mine and flinched back. When he got to a better distance, he nodded, "Thanks for taking her home for me, you're a good friend." He pounded his palm on the door, and screamed, "Get her home safe, this big boy has gotta play superman!"

I wanted to drive away with his head still inside the car.

I peeled the Jeep into the street with squealing tires. I was *pissed off*. I was jealous. I didn't understand why in the world she chose to go out with someone like Tucker. But I didn't say anything. I had to remember that she wasn't Selah, she wasn't anything to me; and she definitely wasn't mine.

We drove back in silence. Complete soundlessness. Yet, I could loudly hear the blood pounding through the veins in my body, hard and angry.

I had to drive the freakin' Jeep around the block about a half dozen times before I found a spot. *Why would anyone in this city own a car? Seriously not worth it.*

I walked her to her apartment, but she didn't go inside. She just walked right past it and said, "Thanks, Shane, goodnight."

"Where are you going?" I called after her.

"I need to have a drink or *few*."

"What? Now? Why?" I stammered.

She pulled out her cell phone and looked at the screen, and then leveled a serious stare at me. "That was just two and a half hours of my life that I will never get back. And in those two and a half hours, I have spent more time with a jerk, than all of my years on this earth. I am kind of hoping the rest of my night will be full of regretful behavior and irreversible decisions." She tried to walk away, but I grabbed her arm and spun her around to face me.

Her face was so close to mine, I had to swallow back a shallow gasp. I managed a small smile. "What? So that *wasn't* the best night of your life?" My heart slammed itself against my rib cage.

"Shut up, Shane, and go home!" She tugged away from me and walked away.

I caught up to her in two steps. I swung my arm around her shoulder and fell in step with her. "I think I need a night of watching you entertain me with your regretful behavior and your irreversible decisions."

She leaned into me but looked up at me and said, "We need to call Lea and tell her and Conner to meet us at Boozer's then."

I'm positive that she didn't realize it, but she knocked my legs right out from underneath me. "Grace, are you afraid of being alone with me?" I didn't even try to hide my hurt. I lifted my arm off her shoulders. "Grace, I get it. You aren't interested in anything with me. I'm not going to try anything, I promise." *Hell, she was breaking my damn heart.* I took my phone out of my pocket. "I'll tell them to meet us there."

Someone like Tucker was okay to be alone with, but not me? This girl was horrible at reading people.

We walked into Boozer's and headed straight for the bar. As always, there was a great crowd and Ryan the bartender nodded to me and shook my hand.

"Hey, Ry, what's up? This is the beautiful, albeit untouchable, Grace." I looked down at her beautiful eyes, "Grace, this is Ryan." She said hello to him. Of course, Ryan, being a man, openly gawked at how beautiful she was. I wanted to slam my fist into his face, and then rip that lip ring of his right off his lips.

"Ryan, everything she gets is on me, whatever she wants; no limits," I said. I gave him a threatening glare, but he was too busy eye fucking Grace even to see me. When I turned back to ask her what she'd like to drink, she had taken her coat off and placed it on the bar. My heart rate tripled; adrenaline spiked in my veins. My eyes slowly took in her body, from head to toe and

110

back again. It took all my restraint not to fall to my knees in front of her and beg her to love me.

She wore a tight silver shirt that shimmered around her body and matched her eyes exactly. The neckline plunged low and the curves and perfect roundness of her breasts sent waves of desire spiking through my entire body. She wore skintight black leggings and those fuck-me knee high leather boots that I had dreamt about wrapped around me.

"What would you like, Grace?" I could hardly breathe standing so close to her.

"Tequila, please," she whispered.

"Ryan, the woman wants Tequila. Line up the shot glasses, salt and limes, sir," I said to Ryan. Then I turned back to look at Grace, "And let the regretful behavior begin!"

Ryan lined up a row of shot glasses, a glass saltshaker, and placed a handful of limes on a napkin in front of us. His eyes never left her. I think I might have growled out loud.

Without a moment of hesitation, Grace licked the back of her hand with her tongue slowly, her eyes meeting mine. She sprinkled salt on it and licked it again, slower. With her gaze still steady on mine, a rush of crimson colored her cheeks. She tilted the shot back and slowly placed the lime in her mouth and sucked. *Instant massive hard-on.* It took every last little bit of my self-control not to slam my lips against that sexy mouth of hers.

"My God," I whispered.

She narrowed her eyes playfully at me. "Why am I drinking alone?"

"Oh, don't worry, Grace, you're not alone," I said as I took my shot, not anywhere near at sexy or sensual as she did it. Her cheeks reddened more though, and I found myself, yet again, wondering what she could possibly be thinking of to blush like that around me.

"Holy shots!" Lea's voice tore me from her eyes.

"Lea!" Grace yelled, and hugged her tight. She pulled away and scolded her friend, "That, my friend will be the last time that you will *ever* talk me into going on a date!"

Lea held up her finger to Grace, I guess to disagree and Grace bit it. *Holy shit, did that turn me on even more.* I held out a shot to her and smiled, believing for the first time, Lea really was the reason she went out with Tucker.

"Last time, Lea. It's my messed up life and if I want to waste it, I will!" She grabbed the shot glass out of my hands and brushed her fingers against mine. Our eyes collided with each other's. Her breath caught and for the second time, I thought I felt there was something there.

After two more shots, I took her hand and entwined my fingers with hers. I nodded to the dance floor and she smiled and came with me, not hesitating for a minute. Lea and Conner followed. I spun her around and held her back to me. I knew if I faced her, she'd run, and I wanted desperately to feel her move against my body for just a little while. And my God, did she. She melted right into me like we were one. Like she found where she belonged. Her hips swayed with mine to the music and she lifted her hands up over my head. My hands wrapped around her, pressing on the flatness of her stomach. I pulled her closer, crushing my body against hers, still moving our bodies to the beat of the song. Sweating into each other, grinding and sliding against each other. I roamed my hands up the sides of her body, grasping her skin, and skating my fingertips along the damp flesh. When she ran her hands through my hair, I couldn't bear not to face her any longer. I spun her around and for a moment, desire pulsed in her eyes, but she pushed me away and stopped dancing.

"Shane," she breathed, through parted lips. Guilt and fear shone through her features, yet she fisted my shirt in both her hands, not letting me move away too far.

I tightened my grip around her waist, pulling her in closer

until she was full fledge up against my body, and had to realize how much I wanted her by what she felt against her. I buried my face in her hair and inhaled those sweet wildflowers. "You're killing me, Grace," I whispered against her ear. Her breathing quickened as I slid my hand slowly up her ribs until my fingertips grazed the underside of her breast. *Damn, she felt good.*

She leaned her face away from me and looked terrified. I *didn't want to scare her, I didn't mean to do anything wrong, but she was giving me signals, wasn't she? Shit, probably not.*

"I know. I know, Grace!" My hands flew up into the air. "I have absolutely no chance at a night with you. I'm not trying to sleep with you. I'm just having fun, you smell awesome, you are inhumanly beautiful, and you're making my heart beat overtime...Shots?"

After a split second of sheer terror, an enormous smile pulled at her lips and she laughed and nodded. "Shots!" I wiped my sweaty palms down my pants as I followed her off the dance floor.

Back at the bar, we did a few more shots. I lost count. The only thing I knew was that I wanted her to want me. I had to know how she felt.

The girls went to the bathroom, as they always do, in packs. The night was speeding by. There had been too many shots drunk and I didn't want things to get any fuzzier, so I ordered a few bottles of water. For the first time since I got thrown into Shane's body, the first time in the nine months that I'd been on earth, I didn't drink myself into oblivion.

"Conner, do you think Grace is talking about me in the bathroom?" I slurred. *Fucking hell, I was drunk already.*

He laughed. "Maybe, if there's some good shit written about you on the walls. If not, she's probably just taking a piss," he slurred back. *Fucking hell, he was drunk too.*

I jabbed him in the shoulder. "I'm fucking screwed, Con."

He leaned against the bar next to me. He laughed, "Why

what's going on? You break both your arms? Get arrested?"

"Worse. I'm crazy about her."

He quirked an eyebrow and snorted, "Yeah. Right. Sure." Then he punched me in the arm. "Whatever you say."

My body went rigid with annoyance. "Hell, Conner! I'm not fucking kidding around. She's driving me bat shit crazy, I don't know if she's interested in me or not. She's Lea's best friend, dude. I don't want to mess anything up." I raked my hands through my hair and held my head, "Bro, I can't even see past her to look at other girls. All I see is *her*."

Conner folded his hands and offered me a thoughtful expression, as if he was my shrink about to give me really expensive advice. "Yeah, I guess I can see where that might be an issue. If you want my advice, I say leave her alone. The way Lea talks about her, she's got bigger demons than you," he slurred.

I highly doubt that.

Conner took another shot and smiled at me through glazed over eyes. "But if you really want to know how she feels, and don't you ever say this to Lea, because then I will have to hurt you big time. Just pick some hot chick at the bar, mess around, and dance with her in front of Grace. See how she reacts."

"So, your drunken ass advice is to dance with someone else and see if Grace says something to me?"

"Yep." He giggled. "Maybe you shouldn't listen to me, cuz I think I'm getting drunk. But, that's how I figured out Lea wanted to be more than friends with me." He looked at the floor with a distant cloudy look to his eyes. "Lea walked right onto the dance floor and smacked me upside the head and told me to *man up, lose the skank, and dance with a real woman*. I haven't been the same since."

On cue, a decent looking blonde waved at me from the other end of the bar. I had seen her a handful of times at shows, so I took a deep breath and sauntered over. *Just talking to the chick won't hurt anything, right?*

Before I even got over there, the blonde started talking to me. From about ten feet away, she greeted me and told me her name, which I didn't hear. I also didn't ask her to repeat it either, because I didn't give a shit.

"You're Shane, right? The singer?" *Well, that's one I've never heard before. Shit, I'm thinking sarcastic drunk thoughts.*

"That's what I've heard," I laughed.

She arched her back, making sure to place her cleavage in my view, and curled her blonde hair around her fingers. *This is stupid, I don't want to be talking with this girl, I wanted to be near Grace.*

"Are you going to sing tonight?"

"No," I kept looking towards the bathroom.

"I've seen your band here a few times. I really like your music. It's hot."

"Thanks." *Um yeah, hot. Yeah that's one way to describe something I have been creating, composing and breathing life into for thousands of fucking years.*

She giggled, "Do you think *I'm* hot?"

Grace and Lea walked back into the room. Lea was oblivious, but Grace saw me immediately. She showed no emotion, she just walked right back to where we were before.

Okay, here goes nothing*, or everything.* I leaned closer to the girl, brushed her hair off her shoulder and whispered in her ear, "One of the hottest girls I've seen."

She giggled and raked through my hair with her long clawed hands. I shivered; I hated grossly long fingernails on women, they reminded me of demons. *Real ones.*

Grace drank a shot and slammed the empty glass back on the bar. She and Lea sat on two barstools, both of them watching me. I couldn't see where Conner was, *traitor.* I hoped he was puking in the bathroom; this was a horrible idea.

The blonde grabbed my hand and pulled me to the dance

floor. Grace watched every step I took. Still she showed no emotion that I could see.

The girl's hands were all over me. I tried to dance with her, but really all she was trying to do was rub her ass all over me and dry hump my leg. It reminded me of my grandmother's dog when it was in heat.

Grace continued to take in our show and her face slowly started changing. I knew because I never looked once at the girl I was dancing with, I only looked at Grace. She downed four more shots sitting there. I wanted to tell her to stop, but I wanted to see her reaction to this too. So far, I liked what I was seeing.

Conner came back and he and Lea started a conversation. Grace glanced at them once, jumped off the stool and headed for the bathroom again. As she passed me, she shook her head and smiled. It was torn, it didn't reach her eyes, and I knew that I must have meant something to her. I watched her walk away into the back hall and I saw her stop short. A dark shadow seemed to wrap its arms around her and yank her away. *What the?*

I threw the blonde off me, "Thanks for the dance. I have to go!"

The girl whined and stood there with a look as if I had just ripped her heart out. *It was one freaking dance!*

I yelled for Conner and Lea to get Marty, the bouncer. I didn't know exactly what I saw, but I knew something wasn't right. Lea collided with me and we both drunkenly stumbled onto the floor.

"What happened? You looked scared, where's Grace?" She was freaking out.

I got up and dragged her up with me. "I saw her go down the hall and I think I saw something, I don't know. Let's just find her!" I couldn't explain that I just knew, for sure, that something was wrong. Maybe I still had remnants of left over angel abilities, I didn't know, all I knew was that *I knew*, deep in my soul, she needed *me*.

Lea screamed her name and ran into the bathroom. "Shane she's not in here!" I tried all the doors, closet, storage room, men's room. The last storage room was locked. Boozer never locks that door, the wait staff needs to be able to get to all the supplies in there.

My skin crawled. "Grace!" Lea pounded her fists on the door. I shoved her out of the way. Backing all the way up, I rammed a front lunge kick right next to the locked doorknob. The door burst inward, the frame shot splinters of wood around me. A guy almost the size of Ethan was hunched over in front of Grace. There were splatters of bright red blood all over the floor and all over Grace's hands. "Get the hell off her!" I yelled, yanking the guy away from her. I didn't even think, I pounded the guys face over and over. I had fought in angelic wars; we knew no mercy. I wouldn't stop until I heard his last breath of life.

Then I heard Grace exhale. That's all it took to make me stop. I needed to know if she was hurt. But the minute I turned my head and looked at her, I felt a sharp pain in my chest, above my heart. The guy stabbed the blade of a knife into my shoulder and yanked it right back out to do it again. He advanced towards me once more, and I easily brushed the weapon away and slammed him in the chest full force. *I was done fighting like I was just human*. The guy flew across the small room, slammed up against the wall and collapsed to the floor, out cold. I grabbed for her. I took her beautiful face in my hands, but she kept looking at my shoulder. Her eyes were wide, but she showed no other emotion. "Grace, are you okay? Did he hurt you? He had blood all over him when I came in. Where are you hurt?"

She clawed at my shoulder, found the puncture wound and held it down hard, putting pressure to it. Then she met my eyes with hers and smiled. *I wanted to die right there in her arms*. "It was his blood, Shane. He didn't hurt me."

I looked at the huge monster of a man lying on the floor.

His blood? I was in complete awe of her. *What did he want from her?* Rage boiled my blood. "Did he touch you? I swear to God, Grace, I'll kill him right now."

She gently placed her hand on my cheek, and my body calmed instantly. "He never got the chance, you came."

Relief. *Pure raw relief* surged through my shoulders. I looked at her beautiful eyes, welling with her beautiful tears and my heart stirred. It was too overwhelming, too awe inspiring. All I wanted was to tell her that I was falling for her, but I couldn't. I was stuck in Shane's body and she seemed to know how much of a jerk he had been. I had no idea how I could change her thoughts about him. "Grace, I just got stabbed to save you. Can I at least have a kiss as a reward?" I wiggled my eyebrows up and down to make her laugh.

She brought her plump pink lips to my forehead and gave me a small sweet lingering kiss.

I busted out laughing, "Wow. A peck on the forehead is the equivalent to being stabbed to you? No way! I'm going to milk this one! You owe me, big time!"

Slapping at my arm, she teased, "Shane, you could take your blonde bimbo home or me, and you wouldn't know the difference. But, I do owe you, so I'll think of something where I get to keep my clothes on."

There were a ton of people in the small room all of a sudden and my head started spinning. The stab wound was nothing much, I could feel that it didn't hit anything important. It looked a hell of a lot worse than it felt, because blood was everywhere. And unfortunately, I was all of a sudden completely sober.

Grace slid my arm around her shoulders and helped me up. All I could do was smile and look at her. What girl in their right mind would pick up a bleeding guy off the floor without flinching? *Someone like Grace.* This only endeared me more to her. *Shit.*

Conner had called 911 and the police were just coming in. An ambulance was pulling up just as Grace walked me outside.

I tried like crazy to refuse going to the hospital, but no one listened to me. Conner and a few of the other regulars at the bar shoved me into the back of the ambulance. Before they closed the back doors on me, the blonde girl I was talking to at the bar and dancing with climbed in. *Why is she here?*

Giggles, giggles and more giggling. "I bet you never had sex in the back of an ambulance before," she giggled even more and slithered her hands up my leg.

What the hell is wrong with this girl? "Um...well, no, I can honestly say that I have not had sex in the back of an ambulance." I stopped her hands. "And, honestly, I *never* will. If you haven't noticed the reason we're sitting here, well, I got STABBED tonight! So, I'm not really in the mood. Do you kind of understand that?"

She licked her lips slow and sensual. "I bet I can get you in the mood," she moaned. "Then I can go home with you and take care of you for as long as it will take. I can be your own personal nurse. I'll even dress up." She giggled *way* more than was freaking necessary.

Ah, no. No thank you, you psycho skank. "Well, even though that sounds really tempting, I think I'm going to pass. But, thanks, really."

"Let me at least give you a..."

The doors opened before she could finish and I launched myself past her and through them. The EMTs walked me into an almost empty emergency room, up to the front desk and right into triage. I was quickly seen, poked, and prodded. Two police officers came a few minutes after I arrived and questioned me about the incident.

I had no information to give them though. I had never seen the guy before. I just saw something come up behind Grace in the darkness of the hallway and I ran to her. I didn't think. I just wanted her to be safe.

"So tell us what happened when you ran back into the hallway," one of the officers said.

"I tried every room. I ran into the men's bathroom. Lea tried the women's room. I tried the storage closets. When I tried the last storage room, it was locked."

The officer asking me all the questions was writing down all my answers. The other officer kept looking through the curtain of my little area.

"I heard them scuffling behind the door and I kicked it in. It swung right open and the guy was trying to attack Grace. I grabbed him off her and started hitting him. All I was really concerned about was Grace and if she was hurt. There was blood everywhere so I figured he hurt her pretty bad. When I went to her, the asshole stabbed me. I never even saw he had a knife on him until it was in me."

"We have two other officers speaking to your friends in the waiting room right now. Grace is the blonde or the brunette in the waiting room?"

I couldn't hide my smile. *Grace was waiting for me?* "Grace is the one with the jet black hair and light gray eyes."

The officer shook his head. "A beautiful girl like that, the guy probably tried to pick her up and she turned him down. It's a good thing you were there."

After a while, someone came in and stitched me up, smiling that no major organs were punctured. He wanted to give me something to kill the pain, but I said no. I never took anything stronger than over the counter medicine, I didn't trust Shane's body to not get addicted to anything again. Besides, twenty-one stitches are like a paper cut compared to having your wings ripped from your body. I didn't even flinch.

I hesitated in the doorway to the waiting area and watched Grace for a minute before anyone noticed I was there. Worry lines creased her forehead and she sat staring at her feet,

120

biting down on her bottom lip. *Was she upset about what she'd been through tonight? Was any of that worry for me?*

I quietly sat down next to her and leaned my elbow on her shoulder, "Were you worried sick about me?"

She rolled those beautiful bedroom eyes, but gave me a dazzling smile. "No, Shane. I knew your big fat ego would block the knife somehow."

Looking at me for a few silent seconds, her expression spoke everything to me. *Thank you. I need you. I want you, but I can't. I won't. But, my God, I want to.*

It hurt like hell.

We shared a cab with Conner and Lea; nobody said a word the entire ride. Conner and I had the driver drop the girls off in front of their apartment.

When the driver pulled up, Grace looked over to me with a sad look, "Oh, Shane. I forgot to mention it, but Brianna wanted me to tell you to call her. We made her call a cab, sorry." She looked to Conner and Lea, "We thought it would be longer, and well, she was annoying to look at really."

"Who's Brianna?" I asked. Oh, was that the blonde girl's name? I hadn't even wondered where she went.

Grace looked even sadder and stepped out of the cab. I watched her walk up her front steps and the thought of not spending the rest of the night with her made me feel like half a man.

The cab pulled away and I wondered why I felt such intense feelings for someone that I just met. Someone I knew almost nothing about. Was it just because she looked so much like my lost love that I wanted to be with her to fill that ache in my heart?

"Hey, you sure you're okay, man?" Conner asked.

"Yeah, bro. Golden." Less than five minutes later, Conner and I were back in our apartment. He patted me on the back and trudged to his room. "Night, knock if you need me," he said.

Before he got there, I heard him telling Ethan everything about my ER visit, and then Ethan telling him everything he knew about Alex.

I locked my door and threw myself onto my bed. I took out my phone and called Grace. There was no way I wanted to call it a night with her. Her phone rang a few times and then went to voicemail; her sweet voice echoing through the line. *I'm not near the phone, leave a message and I'll call you back.* Thousands of poetic stanzas ran through my mind. What message could I leave that would make her call me back? Probably nothing. *This is Grace I'm calling, nothing in the world would make that beautiful creature want to call me back, unless I annoyed her enough.* "Grace, it's Shane. Give me a call back tonight, doesn't matter what time. Call me or I swear I'll ring this phone all night." *Whoa, great going, Casanova, that was awful.*

Okay, I definitely needed to leave another message way better than that idiotic one. Like the freaking stalker that I was quickly becoming, I called her again. Her cell rang and rang. *What could I quote into her voicemail? What words of long ago would move her?* She had looked so sad when we dropped her off in front of her apartment; I wanted to make those beautiful lips smile. What had she been sad about? Was it because of the attack? Shouldn't she have been scared? She wasn't though. She was brave and strong. What had she said when she walked out of the cab?

"What do you want, Shane?" Her voice cut into my thoughts. *It's not her voicemail, she answered the phone!*

"Who is Brianna?" I answered. *How was it possible that those words could have crossed my lips?* This girl made me an idiot. She tongue-tied me like no one else.

"Um, the stunning blonde you picked up at the bar and danced with," she replied. *Was that a giggle I heard?* "She went in the ambulance with you, Shane. How could you not know who I'm talking about? Anyway, why are you calling me and asking about it; more importantly, who gave you my number so I can plot their slow death?" *She was definitely giggling at me!*

"Oh, man. I thought her name was Lori. Did you get upset when I was dancing with her?" *Holy crap, it was as if I had lost the brain to mouth filter in this body! What the...it's like I'm malfunctioning.*

"Shane, why in the world would I care if you danced with someone? Is that why you called me?" *Not the answer I really wanted to hear. How about a HELL YES! It drove me crazy! I want you to come over right now!*

A laugh sputtered out of my damn lips. *A laugh.* More like a girly freaking giggle. I sighed loudly at my own stupidity. Why did I even bother to call her? She would never give me the time of day. What was I hoping for?

"No, I just wanted to see how you were doing. It's not every night that someone attacks you, right?" *And, Grace the thought of someone hurting you almost killed me. The thought that someone had touched you, caused you pain in any way, made me what to bring the heavens down.*

"I'm absolutely fine, exhausted, but fine."

I felt like a chump calling her. "I programed your number into my phone when I called you on Lea's phone looking for Tucker. I didn't think you'd mind." I desperately tried to change the subject. "I was about to grab something to eat and then go to bed, what are you doing?"

"I'm climbing into bed right now," she yawned.

The thought of her slipping her sexy legs under her sheets made my whole body stiffen. I couldn't even wrap my head around the thoughts her words brought to my mind. "Oh," I managed to reply. My chest ached as much as my damn body did at her voice. "That's a thought that's going to last me all night."

"God, Shane! Shut up! Why does everything have to be sexual with you? Have you seriously never had a platonic

123

friendship with a female before?" Even though I knew the words were serious, I could hear the laughter in her voice.

"No. Ah, Grace, look, I just called to see how you were doing. Like I said, it's not every night that someone attacks you, right? Or *does* this happen often?" I asked again in a playful tone.

"I really am fine, Shane, but it's not every night that someone tries to protect me from someone who attacks me. I don't even know what to say, because thank you just doesn't seem to be enough. You kind of amazed me tonight."

Then she just talked with me. At some point, my heart stopped and I could barely breathe listening to her words. When my heart started thundering in my chest again, I let myself fall limply against my pillows and laughed with her until the sun came up.

When we disconnected, I was so much more taken with her than I had been when I first laid eyes on her and my heart felt twisted. The truth was, Grace should steer clear of my cursed life and me. I would never be whole for her. But, that girl had a way about her that made me feel like anything was possible.

Chapter 7

I rolled myself out of bed around five o'clock on Thursday evening. And the conclusion I came to as I stumbled through the hallway into the kitchen looking for coffee: Staying up on the phone all night with a girl that spun your body into a whirl of fucking tense sexual emotions will cause a man to sleep for eleven hours straight. It also made me feel higher than a kite. My body was strung tight and I practically bounced off the walls of the kitchen with a strange euphoric energy.

"Hey, good evening, Sleeping Beauty. Glad you remembered to get up for the auditions tonight," Ethan quipped as I made coffee. "Who the hell were you laughing and talking to on the phone all night?"

Crap, this was going to be a shitty conversation. "Grace," I murmured, slowly bringing my eyes to meet his.

Ethan dragged his gaze away from the coffee maker and directed a threatening look right at me. "Don't go there, Shane," he said grimly. "Dude, you're going to end up crushing her if she falls for you."

"Well, thank you, buddy, for the fucking vote of confidence," I said, finding my black leather motorcycle boots and shoving my feet into them, then glaring back at him.

"Shane. Look me in the eye and tell me you won't hurt her," he deadpanned.

"Drop it, Ethan. I'm just getting to know her; I'm trying to be a friend. I called her last night to see if she was okay after what happened. That's it. We talked. Leave me alone about it."

"Fine. Let's just go down to the studio and see who shows up for auditions. Alex, Bray and Conner are already downstairs. *Waiting,*" he said storming out. "Oh, and while you were sleeping all day, Alex is fine. He didn't have to stay the night in jail. Tucker's dad got him released. Not that you seem to give a shit about anything but your dick."

I took off after him out of our apartment and down the steps to the studio that we had built in the basement of the building. I stopped dead when I reached the doorway. Four people were waiting in the hallway with guitar cases in their hands. *Four fucking people* and Tucker was one of them. My muscles tightened immediately. I had a shitty feeling that Mad World would be out of gigs for the next six weeks.

Tucker barged his way through the studio door when I opened it, carrying a 30 pack of *Budweiser*. He wore a pair of those 1970 nuthugger jeans, converse sneakers and an old worn out *Poison* tee shirt circa 1990. "Hey, posers! Anybodywantabeer? I think I got like eight left in here," he said slurring his words. *Well, if we didn't find someone to replace Alex for the next few weeks, at least we knew the auditions would be very entertaining with Tucker as tanked as he was.* Let's see 30 beers minus 8 equals, yeah, *tanked*.

Walking right in the studio behind Tucker were the three other guys there to play for us. They each took a beer from Tucker, which pissed me off at all of them instantly.

Ethan quietly sat himself behind his kit, and Brayden was already leaning up against the wall with his bass in his hands. Alex sat on one of the couches with his casts lying across his chest, Conner sat beside him. I grabbed my guitar from its stand and nodded at the guy closest to me. "Okay, let's get this shit over with. Why don't you just start playing whatever you're good at and we'll jump in? What's your name, by the way?"

"They call me Axe," he sneered, plugged his guitar into Alex's amp, and played a heavy thrash rhythm. The guy was good, he had really fast fingers and he flew through riffs. I jumped in with him when he played an old school Metallica song and when it was over, Alex gave me a slight nod with his head as if to say he liked him.

Tucker stood up, took a huge gulp of beer and yelled, "That fucking sucked! Next!" Then he threw his empty beer can at the guy. When the guy didn't move fast enough to his liking, Tucker pegged the rest of the applicants with more cans of beer until I grabbed him around the waist and subdued him. By the time I reached him though, it was too late; the three guys wanting to take Alex's place were running down the hallway away from the studio.

Alex jumped into Tucker's face, casts flailing around, "What brand of douche *are you?* If I had my hands out of these casts I would slap you like a little girl."

Tucker tried shrugging himself out of my hold, "You know this is all bullshit anyway. Who knows your shitty ass music better than me?"

I palmed his face and mushed him away from me before I got too angry and started really wailing on him. "Grab Alex's guitar then and see if you can even remember how to hold it."

We all watched in horror as Tucker drunkenly tried to strap Alex's precious guitar on, banging it into the speakers and amps, stumbling and struggling with it as he tried to stand up straight.

"You have got you be kidding me," Ethan growled when Tucker finally got the guitar strapped to him. *Backwards.* Then his legs seemed to buckle under him and he dropped heavily to his knees on the floor.

Alex's eyes widened and his jaw flew open. "Get my guitar! Get it away from him! Get it! Geeeeet Ittttttttt!" he yelled.

Ethan jumped over his kit, symbols crashing to the floor, ran for Tucker and yanked the guitar right off his neck. Tucker's response was to laugh and crawl back to his case of beer and snap open another one.

I watched all the expressions on my band mate's faces and my stomach dropped for them. Since the day we met Tucker, he had always been a royal pain in our sides. I didn't even know why we still put up with his crap.

Shaking my head, I glanced at Conner who was talking on the phone with a giant smile plastered over his lips. "Well, that is going to be awesome to watch. Okay, babe," he was saying into his phone. *Sounded like he was talking to Lea, probably about something naughty. Crap, I envied him.* An amazing fantasy danced before my eyes of those words falling from my lips as I spoke with Grace. *I could think of about ten thousand things it would be awesome to watch Grace do. Ugh. Get a grip, Shane!*

Nodding to the rest of the guys, I sat down hard on the floor of the studio and laid my guitar across my lap. Alex, Braden and Ethan followed suit and started discussing all the many wonderful ways to kill Tucker. All while Tucker sat crossed legged and giggled. *Idiot.*

About ten minutes later, a soft knock at the door silenced the room. With that huge smile still splitting his face in two, Conner opened the door. "Just in time, two beautiful girls in the studio should help ease some tension, I hope." Lea walked in and jumped into his arms. But the sight of Grace walking in behind her was what made my breath catch in my throat.

I stood up, dusted my pants off, and started to walk over. But, Tucker reached her before I could, stumbling wildly. "Hey, are you here to listen to me play? That's cool, my first fan." I shoved him out of the way to see Grace better.

As I laid my eyes on her, a cool shiver passed through my body. She paused right after she stepped through the doorway and slid her arms slowly out of her jacket. My body became restless and alive as I drank in the sight of her like a thirsty man. Her hair fell like a straight silky black curtain outlining the savage beauty of her face. Eyes so light gray, they shined and sparkled like diamonds. The red straps of her shirt eased themselves over her shoulders and plunged down to show the curves and swell of her breasts. I swayed back on the heels of my boots when my eyes slowly traveled down to her hands and watched her open a guitar case. Then, I stopped breathing all together.

"I'm sorry, Tucker, but I'm not here to listen to you play. I thought I'd take a crack at auditioning; see if I could play as good as Alex," she said in a breathy voice. Her eyes were fixed on mine, and I could see the rapid rise and fall of her chest. *She was having trouble breathing too.*

Tucker busted out a drunken laugh, "My fucking mother could play better than Alex right now, both his arms are broken, but she ain't here. But, damn girl, you look hot. I'd like to buy some stock in that ass later. My place or yours?"

I wanted to hit him. I turned to grab him, shake some sense into him, or just shut him the hell up. The way he spoke to her made me want to lift him above my head and throw him against the wall.

Grace narrowed her eyes at Tucker, and then glanced behind him at the cans of beer he left on the floor. "I think you are subhuman when you drink and talk like that, so I'd appreciate it, if when you do drink, you don't speak to me," Grace said to him. I held back a laugh. "Shane, is it okay if I try?" She held her guitar in her hands and I stood there stunned. *Oh my God, that looks like Eric Clapton's guitar.*

"That looks an awful lot like a *1964 Gibson ES0335 TDC*," I whispered.

"Yeah, an awful lot like it. So, can I play?" she said in a sultry tone. Her lips lifted up in a sideways smile. *Oh my God, she's smiling like **it is** Eric Clapton's guitar.*

I wanted to close my eyes and just focus on breathing again. Only Grace was standing there waiting for me to answer her. Standing there, while the most carnal, erotic sensations tore through my entire body. The first woman ever who was capable of making me feel so out of control in this body.

"You tell me, Grace. Can you play?" I asked.

"Give me a fucking break. Don't let her embarrass herself like this. Shane, tell her no!" Tucker shouted to me. One of Lea's shoes flew across the room and smacked him in the head. I smiled to myself as Tucker drunkenly stumbled back as if he'd been punched by a heavy weight fighter.

Grace strapped on her guitar and plugged into an amp. *It fucking looked like she was born with it there.*

Then the earth stopped and tilted rigidly on its axis. I felt the ground disappear beneath my feet as Grace's hands replicated the haunting song I played for her that first time she came to the studio. The song that she unknowingly inspired me to compose, twisting itself from her delicately dancing fingers. Heat swept over my body and an overwhelming need to touch her, to kiss her lips, almost had me throwing myself at her.

A slow tight rhythm floated through the studio. *My song*, the one I wrote for her, was seeping through the strings of her guitar and echoing through Alex's amp, filling the studio with my secrets.

Soft and forlorn, the notes she played reproduced the longing and desperate feelings I secretly felt for her when I first composed the piece. Her entire body, intensely involved with the power of the music, made tears sting my eyes. Then passion, pure and alive burst through the speakers as she sped up her hands and let them skillfully dance along the strings of her instrument. *Dear God, who is this creature? She's captured my heart without even trying. Without me even knowing, I still had one.*

I scrambled for my guitar and added my sounds to her symphony. Eyes locking, we played for each other, to each other. *I knew I would never be the same.* Together, our rhythm quickened, teasing notes and harmony into the air. We exploded in sound and feeling until we stood breathless across from each other, ceasing our melodies and slicing silence through the room.

"What else can you play?" I asked panting.

"Anything you want me to," she whispered.

"Hendrix," I answered.

She grinned wide and blasted through Purple Haze from start to finish, embellishing on Hendrix's infamous guitar solos and deliberate distortions. My heart pounded. Before I could ask for more, she began fingering a soft ballad, unfolding the notes at a slow measured pace. She bounced towards all genres of music, each note giving rhythm and birth to a funky piece of music that soared throughout the studio. A bleak bluesy beginning dripped from each note, transforming into a jazzy composition and weaving into a web of classical eloquence. A sharp shrill rock solo to the heavy chords of thrash then back to the low murmurs of a hushed lonely melody, like a heartbeat unraveling its beautiful ethereal essence into the heavens until there was silence. All the while, her eyes never left mine.

"That girl can play," Ethan's voice cut through the silence. *I completely forgot that everyone else was here.*

Alex chuckled, "Yeah, and I think I'm in love!" His words sent a fire of rage through my body.

"Shut up," I said to Alex, but still glared at Grace, "play more."

A beautiful blush of crimson colored her face. "No. You seem really upset with me for some reason right now and that's not what I had wanted to happen, Shane." She slowly slid her guitar strap over her head and gently leaned the guitar against the amp. Eyes still locked on mine she started packing up.

"Don't go, Grace," I whispered.

She looked away from me, intently stared at something on the ground, and then with a deep breath, met my eyes once more.

"What did you want to happen?" I asked.

"I honestly thought you would let me play for Alex and that you wouldn't be angry. I don't understand what it was that I did wrong, but right now, you look like you want to kill me," she stammered.

"I'm just thunderstruck right now, I'm not angry. That's like the third time in less than a week you've managed to shock me. What else can you do? Fly? Or," I started laughing, "Or, can you also play the piano and sing? Because then I'd understand Alex, then I'd be in love with you too."

Her face paled. "Well, we definitely wouldn't want that, would we? So let's just say that I can play guitar really well and I can't do anything else." Then, a deep red splash of crimson spread across her cheeks and down her neck. *Holy shit, she's lying to me and she could sing?*

"Ha! Don't let her kid you. She can do it all," Lea laughed.

No way.

Ethan jumped up, pulled her over to keyboard, and switched the mic on. Grace looked up at him with a sweet shy expression, but he smiled down at her, brushed the hair off her shoulder, and whispered into her ear. "Go ahead, Grace, make us fall in love with you," his whisper softly echoed through the microphone.

Hell no. Please God, make her suck at singing; please don't give me anymore reason to want her.

A sublime expression brightened her features as she bit her lower lip and closed her eyes. Eyes still closed, she reached for the microphone, cleared her throat, and placed her hands on the keys, knowing where everything was blindly.

Slow and steamy, the lyrics of my song fell from her lips. Her delicate fingers danced like raindrops across the keys. My legs buckled and I dropped to my knees. *She brought me to my damn knees.*

Where do I go from here? What do I do? This had to be the worst part of my punishment. This was going to destroy what was left of my soul wasn't it? Seeing this beautiful being, so much like Selah in every way, but never being able to have her. Anger tore through my body. It crashed over my soul worse than any pain that I had ever felt while being imprisoned in Hell. This was my torment. This would be my end. *Grace.*

"I think I can speak for everybody here, you're taking Alex's place," Ethan announced. "Where the hell did you learn to play like that?"

Grace's eyes met mine and she shrugged in answer to Ethan's question, "I took a few lessons."

Tucker stumbled up to Ethan and looked around to the rest of the guys. "Wait a second; does this mean I don't get to play? That pretty much sucks, Grace."

Ethan grumbled at Tucker to shut up and climbed behind his drum kit and nodded to Brayden and me. "Let's practice with our newest band member," he smiled.

I ignored my anger and rage. I controlled my desperate need to run out of the studio and never return. I picked up my guitar, and like a robot, I watched Grace and played. I needed to stay the hell away from her; the archangels put her here to remind me of Selah. She wasn't Selah. *I was done with this shit, with her.*

Those thoughts didn't help with the fact that I thought I might be falling in love with her.

We played for hours, until I unhooked my guitar strap and just stopped playing.

Ethan pulled me to the side and brought his face just inches shy of mine. "Dude. I can see you, and your emotions are written all over your face right now. Don't go there, Shane, especially if she's going to be playing with us. Don't mess this up for the rest of the guys." He backed away from me and held his hands up. "Bro, just do me a favor and wait until after six weeks is up to sleep with her. Remember, we made a rule, if there's any chick in the band, hands off."

I made my way to the studio door. Ethan was right. Now I had to get the hell away from her. It was like my own personal room of Hell, in a house in the neighborhood of Hell, right smack in the middle of the city Hell. I grabbed my jacket and shoved my arms in it.

"Hey, dude. You're splitting?" Ethan asked. "Where you off to? Shouldn't we celebrate or something?"

"I have plans," I said opening the door and slamming it hard behind me. I stormed out of the building and down the street. I walked past Boozer's until I hit the next bar. There I drank myself stupid until a cute dark-haired girl started yapping at me. I told her I was in love with another girl I would never be allowed to have, and she said she would help me forget about her. She sat next to me at the bar, talked, and slid her hands up and down my back. I barely registered her there. The only time I noticed her and her efforts was when she got too close and her perfume slapped me in the face.

A few hours had passed and my only thoughts were of calling Grace. I just wanted to hear her silky voice. I needed to see that little mischievous smile and hear her contagious laugh. *Fuck, I wanted to tell her how I felt.* How she twisted my insides like nobody else, how I didn't want to spend one more minute without her.

"Hey, Shane? Are you still with me? What are you thinking about, Sweetie?"

I was peeling back the label of my beer, one wet thin silver strip at a time, ripping it into shreds on the bar. My shot glass sat empty next to it. *How much had I drunk already?* The bar was spinning. I glanced at the girl next to me. Her eyes were big and brown, full of pretend sympathy. They weren't light gray. She wasn't Grace.

"Need another shot," I said.

Like drunken magic, a shot appeared before me. I smiled, thinking that was pretty awesome.

"Shane, you want to go somewhere else, baby?" *What the hell was this girl's name again?* Couldn't she see I was in love with Grace? *Shit, I was in love with Grace.*

"I gotta go," I explained.

"I'll come with you, baby."

"I'm going to Boozer's to see if Grace is there."

"You sure you don't feel like swinging by your place, Shane?"

"Fuck no," I slurred.

She must have used that drunken magic voodoo again, because the next thing I remember was walking into Boozer's and my freaking stomach dropping to the floor when I saw Grace. Something invisible was squeezing my heart, making it sputter and thrash. She and Ethan were hunched together in the corner away from everybody else, like they were a freaking couple. No fucking wonder Ethan was so against me liking Grace. He liked her just the same. Backstabbing fucknut. It didn't help me at all to know she was better off with someone as good as him. The big-ass teddy bear would never hurt her. I'd be the only one with a broken heart in that scenario.

The girl I was with dragged me to the bar and ordered more drinks. She was still yapping at me. Giggling, yapping and running her hands all over me. All I wanted to do was walk right up to Grace and tell her I loved her. *Pick me or Ethan, Grace.*

"No, Shane. My name is Ava. Stop calling me Grace."

I looked at her and laughed. "Sorry," I said running my fingers up her arm trying to be sweet and let her down nicely. "Maybe you should leave me alone, especially since I don't care enough to remember your name."

She leaned forward and thrust her tongue right into my mouth. I backed away quickly, only to hear Grace's musical laughter from across the bar. Our eyes caught each other's and the expression she offered me made me feel like Ethan was her choice even though I hadn't yet asked her to pick between us.

135

I downed my drink. Then I downed some more until I watched Ethan walk Grace out of the bar, and I wanted to freaking die. She didn't even look at me when she left. I jumped up and my head swam with the rush of alcohol that surged through my veins. My hands dropped heavily to the top of the bar and I leaned against it to help myself stand upright.

"You ready for some fun, now?" Eva, Evie, Avery, Ava...*whatever the fuck her name was*, asked.

"Going after Grace," I slurred back. *Fuck this shit. If falling in love with Grace was some fucked up shit from my punishment, then bring it on, punish me. Punish me with Grace. I have to take my chances on loving her.*

What's her face's high pitched whines echoed in my ears as I stumbled out of the bar and into the street. Snow covered the ground and was falling in huge flakes across the city. *How the hell did I not remember seeing snow before? And where the fuck was my coat? Not important, I had to get Ethan away from Grace.*

I pulled out my cell and stared down at it, willing it to call Grace. My dumb drunk fingers hit Gary Tompson's icon instead of Grace's. He was my dentist. I hung up. *I didn't need to make an appointment right now.* I walked in the direction of Grace's apartment and kept trying to call her.

"Hello?" *God, her voice was amazing.* It could soothe a man's restless soul.

"Where are you?" I demanded.

"I'm in bed, Shane. Honestly, I just fell getting the phone and right now, I'm on the damn floor. Why are you calling me?" *Oh shit. SHIT, SHIT, SHIT! They were in bed already?* I stumbled down the block faster.

"Is Ethan with you?"

"No." Low. Quiet. Full of *hurt*.

"I'm sorry, I shouldn't have..." I was on her block. I **was** a freaking stalker now *and not about to stop*.

136

"Don't feed me any of your crap, Shane. I have no idea why you think you can call me at any hour and pretend you give a crap about who I leave a bar with." *Pretend? I fucking wish I were pretending. I am in fucking love with you.* I had to tell her I loved her.

"Stop, Grace. Please!" I pleaded into the phone. "I have a whole speech I need to say and..."

"Yeah, yeah, Shane. Four whores and seven beers ago...save it, Shane. I don't care what you have to say to me. It's none of your business if I take home an entire football team. Are you just pissed because you didn't get a crack at it first? You can't even comprehend how someone isn't fazed by your rock god status. Well, get it through your skull, you're not a thought in my mind. So get on with your life. And don't be pissed off at me because I tried to do you and your friends a favor by showing you I can play a few instruments. You don't want me to play with you guys; fine. I DON'T CARE!"

Disconnect.

What the hell just happened?

Did she just fucking hang up on me? My body went numb. Mind reeling. I had no right to this beautiful creature, but I wanted her more than I ever wanted anyone else. I wanted her more than *anybody ever wanted anybody else.*

Standing in front of her door, snow soaked through my shirt, I wondered if I should ring the front bell. Hell no, she would never answer the door for me. *Wow, the city was spinning around me.*

I climbed over her railing and scaled the tall iron gates to the small alleyway between her building and the next. Falling over the garbage cans, I crawled my way to the fire escape. I jumped up, pulled down the rusty ladder, and climbed the rungs. My hands slipped off the wet metal a few times before I got a good grasp and made it to her bedroom window. There was no sensible thought in my brain. I needed to see her. The world spun out of control around me and I felt swept up in its torrents.

I rapped my cold wet knuckles against the glass of her window. Inside, the curtain was pushed to the side and the vision of her, *so damn beautiful*, looked back at me. Heat soared over my body as I placed an open palm against the icy glass near her face to try to touch her.

The curtain fell back, robbing me of my redemption. In my skin, my blood, my bones and my soul the only truth I felt to be real was one: If this creature could love me, and if I could love her, this existence of mine would mean *something*. I would never get to stand in heaven again. Yet, heaven was standing on the other side of that curtain.

"Grace, please. It's freakin' cold out here," I pleaded, letting my forehead fall limply against the window. "Grace, I swear I will ring your doorbell until I wake everybody up. Open the damn window!"

The click of the lock and the harsh creak of the window sliding up was the best sound that ever touched my ears. Well, besides the sound of Grace's voice singing or the music that emerged from her fingers when she played.

I tumbled in, scanning the room to see if she was truly alone. My entire body relaxed when I found no one else. Then my gaze locked on her and I was gulping for fucking air.

The glow of the streetlights fell across her soft skin, making her look ethereal; spectral. My God, did she wear the warmth of that soft light like no other. Her black hair spilled over her creamy shoulders and her exquisite silver eyes shimmered wide into mine. A loose white sheet cascaded around her body, held up only by the hands she held clasped at her breasts. I wanted to devour her.

"You're not dressed, are you? Is that your sheet?" I could feel my own breathy voice puff out of my mouth and I clenched my fists.

138

She tightened the hold on her sheets and her gaze slid away from mine to stare at the floor. "What. Do. You. Want?"

Those four words were all she spoke, yet her presence was overpowering my senses. I was aware of all of her. The smell of wildflowers, raw heat radiating from her body, her breath quickening and the pure desire surging through her body, enveloping me.

A tension beyond anything I'd ever felt coiled deep inside me and my body shook violently. I wanted to taste her, touch her; completely make her mine. I wanted to feel her heat seep right into my skin and kiss her perfect lips until they were raw.

When she slowly pulled her bottom lip between her teeth, I came undone. I stalked towards her, backing her up against the wall. Her body responded to mine, arching off the wall to touch me, answering greedily. I leaned both my hands on either side of her face against the wall, and watched her lips slowly part. Instinctively, her hands came up to my chest, but it wasn't to push me away. I knew this because they slowly slid up and fisted my shirt and pulled me in, dropping the sheet from her grasp. She wore nothing but a tiny bra and panties and the feel of her skin so close to me made my mouth water.

"Shane, stop," she whispered between throaty breaths. Yet, her body continued to press itself into mine with need.

Hovering my face over her skin, I breathed her in and gently let my forehead rest against hers. The touch was erotic, sensual and loving. Skin against skin, mouths open, savoring each other's scent and feel.

I skimmed my fingertips slow and gently over her bare shoulders and down to her waist. She felt like warm silk shivering beneath me.

Brushing my lips across her cheek, I buried my face in her hair. A soft gasp fell from her lips and they tilted up towards mine.

"Grace, all I want to do is kiss you right now," I whispered. I softly pushed her hair back and grazed my lips along her neck. I couldn't help but slip my tongue out to taste her sweet warmth. *Delicious.* She pressed against me harder and moaned softly against my ear.

"Shane, please," she whispered. I knew her mind was asking me to stop, but I knew every other part of her body was aching for me to continue. I felt it in her clenched fists holding me tight, her small whimpers, and her warm skin against mine.

"Just tell me why I got crazy thinking you were going home with Ethan? Tell me why I want to kill any man that looks at you? Grace, I don't want to feel this way." Pulling my head back, I locked my eyes on hers. I slowly slid my fingertips back to her waist, hooking one under the silky lace trim of her panties, tracing a circle on the skin hidden beneath.

She sighed softly. "*So tempting,*" she murmured barely above a whisper.

I searched her eyes and watched as tears pooled in the bottom of them. I wanted to wipe them away, but I watched as her features hardened again and I knew our moment was over, but I knew it wouldn't be our last. I didn't know what force stopped her from taking a chance on me, or what she was afraid of, but I would be spending the rest of my time here making her mine.

"Shane. Stop, you're drunk, you're soaking wet, and you are so cold you're trembling."

The room spun around me as if I was on an alcohol fueled merry-go-round. I stumbled to her bed and sat down, hanging my head in my hands. "I'm not trembling from the cold, Grace," I whispered as she walked out her door. She left me alone for a few minutes with my own thoughts. They were dark and disturbing and I wanted to crawl out of this skin. There was no way that I could ever replace Selah in my heart, but I desperately longed to ease the pain of losing her. The wounds still felt fresh, even though she was taken from me lifetimes ago.

Grace came back into the room fully dressed, carrying an armful of clothing.

A sudden sweep of fear flushed through me. *Did I just go too far?* "Did you wake up Conner? Oh, God. Grace, did you call the cops?"

"Shane, you are a real ass sometimes," she giggled and knelt down in front of me and lifted my wet shirt over my head. She struggled a bit with the wet material and I laughed. She gently touched a hand to my face and smoothed her knuckles along my jawline. Waves of heat spread through my body and I clutched at the sheets of her bed to keep me from throwing myself on her like an animal. "I have dry socks, boxers and pants for you too, but you need to dress yourself." Again, she left the room and I changed out of the rest of my wet clothes quickly.

When she didn't return, I walked down the hallway and into the living room in search of her. She stood in front of the couch that she had made into a bed for me, with her hands over her face, body shaking, silently sobbing. It killed me to think I did that to her. She was plainly hiding so much from me, and I ached for her to let me in.

She lifted her head and her body straightened immediately when she saw me, not wanting me to see her humanity or her moment of need. *Shit, how damaged is this creature?*

"What?" she asked me exasperated. "There's no way you should be going home this intoxicated in the snow with no jacket on." She seemed to be trying hard to act pissy. It wasn't natural for her; Grace didn't come with a bitch bone in her body. She was hiding things, from me I knew, but mostly from herself.

"I really screwed things up with our friendship, didn't I? You're standing here looking at me the way you look at Tucker."

She laughed.

"Why are you laughing at me?" I asked moving closer to her.

"Shane, you can't ruin a friendship, if you were only pretending to be my friend to get into my pants."

That was so easy for her to believe. Such a human jealous, self-pitying emotion. And I loved her more for it. I took her wrist and led her back to her bedroom, and she let me, placing her other hand on my back, as if she *needed* to touch *me*. I stopped in front of the door to her room and faced her, lifting her wrist to my lips. Her body trembled and her breath caught.

Her eyes fell to her wrists with a fear in them, and I followed them down. A tattoo darkened the soft skin. "You have a tattoo?" My thumb lightly swept over her skin and my heart raced. *What the hell?* "It's covering up a scar?" I grabbed her other wrist fumbling for it; she gave it to me easily. A horizontal jagged scar ran across both of her wrists. "Why would you do that?" I asked.

She pulled her hands back slowly to her chest. "You know, Shane, the people that walk around you every day? Each of them has a life separate from you. Pasts, pains, loves and losses. You don't know me. I am a hell of a lot more than a fifteen-minute screw, and sadly, most of your other *friends* are too. You just don't ever see that from between their legs," she whispered.

You are so right, Grace. You are so much more to me. So right, and I'm going to prove that to you over and over again. "Goodnight, Grace," I said walking back into the living room.

Chapter 8

The next morning, I woke up with my brain hammering against my head. It was late morning and I was alone in Grace's living room underneath blankets that smelled of wildflowers and summertime.

My entire body was stiff, and certain parts could rival the hardness of a diamond as soon as thoughts of Grace wrapped in her sheet came to my mind.

The coffee pot in the kitchen was half full and still on. I figured Grace had already been up when I saw her favorite mug turned over in the sink. I walked through the apartment looking for her. *Empty. Silent.* I walked softly to her room and knocked on the semi-open door. *No answer.* I pushed the door open wide enough to stick my head in.

I struggled to swallow the huge-ass knot in my throat and sweat broke out all over my body. Grace lay across her bed curled into a ball on her side facing away from the door. Ebony strands of glossy hair spilled across her pillows. The hem of her black shirt had ridden up high on her ribcage showing off a line of dark scripted tattoo across her back. From where I stood, I couldn't read the words. Without even thinking, I walked closer.

Latin, the ancient language scrolled deep under her skin. *Nullum Desiderium, Deus solus me iudicare potest* (No regrets, only God can judge me). What was this creature's story? I held myself back from touching the black inked lines. *Who the fuck was I kidding, I was holding myself back from licking them.*

The waist of her pants hung low against her skin and the most exquisite curve of a hip peeked out and traveled tightly into the soft ivory skin of her waist. I stood over her and took in her features in rapt desire as she slept. I studied every inch of her face. The smoothness of her skin, the plump pink curves of her lips and the shape of her nose were pure perfection. Under her closed eyes, her skin was a pale pink and a thin tear streak stained her perfect cheek. She took my breath away.

Her hands were clenched around some papers, no doubt containing the reason for her tears. I didn't look at them further, whatever was in them, whatever pain they caused was her story to tell. Not mine to take.

I couldn't help but stay and watch her. *Could you blame me?* It was one of the only times I could really look at her without her biting my head off or giving me those sexy little smiles that she pretends she doesn't make when she looks at me.

I may or may not have watched her for thirty minutes.

I only touched her shoulder to wake her when more tears spilled from her eyes and small whimpers passed through her lips. Whatever she was dreaming of that made her cry; I wanted to save her from.

"Grace? What's wrong, are you sick?"

She shot up and wiped at her eyes, "I'm fine. How are you?" She turned her head away from me and brushed away her tears.

Crap. I needed to make her think of something else and not her crying in front of me. I raked my hands through my hair and figured I should just act like I didn't remember shit from last night. *Hopefully that would make her pissed off at me and get her mind off why she was crying.* "What the hell did I do last night?"

That did it. She glared at me and laughed humorlessly. "That's great, Shane. No, really. That's perfect. Why don't you go home now, okay? Goodbye," she snapped. Her head turned away again and her hand reached to wipe another tear.

Okay, I need to be a bigger dick right now. "Grace, I know we didn't…did we?"

Yeah. That stopped her from crying. She wasn't sad anymore, now she was pissed off. Whatever she was upset about and hiding from me was not the problem anymore. *Now my complete douche-ness was the problem. Maybe I didn't think this through.*

She jumped up, grabbing all the papers and shoving them into one of her drawers. Then she bolted out of her room. *Shit, I went too far!*

I ran after her, caught up to her in the kitchen and swung her around to face me. "What did I do? Why have you been crying?" I leaned my face into her so all she could see was *me*. The face off lasted about five full minutes. Her expression softened.

"You didn't do anything, Shane. You called me last night. You thought I was with Ethan. I hung up on you and you climbed up the fire escape in the snow, with no coat on and banged on my window until I let you in. Now please, just leave."

"No. I'm not leaving until I know I'm not the reason you're crying." I stopped talking and looked intensely into her eyes. "You were wearing a sheet? You...you got me dry clothes," I said, pretending I was just remembering.

"No big deal, see?"

"No big deal? I leaned you up against a wall; I can still taste your skin on my mouth. I can still feel your body against mine."

My God, did my heart almost stop when I saw the shy smile that she tried desperately to hide from her lips. *Now, if I ask why she was crying, she'd tell me.*

Gently, I took her wrists in both my hands and skimmed my thumbs against her scars. I could feel the pulse quicken from my touch. "Why were you crying this morning?"

"I received a letter in the mail today from the hospice where Jacob passed away. Inside was a letter that he had written for me before he died. It was just hard to read it." She slowly dragged her hands from mine and let them limply fall in front of her.

I scooped them right back up, "Grace..."

Her eyes searched mine and she blew her cheeks out in a puff. The tears poured down her cheeks right after. I pulled her in and held her tight. Holding her until the tears stopped and she looked up at me, and smiled timidly, "I'm sorry, Shane. I didn't mean to snap. I'm not used to all this emotional crap."

I closed my eyes and leaned my forehead against hers. I loved feeling her skin on mine like that. I moved my head just enough to look into her eyes, and breathed her in softly, our lips almost touching. It took all my strength not to kiss her. I closed my eyes and stepped back finding my resolve. I almost lost it again when her body followed mine. *Damn it, then why the hell does she fight against me all the time?* I stepped forward. *Damn this restraint, I needed my lips on hers.*

Before I could close the space between us further, the damn doorbell rang. "Please don't be sorry, Grace," I said before I let her answer the door. "I *am* your friend and I'm here if you need to talk about anything or need a shoulder to cry on."

"Thanks," she whispered and spun around to answer the door.

I tore my hands through my hair. "Especially if that's the only way I'll ever get to hold you," I whispered looking up to the ceiling. I leaned back heavily against the wall making a soft thud, causing the pain in my head to throb harder and sharper.

"Good afternoon. We're detectives from the 19th precinct. We're looking for a Grace Taylor," a man's voice sliced through my thoughts.

I ran to Grace's side instantly.

Grace offered the detectives a tight smile, "I'm Grace Taylor. How may I help you?"

"Miss Taylor, may we come in? We need to speak to you about the incident with Carl Sumpton."

Next to me, Grace's body went rigid. Nodding her head, she directed them into the living room. "I'm sorry, Detectives, but I'm not sure who Carl Sumpton is, unless you are referring to the man who attacked me in Boozer's late Wednesday night?"

I walked ahead of them and yanked the blankets and pillows I slept on the night before off the couch, so they could sit. Folding the blanket up, I piled it on top of the pillows on a small antique style table that stood in the hallway. In the kitchen, I made a fresh pot of coffee, grabbed four bottles of cold water from the refrigerator and walked back into the living room to offer the detectives some. "I made some coffee, if you'd like," I said.

One of the Detectives, he said his name was Ramos, accepted the water, "Thank you. I'm sorry, I didn't catch your name." He twisted off the top of the bottle and sipped the water, waiting for me to reply.

I held out my hand to shake the Detective's. "That's because I never said it. I'm Shane Maxton." I smiled at him and sat down next to Grace, placing a water bottle on the table in front of her. Without thinking, my hand slid to the small of her back, giving her the slightest touch of pressure. I wanted to nuzzle my face in her neck when she moved in closer to me. And I freaking would have if those damn detectives weren't eyeing us like we just robbed a bank.

Ramos looked at me deadpan, "You're the one who helped to stop the attack."

Grace's body stiffened under my fingertips. I kneaded small circles over her back and she slowly relaxed back into my touch. "Grace was doing a pretty good job of defending herself. I think she could have taken care of him all by herself if I hadn't gotten there in time. But I'm confused, we already spoke with the arresting officers at the hospital that night. Has something changed?"

Ramos glanced at his partner. Then the older man nodded his head and Detective Ramos gave me a somber expression. "After Mr. Sumpton was arraigned, he was remanded and housed in Riker's Island. We don't know how it happened, but he was put in his cell at 1400 hours and at the evening head count after meal, he wasn't accounted for." He hesitated for a moment, letting the news sink in. "The cell was still locked when they went to feed him. No one understands how he escaped, since the cell hadn't been opened since his arrival. Furthermore, when questioned, none of the other prisoners even remembered seeing him inside his cell."

What the hell? They let that piece of shit escape?

"Like he just vanished?" Grace asked.

The hand I held on her tightened and she moved in even closer to me. The level of my anger was about to explode through the roof. If it wasn't for my hand touching Grace, which in some weird way was calming to me, I know I would have punched the detective in the face. *These fuckards let that guy get away, the guy that took Grace into a back room and tried to hurt her!*

Detective Ramos gave Grace a tight smile. "No. Most likely, he found some way out with help from someone on the outside of the cell. He probably terrified the other prisoners so badly that they pretended to see nothing. He was a monster when they brought him in. They needed a few corrections officers to settle him down when he was left in his cell, but there's an even more disturbing part," he explained. He sighed and continued, "When we ran his name through our system, nothing came up. Investigating further, we found him to be an outstanding citizen until the last five months or so."

My blood pressure soared; I could feel it surging faster through my veins. Sweat was breaking out over my cheeks and across my forehead. *Weren't these people supposed to be trained in containing criminals?* "What happened five months ago?" I asked through clenched teeth.

Taking a deep breath, Ramos' partner stepped forward to answer, "He was admitted to the Sans de Barron Hospice; he was terminal. His doctors had given him only a few weeks to live. He'd been comatose and unresponsive for weeks, and then sometime last Sunday, he just walked out of the hospice." He gave Grace a curious look, "Am I right in saying that you had been living at the hospice with your brother Jacob for approximately six months?"

Grace nodded and leaned into me further. *I didn't even think she realized what she was doing, but thank God she was doing it, because it stopped me from pummeling these two cowards to a bloody pulp.*

"There must be a mistake though. The man that attacked me, there was no way that he could have been that strong and dying of some disease at the same time. Maybe the guy stole the real Carl Sumpton's identity or something," Grace offered.

The detectives both nodded their heads, and then Ramos cleared his throat and continued, "When a perpetrator of a crime of this magnitude is arraigned, the District Attorney on the case usually requests a temporary order of protection to be issued to the victim. This is your copy of the order." He placed a paper on the table from his briefcase in front of Grace. "I wanted to say that I'm sure this matter will be resolved soon."

That's when I snapped. "And you think a piece of paper will stop this lunatic from trying to hurt Grace again? What should she do if he comes up to her when she's walking down the street? Should she say, hold on while I look in my purse for the piece of paper that will stop you?"

Grace grabbed my knee and her touch sent an electric current straight to my freaking dick. The feeling was so strong that I almost jumped out of this damn skin. Our eyes collided and she held my stare for a moment, "Stop it, Shane. I'm sure they will do everything they can to contain him again." I knew she meant to calm me down, but anger tore through my veins, as my protectiveness over her was all I could see.

Then she looked at both the detectives, "Thank you both for coming here and telling me instead of calling me on the phone. I appreciate the paperwork and everything. Is there anything that you think I could do in the meantime, while you...um...work on this matter?"

Her face was stoic. *Like she didn't care.* That's different, wouldn't most girls cry and whine about being afraid? *Yeah, they would.*

"We understand your anxiety, Mr. Maxton. For the next twenty-four hours, there will be a uniformed officer sitting outside this apartment in a patrol car. Just be aware and keep your eyes open, Miss Taylor."

After a few more words, Grace walked the detectives to the front door and locked the deadbolt. She stood there staring at it, so I walked up behind her and laid my hands on her shoulders and pulled her towards me. She freaked. She moved away and shoved my hands off of her, "I'm fine, Shane," she snapped.

"Yeah, well you definitely will be, because Conner and I are staying here with you and Lea until that asshole is behind bars again," I said as I left her in the hallway. I was freaking livid. I should have broken the guy's neck when I had the chance. I stormed down the hallway and locked myself in the bathroom. I needed to calm the hell down before I found that worthless bag of flesh and ended his existence. "I'm taking a shower! Do not leave this building without me!"

"Make sure you scrub yourself real well, Shane! That perfume you were wearing when you came here last night stinks!" She screamed, slamming her bedroom door.

Where the hell did that crap come from? Oh damn. *Perfume from last night?* Well, fuck me, isn't that interesting. Grace was acting jealous.

I regulated the temperature in the shower with a big-ass grin on my face and jumped in. All thoughts of tearing Carl

Sumpton to shreds were gone because the images of Grace's words filled up my mind. I heard a door slam somewhere in the house and an icy blast of water hit me full in the face. I let out a startled scream, *okay so it wasn't one of my more masculine moments*, but it felt like someone was pouring ice cubes *and* glass over me.

She either flushed a toilet somewhere or she was using the hot water. *On freaking purpose!* Grabbing a towel and wrapping it loosely around my waist, I jumped out of the shower and ran through the house looking for her, dripping a stream of water everywhere I stepped.

The basement light was on. I could tell by the illumination that seeped through the bottom of the door to downstairs when I looked in the kitchen. I flew down the stairs, almost losing my damn towel, and shoved open the laundry room door and charged at her. Only stopping right before my body collided with hers, our lips but an inch apart. "You really need to do your laundry right now? What? Are you mad at me for wanting to stay here? Ticked off because I might actually care if you are okay? What? Will it ruin your high expectations of me?" I cupped her face in both my hands. I could feel her heart pounding against my chest and the heaviness of her breaths. "Or, maybe Grace, you want me here every freaking bit as much I want to be here and that scares the shit out of you?"

Her eyes traveled down to my towel and rose slowly over the skin of my stomach and chest; lingered over my tattoos and right into my eyes. Her pulse sped faster. I felt it beat little drum solos beneath my fingertips. Her mouth was about to lie to me, but her eyes were telling me the truth.

"Nothing about you scares me, Shane. I just don't want you getting the wrong idea about us." *Why the hell is she pushing me away?*

"I know, I know. There *is* no us. I'm not talking about staying here to...Grace, you really think so little of me to think that I want to stay here so I could try to...forget it, Grace." I shook my head and walked to the stairs. "I'll break down your walls, Grace Taylor. You aren't going to know what the fuck hit you," I said, continuing up the stairs. Then I took the coldest shower anyone has ever taken in the history of the universe. And it didn't help me one damn bit.

I left her alone for almost three hours, sat my ass down on her couch and stretched my feet up on her coffee table. I caught up with my favorite television shows and watched two episodes of *Sons of Anarchy* and two episodes of *Family Guy*.

Then I made some grilled cheese sandwiches and brought them down to her as a peace offering. "I thought you'd be starving by now," I said as I knocked on the laundry room door.

She lifted her head off her arms and smiled. "More bored out of my skull than hungry, but thank you."

I matched her smile. "You know, Grace, you don't have to stay down here. I promise you I won't bite," I smirked. "Well, unless you ask me to," I teased to lighten the mood.

"Shut up," she smirked back at me. "I'm sorry about before," she said digging into her sandwich. "I guess I'm just a little freaked out by the whole Carl Sumpton thing." The girl was blatantly lying to me and it was killing me to know why.

I shrugged, playing at her game. "Do you remember him at the hospice?"

"Not at all," she said, hiding her mouth with her hand because she was chewing. "He did look familiar, but not from anywhere I could pinpoint." She threw up her hands. "There were so many people there. I used to play my guitar for Jake every night, well, up until the last few days. There was always a different crowd of people surrounding the door listening. But if he was comatose, he shouldn't have known anything about me. I barely left Jake's room, let alone walk into other patient's rooms." She stuffed her face with the sandwich, it was freaking adorable.

"Maybe he thought your playing stinks," I said taking her empty plate.

"Probably. I mean, I am almost as horrible as you!" She was laughing, no trace of the tears from that morning or fear of Carl Sumpton. Her strength and non-whininess was kind of non-girlie. There was something different about Grace Taylor that made me so intrigued. Maybe that's what these feeling were, and not just the simple fact of her looking like Selah. I just couldn't help wondering what the hell she was hiding from me. If only I could put my lips to hers, I might be able to gauge her feelings a little more. If I still had my wings, I'd know everything through her lips. *Not having my angel abilities sucked, but being human and not in control of human emotions was worse.*

The shrill buzzing of the dryer echoed through the small room. Grace didn't even flinch from the startling sound. She just sauntered over to the machine and took out her clothes, deep in thought. Piles of clean freshly folded clothes lay on the small table near the wall.

The little red lace bra from the first night I met her sat on top of one of the piles. My body stiffened. I had to touch it. *Sue me; I am just a man after all.* I won't lie, even if I was still an angel I would still try to touch it. I held the bra and panties up. Damn they were soft, silky, and lacy. Okay, this shit is new to me; I never got excited over a freaking piece of material before. No, it wasn't the damn material. No. It was the thought of it being on Grace's soft skin. *Shit. This was freaking bad. I had to snap out of this.*

I heard her gasp when she saw me holding her things. She had a sexy smile on her face too. *Real sexy.*

"Hey, Grace. Maybe getting an eyeful of your lingerie woke up our friend Carl from his coma. These are pretty intense undergarments. I know I'll be thinking about them later tonight!"

Walking over to me, she gave me a friendly shove. "You are a jerk, Shane Maxton," she laughed.

The shove was more than friendly too, because she kept her hands on me and my skin burned right through my shirt where her hands were. Yeah, there was something really different about Grace Taylor. I wondered again if she was part of my punishment. Well, if she was, then I was going to enjoy *this* hell. "Thanks, that's like the nicest thing you've called me so far."

Biting her bottom lip, she just shook her gorgeous head at me.

I helped her fold the rest of her clothes and carry everything upstairs. I kept the red lacy crap on top of the pile I carried just so I could look at it some more. She smiled at me knowingly.

When we got to her room, I collapsed on her bed and watched her as she quietly put her clothes away. I kept the red lacy goodness on my chest, holding it hostage, smiling. I laid back, folded my legs across her bed with my hands behind my head.

After everything was put away she stood above me and grabbed her bra and panties, but I grabbed her hand instead and didn't let her go. She didn't struggle. She just looked right into my eyes.

I nodded my head toward her guitar, "Will you play something for me?"

Seeming to think about it for a minute, she nodded her head and I let her hand that held her red lingerie go. Then the damn girl bit her bottom lip at me again and flicked the red lacy lingerie in my face, turned and grabbed her guitar from its case. I'm not freaking lying when I say that I have had a raging massive hard-on since I woke up. *I might need to visit a hospital if I didn't find some sort of freaking relief soon.*

Guitar in hand, she pushed me over across her bed and sat cross-legged in front of me. "What are you in the mood for?" *Finding out what it feels like inside you.*

154

"Surprise me," I said instead.

She started with the theme from *Sesame Street*, then played *You're so Vain* by *Carly Simon, Lost Cause* from *Beck,* and ended with *(I Hate) Everything About You* by *Ugly Kid Joe.* I smashed her in the head with one of her pillows. "Nice, Grace. What was that, a montage of how I feel about Shane songs?"

Grace smiled wide. "Gee, am I that easy to read?" She teased.

"Play something that means something to you," I whispered.

A slow sexy mischievous smile crossed her features.

Her fingers whipped up a soulful jazzy melody with an edge to it. She locked her gaze on mine and the rough raspy lyrics of *Piece of My Heart* fell from her perfect lips.

Tense. Deep. Fiery. The music was emotional, but the way her voice reached out and claimed my soul was maddening and fierce. Feelings bubbled to the surface of my skin and I felt like screaming out. I clutched at the blankets covering her bed. It was as if Grace was gone and the spirit of Janis Joplin was singing right in front of me. When she finished the song and her lips were parted from her breathlessness, I strained my muscles trying to hold myself back from her. My entire body ached to ravage her. *It was insane.*

"You are simply the most amazingly talented person I've ever met," I whispered.

"Eh. I bet you haven't met too many people then."

We stayed there, searching each other's eyes. She slid her guitar off her lap, thumped it down on the floor behind her, and laid her body on its side face to face with mine.

When I looked down to her lips, they parted and I lifted my hand to her neck gently and pulled her closer. I could hear the fast draws of her breath and feel her pulse racing through her veins under my thumb. Her body leaned in and her hand glided slowly up my arm to the hand that held her neck,

155

entangling her fingers with mine. My chest was thrumming wildly for the taste of her lips.

Then fast footfalls ran down the hallway and she broke away from me and sat up quickly. Lea slammed open the door demanding to know why there was a police car outside their apartment. Conner came running in about two seconds after her yelling the same thing.

I freaking needed another cold shower.

Chapter 9

"Dude, I'm telling you. I don't think it's a good idea," Conner said as he flipped through the channels.

We had been sitting in Grace's living room for about an hour talking about the Carl Sumpton situation, and the girls were showering and getting ready for Grace's first gig with Mad World.

"Yeah, well, I really don't care, bro. I'm staying here to protect Grace until they find that guy," I explained.

"You're going to push her away, dude. Grace isn't like all the other girls you're used to. And you're kind of scaring the shit out of me," he gave me a serious look and leaned in closer to me. "You look like you can fucking inhale that girl. Look, Shane. I know you've been clean for like eight months, but when you're around Grace, you look *high* again. Are you *using* again?"

You have got to be kidding me. Everybody just always assumed the worst in me.

I bolted up and paced the room, Conner paced with me. *I have no clue why.*

"Conner, I haven't touched a drug in *nine* months!" I raked my hands through my hair. "Dude, you *know* me. You *know* I've changed, and the freaking way I feel about that girl is so much different from all the others. I'm crazy about her." I leaned back heavily against the wall.

Conner jabbed me in the gut, "Alright, Shane. I'll talk to Lea and we'll see what Grace really thinks of you and we'll go from there." Smiling he looked away from me towards the doorway, his eyes got wide and his face turned serious. "Oh hell no! No way, Lea! Take it off!"

I followed his gaze and my mouth went dry. *She was absolutely exquisite.*

Grace hesitantly stepped into the room sidestepping the now fighting couple. I didn't even look at Lea's outfit; I couldn't take my eyes off of Grace.

Her hair fell down in wild black waves with streaks of deep purple that reflected into her lavender-silver eyes. A silky deep purple shirt plunged daringly down her chest showing the perfect perky roundness of her very full breasts. A short fringed up denim skirt hugged her hips that showed off a pair of legs that went on *forever*.

I pulled myself off the wall slowly and greedily examined every inch of her bare skin. I lingered my gaze on her eyes and lips the longest and I knew she noticed because of the breathtakingly shy smile she gave me. I slowly walked over to her and gently reached for her hand. I entwined her fingers in mine, lifted my hand over her head, and twirled her around slowly.

"I have never seen anyone more exquisite in my entire life, Grace. You seem to have this knack of making me completely...breathless." I spun her around again, brushing the silky hair off her soft shoulders. My breathing stopped; caught somewhere deep in my lungs. Lightly touching the skin on her shoulder, I inhaled deeply, "You have another tattoo," I exhaled in a whisper. I traced the lines with my fingers, a pair of broken angel's wings.

The corners of her mouth slowly lifted upward sexily. "I bet that's your signature line to try to pick up women, huh?" She looked right into my eyes, as if she was actually looking at the real me, *Shamsiel*, for the very first time. "They are my angel wings. To remind me and to honor what I've lost."

I flinched as if she smacked me. Selfishly, I wanted her to be talking about me. I wanted her tattoo to be the pair of wings that I wore when I was an angel. The wings that were broken and taken from my body because I had fallen in love with a human girl who looked just like her over two thousand years ago. But, I knew it wasn't for me. "Your family," I murmured.

158

Was my selfishness a sin? What man could stand before this creature and not want the same thing? I will never regret how I longed for her like I would never regret how I felt for Selah.

What Selah and I shared was completely innocent; a simple kiss. Before the world was what it is today, when there was paradise on Earth and angels walked among men. A simple kiss which gave me an eternity in hell.

I held Grace's hand as we walked the snowy streets to the bar. She kept her bottom lip tightly between her teeth the whole way as if she was holding back a secret. And Lea kept giving our hands a sideways glance and a smile.

Boozer's was the most crowded I had ever seen it. When we walked through the doors, Grace gasped and squeezed my hand tighter. I slid my hands around her waist and pulled her in close. "You nervous?"

Her sparkling eyes scanned the crowd, "Excited." Her eyes looked up to meet mine. *God, I wanted to kiss her.*

"You know, for the first time in a long time, me too. I can't wait until they hear you, and I can't wait to play by your side up there."

The way she smiled back at me was heart stopping.

The place was crowded enough that we couldn't even get our regular table, so we crowded around a booth that Alex had taken over from a bunch of college girls. He sat in the middle of them with a Burger King crown on his head. I grabbed a few chairs from one of the back rooms and we were all having a great time, until Tucker showed up.

He sauntered in with his Gucci suit, tie undone, and his hair slicked back. He brought an entourage of people from work, escorting them all right to Grace. *All men of course, I was surprised he didn't bring his piece of shit drug addict cousin Blake.* I knew Blake was back in town because he kept hitting me up on my phone trying to get me to party with him again. But I wasn't ever going back to drugs, hell no. I just ignored his calls.

159

Tucker's friends openly ogled Grace, and it fucking killed me. "Your girl has a great ass, Tucker," one of the guys who was about to get a fist to the head said. I held my tongue though; I was waiting to see what Grace's reaction was. I was waiting to see if she wanted me to say something or see if she was getting uncomfortable. *Fuck, I had no idea what the hell I was doing.* My damn leg was tapping up against the leg of the chair and it shook the whole freaking table. I clenched my fists and I knew I was about to blow. I knew I had no rights to her, but I also knew there was something going on between us. I just didn't know what yet. I really needed to follow her lead because I didn't want to mess anything up.

Then Tucker touched her.

He put his greasy fucking hands on the bare skin of her back and slid them down towards her ass. *MY ASS! Hell, I know it's not really my ass, but it's...no it's MY ASS!*

I flew out of my seat and launched myself between them. *Man insane.* I shoved Tucker away, not hard, because I didn't want to kill the jerk. I grabbed Grace by the waist and pulled her towards the stage, "Okay. Almost time to go onstage, so let's have a band meeting before we do this!"

I knew that Ethan and Brayden were looking at me as if I was messed up. God, no wonder why everyone thought that I started using drugs again. *I was acting like a lunatic.* I didn't care. *Tucker wasn't allowed to touch her like that.*

Ethan and Brayden both raised their eyebrows. Ethan chuckled and shook his head. Brayden froze in surprise. "Huh, why?"

"Just shut up and let's go!" I snapped. *Holy shit, I'm bat-shit crazy.*

"You guys go ahead; I'll be there in a few minutes. I think I need to talk to Tucker *alone*," Grace said. Holy crap, her words felt like they were a *KNIFE STABBING ME IN THE GOD DAMN HEART!* "Go ahead, Shane. I'll be right there."

People would call the cops if I dragged her away right now, right?

Tucker stepped forward and shoved his face in mine, "Yeah, Shane. Give us a few. She'll still be able to play when I'm done with her, I promise. She just might not be able to walk straight," he laughed exhaling his putrid beer breath all in my personal space. *I will kill him. Kill him dead, the drunk douche.*

Before I could grab him by the neck, Grace yanked him past me.

"Whoa, she definitely wants me right now!" Tucker disgustingly called to his friends.

Ethan and Brayden were behind me shoving me to the stage. "Shane, walk away. Let her make up her mind herself. You can't just kill all the competition until you're the only one left," Ethan said.

When we got to the stage, I turned on him. "What if he tries to hurt her? What then, Ethan?"

He got close to my face, "And what if she takes him in the bathroom and fucks him, Shane? He'd be doing the same thing you want to do. She's too good for either of you. She is not a toy that the both of you could fight over just so you could play with her for one night." He turned around and was about to walk away, then his shoulders relaxed and he turned back around to face me. "Unless you willing to be more to her, Shane, then I got your back, bro." And he walked off to get a drink.

Damn it! I paced the back of the stage. *Holy crap, is she doing something with Tucker in the bathroom?*

Ethan came back about fifteen minutes later with four shot glasses of whiskey and placed them on one of the amps, shook his head and walked away.

I started plugging the guitars in and flipping the amps on when Grace climbed up on the stage. My eyes quickly scanned over her, her hair looked a little tousled. I saw red. "I guess

Tucker's pretty fast, huh?" I sneered. I knocked back one of the shots, slammed it down empty, and glared at her.

Her face was utterly indifferent. My stomach dropped.

She walked towards me slowly and shoved me lightly against the wall of the stage, behind the tall speakers, where no one could see. She left her hand on my chest and spread out her fingers. I knew she could feel how hard my heart was thrashing against her fingertips, and I wanted her to know. I begged for it to just explode under her touch, so she would know what the hell she was doing to me.

"Are you angry with me or Tucker, Shane?"

My heart sped up. "Did you fuck him?"

She bit down on her lower lip, smiled and tilted her head. "Yeah, right in the hallway to the bathroom. I just let him have me against the wall." *She wasn't gone that long, could they have?* The douchebag *would* only last five minutes with a girl like Grace.

My heart stopped, and then it started wildly drumming under her hands. Beads of sweat formed on my forehead and over my lips. *She wouldn't have, would she? I'm going to be sick.*

I pushed against her hand; I needed to get the hell away from her. But when I tried to pass, she slammed her arms into mine and pushed her lips to my ears.

"Is that what you think of me? Is that what you need to hear? That I'm like all the other girls? Tell me, Shane," she whispered, pulling her head back to look into my eyes then down to my lips. Her eyes welled with tears and I knew, I knew she couldn't have done anything with him.

We stood inches apart, breathing each other in. Her heart pounded just as fast as mine.

I lifted my hand and traced the edge of her jaw down to her neck with my fingers. When she shivered, I grasped my hand around the back of her neck and pulled her closer to me so all she could see was *me*. Her lips parted and her breath hitched.

162

"No. I want you to tell me why you have a pair of broken angel wings on your shoulder. I want you to tell me why you cut your wrists and I want to know why and how you play and sing the way you do, but most of all, I want you to tell me what I need to do to be a good enough man for you."

She stepped back immediately, her eyes wide. Grabbing one of the remaining shots, she gulped it down. "Shane...I don't want to be just another one of your girls. I have other...things, too many things in my life. I really just need a friend right now."

"Then, that's where I'll start," I whispered.

"Hey!" Ethan's voice called from in front of us. "You guys about ready?" he asked, coming over to stand next to us. Brayden followed. They took the last two shots and drank them. "Next time, we do them together," Ethan said, holding up the glass. "That will be how we start each show with Grace."

Grace laughed. "Sounds good to me. Shall we amaze them?" she said, looking out into the crowd and shyly back to me.

I smiled down at her. "Grace, trust me, they were amazed just by you walking in."

The crowd roared when we were all visible. Grace ducked her head and laughed as a hot pink lacy bra sailed onto the stage. She plucked it off the floor, flung it at me and winked, "I believe this is for you?" she teased into her microphone. Howls erupted when I tucked the bra into my front pocket, letting it hang down my leg.

I covered my hand over my mic and winked back at her, "Grace, they don't turn me on like yours do."

She hip bumped me and laughed.

"Hey, everybody!" I screamed into the crowd. "I'd like to introduce you to the gorgeous Grace Taylor on guitar!"

The place erupted. *Yeah, because that's the effect she has on people.*

I fixed my gaze on those stunning silver eyes of her and nodded her cue. My heart fucking exploded when her hands flew like lightning over her guitar. I swayed back on my heels watching the powerhouse that she turned into on the stage right next to me. The music came alive and the audience detonated into roars and screams for her. A smile split across her face and she winked a sparkling silver eye at me. I almost dropped my guitar.

Grace rocked through the rhythm and stepped forward towards the audience and the edge of the stage, looking out over the crowd. People screamed louder. Strangely enough, I could hear Lea screaming, "That's my best friend, bitches," over everyone. I almost missed my intro watching her play. I was in complete awe.

Grace caught my eye and laughed as I joined in playing by her side and our harmony twisting together left us both gasping for air. She glided over the stage, eyes locked on mine and I could swear she played her guitar just for me. We played as one, staring at each other, neither one of us looking away. The crowd was somewhere in the distance, but we were in a place all our own. The intense feeling of something so ancient, so old, so beautiful overwhelmed my senses. *If I could end my existence right now, I would die the happiest soul to have ever walked the earth, because I knew* **this**. *Because I had felt* **this**. *Because I had known Grace.*

We played the entire set of Mad World songs side by side. When the set was over, we all looked at each other and acknowledged without words that none of us wanted to end playing for the night. I glanced over to Ethan and Brayden and nodded towards Grace. I knew that whatever I decided to play, my bassist and drummer would immediately be able to improvise and play. *Yeah, we were that talented.*

I touched the small of Grace's back and her soft silky hair brushed over my fingertips. "Let's introduce them to Janis," I whispered to her through my microphone.

Tears glistened in her eyes and she slid up next to me, touching her back to mine. Leaning her head against the back of my shoulder, her long hair washing over the front of my arms and chest, she begin the intro riff to Janis Joplin's *Piece of My Heart* and sang to me with all her soul to come on and take another little piece of her heart. *And I wanted to.* I wanted her whole heart, and I promised myself right then and there that I would never stop until I had her whole heart, because she already had mine.

The set ended in a riot of noise and applause. I jumped off the stage, turned and reached both hands out for Grace to jump down. Without a second of hesitation, she dove into my arms. I caught her easily, cradling her in my arms and I kissed her on the cheek. "That was...*intense*. I think I need a drink," she breathed.

"Yeah, well, I need another ice cold shower. Tequila?" I asked, sliding her down my body so she could stand.

She gave me a little friendly jab in the arm, "I'm sure in a few minutes any one of these girls will cure you of your need for a cold shower." *Pushing me away already? Tough, you're the only girl that will cure me.*

At that point, everyone surrounded us, and I walked away.

Grace was grabbed by Lea, so I separated myself from everyone. I walked down to the end of the bar and nodded to the bartender.

Ryan leaned over the bar and shook my hand. "Shane, you guys sounded awesome. Grace is amazing. What can I do you for tonight?"

"Just put a bottle of our best tequila in front of me and one glass, *for now*."

I slung back my first shot, leaned my elbows against the bar and watched Grace. She worked the crowd easily and detached herself from them even more easily. When she locked eyes with me, it was like no one else was in the room.

Out of nowhere, a dark haired girl slithered up in front of me and brushed a piece of hair from my forehead. I leaned back away from her hands and asked her simply, "If a complete stranger walked up to you and did what you just did to me, wouldn't you feel the need to call the authorities?"

"Are you not in the mood for some fun?"

"Nope, not with you," I shook my head.

"Whatever," she said and stormed off.

I kept watching Grace.

A blonde girl walked in front of me next. "Hey, you need some company over here? You were really great on stage..."

"No thanks, I'm waiting for someone," I smiled, cutting her off.

Grace smiled at me when the blonde walked away. Lea and Conner stood next to her, all three obviously talking about me. When they started walking towards me, I reached over the bar and pulled up three more shot glasses, the saltshaker and a handful of limes on a napkin.

We each did a shot in silence. Then Lea winked at me and grabbed Conner to the side, leaving Grace and me alone. Lea silently mouthed to me that her and Conner were going home and to have fun. *I have to remember to buy that girl chocolate. Chocolate, flowers, shit, I'll buy her diamonds if she would help me break down Grace's walls.*

I poured two more shots and gently took hold of her hand. Taking a deep breath, I stuck my pinky into her shot glass, slid my wet finger over the back of her hand, and then salted it. She watched every move I made, biting down on her lip. Slowly, her eyes rose to meet mine and she licked the back of her hand and tilted back her drink.

166

"I bet you make that taste like heaven," I said having trouble swallowing.

Smiling, she placed her glass back on the bar and looked down at it. Then she tilted her head up at me. "Shane, I watched you before. You didn't have to say no to those girls because you think you have to stay with me tonight. You don't have to stay over to babysit me instead of doing your usual thing."

I could seriously just kiss her mouth shut right now. "That's what you think?" I turned around to face her, shifting my body closer to her.

A flash of crimson flushed through her cheeks. "It's what Conner said when he saw you standing here letting those girls walk away from you."

"You didn't answer my question. Is that what *you* think?"

"I didn't think about it at all. I just don't want you to do something you don't really need or want to do."

I leaned in closer, brushing my cheek against hers, to whisper in her ear, "Funny thing is, Grace, needing and wanting is exactly what I am doing right now. And, just for the record, it's *not* those girls I need or want."

I gently took her arm and sprinkled a small pinch of salt on the soft skin of her inner wrist. I slowly raised her arm to my mouth and I lightly pressed my tongue against her skin, skimming it across the surface. She tasted as sweet as fucking honey. Her breath caught and her body shivered. I downed my tequila and squeezed the lime into my mouth, "God, Grace. You do taste like heaven," I whispered breathlessly.

The splash of crimson that had fallen across her cheeks before, deepened and traveled down, spreading itself across her chest. "I think I should go home now. I'm...really...tired." She whirled around and practically ran towards the bathroom.

"Then I'm going too," I yelled after her, but I lost her in the crowd.

I ran all over the damn bar trying to find her for a good fifteen minutes. Her guitar was still on stage where she left it and I didn't think she would have left without it. I grabbed my phone and texted Lea.

Shane: *Is she home already????*
Lea: *Yep, she just ran in*
Shane: *On my way*

I grabbed both our guitars and ran to Grace's without saying goodnight to anyone. Ethan saw me on my way out the door and nodded to me, but that was it.

When I got to the apartment, I banged on their front door. Conner let me in with a scowl on his face, "Shane, what the hell? Are you trying to knock the damn door down?"

"Where is she?"

Lea smiled at me. "Bedroom."

I started to make my way down the hallway, but then I ran back to Lea and grabbed her by the shoulders, "Lea, tell me right now. Do I have any chance whatsoever with her?"

Lea looked into my eyes and I could see a dozen different answers there, but she offered me just one. "Yeah, Shane, I think she's got some sort of feelings for you, but she isn't going to ever..." Then she stopped and searched my face for something and gave me a tight smile. "If you could make her forget her past, Shane, then yeah, you have one hell of a chance, because I've never seen her look at anyone like she looks at you. But she will fight you every step of the way. Now go in there and make her forget her past, you sexy bitch."

I smacked a kiss on her forehead and left her standing in the hallway. All I needed to hear was that I had a chance. I ran down the hall to Grace's room. "Grace..." I thumped my forehead up against the door. I knew in my soul that in some way she was touching the other side of the door trying to keep that inch of wood of the door between us.

"Grace. Please let me in. I'm...sorry."

I heard her move away from the door, sliding her hands along the grain of it. I kicked my foot at the door, turned around leaning on it heavily, and slid my body down to the floor against it. "I'm sleeping on the floor then. Right here." Thumping my head against the door again. "Oh. Man. This is so comfortable, Grace. *Really. Very.*" I said sarcastically.

I watched under the door as the light went out in her room and heard the click of her bedside lamp being turned on. I listened to her drawers open and close and to the sounds of her changing.

She wasn't opening the door. Fine. *I was going to make her.*

I ran back down the hallway and grabbed her guitar case from where I had left it when I came in. I ran back to her door and fumbled to open her case as fast as I could. The case flew open and I almost lost the grip of the instrument and cursed loudly as the case fell to the floor. *Well, at least I didn't drop the guitar.*

From her room, I could hear the rustle of her covers and the creaks of her bed as she slid in. *I'd be shit out of luck if she had her ear buds in.*

I cleared my throat, kicked at the door again and then played her guitar.

I played a slow melody I knew she had never heard before. Its beginning was low and wistful, transforming into a passionate yearning melody. I hummed along with the tune, whispering the words about how much I wanted to be with her.

Her door flew open and she stood there with a small little tank top and those insanely sexy boy shorts on.

Her eyes were glued to her guitar as I walked in. *God, she was so damn beautiful.*

I pulled the strap over my head and carried the guitar into her room, kicking the door closed behind me. "Please, look at me, Grace."

Sliding the guitar out of my hands, I leaned it against the wall. Her eyes stayed on the instrument.

"Grace, please look at me." I stepped closer to her, blocking her from staring at the guitar. I kept moving closer to her as she moved backwards, still staring at her guitar, until I got close enough to touch her chin and lifted her face to mine. "Grace...I'm sorry. I didn't mean to..."

She backed up another inch and gently hit her back to the wall. Smiling down at her, I rested my forehead against hers.

"Tell me. Tell me, Grace, that you don't feel this. *Please.* Tell me and I will walk right out of here." I touched my lips to her jaw and listened to her jagged breaths. Slowly, I melted my body against hers, one hand slowly sliding down her arm to her waist, feathering my fingertips along her skin. She felt like silk.

I pulled my head away to look at her and pleaded, "Talk to me, Grace, please."

Her body moved with mine and she slid her hands up my chest and grasped my shirt tightly in her fists.

I couldn't take it any longer; I twisted my fingers through her hair. "Grace...One kiss, please. Let me taste you," I pleaded, pushing my body harder against hers.

Her heartbeat raced in her chest and she arched her body against mine. A small moan escaped from her lips. "Shane..." Then she stood on her tiptoes and brushed her lips slowly over mine. Both of us hesitated, breathing in each other. My entire body came alive and I tightened my hold on her.

"Say my name again," I said, as I slid one of my hands down to her hips and pulled her leg up around me. Her breath came out in soft desperate pants and her scent surrounded me.

"Shane," she whispered, moving her lips over my mouth. My whole fucking body trembled.

My head was spinning and my skin was on fire. I couldn't hold back anymore. I growled low, and crashed my lips into hers. She moved her lips with mine, opening them to let me in. I skated my fingers beneath the lace of her panties and she answered me by sliding her hands through my hair and down to my shoulders. She dug her fingers into my skin, which made me kiss her deeper and harder. She tasted sweet and delicious.

I tore my lips away, panting, and stared into her eyes. My fingers slowly slipped deeper under the very wet lace of her panties. I wanted to watch her expression as I slid my fingers inside her.

"Shane. Stop. I can't..." I saw the tears brimming in her eyes. She didn't want me to stop, but she couldn't let me go further either.

I let her leg slowly slide down my hip and moved my fingertips up to her neck, until both my hands cupped her face. *I love you, Grace*. I looked into her eyes, "Grace...I think I..."

She stretched her fingers across my chest. "Please. Shane...don't. This was a huge mistake." Yet, she still tugged me towards her as her fingers closed into fists clenching at my shirt. One tear streaked down her beautiful face.

"Grace...please. You would never be a mistake to me."

She let go of her hold on me, walked to the window and pushed the curtain back. "Shane, drop it. I'm not one of your groupies that you just met at the bar, I wasn't screaming for you and throwing my clothes at you, and I don't give a crap how good you play or how sexy you look on stage, none of it will make me sleep with you. So just keep the normal line you feed to your skanks to yourself," she snapped. She wiped at the tears in her eyes.

I grabbed her by the waist, lifted her off the floor and tossed her on the bed. I dove on top of her, straddling her, pinning her arms above her head. She bit that plump little lip of hers the whole time.

"Shut. Up. Don't. Just don't say anything else." I moved my body next to her and grabbed her into my arms. "Just sleep, Grace," I whispered, pulling her closer to me. Then I gave her one single kiss on the tattoo of her angel's wings and her warm body relaxed and snuggled into mine.

I tangled my legs with hers and clung to her, aware of every inch of where our skin touched one another's. My heart pounded against her body and my fingers burned each time I slid my hands across her flesh. She stole my breath away and crushed her body to mine, until we both fell asleep in our desperate embrace.

Lying with Grace in my arms all night was better than heaven.

Chapter 10

I woke up slowly and not alone. I smiled to myself since it was completely the first time in any of my existences for that to have happened because I wanted it to, not because I passed out the night before by mistake.

Grace shifted a little in her sleep and a sweet moan escaped quietly from her lips. The lips that were gently brushing my chest as her body lay tangled comfortably over mine. I brought my hand softly through her silky hair and slowly slid it down her back. She nuzzled closer to me. God, my entire body was awake and completely aroused, *and* moving from the raw ecstasy of being underneath her was not what I wanted to do.

I watched her sleep for a while, and then I slipped out from under her. I think my heart broke when I was no longer touching her. I walked through the apartment silently, visited the bathroom, and then made Grace a cup of coffee.

I climbed back into her bed and slowly traced my fingertips down her spine to wake her up.

She bolted up; hair tumbled wildly around her face and her eyes were wide.

"Hey, I got you some coffee," I said.

Without hesitation, she grabbed the coffee and sipped it. A blank look crossed her face, and then she slightly shook her head and narrowed her eyes. "Thanks. Did you make this or did Lea?"

My body tensed and a wave of heat flushed through me, causing me to break out in a sweat. I stood up, yanked off my shirt in anger, and threw it in her hamper. "Don't worry, Grace, they're still sleeping. No one will think we had sex, and if anyone asks, I'll make sure everyone knows you don't want me," I snapped, as I rummaged through a bag near the door I had Ethan bring over the day before.

Indifferently, she took another sip of her coffee and placed the cup on the nightstand. She untangled herself from the sheets slowly. "I didn't ask that to see if Lea or Conner thought we slept together. I was just wondering if *you* or *Lea* made the coffee, exactly like I asked." When the sheets were untangled, she stood up from the bed and stretched her arms over her head.

Oh fucking hell.

I was so aroused that the muscles of my body quivered just from looking at her in her little bra and panties. Like a fucking bull in heat, I charged at her. I was beyond angry; I was tormented; *fucking tortured.* No one deserved to hold this fucking kind of power over me. *No one.* She fucking twisted my soul and left me struggling to breathe all the fucking time. This had to be the cruelest punishment, never to be able to have her believe I was more than the piece of shit she thought I was. "Right, sure. Well, why not, let's talk about shit that doesn't matter. Lea is sleeping and I made the freaking coffee! What is it, too strong for you? And let me just put this out in the open, so that I don't get accused of playing games or whatever the hell your warped mind thinks I do. I am so freaking glad I *didn't* sleep with you, Grace, because you and me would be horrible. The sex would suck and I wouldn't have to look at you and pretend you were more than a hole to stick my dick in for the next six weeks! There, happy now? That's all you want to believe of me, right?"

Swallowing hard, I could feel all the color drain from my face. I gave her exactly what she wanted to hear. Let's see how she freaking handled that. I grabbed her robe off the closet door and threw it at her. Looking at her was ripping me apart.

Catching the robe, she walked right in front of me and dropped it at my feet. She looked me deadpan in the eyes. "Thanks for the heads up on how sex would have been with you. But, honestly, Shane, I just wanted to know if you actually had gone out of your way to know the exact way I take my coffee, because that just would have been...*sweet.*"

What. The. Hell?

She grabbed an armful of clothing, without even looking at any of it, from one of her drawers and dashed for the door.

"Grace, stop."

"Go screw yourself, Shane. Consider your duty to babysit me done, since you stayed here last night to protect me and I still ended up hurt," she whispered as she walked out the door and closed it behind her. *Yeah, she actually whispered it, like I really did hurt her.* Shit.

I ran after her but she locked herself in the bathroom.

My shoulders collapsed and I dragged myself into the kitchen. Lea was leaning against the counter, arms crossed, with a steaming cup of coffee next to her.

"What the eff are you two screaming about?"

"I messed up. I said a bunch of bullshit to get her pissed off, because I was pissed off at something she said. I'm like fucking Tucker right now. I. Am. A. Douchebag."

Then Lea hugged me. It felt so fucking weird, because she squeezed the muscles in my arms and asked me to flex. *I'm surrounded by sixteen years olds.*

"What am I supposed to do now, Lea? She's driving me crazy; I can't take the shit I said back. She's fucking killing me."

"Well, I don't know what you said, but I do know that whatever you did last night had to have been pretty packed with all sorts of awesomeness, because she's never had a guy spend the night in her room with her since we've lived together."

"Yeah, but how long have you lived with Grace?"

She gave my cheek a pat. "Since we were fourteen. So yeah, Shane, whatever you did last night, keep doing. But, um...what did you guys do last night?"

"Nothing. We kissed, that's it but...*God, Lea.* I don't mean to sound like I grew a pussy, but it was the fucking best kiss these lips ever felt."

"Wow. She aced on your slutty lips. That's just...wow," she laughed.

I chuckled too.

Grace chose that moment to rush through the kitchen and grab a bottle of water from the refrigerator.

"Where are you going?" Lea asked.

"For a run," she said, completely avoiding my stare.

"Alone?" she asked looking from me to Grace.

"Lea. This is New York City. Eight million people live here, I won't be alone," she laughed and walked out the front door.

I talked with Lea for a few more minutes and then made my way back home. I sat on the couch in my living room and stared at some movie on the television that I wasn't paying any attention to. I just knew it sucked.

One movie blended into the next and before I knew it, Ethan and Brayden were throwing our beer pong balls at me. *Hard.* I'm talking whaling them at me. Ignoring them, I jumped in the shower, threw on a pair of jeans and an old shirt and walked to Boozer's. It was snowing again, but the hushed silence of the falling flakes did nothing to soothe my soul.

Boozer's was empty, thank God, because I wanted to wallow alone in my self-pity. I grabbed a beer from Mollie, one of the waitresses (NO! I never banged her- Alex has a huge crush on her) and climbed onto the stage. I sat on one of the gray metal folding chairs and played my guitar.

I stayed there for four hours.

Yeah, four hours.

I realized the bar was getting full and it was closing in on the time for our gig when Grace walked to the back of the stage and stopped abruptly in front of me. Probably startled at me being there.

I lifted my head only slightly when I noticed her, but I didn't stop playing.

"Hey," she said. "What's doing?" Then she pushed my legs off the second chair I was leaning them on.

"Oh, are you talking to me? I thought we hated each other." I knew I sounded pathetic, but I didn't care.

Then, you know what she freaking did? *She SMILED AT ME!* She smiled at me, and a deep fiery-red splash of crimson colored her cheeks.

My heart thudded to a stop. "Stop smiling, Grace." I leaned forward, giving her a slow sexy smile. "A smile like that can give a man hope."

Neither of us stopped smiling. Smiling and staring into each other's eyes, until Ethan walked up to us and cleared his throat. "What is with the two of you?"

The crowd screamed for us to play, and when we emerged from the back of the stage, the sound was deafening. Looking at Grace, I struck a chord that silenced the audience. We played as if we were on fire, a scorching inferno tearing through the crowd as they screamed for more.

We kicked the set off, immediately bursting with raw energy and power. We played each song like we danced through our friendship, full of angst and intensity. *I would never get enough of playing next to Grace.*

After the set, we all jumped off the stage. Once again, I held my arms out for Grace and without hesitation, she dove right into me. Sweaty and on fire, we ran to the bar to try to quench the flames.

At the bar, Ryan lined up shot glasses of Kamikaze shooters for us, *dumbass fruity girly drinks.* I gulped one back anyway and slammed it on the bar, not taking my eyes off Grace. I was freaking thirsty.

Then some fucknut walked right past me like I wasn't standing there. He leaned against the bar next to Grace and asked, "May I buy you a drink?"

Grace looked at him as if he had grown a dick right out of his forehead. Which probably would be useful in other situations, however, *not this immediate one.*

"Hi, I'm Steve," the fucknut said, then pointed to her empty glass, and repeated the question, "May I buy you a drink?"

She smiled politely at him, "Thank you, but the band has a running tab at the bar, so there's no need."

Damn that was hot. She said *NO FUCKNUT!*

Yet, fucknut did not get the hint. He stayed.

Steve the fucknut, smiled down at her with wagging Tucker-like eyes. "You were amazing up there," he said. "I'm sure you hear this all the time, but you are incredibly sexy and your eyes...I've never seen a more beautiful color."

Grace smiled at him. And before I could think clearly, yes, I know I was showing blatant signs of psycho-like-possessive-violent-bat-shit-crazy tendencies, I shoved my body between the two of them. "Hey, excuse me, um, Steve was it? Yeah, well Grace and I have band things to take care of, so goodbye." Then I stood there glaring down at him (like a foot down, he was even shorter than Grace) until he backed away. "Walk the fuck away from her right now; she's not up for grabs, *Steve.*" Okay, so I may have acted a bit immature.

Steve kept his hungry little eyes on Grace, "She's not up for grabs? Calm down, jackass. I just wanted to buy this beautiful woman a drink." *This guy was seriously trying to commit suicide.*

I stepped in closer to Steve, blocking his view of Grace. "Just walk away, dude."

Steve shook his head, laughing and he held his hands in the air. He leaned past me and spoke directly to Grace. "Listen,

178

my friends and I will be here for a while, so if you'd like to dance or something, come and find me."

Oh, no. I'm going to start a bar fight.

I balled my fist and pulled back.

Immediately, Grace was off her barstool, smiling at Steve and placing her hands on my chest, softly. All the anger in my body instantly evaporated. "Thank you, Steve, but I'm wiped from the show, so I'm calling it a night. I'm Grace by the way. It was nice to meet you and I'm glad you enjoyed the music." Then she turned her back to him until he got the hint and walked away.

Our eyes were locked on each other's the whole time.

Her hand still lay on my chest. "I am leaving now. Don't ever do that again to me. Don't ever stop someone from speaking to me. I'm not your property. I'm barely even your friend," she whispered.

I wasn't letting this go. "Do you want to go home with him?"

"What the hell is wrong with you, Shane? Are you serious right now? You're the guy who has slept with almost every girl in this bar, and I can't have someone buy me a drink?"

"You told him no thank you and he didn't listen. And Grace, I haven't slept with anyone since you walked into this bar that first Friday."

"Liar. You've been here with girls, sucking their faces off right in front of me," she replied crossing her arms.

"I haven't slept with any of them, Grace. Last night with you, Grace, was the best night of my life, I'm sorry about the coffee thing...this is all new to me..."

"Please don't say anything else. Please don't. I have to get out of here. I'm exhausted and I don't have the energy to fight with you."

"Then, I'm taking you home and I'm staying."

"Excuse me?" she asked.

"I'm not letting anything happen to you, Grace. Carl Sumpton is still out there somewhere and it would completely fucking crush all the guys in the band if you got hurt."

"All the guys in the band, huh?" she asked with a coy smile.

"Yeah, Grace. Especially me. The insanely possessive one."

Grabbing our guitars, we left and walked back home through the snow in silence. Once inside her apartment, we raided the refrigerator.

With us both standing in front of the open refrigerator, cool air drifting against our skin, I grabbed her by the waist. "How about I make some pancakes while you jump in the shower and get comfortable."

"Sounds yummy," she whispered.

"Yeah, the pancakes do too," I teased.

I swear I think she giggled all the way to the bathroom.

I was mixing the second batch of pancake batter when Grace walked into the kitchen, wrapped only in a towel. The spatula fell to the floor splattering pancake batter all over. "Pancakes are almost ready," I whispered.

"There should be more hot water in about five minutes, if you want to jump in the shower," she said.

I turned the burners on the stove off and lifted my shirt over my head. Forget pancakes and showers, all I needed was her. "Why, Grace? You think I'm dirty?" I stalked towards her slowly.

"Oh no, Shane, I'm betting on you being filthy," she laughed.

Our bodies moved closer, until our lips hovered over each other's and I could smell the soap she used on her skin. She hooked her fingers through the loops in my jeans and pulled me closer.

"Woowhoo! I smell pancakes in here!" Lea screamed from the front door. Then *lots* of voices seemed to come from the direction of the front door.

"No. No, no, no. Those sounds are just our imagination," I said as I watched the most beautiful girl in the world walk away from kissing me.

So, yeah. Five batches of pancake batter later, everyone was eating pancakes. Thankfully there was only minimal food fighting. Only one pancake was called in to combat on Alex's face when he came in and asked me for *eggs and bacon too* and to *hurry it up*. Jackhat.

A short time after, Grace walked in, joined us in the living room, and then she sat right next to me. I reached out to her and rubbed my hands over the small of her back. Her skin was so soft it melted under my touch. I almost dropped dead right in front of everybody when she ran her hand through my hair.

"Are you okay?" I asked.

"I'm just tired. I think I'm going to call it a night." She smiled at me. "Goodbye, Shane."

I watched her walk away, thinking I'd give her a little time and then I'd crawl into bed with her later, when everyone left. No one needed to see me follow her to her bedroom and start wondering about us. After all, they were already looking at us weird.

It was really late when everyone left. Lea had gone to bed already, and Conner and I ended up falling asleep on the couch in the living room, trying to watch the end of a *Walking Dead* episode.

A little while later, I woke with a start and my body hummed with energy. Conner was sprawled out on the couch next to me snoring. Loudly. But that wasn't what woke me up. Something was wrong. *Something was wrong with Grace.*

That's when I smelled the smoke; smoke that was billowing dark and thick from down the hallway. I shook Conner awake and we both ran to the girl's rooms. Lea's room was filled with smoke, but Grace's room...Grace's room was filled with fire that licked its orangey flames from under her door. I ran to the hall closet, yanked a towel off the shelf, ran to the sink in the bathroom, and soaked it under water.

Crouching low to the ground, I made my way back to Grace's bedroom door, while Conner took Lea out the front to call for help.

"Grace!" I screamed. I screamed her name until my lungs burned with the heat from the fire. With the towel wrapped around my hand, I turned the knob and flames exploded along the ceiling and into the hallway and a blast of heat scorched my skin. Jumping right through it, I didn't care. I needed to get to Grace.

Bright hot flames engulfed her room. Grace lay still on her bed; I could barely see her through the dark, thick smoke. I slid into her bed covering her body with mine to shield her. "Grace," I begged. "Grace, please wake up!" I shook her, but she lay limp in my arms.

Flames spread and raced across the ceiling and floor, circling us. In a perfect fucking circle? *What the fuck? How the hell are flames traveling in a perfect fucking CIRCLE?* I could hear Lea screaming from somewhere, but within seconds, her cries were suffocated by the hissing and crackling of the flames. I cradled Grace in my arms. There was no time even to think straight. *How the fuck am I getting her out of here?*

The air was getting too thick and the flames were closing around us, beginning to burn the sheets of her bed. "Grace, baby, please, *please wake* up. Grace, please don't leave me, please. *I love you.*"

Sirens pierced through the rumble of the burning flames.

I carried her listless body through the heat and flames. Tears fell down my cheeks that evaporated within seconds from the scorching temperature. I could still feel her pulse thudding strongly under her skin, but the thought of losing her as I lost Selah was *crushing*. I kicked my steel toe boots through her bedroom window until I felt the glass shatter and fall around me.

The cold air filled my lungs painfully as I slid Grace and me down the fire escape ladder and coughed out a scream for Conner and Lea to open the front gate. Firefighters immediately surrounded us and Grace was ripped from my arms. I stumbled to the curb, threw up fucking tequila-flavored pancakes, and wept like a child.

I didn't move until Conner placed his hands on my shoulders and squeezed, "She's gonna be okay, bro, she's breathing. They're going take her to the hospital and look her over, but it just looks like smoke inhalation." He knelt down behind me and knocked the front of his head to the back of mine, still holding onto my shoulders tight. "Shane, if you hadn't woke up. Grace and Lea..." He inhaled deeply and coughed out a choked cry, "Thank you, Shane, I couldn't live without Lea in my life. I just couldn't. I wouldn't want to."

Conner helped me up and gave me one of his big man hugs. With his arm still over my shoulder, he helped me over to Grace who had an oxygen mask over her beautiful ash covered blackened face.

I turned to one of the EMTs who started cleaning her face off with some sort of wipes, "Any burns?"

"No sir," she smiled. "This is a very lucky girl."

When the fire was extinguished, I walked over to the fire chief to see what he had to say. *Definitely arson.* It was a simple glance at the burn patterns and the smell of gasoline, thick black smoke, oh, and let's not overlook the *fucking melted gas container someone left by the foot of her bed.*

Carl fucking Sumpton.

How do you want to die, Carl? Because I'm going to make sure that happens. Slowly.

I watched from a distance as Grace sat up with the help of Lea. *Why would this guy want to kill Grace?* I stayed in the distance watching over her and wracked my brain for what I needed to do to keep her safe. Ethan and the rest of the guys were running down the street to her. Tucker, of course, reached her first and grabbed her into his arms like a rag doll until the paramedics separated him from her and rolled her gurney into the ambulance.

The ambulance pulled away taking Grace to the hospital, while Conner and I spoke to the fire chief and police about Carl Sumpton and the events of the night. Even the two detectives that came to Grace's house to tell us about the dick escaping showed up. I eyed them as if I was going to stab them both in the eyes with my bare fingers. This shit wouldn't be happening if they could hold a damn prisoner, one who supposedly has only a few weeks to live. Nothing made sense.

I talked the fire chief into escorting me back into the apartment to get Grace and my guitars that we left in living room. The apartment stunk, but the damage was really contained to only Grace's room, and I wondered how someone could look at Grace and not want her around. It seemed impossible to me.

Tucker, Ethan, even Brayden and Alex were out in front of the apartment with the firefighters and police discussing the situation when I came out of the apartment with our instruments.

"Look at the fucking hero, even saving her guitar!" Tucker sneered.

"Shut up, douche."

Everyone fell silent as I approached them on the sidewalk. "You know there's no way she'd want to keep her guitar here." I looked at Ethan and Conner. "She and Lea are going to be staying with us. This is too messed up. I'm not letting her out of my sight from now on," I said flatly.

Ethan and Conner both silently nodded their heads. There was nothing else to say.

Tucker coughed, "I was thinking that maybe I should take her to my winter house. Get her out of the city for a while; no one will know where to find her."

Laughter bubbled out of my mouth, "Why, you think she would want to be *alone* with you? Is that your plan? Someone is trying to kill her and you're busy still trying to get in her pants. I should staple a fucking diaper on your face because you are such a shithead sometimes. She's staying with Conner, Ethan and me. Period." I was practically foaming at the mouth with anger.

Conner placed his hand on my shoulder. "Shane, I agree with you that the girls are with us tonight. But we need to get them out of the city until this shit is over." He looked Tucker straight in the face and folded his arms across his chest. "We *all* go, Tuck."

Tucker offered to pick up Lea and Grace at the hospital, while Conner and I explained the entire Carl Sumpton situation with the authorities more. Ethan left to start packing a bag to go to Tucker's place and I think Alex and Brayden both had chicks they were trying to get back to.

I hated the fact that Tucker would be picking her up. That was something that I should be doing, but protecting her and making some sort plan for keeping her safe was my job too. Besides, he was the only one besides Grace that had a car. *Jaguar driving doucheball.*

While the cops and the fire department were wrapping everything up, Ethan texted me that Grace got back to the apartment.

> Ethan: *Tucker had girls in his place*
> Shane: *Don't want Grace there*
> Ethan: *Duh, got them with me now*
> Ethan: *Ass was trying 2 give her champagne*
> Shane: *Leaving now*

When I got home, Grace was taking a shower. The sound of the running water behind the bathroom door was hypnotizing. Small swirls of mist floated up from under the door and the smell of soap filled my senses. Walking into my bedroom, I searched through my drawers to find something Grace would be comfortable wearing until I could get her some clothes. One of my small tee shirts and a pair of new boxers was all I could come up with.

Passing by the bathroom door to go into the living room to tell Lea to give the clothes to Grace, I heard her soft, sultry voice singing the song I had written for her and it made me breathless. I never made it into the living room.

I knocked softly and opened the bathroom door.

"That better be Lea," she sniffed.

I gave her a low, raspy chuckle, "No, sorry. Just me. But, if you want me to get Lea to come into the shower, that's a really entertaining thought."

"Shane, get out of here!" she squealed.

"Relax, Grace, I'm not going to jump in with you. I just came in to give you some of my clothes to wear. Unless you want to traipse through the apartment with just a towel on in search of clothes, because that's just...Hey, you know, *you are absolutely right*, that's a much better idea than me giving you something to wear...I mean, *I clearly* remember the first time I saw that at your place. That image is definitely burned into my brain. I wonder if it would have the same effect on everyone else here." *Just the thought gave me an instant hard-on.*

"Okay!" she yelped, poking her soapy head out through the shower curtain. "Thank you! Please just leave the clothes and go!" *Damn, her lathered up like that was more fuel for my fantasies.*

I leaned back against the sink, folded my arms across my chest, and stared into her eyes. *Stop thinking about her naked behind that curtain, you perv, she was just in a fire.* "Are you okay, Gray?" *Damn, I called her Gray, Lea's nickname for her, think she'll be pissed off?* Do. Not. Move. The. Curtain. Away. Stand down, man!

She stuck her face back in the shower, rinsed, and turned off the water. Then held out her hand from the other side of the curtain, "May I have the towel, please?"

I probably hesitated a little, but I *did* give her the towel. I wasn't a total jerk. Well, maybe I was, because I still waited there, and I wasn't leaving until I saw her.

My heart slammed against my rib cage when she slid the curtain aside and I could just see her bare shoulders. *Stunning.*

"You're still in here," she whispered. Her eyes were wide and frightened.

"Yeah. I'm having trouble moving," I murmured.

I heard a small gasp. Sliding the shower curtain all the way to the side and stepping out, she whispered, "Did you get hurt before?"

Oh my God.

She was wet.

In a towel. *Wrapped only in a towel.*

Wet.

"No," I murmured. I took the shirt I had brought for her and gently pulled it over her damp hair. She slowly lifted one arm at a time into the sleeves, strategically keeping the towel wrapped around her body. When the shirt fell to her knees, covering her fully, she let the towel drop to the floor. "Well, *that's* something I've never done before," I sighed.

"I guess you do mostly the undressing of women, huh?" she teased. A tired smile peeked out from her lips, but the look of sheer exhaustion lay heavily across her beautiful features.

I reached out my hands toward her face.

Her eyes were bloodshot from crying and the skin beneath them was pink and puffy. My entire being craved to take her pain, to take it all for myself, but I didn't have that power anymore. *I wanted to punch myself in the face for all the times this week I had to remind myself of that.*

I laid the palms of my hands lightly against her cheeks and with my thumbs, I gently wiped the moist skin below her eyes, wiping away the tears. "You were crying," I murmured. I trailed my fingers softly along her skin.

"Well, I was just in a fire that Tucker says someone purposefully set, so yeah, I've been crying."

My hands stilled on her face, "Tucker said that, huh? That ass couldn't just give you one night of rest?" I glared at her, "I swear, Grace, I will not let anything happen to you here, and tomorrow we'll all go up to Tucker's place and get away from Carl Sumpton and his sick twisted games. No one will know where we are."

Grace opened her mouth to say something, but stopped the words before they could reach my ears. *Why did she always hold back with me?*

Sliding my hands slowly down her arms and around her back, I pulled her in and held her in my arms. *Dear God, she shivered under my touch.* The shivers became tremors when her hands slid up the length of my arms and gripped my shoulders. The material of the shirt she wore rode up her back as she lifted her arms, and the knowledge of her not wearing any underwear made me freaking dizzy. Hating myself for what I was about not to let happen, I leaned back and grabbed the boxer shorts I brought for her to wear and shoved them in her hands. "Here, I can't stand here with you like this, so wear a pair of my boxers, *please.*" *YES, I am an ass.* My dick was screaming profanities at me from behind the zipper of my jeans, and then blatantly asked me if I might be gay and just didn't tell him yet.

Without taking her light grey eyes off me, she slowly slid the boxers up her long legs. My jaw clenched tighter, I wanted desperately to rip them right back off her.

We just stood there, face-to-face, eye-to-eye knowing something could be about to happen. Her eyes clouded over, her lips parted and her tongue slowly ran across her bottom lip, tasting what I wanted to taste. *She was just in a fire. She was just in a fire. She doesn't need you poking her with anything right now. She's exhausted, she's been through a horrible night, and she probably isn't in the mood even for a kiss. I'm going to try to kiss her anyway, aren't I? I'll ask her if she wants to...*

"I'm really tired, Shane. In fact, right now, I kind of feel like I'm going to pass out." She leaned her hand on the sink heavily as if she was having trouble standing upright.

And there's my answer.

I scooped her up and cradled her in my arms. Her eyelids fluttered closed. She wrapped her arms around my neck and dropped her head heavily on my shoulder.

With her held tight to my chest, I opened the bathroom door and watched as the cold air from the hallway sent goose bumps up her arms; I hugged her even tighter. *I never wanted to let her go.*

Ethan was walking down the hallway towards us with a concerned expression across his face.

"She just conked out in my arms," I explained.

"Yeah, Lea just passed out on Conner in the living room. He had to carry her to bed. Where are you going to put her to sleep?" *Yeah, like he didn't know the answer I was going to give him.* Grace isn't a girl that deserves being put in the Bone Room. I don't want her ever to see the inside of it.

I was moving through the hallway with her, heading right towards my bedroom. "Open the door to my room," I said.

"Shane, that's not the best idea. She's going to wake up pissed at you."

"I'll sleep in another room. I'm not putting her in the Bone Room, Ethan."

She opened her eyes as Ethan flicked the light on in my room and she lifted her head off my shoulder. Scanning the room with her eyes, she smiled.

"Hey, Grace, can I get you anything?" Ethan asked her.

"No, Ethan, thank you. I'm just wiped out. I don't care where I sleep, I just need to sleep." She was still looking around and then her eyes widened when they registered what lay in the corner up against the wall. She turned her face into mine, our lips not even two inches apart, "You saved my guitar?"

Pulling back the covers of my bed, I delicately laid her down and sat beside her, giving her a slight nod and a smile. She closed her eyes and nestled her head into my pillow. *Damn that was beautiful; her head on my pillow.* "Get some sleep, Grace. We'll be right outside if you need anything," I whispered.

Before I could stand up, she reached her arm out and tugged me toward her. "Don't leave, Shane," she whispered.

Those three words where like a drug, pure and electric, coursing wildly through my veins. There was nothing in this world that I wanted more than to spend another night with her wrapped around me.

I squeezed her hand softly and moved off the bed. Ethan gave me a goofy smile and slipped out of the room. I walked to my dresser to change. I threw my clothes into my hamper and threw on a pair of pajama bottoms and nothing else. I wasn't putting a shirt on. I wanted to feel her skin against mine when I held her all night, because that's what I was going to do. I was going to hold her all fucking night. *I might never let her go.*

I switched off the light and crawled under the covers right beside her. I ran a single finger along her arm from her shoulder to her elbow. "Are you okay?" I asked.

"Yes, I just didn't want to be alone. I'm sorry," she whispered.

I pulled Grace closer to me, "Don't be sorry. I get to hold a beautiful woman in my arms all night, so I'm definitely making out on the deal."

"Thank you," she said. I could feel the smile on her lips.

I nuzzled my face against the back of her neck and between her shoulder blades. She arched her body into mine. "For what, saying you're beautiful? Like you don't hear that from every freaking guy that looks at you."

"No, not that. For saving my life tonight. You could have gotten killed, Shane. Don't do anything like that for me again."

I softly placed my lips on the nape of her neck, and kissed her. "Shut up and go to sleep, Grace."

I didn't think I'd ever get to sleep that night, with her in my arms, her body so close against me, and the terrifying thoughts that somewhere, there was someone trying to hurt her. However, when her body settled and her breaths evened out, my eyelids became too heavy and I drifted off to sleep. It was a dreamless night, but I kept waking to make sure she was still safe in my arms.

Chapter 11

Grace was poking me and giggling quietly to herself. I could see from behind my closed eyelids and the brightness that hit them, that it was daytime on the other side. She tried to slide herself out from my arms, but I only smiled and held her tighter. While she was trying to roll over and fling her legs onto the floor, I rolled my body on top of hers and started a full-fledged wrestling match. She finally pinned me down and flung herself off the bed and onto the floor laughing. *So*, I dove on top of her.

There was a loud knock on my door and both of us bolted off the floor laughing like we were afraid of getting caught all over each other.

Without another knock *or anything*, Ethan came barging in holding a steaming cup of coffee, "Hey, I got coffee and bagels inside!" His eyes looked back and forth between Grace and me. His face reddened and he looked down at the floor, "Ah, sorry, I didn't mean to interrupt anything."

Yeah, right.

"Ethan, you didn't interrupt anything. We were just wrestling to get to the door first. There is absolutely nothing going on between Shane and me." Her cheeks were stained crimson.

What the hell? Absolutely nothing going on? She was rubbing that gorgeous ass of hers against my rock hard dick all fucking night and there's nothing going on?

Ethan shrugged, nodded his head and gave me a serious look. "Well, breakfast is inside anyway. Everybody is packing up now, so we should be heading out soon." Not waiting for a response from either of us, he just turned his back and left the room, closing the door behind him.

Her eyes caught mine, and I'm sure my emotions where screaming loud and clear at her. *I was livid.*

"What's *that* look for?" she asked.

"Why do you do shit like that?" I said, pointing to the door Ethan just closed.

"Like what?" *Now she's playing all innocent?*

"Pretend that you don't give a shit about me. You're the one that asked me to sleep in here last night. I get a lot of mixed signals from you, Grace."

I could see her mind scrambling for an excuse, wracking her brain for something to tell me so we couldn't continue on this tense rollercoaster ride. Wrapping her arms around her stomach, she tilted her head down and sighed, "Look, I was with someone for a long time. We had to go our separate ways, but I'm *still* in love with him. I don't...want anybody else. So...this is weird for me. I'm sorry if I'm giving you *any* signals. I really don't want to be with anyone but him." Her eyes dropped to the floor, she couldn't even fucking look at me.

I call BULLSHIT!

Nevertheless, she continued with her *bullshit* story, "*Ever*. Especially with anyone who would think I was only worth one night of their existence," she whispered. She still looked down; cheeks blazing red.

That was the reason, plain and simple. My, *well, really mostly Shane's*, history of being a player. There was nothing I could do at the moment to prove that she was wrong. It was going to take me just being her friend and earning her trust to get her to understand me and let me in.

So I let her walk out of my room. When she got into the hallway, I called after her, "Every fucking breath I take from now on will be solely to prove you wrong, Grace, *every last one.*"

Grace strolled right into the bathroom and softly closed the door behind her, pretending she couldn't hear me, ending our discussion.

Frustrated, I stormed into the kitchen. Everybody was there; even Tucker's asshat of a cousin, Blake, was there. Maybe a year ago, the real Shane would have thought that was cool, having Blake around. The real Shane and Blake were once tight. *Of course*, drug addicts stick together and party hard. *Freaking junky*.

Bagels and a big *Box of Joe* littered the table and counters.

"Hey, there's my partner in crime. You got a little hottie in that Bone Room of yours?" Blake fist bumped me with a coffee and bagel in his hand.

Pounding his fist back, I said, "Hey, Blake. What's new?"

He sipped his coffee and swallowed, "Great shit. Tucker's father has me in his firm now. I've been staying with Tuck for a few days until I get a place set up for myself."

"Great," I said through clenched teeth. Didn't he realize I didn't even want to look at him, let alone talk to him? I pulled myself up to sit on the counter. There was no room around the table, since Tucker, Ethan, Conner, Alex, and Brayden sat in each seat.

"Dickbag, where's Grace?" Tucker cut in.

I shrugged. "Bathroom maybe."

"Thanks for helping Grace last night," Tucker smiled. "I plan to make my *girl* really fall in love with me this weekend, going to sweep her right off her feet."

"She's not your girl, Tucker," I said flatly.

Everyone just sat back and watched our exchange, laughing. Even I laughed at Tucker's stupidity and arrogance.

Then Grace walked in. I could hear the audible gasp from Blake's lips when he saw her, and saw how his whole body went rigid. I completely understood what the guy was going through, but it would be over my dead body before I would let *that* drug addict loser lay a finger on her.

"Hey, there she is! Good afternoon, beautiful! It's about time you got up!" Tucker called out, shoving a bagel in his mouth. I pulled myself up onto the countertop quietly and didn't even lift my head when she walked in. Lea walked in behind her, patted me on the knee, and smiled. *I wonder what Lea is thinking, is she encouraging me? I wish human women came with a book or even a little tiny pamphlet of instructions…just something to explain them to me.*

Grace nodded in Tucker's direction, walked straight to the Box of Joe, and poured herself some coffee. I tossed her a packet of sweetener, and even though she kept her head down, I watched her bite her bottom lip and smile, knowing I remembered how she liked her coffee.

Tucker jumped out of his seat, food falling all over the floor, cleared his throat and started barking out commands, "So, Grace, we are going to be taking your Jeep and Blake's truck. As soon as you are ready, we can leave. I'll drive your Jeep and you can just sit and enjoy the ride."

Stirring in the sweetener, Grace looked up towards Tucker with venom in her steel colored eyes. "*I'm* driving my Jeep, Tucker. And I have no clothes, since my bedroom somehow caught fire last night, *so* before I go on your little trip, I'd like to stop at a store to buy some clothes, so I don't have to stay in Shane's tee-shirt and boxers the whole time I'm there. When you guys are ready, *you* can leave, and I'll be about an hour behind you. Just give me the address. I have a GPS, so I'll be fine."

Curt. Cold. Hiding emotions. She was hiding from me.

Lea stepped up, "No way…"

Blake cut her off, "Well, that sounds like a plan then. If you'd like, I can stay behind and keep you company, and make sure nothing else happens."

Not a chance.

Grace snapped her head in Blake's direction; her eyes widened a bit, as she looked him over.

Oh, hell no, why the hell was she looking at him like that?

He stood leaning his back casually against the countertop watching her. Grace stared back at him fixating on the asshat's blue eyes.

What. The. Hell?

"Hi," he said with his cheeks turning bright red. "I'm Blake, Tucker's cousin."

Grace looked like she was having trouble breathing. My heart felt like it was ripping out of my chest. *Why the HELL DID SHE LOOK AT HIM LIKE THAT?*

Tucker shot up and leaned into the space between Blake and Grace, folding his arms. His face was tight and possessive. "Thanks, *cuz*, but I don't want to be responsible for your brand new truck," he said eyeing Blake. "Besides, Grace doesn't even know you, so I don't think she'd be that comfortable driving with you, since her feelings for her safety have been in question lately."

I acknowledge now, that it was all kinds of fucked up that I wanted to kiss Tucker at that moment. I didn't though, then Tucker would get all Bad Bromance on me, yet I was grateful for his big lawyerish mouth then.

Blake pushed himself off the counter and looked down at Tucker as if he was trying to scare him. Tension filled the air. Everyone in the kitchen had stopped talking and watched the exchange between them.

Alex chuckling low in the corner was the only sound in the room.

I toyed with the idea of letting them kill each other and get all the competition out of the way. Instead, I jumped off the counter and strolled past them as if nothing was going on. "Wow, this is like mating season at the zoo. Why don't I go with Grace later after she picks up what she needs? After all, everyone knows there will *never* be anything between Grace and me. *Ever.*" I leveled my eyes at her and her cheeks flamed.

Tucker backed off, but Blake was humming with angry energy. He charged towards me, but I sidestepped him and ignored the advance. I walked over to Grace and gently escorted her out of the kitchen and back down the hallway to my room, "You have a strong effect on people, don't you?"

She said nothing, just followed me into my room.

Lea walked in right after us and shot Grace a wide-eyed look that expressed her concern about what had just happened. "What in the world was *that* about?"

Grace grabbed at her hands and whispered, "Did you see the color of his eyes?"

The freaking color of his eyes? What, drug addict blue?

Grace glanced at me and moved closer to Lea so I wouldn't hear, "He has the exact color that I've been looking for."

I heard anyway. *What the hell was this about?* Oh, hell I was going to be asking Lea later.

"Are you *effing serious*? Are you positive?" She started pacing and dancing around.

"What are you two whispering about? What have you been looking for?" Conner asked walking in.

Neither of them answered. They just gawked at him as if they were waiting for him to leave. Well, *I* wasn't leaving. *This was my damn room, and I wanted to know what the hell was going on.*

Conner nodded at me, "Someone has got to talk to Tucker, he's obsessed. And did you see him and Blake? Dude, I thought it was going to come to blows."

I didn't bother to answer him. I just watched Grace. Her eyes locked on mine and a sadness spread across her features, like whatever was bothering her could hurt me.

Then a small smiled appeared on her lips, but never reached her eyes. "I just think that everyone is a bit nervous and out of sorts because of what's going on, that's all. Everyone's on

197

edge, so we definitely should get out of the city and up to Tucker's as soon as we can. It'll make everyone relax and we won't have to look over our shoulders for a while." She watched me carefully looking lost and defeated.

"Do you want me to stay here and drive up with you? It's up to you, nobody should make the call for you," I said.

"That's fine," she answered. She gave Lea a smile, "I'll just run to the store quickly. I promise I'll be right behind you guys."

Conner and I left the girls to their girly talking and helped pack up the cars. My mind kept wandering back to the words Grace said to Lea when she thought I couldn't hear. *Did you see the color of his eyes? He has the exact color that I've been looking for.* Look, I know some women have those stupid checklists with all the traits a perfect guy has to have, or a dumbass test *Mr. Perfect* has to pass to prove he *is* the real freaking Mr. Perfect. But if Grace's only *thing* is the color of the jackasses eyes, then that's just messed up and shallow. Besides, his eyes are blue like mine. Does the color of his hair, light shit brown, make him more attractive to her than my dark hair? What the hell is wrong with women?

I watched Grace closely as everybody trudged through the snow and got in Blake's grotesquely enormous black Cadillac Escalade. She couldn't take her eyes off Blake. She kept twisting the hem of my tee shirt that she was still wearing like she was nervous or anticipating something big. It made me insane. She just met this guy. When she finds out what an ass he is and the bad crap he's messed himself up with, she's going to hate him. *I hoped.* I wanted to scream out that Blake used to be Shane's dealer. I wanted to let her know what a junky, lowlife piece of trash he was. I wanted to, and I freaking should have, but I knew she'd fight me on it and I couldn't stand the thought of us fighting anymore.

Dressed in my leather jacket, tee shirt, boxers and a pair of Lea's sneakers, we treaded through the snow across the avenue to a department store that was empty (thank God) because of the snowstorm. Grace didn't even bother to try anything on. She just told me her size and asked me to help her grab as much crap as I could. Yeah, so I picked up some sexy underwear and low cut shirts. I made her laugh every time I brought something to the register that was *revealing*, yet she bought it all. Thirty minutes later, we were back at my apartment. That had to be some sort of women's shopping record or something.

Grace started throwing everything she bought into a backpack she also purchased at the store, when her phone started ringing. She ran into the bathroom with it immediately. Feeling a little jilted, I sat on the couch and flipped on the television. Every station I turned to had news on about the blizzard that was about to hit the city. It looked like it was going to be a bad one too. There was already a decent amount of snow on the ground and the weather center was saying the storm hadn't even hit us yet.

My phone alerted me to a text message.

Conner: Blake and Tucker are dicks

Shane: Y?

Conner: They r in car placing bets who can bag Grace first

Shane: Serious?

Conner: Up to $1000

Conner: Lea is showing Grace now

Shane: Showing?

Conner: Lea got whole convo on video ☺

Shane: I have to see it

Conner: Sending you two videos we just sent Grace

Conner: Alex and Ethan are throwing crap at them as we drive

My phone alerted me to a new multimedia message. A video. Lea had recorded some of the conversation in Blake's truck. The conversation was between Tucker and Blake placing bets on who would *bag* Grace first. They were fighting and shoving each other in the front seat as Blake drove through the snow.

It was pretty damn comical.

The next multimedia message wasn't. Before I saw anything, I heard Grace playing her guitar. The camera phone scanned across the studio from Grace to me. My expression was complete and utter awe, and I was on my knees. The camera focused in on my face and tears welled in my eyes. Conner had recorded the night of the auditions, when Grace played to me the very first time. I clicked the phone shut instantly. I didn't want to watch the expression on my face when I was falling in love with her, not now, not when I'd never know if she'd ever be mine. And this is what she's in the fucking bathroom watching right now, Blake and Tucker placing bets on her and me falling on my God damn knees in front of her.

Kill me now.

I banged on the bathroom door. I needed to see her face; I needed to see what the fuck was going on in her head.

Grace flung the door open with red teary eyes.

"Aww, Grace. Are you okay?" I asked raising my hand to reach out for her.

"I'm fine, but I really have to go now. I've wasted way too much time and waited too damn long."

Waited too long? Wasted too much time? What the hell was she talking about now? It's been like forty-five minutes.

She squeezed my hand as she walked past me, grabbed her backpack from her bedroom and jingled her keys. "I am so ready for this to be over," she said.

But the tears still poured down her face.

Chapter 12

I brushed off the snow that had collected on the front and back windshields of Grace's Jeep, amazed how this city sparkled under the foot of snow that accumulated over the past few days. The news said that the snowstorm would reach us in about an hour, and that no one should be driving in the city unless it was an emergency.

Grace flung the driver's side door open and threw herself in the Jeep like a mad woman. Yeah, I think getting away from Carl Sumpton was definitely an emergency.

I opened the passenger side door and knocked my boots on the side of the well, spraying snow all over.

She glared at me. "Hurry up, just get in, I want to get out on the road ahead of this storm if we can."

I rolled my eyes. "We could just stay here, Grace. We don't have to go to Tucker's. I promise, I'll keep you safe."

"Shane, I'm going. If you want to stay, then stay."

Grace shivered, turned on the heat and defrost, and tried to blow some warmth into her hands. She plugged in her GPS system and keyed in our destination. Outside, the snow fell faster.

I pulled my door closed and the bang echoed through the silence of the night. She stomped on the gas before I could even get my seatbelt on.

She pulled the Jeep over the snowdrifts in four-wheel drive; the wind howled against the car. "Looks like the angels are having one hell of a pillow fight," she laughed nervously.

"Pillow fight," I whispered. I cringed inside myself. Why did humans believe that angels had pillow fights? Why did they even think that they acknowledged humans any longer? This earth had long been forgotten about. I was once one of their kind, and even I was forgotten about.

"Yeah, it's an old saying, but Conner said it when it started to snow the other night. What's wrong? You don't believe in that stuff or just not in old wive's tales?"

She stopped at a red light and looked at me for my answer.

I shrugged and looked out the snowy window. "I don't give much thought to angels," I said. *They are mean, greedy, selfish beings. Trust me, I knew.*

She took the Lincoln Tunnel and emerged into a wintery wonderland worse than what we came from, nothing on that side of the tunnel seemed to have been plowed. I finally buckled my seatbelt, but still sat at the edge of the passenger seat; knuckles white and clutching the dashboard. I seriously thought she was trying to kill us with the sliding and driving she was doing. I kept asking her if she'd like to stop and go someplace safe until the storm was over, she ignored me.

My cell phone rang. *Conner.*

"We made it here without Tucker and Blake getting throttled by Ethan or Alex. I swear, I think Ethan is really going to kill them both. But, for now, we're all safe out of the storm."

"That's good; we just got out of the tunnel, so we aren't too far behind you guys."

"Shane, they are talking about white out conditions on I-80. Maybe you guys should stop somewhere. It'll give you a chance to talk to Grace about stuff. Tell her how you feel. Lea really thinks you should. Something is going on with Blake and Tucker, and Lea is freaking the hell out. If you really have feelings for her, dude, you really need to step up to them, man."

"I wish that I could, bro, but she won't stop." I glanced at Grace, who was leaning at the edge of her seat trying to see through the front windshield. "I think this is her way of offing me. I'll see you in a bit, hopefully. Later."

"Later, bro, stay safe."

I clicked off my phone. "They made it there okay. Conner says the roads are getting worse. They are talking about white out conditions on I-80."

Thick chunks of snow collided with the windshield; the wipers could barely stand against the attack. "We can't go back now. It's fine. Look," she pointed through an almost opaque windshield. "The roads aren't so bad."

"Oh my God, you *are* trying to kill us. Lea is right, you really do have some sort of a death wish," I said.

Eye roll.

"Do you want to explain to me why you are driving in this insane blizzard to get to someone you don't want to be with? Or am I wrong about you and Tucker? Or Blake, you know the guy you don't know anything about but the fact that he has blue eyes."

"I don't want to be with Tucker. Let me just concentrate on driving."

Shit, she didn't say anything about Blake. I should just tell her what a freaking dirty drug addict he is. "Grace, just listen to me..."

"Please, Shane, I won't be able to drive if I have tears in my eyes."

Aww, shit. I glanced over at her profile. She was white knuckling her steering wheel, biting her bottom lip and I could tell she was fighting back tears. I couldn't be the one to make her cry. I leaned my body against the door and watched her as she drove. After an hour, I had to bite at my fucking knuckles not to scream about how much I was in love with her. It was killing me not to tell her, not to let her know how much I was dying to be with her. *Grace could make me forget. She had this strange power over me, she made me want to stay human, and find a way to become a better man for her.*

Slapping me from my thoughts, the explicit voice of Drill Sergeant Hartman screamed through Grace's GPS telling her to take the next exit or he would unscrew her head and shit down her neck, *HOOO-RAAAA!* *Shit like that is why I freaking think I love her.*

The Jeep skidded onto the off ramp and almost slid into a snow embankment. I grabbed the steering wheel, turning it into the skid, and somehow managed to straighten out. "Damn, Grace, let off the gas!" I cursed under my breath.

She let out a low gasp. "We're almost there," she said. "The GPS says we'll be there in three minutes. And, um, thanks for saving our asses," she laughed, merging slowly onto a completely whited out road.

Drill Sergeant Hartman's voice screeched again, "What is your major malfunction, numbnuts? You have exactly three seconds to get the hell out of this car. You've reached your destination, you piece of amphibian shit! Hoo-rah!" Outside the windshield was pure white. Grace's mouth was positioned into a perfect *'o'* and her eyes were wide with terror.

"Tucker's driveway is right off this main road, so we are probably at the entrance," I explained.

Her answer was to drive right into a damn snow bank and cringe.

"Looks like the drive is plowed in," I said laughing. "Try to pull up to the right more so you're off the main road in case another plow comes by and doesn't see us."

For probably the first time ever in this twisted friendship, she took my advice and pulled her Jeep closer, shifted into park and pulled up the brake. "Should we get out and walk from here?" she asked.

Suicide mission? Fuck no! "Tucker's driveway is at least three miles long because it's part of the ski resort about a half mile up. The driveway even has its own name, and there's no way we can walk in this for three miles. I'll call them and see if he can get to us with the snowmobiles."

I tried calling, but I got no reception at all and when Grace tried, it went right to voice mail, so she left a message. "Hey guys, we're here, but, we're stuck at the entrance of the driveway. Um...can someone tell Tucker, so he could come get us with the snowmobiles?" She glanced up at me and continued, "Kind of hurry, because it's flipping cold out here." Then she hung up and stared at me. "What should we do?" she asked anxiously.

"We should stay in here until we can get them on the phone. That way, Grace, we won't die out there in the pretty white stuff," I teased. "Kill the ignition, so you don't waste the gas."

A tremendous gust of wind blew hard against the Jeep making it sway, which caused Grace to try to call Conner and Lea on her cell phone again frantically. She still couldn't get through.

I was hoping they wouldn't get any of the messages; I liked being in a tight confined space with her. I shifted around in my seat to face her, "My ass is asleep from sitting so long. Is that even possible? Wanna rub it for me?" I laughed teasingly.

"Shut up," she laughed back shaking her head.

I tried to make myself more comfortable in the small box she called a vehicle, but no deal. I was way too big for the Jeep. As I moved around, I skimmed my hand lightly across her knee, and I watched as her entire body shivered. *Fuck me, it wasn't even cold in here yet.* Was that from my touch?

I bent forward, sprang the handle on the seat, and pushed it all the way back. "You're cold already, climb over here," I whispered, locking my eyes with hers.

She held my gaze for a moment before she looked down and whispered sadly, "That's not necessary." *I could plainly tell she wanted to, but just wouldn't let herself.*

Outside, the wind screamed louder, and inside, an icy draft blew in, dropping the temperature faster. "What's in your glove box?" I asked, wondering if she had any supplies we could use like a flashlight, or matches or even a freaking umbrella. A damn blanket would have been useful too.

"My glove what?" she asked, confused.

I shook my head, laughed and pointed to the dashboard right in front of me.

"Oh, you mean my *glove compartment*. Trust me, there's nothing in there you'll want to see," she explained teasingly. *Now she's flirting with me? Women really do confuse the hell out of me.*

"Glove BOX. And is that supposed to make me *not* want to know what's inside it?" I laughed and flirted back. "Because, trust *ME*, it doesn't."

We both reached for it at the same time, but I got to it first and flung it open. About half a dozen tampons flew out at me. *Ugh. That's the freaking equivalent of taking an ice cold shower.*

Grace laughed uncontrollably. "I told you it's nothing you'd want to see, so why do you always have to try to get your way?"

I reached my hand in and felt around, throwing the last tampon on her lap. "Because I was hoping you had one of these," I said smiling, holding up a flashlight to taunt her with it. Our eyes locked when I lobbed the flashlight back inside and closed the *compartment*. A loose strand of silky hair fell against her cheek and I couldn't help but tuck it gently behind her ear. Another shiver rocked her body. I pressed my lips together tightly and closed my eyes for the briefest of seconds so her beauty wouldn't blind me to my senses. I was desperate to kiss her but I still needed time to earn her trust. However, as I opened my eyes to her heart stopping gaze again, she shivered once more.

I unzipped my jacket and slowly peeled it off. "Come here, Grace, you're freezing." I reached out for her, gathered her into my arms, and gently pulled her onto my lap. I breathed her scent in deeply and held her tight in my arms, draping my coat over us.

Just like we were a perfect fit, she nuzzled right into my chest under the cover of my jacket. *Right though my damn skin and into my heart.*

She snuggled closer and giggled. *Okay, now she's really just trying to kill me.*

Loving the feel of her body against mine, I moaned and held her tighter, "What are you giggling at under there?"

She poked her head out from under my jacket, our faces so close to each other I could barely breathe. Our lips were so close that, one more inch and they'd touch. *I never wanted one more inch so much in my life.* And don't let your mind go anywhere else about me wanting more *inches*, because I don't need any more inches anywhere on my body. *Trust me.*

"I'm losing it," she laughed. "I'm desperate for some hot cocoa; you know the thick and creamy kind with those sweet sugary little marshmallows. I want to sit near a roaring fire with my hands wrapped around the warm cup and I want to feel the velvety heat coat my mouth and slide down my throat," she ranted. *I freaking pictured it. Thick? Creamy? Her hands wrapped around something and velvety heat coating her mouth, sliding down her throat?* I was having sex with her already in my head.

"God, Grace, you can seriously make anything you say the sexiest thing I've ever heard." My eyes lowered their gaze to her plump lips, and without another clear thought in my head, I unzipped her jacket. We locked eyes as I helped her slip her arms out of its sleeves. Her breath pitched. Wrapping both our jackets over us, I pulled her closer and nestled my face into her thick hair, and breathed her in deeply once more.

I slid my hands under her shirt and slowly traced my fingertips along the small of her back and up her spine. Her skin was so smooth and warm it felt like she was melting in my hands.

I nestled my face in her neck and along her jawline as my own breath faltered.

She slowly slid her hands up the front of my shirt, and a soft moan escaped from between her lips. *There was no way in the world I could stop myself now.* I had to hear her moan like that again. I pushed myself up against her, nuzzling closer into her neck and gently pulled her into a sitting position with her legs straddling me. Her body slowly rocked against me. *Holy hard-on.*

She leaned her head back slightly and looked down into my eyes, and rocked her hips against me again. I raised my hand to her face and traced my thumb softly against her lower lip.

"One kiss, Grace, just one simple kiss. Baby, please," I begged her. I *needed* to taste her. "Just one." I reached up, grabbed her hair and pulled her towards my lips. Our lips were almost touching, breathing each other in as I ran my fingers lightly down her neck. Then her lips touched mine. It was barely a kiss; her lips gently brushed over mine, taking the briefest of moments to savor the intensity. Her body trembled against mine. "Damn, do you have any idea what you do to me, Grace?" My voice was low and husky, and our eyes were locked. She simply took my breath away. "Just one. Grace..."

As soon as the corners of her lips lifted slightly, I just fucking kissed her, crushing my lips to hers. She hummed deeply into my mouth. I clawed at the hem of her shirt and pulled it over her head. I leaned my head back to look at her, all of her in front of me, and let out a long faltering sigh. Pulling her in, I trailed kisses over her neck and shoulders, and across her torso. Gently, I grazed her skin with my teeth, biting her softly. I could barely fucking breathe, I wanted her so much.

Gently, I tugged the cup of her bra down, taking her to my mouth and licked her in slow circular motions; her nipples hardened under my tongue. She shuddered in response.

Her fingers ran down my chest and settled on the button of my jeans, undoing them with a quick snap of her fingers. With my tongue still working her, I slid my hands over her legs, up to the button of her jeans, unbuttoning it slowly. I couldn't stop the growls that were coming from the back of my throat. I had never wanted anyone like that before.

I tilted my head back to watch her as I laid my right hand flat against her belly and dipped my fingers slowly between the material of her panties and her skin. Her hips hitched up towards me and rocked against me. My fingers continued to travel down, ever so slightly, and I throbbed to be inside her. Our breathing amplified in the small confines of the Jeep. I caught her bottom lip between my teeth and moaned; she rocked against me again when I reached the wettest part of her lacy panties.

She slipped her hands past my waistband and gently wrapped her hands around me, grasping and tugging my rock hard skin. I closed my eyes, trying desperately to catch my breath and not explode from just her touch, like a twelve year old.

Our lips devoured each other's again until I pulled myself away. "Please, Grace, whatever it is you're going after, please try to find it here in me. I will try my best to be the man that you need me to be." As soon as the words left my lips, I knew I shouldn't have said a word. Her eyes widened as she pushed against me and leaned back.

She tore her hands out of my pants and cupped them over her swollen lips. She flailed and tried desperately to get off me. "Shane, I'm sorry," she whimpered as her eyes filled themselves with tears. Frantically, she looked everywhere trying to find some sort of way to escape. She started the engine and blasted the heat; ice-cold air filled the small space. She squeezed her hands around the steering wheel and sobbed loudly.

209

Gently, I placed my hand on her chin and pulled her face towards me. "Grace, you have to know...I lost myself in you that night, lost myself somewhere in that kiss," I said.

Tears streamed down her face as her eyes locked with mine and my words penetrated her brain. "I told you *I can't* do this. I told you I was in love with someone else."

"An ex-boyfriend, right? Not Tucker or Ethan or Blake?"

She nodded her head and I lightly wiped the tears from her cheeks with my fingertips. Thousands of thoughts seem to flicker across her face, but she said none of them. She just leaned her body back towards me like we were magnets that had been pulled apart from someone else's hand.

"Let me help you erase his memory," I whispered pulling her in closer to me.

I didn't even see the slap coming, but the sting of it echoed and rattled in my skull. *What the hell was that for? Aren't ex-boyfriend's exes for a reason?*

"You cold fucking bastard! What will you erase it with, your *dick*? You really think sleeping with you is that fucking awesome? I love someone, Shane, with my whole heart. Don't you understand what that means? Do you even have a heart inside that body of yours?" She cried. Thick tears poured down her face. She grabbed her shirt off the dashboard and pulled it back over her head, covering herself.

I knew better than anyone who had *ever* fucking walked on this God forsaken earth what love was. I had burned in hell for it. I yanked my hands back and leaned against the door, looking right into her teary eyes. "No, Grace. I don't have a heart. I did once, but I gave it to a girl and I let her keep it when she died. That's why I am the way I am, why every girl is just another piece of ass to me. No one has ever come close to making me feel the way she did, *until now*. Shit, Grace, I would do anything to erase her, not to feel that fucking hole in my life."

She looked away from me, sobbing and shaking. Then, in an instant, the tears stopped and her expression hardened. "Let's just keep trying our cells, so we can finally get out of this box, forget everything that's happened, and move on with our lives. You can go back to your adoring *Pieces of Ass*, and I can go back to being alone. Everyone gets to live happily ever after."

"Holy shit, Grace! Do you not listen to anything? Grace, that's not a kiss I'm ever going to forget. Looking at the way I fucking make you cry, I wish like hell I could forget it, but I freaking can't! I want *you!*" I grabbed her hands and pinned her wrists together to keep her from turning away from me.

"Don't do this, Shane."

"Why? Lie to me and tell me you don't fucking feel the need between us," I yelled.

"Really, Shane? You want to go there? What are you asking me for exactly? You just want me to spread eagle for you right here, let you have your way with me, get me out of your system? Then we get out of this and you get to treat me like nothing but a PIECE OF ASS? You can have a great story to tell the guys, all about how you tapped that ass stuck in a snowstorm."

I pulled her hands closer to me. I wanted to put them against my heart, to make her feel how it beat for her.

"This is a nightmare, Shane, you and me. I woke up crying the other night thinking about how you kissed me!"

"Really, Grace? Why don't you go ahead and ask me what wakes me up sweaty and trembling every freaking night! Go ahead, Grace, ask me!" I demanded. I pulled her even closer so our lips were almost touching. Her breathing kicked up and she struggled between looking down at my lips to kiss me and getting the hell away from me and out of the car. Getting the hell away from me won the vote.

"Get away from me, Shane," she moaned softly, moving away. She expertly got out of my hands, which *once again,* caused me to wonder why she hadn't done it sooner if she had the ability to do it all along, and she tried to yank the Jeep door open. It wouldn't budge, so she shifted her body and kicked at it until it opened enough for her to climb out.

No, I can't let her go. "Grace, please, I'm not the person you think I am! Shit, Grace! Get back in here!" I screamed as she climbed out of the Jeep.

When she fell out into the snow, she stuck her head back in the car and yelled, "I'm a fucking novelty to you, just because no other girl has ever had the self-esteem to say no to you!" She pulled her head back out and lifted herself up onto the roof of the Jeep as if she was some sort of fucking bionic woman. *Holy shit, how the fuck did she do that?* Fumbling, I tried to open the door, but the snow was too deep outside my door too, so I kicked and kicked at it until it opened just enough to get my whole body through, just like she did. By that time, Grace was on the roof of the Jeep trying to jump off.

I grabbed her flailing arms, and dragged her off the Jeep's roof and into the snow. "Get away, Shane!"

I lifted her up and tossed her over my shoulder like a damn two year old. Carrying her, I climbed the snowdrifts, as she pounded her fists hard against my back. Cold. Cold fucking wet snow was everywhere. Everything was white. *Where the hell was I going to take her?* She was going to freeze that perfect little ass of hers off out there. When I found an area sheltered by a tree, I eased her slowly off my shoulder, sliding her down the front of my body. It was like warm butter melting over me, I just about came undone. She tried to walk away sobbing, but I held her tight against me with one hand on the small of her back and the other grasping her neck through a fistful of that thick sexy hair of hers.

She grasped her fists in my shirt and clung to me silently, crying into my chest. Pressing her body into me, I knew I had to tell her. I had to tell her everything.

I gently tugged her hair back and lowered my mouth down to hers, kissing her once on the lips. I brushed my lips along her soft cheeks to her ear and whispered, "Go ahead, Grace, ask me what dreams I wake from at night." I pulled my head back, fixed my eyes on hers, pleading with her to believe me. "I wake up with you as the last thought in my dreams. I dream about your lips, the smell of your skin and hair, and the freaking fire that burns inside of me to be inside you. I want to bury myself inside you and never climb out, *my sweet death*. Grace, I'm so fucking in love with you."

She pulled me in closer and blinked back tears. "In another life, Shane, if I was anybody but me, I would have loved to be loved by you."

Um, what the hell did that mean? I seriously looked down at my chest to see if the Goddamn knife that I just felt had actually been real and pierced right through my heart. Her rejection literally *hurt me*. It hurt my chest and made me want to tear off my skin and bleed out all over the pure white snow. *This isn't real.*

Yet, Grace still clung to me, eyes wide with tears. I held on to her as if it was the last time I'd ever get to touch her. A burning scorched at the back of my throat and I felt the need to gag. I looked away from those beautiful silver eyes that I loved and my heart broke even further when I heard the distinct sounds of the motor of a snowmobile.

I stepped away from her and raked my hands through my wet, snow-covered hair. Two snowmobiles appeared out of the blinding whiteness and skidded to a halt in front of us. *No. God, please no. I can't do this punishment. I can't be here and not have her. I can't be this close to her and not love her.*

Sitting on top of one of the snowmobiles was Tucker who lifted the stupid visor to his flaming red helmet and yelled, "Hey, baby! There's nothing to fear. Your superman is here." Then the fucknut winked at her.

The visor to the second snowmobiler was lifted and Blake's drug addict blue eyes peaked out. He rolled his eyes, jumped off the snowmobile and reached his hand out to Grace. My insides almost exploded when she took his hand and let him help her straddle the snowmobile, then got on behind her. *Wasn't she just fucking straddling me? AND why is she smiling at him like THAT?*

Rage surged through my veins making me break out into a cold sweat and ball my hands into tight fists.

I growled and waded through the deep snow back to the Jeep and yanked the passenger side door open. I pulled our packs and jackets out, and slung both our guitar cases over my shoulders. Then I climbed back over the snowdrifts to Blake's pansy-ass colored snowmobile. I angrily glared into her eyes, and shoved her jacket into her arms, "Here you go, wouldn't want you to get any colder than you already are."

Grace's eyes widened at my words and tears filled them again. Why was she crying if this was her choice? Why was it hurting her *NOT* being with me? She looked down at the ground, pulled on her coat and zipped it up. Blake wrapped one arm around her waist and the other on one end of the handlebars. He took off without even waiting for her to hold on. *Major fucknut.*

I stood there, with everything in my arms and talked myself into not walking in another direction, completely away from Grace.

"Dude, did my cousin just jump on my shit?" Tucker asked.

"Grace isn't your *shit*, Tuck. And it sure as hell doesn't look like she wants to be your *shit* anytime soon."

"Hey, dillweed. It doesn't look like she wants to be your *shit* either. *That* I can fucking see loud and clear."

Without having any other option, I was forced to ride bitch behind Tucker. On a snowmobile painted with bright red flames. While he wore the most feminine pink-flamed helmet ever, as I got to watch the love my life speed away with a piece of crap drug addict who she seemed to be smitten with. *Damn it.*

Chapter 13

Seems that Tucker wanted to get Grace away from Blake as much as I did, because he drove his snowmobile so fast, we almost slammed into the back of Blake's snowmobile before I saw her jump off and run to Lea who was waiting on the porch for her.

I caught up to her, shivering violently in the foyer, while Lea tried to hug her. I dropped all of our belongings on the floor in front of me, closed my eyes, leaned back and rested my head against the wall. Without looking at Grace or Lea, I just whispered "Lea, get her out of those wet clothes."

"I'm fine," Grace stammered. Even with my eyes closed, I could tell how cold she was by the sound of her teeth chattering.

I snapped my eyes open and glared at her. "You're impossible!" I stalked towards her, picked her up with one hand, and flung her over my shoulder, ass to the ceiling, *again*. "Bring the bags for me, will you? My hands seem a bit full," I said, locking eyes with Lea.

I carried Grace through the house, down a long hallway and into a dark room. Lea switched on the lights and I threw Grace down on a beautiful king-size four-poster bed. "Get out of your clothes," I seethed. Rage washed over me in thick heavy waves. She sat there with a defiant look across her cold, pale, shivering face. "Do you know what hypothermia is? Get out of your clothes!" I yelled.

She clamped down on her chattering teeth and began taking off her sneakers and socks. My eyes never left her, as I peeled off my own wet shirt and pants and stood in my ice-cold boxers in front of her. "I meant every word I said, Grace. And you cannot sit there and tell me that you don't feel the same." I looked away from her stoic expression and leaned over my bag, searching through it for dry clothes.

Before I could stand up straight, she picked up her bag, and walked into the bathroom, clicking the lock on the door. I rushed up to the door and tried the knob, but I knew before I even put my hand to it that it wouldn't turn. I thumped my head against the wood and my stomach clenched with the thought of her not being with me. "Come on, God. How can this be wrong? It feels too right. *Please*, I don't want to do this shit anymore," I whispered.

I kicked at her door softly and continued dressing. I packed up my bag when I was done, threw my crap in the next empty room and went to find Lea.

I didn't have to look too far, because she was waiting at the end of the hallway for me.

Her face was covered in concern, "What the hell, Shane?"

"No. You tell me what the hell, Lea? Why the hell does she want Blake all of a sudden?"

"I don't know. I thought you and her would..."

I stalked past her and into the living area where everyone was waiting, "Yeah, well you thought wrong. She doesn't want me so she pulls me close, holds on to dear life and lies to my fucking face." Everyone looked up when I walked in from being with Lea in the hallway. "I'm going to the resort bar on those stupid snowmobiles and I'm getting so drunk that I can forget the damned person I am when I look in the God forsaken mirror."

Brayden hung his arm over my shoulder and Tucker nodded his head. Blake took up the rear and the four of us walked out of the cabin and jumped onto the snowmobiles. I was surprised that Blake didn't feel the need to wait for Grace. *What the hell game was he playing?*

The bar was packed, despite the blizzard raging outside. People were dancing to someone horribly singing karaoke, crowded around the bar ordering drinks, and every table was full with laughing noisy drunks. I itched to start a fight.

Brayden grabbed a huge empty table in the back and pulled in enough chairs for everybody to sit. Tucker and Blake ran to say their hellos at the bar and came back with three bottles of whiskey, a bunch of glasses and a beer for everyone. Perfect. I felt like drowning myself tonight, and the bottom of an empty whiskey bottle was the perfect place as any to do just that.

After three shots and a beer, my gut twisted when Grace walked through the crowd. I broke a wooden spindle off the back of the chair when I watched Blake and Grace's eye meet and the glow that lit up her face. I slammed back my drink, draining the last of my beer and then slammed the bottle on the table. Hard and loud. Everyone at the table stopped their conversations at the jolting noise it made. I stood up, looked around me for the first time and noticed some chick sitting next to me. I grabbed the girl's hand, fixed my stare on Grace and walked the girl out to the dance floor. The girl looked back at her friends, waved and giggled. *Come on, really?*

Grace didn't look away. Her perfect plump little lips made a shocked little 'O' shape and her features darkened. *If she didn't care, why was she mad?* I grabbed the girl's waist and started dancing really close to her. Grace watched. Stunned.

"Wow, I can't believe I'm dancing with Shane Maxton from Mad World," she squeaked. *Oh, crap. Did I freaking need this right now? No.*

She ran her claws all over my body and started dry humping my leg. *Yea, this is fun.* I choked back vomit as the girl kept rubbing herself on me. My eyes never left Grace's.

"Aren't you going to ask me my name?"

"Nope."

"Wait, what?" She stopped dancing and tried to pull my chin away from facing Grace's direction. Grace squeezed her eyes shut, covered her hand over her mouth and looked away.

Fuck, I can't do this if it hurts her. Why the hell can't she be with me if this affects her?

"Why did you want to dance with me if you didn't even want to know my name?"

I looked at the girl for the first time. She was adorably cute and innocent. "Shit, I'm sorry, but did you see that girl who walked in before I grabbed your hand?" She nodded. "I'm so fucking in love with her that I can't see straight. And she is smiling at some other guy, and when I told her I loved her, she..."

"Oh, I get it. Would you like to make her jealous?"

"No. No, I don't want that...I didn't mean for that to happen. I just...shit. What the hell am I doing?" I spun around on the dance floor to walk back to Grace.

Blake and Grace were dancing right in front of me. Blake held her close and she danced with her arms wrapped around his neck. Someone was singing Karaoke to Adele's Someone Like You, and Blake noticed me watching them, winked at me and roughly grabbed her chin and pulled her lips up to his. His mouth devoured her and I wanted to kill him, then he spun her around to face me. Blake pulled her closer against him and kissed that neck that I love; pulling her hair that I dream about splayed across my pillows, and trailed his lips over it.

Her face looked stunned and a tear fell from her eye.

I swallowed the hard sharp knot that was caught in my throat and watched Blake slide his hands around to the front of her shirt. He lifted the fabric, placing his hands on the bare skin of her stomach, the stomach that I had my hands on just a few hours ago. I looked back into her eyes and more tears fell. *The hell with this. I surrender.* I put up my hands, turned around and slowly made my way through the bar towards the front door. *I wasn't going to suffer and watch her do this.* I'm out of here. I'm done with this. She definitely wasn't anything like my Selah. Selah would never do that shit to me.

The crowd was so thick it took me a few minutes to find my way through.

When I finally reached the front door to the bar, I heard Grace's voice sing over the Karaoke machine. Of course, the crowd was so amazed by her voice they went quiet. My heart pulled when I turned and looked at her. It clenched in my chest when I saw she was singing it just to me. Katy Perry's The One That Got Away. *I didn't understand this.*

I flung the doors open to the howling wind and snow outside. I jumped on the snowmobile that I rode to the bar and I felt a small body slide in behind me.

"What the fuck are you doing?" I asked the girl behind me.

"Well, I can't leave you alone after seeing the girl you are in love with suck face with another guy. So just drive."

I hopped off the snowmobile. "Look, there is no way in hell anything is going to happen between you and me tonight. So just stay here with your friends, okay?"

"No way, you shouldn't be alone. Even if nothing happens between us, I could always lie to my girlfriends and tell them some awesome stories about how hard you made me come."

"What the fuck is wrong with you? Whatever, I don't have time for this shit." I hopped on Tucker's snowmobile and left her.

The nut followed me on another snowmobile.

When we got to the cabin, I tried to slam the door in her face but her body was halfway in. I paced the living room area and called her every insult I could think of to get her to leave me the fuck alone. Then I sat next to her on the couch and for a good fifteen minutes, tried to explain that I wasn't going to have anything to do with her.

She laughed and showed me her tits.

When the front door opened, she covered herself and Grace and Blake stumbled through the door. Blake laughed as his eyes narrowed at me. "Crap, I thought we'd have the house to ourselves," he sneered.

I jumped off the couch and stormed over, putting my body between them. "I want you to come with me, Grace." I held out my hand and touched my fingertips to her chin.

She flinched back. "Are you serious, right now? What, am I supposed to join you and your friend over there?"

I leaned in closer. "Don't do this."

Blake yanked her away from me, "Take a step back, Shane, this has nothing to do with you. You have a pretty girl over there," he said, pointing to the girl quietly sitting on the couch. I still hadn't asked her name.

I reached out for her again and touched my hand to her elbow. Her eyebrows pulled together and her silver eyes pleaded with me. But I couldn't figure out what they wanted me to do, all I know was that they needed me to do something.

Blake stepped closer to her and shoved her body behind his. That made the hairs on the back of my neck stand up. It was too harsh, too violent, but Grace said nothing. "Back the fuck up, Shane, she's with me," he growled.

I stepped even closer to Blake, staring him right in the eyes. "Let her decide," I snapped back. I leaned past Blake and grabbed her by both wrists. "Come with me," I said to her. She leaned toward me.

"Okay, that's enough. Get the fuck away from her," Blake screamed. Grace looked down at the floor, breaking our eye contact with each other.

Then she pushed off Blake with tears in her eyes, "I'm not a fucking pretty little shiny toy, both of you get the fuck off me!" She looked at me deadpan, all feeling gone. "I'm going with Blake into my room. You seem to have a visitor with you that you've forgotten about."

No. No, no, no.

"If you do that, you're like every other girl that you fight so hard *not* to be."

"You know what, you're a fucking asshole!"

I laughed. I had to, because it was better than being a pussy and doing what I was really fighting myself from doing, which was crying like a little bitch. "In the past few weeks that I've known you, you're called me a hell of a lot worse." I raised my hand to her face one last time and gently touched her cheek. "Call me anything you want, as long as you don't do this. This isn't you."

She stepped back from my hand. "What? You're here to save me, Shane? I'm sure the answer to all my problems is to lower my standards and go with you and your friend."

With tears pouring down her face, Blake pulled her down the hallway. I watched as she walked backwards with her eyes on mine and closed herself in her bedroom with Blake.

I stood there broken. Watching the closed door. *How can you fight for someone who doesn't want you?* My hands wrapped around the vase that was on the table I was standing next to. It was such a beautiful thing. I smashed it hard in my fist against the wall. The sharp glass sliced my hand open. The pain felt good, it was intense and clear. It was the only thing I knew and the only thing I could understand.

"Oh my God, Shane! You need to get that looked at!" the squeaky voiced girl yelled.

I looked at her and laughed. "Come on. Let me get you back to the bar, so I can deal with this without an audience."

The girl followed me out with a terrified look on her face. Good. She should be fucking scared. I pulled her onto a snowmobile, drove her to the bar, and hauled her ass off my seat as quick as I could. The engine of the snowmobile sputtered and stopped. I probably turned the engine over a dozen times to get it to start again. *Damn, if he was screwing her already, I didn't know what the hell I would do to him.*

"Wait. Shane, what are you going to do?"

I smiled at her. I saw her body melt at my expression. Then I laughed, "I'm going to go back there and probably kill him." With that, I left her there and drove over the snow back to the cabin.

I never made it back.

Halfway between the cabin and the bar lay a small rumpled mound in snow. The splash of bright red against the whiteness of the snow was what caused me to stop the snowmobile and walk over to it. The smell of sickly sweet blood, mixed with the freshly falling icy snow, filled my nose.

Thick dark hair spread out across red snow.

Grace.

Grace?

Red snow?

Grace's body. My beautiful Grace, *bleeding* into the snow.

There was bright red blood all over the snow.

No. This isn't right. That can't be real. That CAN'T be blood. The snow is too red.

Grace. What the hell happened? *WHAT THE HELL JUST HAPPENED?*

"Grace? Grace!" *I could hear my voice screaming. Breaking, sobbing her name.*

Blood.

There was blood *everywhere*.

I knelt in front of her and cautiously placed her head on my knees. Her life was pouring out of her. Leaking all over the white snow.

A knife.

So much blood.

Tears blurred my eyes and I squeezed them shut. *Please God. Please God. Please God, hear me. Please God, save her.*

I put pressure on her side where I thought the blood was coming from, but the wound was too big. *There was too much blood.* It was warm on my hands.

No, no, no. *Grace.* Please don't leave me.

"Grace, hang on. Grace, stay with me. *Please GRACE!*"

I looked across the snow where Blake's body was slumped in a huge heap a few yards away. Buzzing sounds of snowmobile engines surrounded me as I lifted Grace's limp body into my arms and cuddled her close. Her blood oozed warm and thick over my hands; *too much blood. Please, God, please spare her.*

Her warm blood was spreading across the material of my jeans, soaking through my coat and onto my shirt.

Lea's screams echoed in the background, but the only thing I could distinctly hear was the slowing weak rhythm of Grace's heartbeat. "Please, Father, let me be the angel you created me to be. Let me take her pain," I cried. "Too much blood, Grace, there's too much blood."

"Shane, Shane! The ambulance isn't going to get through this snow! We have to carry her inside," a familiar voice called to me.

I knew it was probably too late, but I gathered her in my arms and stood up. "Don't be scared...heaven is breathtaking," I whispered in her ear as I carried her dying body over the snow to the resort.

Chapter 14

The bright lights of the emergency room's waiting area stung my eyes. Doctors and paramedics had rushed Grace's body through the hallways and into surgery, while I stood by helplessly; Grace's blood was dry and crusted over my hands and arms. Her skin looked pale and lifeless when they wheeled her off the ambulance. Blood was splattered across her forehead and cheeks. It dried in clumps through her hair and on her cold wet clothes. So small and still, she laid on the gurney. When my eyes lost sight of her behind the closed doors of the emergency surgical unit, my legs just gave. I slumped back from the doors and slowly slipped down against the wall until I hit the cold tiled floor of the hospital. I held my head in my hands and cried. "This is all my fault," I said.

Lea's body slumped against mine and her arms wrapped themselves around my shaking shoulders. Everybody was in the waiting room with us, but my words were the only words anybody had spoken.

As minutes slowly dragged into hours, I was vaguely aware of people offering me coffee or water. My stomach churned so violently that I didn't think I would be able to hold anything down. I never moved from my spot on the floor. I just kept thinking that I needed to hear her laugh again. I needed to see her smile again and I needed to hold her and never let her go.

Eight hours. Eight hours, thirty-nine minutes and twelve seconds later, the doors to the surgical unit swung open. Three surgeons with vomit green scrubs walked through, pulling their surgical masks off but still wearing grim expressions. I searched their faces frantically for any indication of how Grace was. *Nothing.*

I bolted to my feet and ran towards the doctors just as the rest of my friends did. "What's going on? How is she?" My words sputtered harshly from my lips, coming out raw and angry.

"Which one of you is part of Grace Taylor's immediate family?" The words slapped me hard, open handed-like a bitch, across my face.

"She lives with me, my parents raised her. She doesn't have any other family," Lea coughed out through tears. "Can you just tell us what's going on, Doctor? It's been like almost nine hours and we haven't been told anything, and honestly, I'm afraid of what I might start doing to this waiting area and all its furniture if somebody doesn't start talking real soon," Lea threatened through sobs. Ethan, Tucker and Brayden actually crowded in around the doctors at Lea's threat, menacingly.

The oldest of the three surgeons motioned Lea to the seats, "Please, come and sit and I'll explain." Together, we moved as one unit to the seats, all watching the doctors cautiously.

"Your friend is in recovery right now. We had to place Miss Taylor in a medically induced coma so we could repair all the damage that was done due to the wounds she sustained. She has youth and good health on her side so we are *hoping* she recovers and heals correctly from the lacerations. She lost a lot of blood, *almost 40 %,* and it might take days, weeks or even months for her to wake up and get back to the person she was, *if* she ever does. It's too early to tell how much damage was done when her heart stopped...two blood transfusions...pierced lungs...major organ damage...life support...miracles..." The words jumbled all together, but I knew exactly what the surgeons were saying.

"Her heart *stopped*?" Lea cut in. "But, what happened? What *happened* to her? I don't understand!"

"We don't know the circumstances of the attack, but what we do know is that Miss Taylor came into the ER with a puncture wound under her arm that traveled straight down to her hip bone, which damaged numerous vital organs. Now if you will excuse us, we need to meet with the police who have been waiting for our statements on this matter."

While everybody else went to go eat and wait some more, Lea and I waited to be let into the Intensive Care Unit.

Two hours later, Lea and I silently entered Grace's ICU room, each taking a seat silently next to Grace's hospital bed.

I raked my hands through my hair. "This is all my fault, Lea. I should have been there. I shouldn't have left her. I pushed her. I pushed her too far. I practically pushed her right to Blake," I whispered.

"No, Shane, trust me. You don't understand," Lea's tears blurred her words.

I leaned my forehead into my hands. "I told her I was in love with her."

Lea looked up at me, eyes wide in shock.

I slid my hands through my hair and gazed up at the ceiling hoping for some sort of divine help.

"Hold up...*What?*" Lea gasped.

"I messed up. I thought she felt it too. I didn't know she was really into her ex-boyfriend. I messed up and we fought. I pushed her away and now she's here. I wasn't there to protect her."

"Ex-boyfriend?"

I wiped at the tears that were forming in my eyes. "Yeah, that's what she said in the Jeep when we were stuck in the snow. She didn't want anyone but him." I laughed roughly. "My fucking luck, the only time I let myself feel something for someone and there's no chance, and now she's got fucking machines breathing for her."

"Do you think she'll make it, Shane? Do you think..."

I stood up, suddenly filled with a fury and rage. "No. Life isn't made of miracles, roses and cotton fucking candy, Lea.

She's in *a coma*. That sick bastard knew exactly where to cut her to make her bleed to death, to weaken her entire body before we could get her to a hospital. Think about what she felt! Think about what she suffered the whole time. How many times did they have to revive her? Even the doctor said to pray for a miracle in the same sentence he said how long we should wait before stopping the machines breathing life into her! There's no such thing as miracles. Life doesn't work that way. There's no beauty in it, there's no *hope*."

Lea stared at me with those big brown eyes, pleading for me to take what I said back. *Well, I can't, Lea. This is all part of my punishment, to have someone else I love taken from me. You, Lea, you're just some collateral human damage that those selfish winged fuckers that you pray to, don't even give a fuck about.* I walked over and sat next to Grace on her bed. Leaning over her, I brushed a dark lock of hair off her face.

Lea walked to the other side, took Grace's hand, and held up her wrist. "Hope. It's what's tattooed on her wrist."

"Love on this one," I sighed. I knew what was Lea was trying to do, give herself hope despite all I had just said. *My God, how blind human faith runs so deep.* Ignorance truly is bliss.

"Faith is on the back of her neck," Lea whispered. "Do you believe in heaven, Shane?"

Agony twisted through my soul, tying it into knots.

"She'll go right to heaven, Lea, and I bet it's the most beautiful place ever created. She'll sing and all the angels will turn their heads to listen."

Lea gasped and her tears fell faster; thicker, her body started shaking with uncontrollable sobs. "No, she won't. She doesn't ever get to go to heaven!"

I brushed a finger over Grace's pale cheek. "She was a good person, Lea. She'll go to heaven."

Lea's face reddened and she stood up demanding my attention. "No, Shane. You don't get it!" She closed the gap between us and through her tears, she hissed, "You don't know who *she really is*, where *she's really from*. She was *there*, before Noah, the Ark, and the flood. Her soul was there when the angels fell in love with the humans. They called them the Watchers, The Grigori. Together, they made a pact to marry the human women, to teach them to see clearly. There were like two hundred of them. They became fallen angels and when they married the women, they gave birth to the Nephilim, and they were all punished. She was the only one who never had a child. That's her so-called ex-boyfriend, Shane. She's been looking for an angel for centuries...some angel named *Shamsiel*. And her name...her *real* name was *Selah*. She doesn't ever die and go to heaven, Shane. She goes from dying body to dying body, living all these effed up lives looking for some...some angel that she hasn't seen for thousands of years!"

She took a deep breath and her body shook. "She told me before we left for Tucker's that she thought Blake was *him*. She says that angels have a distinct eye color. And they..."

No. Oh God, no.

"Stop," I whispered. I slid up to Grace's face and cupped her chin. "That's fucking impossible! Grace! Wake up!" I grabbed her shoulders and shook her body, trying to wake her up.

Lea tried pulling me away, "What the hell are you doing! Get off her. You're going to kill her faster!"

I flew off the bed, hands covering my mouth; I dropped to my knees. "Gabriel? Michael? Raphael? *What did you do?*" I whispered.

"Stay over there, Shane, I swear to God if you touch Grace again like that you are going to watch me morph into Lea circa 2005, gangster bitch and go postal on your ass. You need to calm the eff down, I'm getting Conner!" She seethed as she stomped out of the room.

I walked back toward Grace's bed and swept my eyes

over her tousled mess of hair that framed her flawlessly exquisite face. A face that I now knew would haunt me *forever. It's as if I were seeing her for the first time again.* Not being able to fight the impulses that hammered through my body, I reached out to run a fingertip along one unruly strand of that black hair that curled silkily against her pale skin.

My fingers trembled when I withdrew my hand. How I marveled that anyone could cause my body to react this way again over the past few weeks. *Now I understood why.*

I sat listening to the slow rhythmic cadence of the ventilation machine that helped sustain life in her precious body. I inhaled and exhaled along with the tempo of the dreadful sounds, trying to bring my violent rage under control.

I should have known. I should have known that the only fucking person on this God forsaken rock to make me ever feel like that would be *her.*

I scowled at the thought of how messed up I was, how selfish and arrogant I had become. Each day I lived had become blurred and mixed together, with no distinction to any of them. The only solace I found, the only time I felt my existence counted, was when I played my music. Although, the truth was, even that was fading. I became restless with this life, with all the meaningless women, none of which could ever satisfy the hunger I had; I was fed up with everything. I scowled again at myself as I sat before this beautiful dying creature. I had become a sulky ornery human trapped in the damaged soul of a fallen angel. *But she was here.* She's been here *the whole fucking time.*

Michael had told me they took her to heaven, promised me they wouldn't allow her body to die and rot in the earth. Now I was being told by a mortal that this soul, trapped in this body, the one that was hooked up to life support in front of me, had been traveling through millenniums in search of me. *How fucked up was this punishment?*

Should I have realized when I was torn out of my rotting

prison and thrown into Shane's dying body that some other kind of punishment was in store for me? Maybe, but I would have never thought about them involving the humans. How sick and twisted the angels were to punish me after my imprisonment, with the very person who I was punished for loving. *I liked it better in hell.*

I should have known she was Selah. Grace looked so much like her, almost identical. I should have grabbed her and kissed her the very first night I saw her. I would have never let her go. I should have told her who I had been. But, I just thought she was another girl, who just looked as breathtakingly beautiful as my Selah.

I should have known.

I could hear Tucker's dumb ass voice all the way down the hallway of the hospital. He came in with an enormous bouquet of the foulest smelling flowers I'd ever seen. Lea and Conner walked in a few steps after him, holding coffee cups, and wearing the same pinched lips. *Obviously, the flowers had offended them as well.* Or Lea told Conner I freaked the fuck out.

Lea handed me a coffee watching me cautiously, "Feeling better now? Anything new with Grace?"

I shook my head. "I've been just sitting here, quietly talking to her. People who are in a coma can hear everything around them, so we should constantly be talking or just reading to her." I looked directly at Lea pretending I was the calmest person alive. "She'll fight harder to come back if she knows how much she'll be missed here."

Lea sat next to Grace and began whispering in her ear. I took the opportunity to leave, because I needed to find Gabriel or Michael. Any of the archangels. *I needed to know why I had been lied to, but even more importantly, I needed to know who was trying to kill Grace and how I could save her.*

I knew undoubtedly that Carl Sumpton was not an option any longer, since I had received a message on my phone that his

231

body had been found near one of the entrances to Central Park while Grace was in surgery. So why had we traveled all the way in a blizzard to run from an already dead man to have someone else try to kill Grace?

Blake was no help either. He sat in another hospital room, ranting like a blithering idiot. He told the police that he had no recollection of anyone named Grace, or even how he got up to the vacation house. The last thing he remembered was drinking in a bar after work with Tucker and his uncle two days prior, some sort of celebratory thing about a case they had just gotten. He admitted to shooting up heroin in the bathroom of the bar and believed the whole situation was a bad high.

Nothing made sense.

I slumped past the nurses' station. One of the young nurses eyed me and smiled a mouth full of bright white teeth. "Sir," she called. "Did you know we have a chapel on the first floor of the hospital?" I stopped in my tracks. *Why in the world would she think someone like me would want a chapel?* "Many of the families of our patients here find peace with their situation after they've lit a candle there or said a prayer."

A large golden cross lay against her collarbone; it rose up and down with the rhythm of her breathing. Once again, it never ceased to amaze me, the well of faith that most humans had despite their ignorance of heaven. How they could believe in something but had never laid eyes on it; maybe that was what was so special about humans; that complete blind faith.

"Thank you," I nodded. I followed her pointed fingers to the elevator and pressed the down arrow. *Some sort of angel better be there to make sense of all this to me, because I was seriously starting to formulate some major apocalyptical visions in my head.*

The elevator doors opened to the harsh stench of alcohol and whatever cleaning fluid hospitals used to try to cover the smell of death. I choked back my gag reflex and stepped in. If

Grace's body was going to die, I needed to take her out of here. This was no place for her soul to linger. My body shuddered with fury at the thought of her dying here. It took every ounce of my strength not to scream out.

When the elevator ceased its downward motion, I could wait no longer, I pried the doors open with my hands and thrust them into the sleeves of the wall. The reoccurring beeping sound vaguely alarmed me that I might have broken the doors, but I didn't stop to care; there would be a hell of a lot more shit broken if I didn't find the answers to my questions.

I followed the faded brown signs towards the hospital chapel and yanked the doors open furiously.

The only source of light in the small room was from the blaze of glass-covered lanterns that posed as prayer candles. Leaning against the farthest wall was the archangel, Gabriel, with his mighty arms crossed in front of him.

I stormed towards him and got right in his face. Of course, the idiot made no move, not even an expression creased his features. *Heartless angel.* "Tell. Me. Everything." I growled.

Pushing off the wall, Gabriel took a step forward. Something about the slow way he moved made me think he wouldn't put up a fight. But, I felt a burst of raw energy pulsate from his body warning me to step back. I didn't. I wouldn't step back, *not now; not ever.* Not from *him.*

"I will not cower before you when it comes to her!" I hissed. "Tell me what's going on, Gabriel!"

He searched my eyes for whatever answers he needed to find. I felt the energy that pulsated off him in waves recede; my heart receded with it.

"Michael told me she would be taken to heaven; *spared*," I whispered.

Gabriel shrugged his shoulders awkwardly. "She was supposed to be, but she didn't want to go without you. So, I gave her a chance to try to find you."

I staggered back at hearing his answer. "She chose *me* over heaven?" I let my body collapse onto the rickety wooden bench that acted as a pew. I crossed my arms over my stomach to try to stop myself from heaving on the floor. All the anger drained out of me, only to be filled with the deepest sorrow I'd ever known.

Gabriel sat beside me and tilted his head to watch me. "I do agree with your thoughts, it was a foolish decision on her part. You are far from worth it. *Even when you did have wings.*"

"I was never *with her,* Gabriel. You *know* that, you saw what happened between us. You. Watched. Us. We kissed once, yet we were punished as harshly as the rest. We were INNOCENT! I didn't *violate* her. Now you're telling me that she's been searching for me? For two thousand years? *ALONE!* That's worse than anybody has ever been punished. That's worse than MY punishment."

Gabriel laughed heartily, which made my fists clench. "I disagree with you. If I didn't stop you, you would have been with her, *tarnished* her." He rubbed the back of his neck with his hand, making him look almost human. "I couldn't let you. And no, she wasn't alone, because she *always* had me here."

I snapped my eyes wide as his words touched my ears, "What the HELL does that mean?"

"She had my companionship. You know we are not supposed to really get involved in the affairs of humans, so I could only do so much to help her. I did lead her to you though, *eventually.*"

I jumped to my feet. "And in all your divine glory, it took you *over two thousand years?*" I could no longer control my rage. "You were my *brother,* Gabriel! And you BETRAYED me! *YOU KNEW I LOVED HER!*"

Gabriel offered me a small tight smile. "Well, let's just say I've struck out on my own for a while and I don't believe in that *angelic brotherly bond* any longer. Enough. Go sit by your human. Pray as hard as you can. See if *he* answers *you*. Then, if *he* does and Grace lives, see if she will forgive you for all your *time spent* with other human women. And after that, try and keep her alive as Grace."

"You won't help me, after everything you did? Do you want the apocalypse to come?"

"You wouldn't understand Shamsiel, or should I just call you *Shane*? You are more human than an angel now; you could do nothing to stop me. Apocalypse, very funny. You've been imprisoned in hell for thousands of years, how do you know that already hasn't happened yet. Good luck, you weak pathetic human." He took a step away from me to leave.

"Gabriel, I *need* her. I love her."

Gabriel snapped his head back and glared at me. "You're not the only one. *Shane*, forget the girl. *She's with me now.*" Then he was gone.

And so was all my hope forever seeing Grace open her eyes again. And there was a whole hell of a lot more to this story than Gabriel told me. None of it made any sense. *How was she with Gabriel now?* And the slight thought of why would she turn down paradise to search the world for me made me want to tear my own skin off. Someone was lying. There had never been a thought in my mind about her being left on earth. I would have never thought that was a possibility. Michael wouldn't have lied to me, he would have told me. He had agreed that I had done nothing wrong. I never pledged an oath with the other Grigori. I never took a human for a wife. I never fathered a Nephilium. I just kissed the human girl that I had fallen in love with on the last day I was to see her. Yes, if given the chance, I would have done so again. How could any man, human or angel, think past those lips? Even before the kiss, I went to the archangels Michael and Rafael for guidance. To try to find some way I could *become* human to be with her, or for some way to grant her immortality and wings. *Michael knew I loved her.* Why would Gabriel betray me? Confused anguish and chaos raced through my mind. Nothing was clear. Michael told me she'd be spared.

That's what was told to me, from the lips of an angel. *"The child will be brought straight to paradise."*

But she's been on earth the whole time while I was imprisoned in hell.

She was with Gabriel.

"She's with me now."

Chapter 15

When I returned to the room, Lea was alone, curled up next to Grace on her hospital bed. Life support machines chimed their morbid musical compositions in the background. Lea raised her tear-streaked face toward me; it pulled at my gut because I understood how desperate she felt for Grace to open her eyes.

I pulled one of the chairs that was lined against the wall right next to the bed and collapsed on to it. I slumped forward, leaned my elbows on my knees and pressed my forehead onto the hospital bed.

"Where did you go?" Lea asked sniffling.

"To the hospital chapel," I answered looking up at her. Her jaw dropped. *Well, that says a lot about what she thinks about my character.*

She's with me now.

She's with me now.

With me now.

Fuck me.

Gabriel did this.

Chapter 16

I woke to the soft sounds of rustling at the foot of the bed, the putrid hospital smell still assaulting my nose; beeping machines still ringing in my ears. I lifted my foggy head off of Grace's bed, where I had somehow fallen asleep holding her through all the tubes and wires that invaded her body with my ass still planted on a crappy hospital chair. I looked at her face in hopes that she had a smile to give me, but she didn't. My heart sank deep into my stomach; she hadn't moved at all.

Someone behind me was clearing their throat. *I didn't give a damn if someone was choking; I wasn't leaving Grace.*

"Shane? Shane Maxton?" The voice slowly dragged my attention from Grace's closed eyelids.

"Yeah?" I dragged myself back and sat fully up on the chair that I had pulled close to Grace's bed and fallen asleep on. My back was on fire from the position I had been in and I twisted and turned trying to get all the aches out of it. It didn't help.

"Stand up," the voice demanded harshly.

What? I snapped my eyes to the asshole that thought he could tell me what to do. Two uniformed police officers stood threateningly over the end of the bed. Both had their hands hovering over the open strap of their holsters; guns ready. *A bit trigger happy?*

"What's this about?" I asked calmly. I wondered what kind of music they listened to. Mad World fans? *Nah, probably just two disco-house-music-fist pumping prissy ass humans.*

"I told you to stand up! STAND UP!"

I laughed. Yeah, that just made them come at me. "Whoa, officers!" I said smiling. Lifting both my hands above my head, palms up, so no one decided to light me up with holes, I stood up. Slowly.

One of the officers tried to grab my arm while the other pulled out a pair of shiny silver cuffs. I felt my entire body turn rigid and on edge. I couldn't control the response that was about to surge from my fists. *There's no damn way I was going to let someone cuff me.* I lunged forward, barreling through both officers, causing them to bounce off me and flop to the floor on their asses. It was too hard not to laugh so I didn't even try to hold it in. The officers were screaming behind me telling me to stop. Laughing, I ran to the door and slammed up against Ethan's solid body. The look in my best friend's eyes told me I was screwed.

"I swear, Shane, I hope everyone is fucking **wrong** about you and you didn't do this to her. But in the meantime, until I know for sure..." That's when his fist connected with my face and the world went black.

* * * *

A feathery soft *something* brushed itself along my skin; *all of my skin. Every inch*, as if I were lying naked on a beach, feeling the first rays of the sun fall gently upon my body. It prickled all my hairs and aroused a deep desire of need in my soul; a need long forsaken. Warmth and light surrounded me, and then a complete and utter *love* engulfed me until I could no longer breathe correctly. I blinked my eyes open. What the hell did Ethan just hit me with? *His fist must be made of steel. I'm somehow going to have to find a way to get him to hit Tucker like that.* I would definitely pay him for it.

There were smells and sounds of thousands of familiar things; choirs of angelic voices and *purity; innocence.* My old dead heart stirred as my eyes opened towards the heavens and the shadowy passengers traveling home.

"Shamsiel? Shamsiel. Shane!" A voice called; a voice that I had longed to hear for centuries, *Michael* the archangel.

My eyes met Michael's. A fierce expression covered his usual stoic features. His brilliant blue eyes shined with pure light as his wings lay over my body. The touch of the angelic feathers stirred an ache in my soul of what had been taken from me. A tall man, *a human*, stood next to him; his features so familiar to me. I looked at both beings, folded my arms across my chest and narrowed my eyes. "Oh, this should be *entertaining*. Does anyone want to let me in on the joke? Am I being *punked?*"

"Shamsiel." Michael's features softened and I could feel the empathy roll off him in waves. *Interesting*, considering that he did nothing to stop me from going to Hell.

"Michael, just tell me what's going on," I said, standing up.

Michael looked toward the human standing next to him, "Shamsiel, this soul was Jacob Taylor, Grace's earthly brother. He has come to me in hopes of helping his sister."

My eyes flew to Jacob's and watched as he exhaled a harsh breath. "You're *him*? You're the angel that Grace was trying to find."

I smiled back. "I'm no angel. But, yes, I do believe that Grace was looking for me." I turned to Michael, "Why am I here in heaven? I was just in a hospital room, almost arrested, and punched in the face, so how did I get *here*? Oh, yeah and let's not forget my little visit with *your brother*, Gabriel."

"I brought you here, Shamsiel," Michael breathed. His eyes seemed full of love and desperation. "Shamsiel, Gabriel took all this upon himself. Your punishment. Selah. Everything. *I had no idea*." His hand ran softly over my face. "My brother, how I have missed you. Thousands of years..."

"Yeah, Michael there's nothing like thousands of lonely years to freeze your heart until it turns into the cold dead organ I hold in my chest. Let's not pretend that you care."

"You weren't supposed to be punished like the rest, and she was supposed to be spared..." Michael murmured.

Rage. Human blind rage took over. *And I let it*. After all, that's all I am now, *human*. "Well, LA-DE-FUCKING-DA, Michael! You promised me she'd be spared. And I've been in HELL, and Selah...Selah has been in Hell on earth! Forgive me if I don't feel quite so happy to see you!"

"Shamsiel, the archangels…"

"Don't! Just stop! Enough of this angel crap! It's so far from my real world, so far from any human's reality! You and the rest of them are so far-removed from us that you have no idea what is going on down there! You are supposed to be watching over us, protecting us! This is like being stuck in a really bad paranormal book that doesn't freaking end. Just tell me what to do to save her!"

Michael stood statuesque before me. His brows crumpled together and his eyes offered me a pained stare. "Shamsiel, we've been at war in the Heavens for thousands of years." He clenched his teeth and the muscles under his skin hummed with anguish. Drawing his fists together, he began pacing back and forth. "It all started with the Grigori and the human women marrying and creating the…Nephilim…"

Raking my hands through my hair, I huffed with impatience. *What good was this conversation doing for Grace? She was on earth dying and I'm having a history lesson an idiotic angel who doesn't remember that I WAS ACTUALLY THERE* when all this history went down. "Yeah. *Mikey.* I remember. I. Was. There." My fists tightened in my anger. "Do you remember? That's what I was condemned to Hell for, even though Selah and I did nothing wrong! All we did was kiss…we kissed *goodbye.*"

Michael was still muttering and rubbing his wrists and hands together. I must say that I had never seen this kind of behavior in an angel. Given that I was so freaking pissed off at Michael, I was quite enjoying his discomfort. *Greatly. Screw it, I mean really, what was going to happen to me? I'd go to Hell? Well, I had been there longer than any other place, so what-the-fuck-ever.*

Jacob stepped between our advancing bodies, jerking his hands in the air separating us. "You both have got to be kidding me! Look, Shamsiel-Shane, whatever you want to call yourself. I know you want to help save Grace and do whatever you need to be with her. And Michael, we understand that you had nothing to do with Shane getting the shit end of the stick because you were preoccupied with whatever it is you were doing..."

I barked out a laugh. "Holy crap. Are you patronizing us right now?"

Jacob's chin jutted out and he crossed his arms. Cocking his head, he deadpanned, "Well, if it shuts you both up and gets you to help the most innocent person out of all of this, then *yes.*"

I couldn't help smiling and nodding my head at him. "I see where Grace gets her tenacity from. You're right, I will do *anything* for her."

"No, Shane, she gets her tenacity and strength from years of torture."

Right.

Michael's hand grasped my shoulders and the weight of the world and all my hate and rage *disappeared.* Sliding his hand to lie against my chest, he sighed heavily and a tortured expression crossed his features. "Gabriel has laid claim to the girl. He thinks that if Grace and he...unite...that another generation of Nephilim will be created. It's his way of winning the war."

"NO. No one *UNITES* with Grace but ME! Now get me back down there and do some abracadabra angel magic and heal her!"

Michael's arms became heavier on me and his voice seemed to lose all its power, "It's isn't like it used to be, Shane. We can save her from where Gabriel is keeping her, *but* Grace will only heal if she wants to. The only thing that I *could* do with what you call '*my abracadabra angel magic*' is to return you home to be *what you were created to be.*"

My heart seemed to freeze, then pound and hammer against my chest with rushing blood, "I could go *home*?" My damn skin started to tingle. *TINGLE.*

Michael leaned forward, his pupils large, swimming in oceans of heavenly blue irises. "Yes, Shamsiel. You should have never been punished so harshly. You could take up arms and fight alongside me."

The muscles in my body, all of them, trembled and warmth radiated throughout my body. *Home?* Return home to be *what I was created to be.*

"And Grace?"

His chin lowered into his chest and his hands fell limp at his sides. "Grace will live out the rest of this life and will eventually die like any other human before her."

"And we don't ever see one another again, *right*? I stand guard and stay out of the lives of the humans and I never lay my eyes on her again, right?"

His voice was thick and low, "Yes."

My chest heaved, ears roaring with the rising pressure.

My heart pounded. It was all I could hear.

Thud.

Slammed against my chest.

Thud.

My skin tightened.

THUD.

Sweat poured from my pores.

THUD. THUD. THUD. THUD-THUD-THUD

Thud.

"Hell. No. An existence without Grace by my side is not acceptable. I stay human. We die human together. I'm no longer an angel, you ALL took that away from me. I'm not helping to fight in a war that isn't mine any longer. There's too many more important things on earth to fight for instead of all your bullshit – who wants to play God – when there is no way anyone could ever replace *him*."

Michael backed away, posture sagging. "You sound so...human...with your faith in a God that hasn't spoken to his angels...in millenniums."

I swallowed the painful lump in my throat, "That's because *I am* human. And maybe you should have as much blind faith as humans do. You'd be amazed what things their belief and faith can help them overcome."

Michael breathed in deeply and his eyes went vacant. "What if she doesn't want you any longer because you're *not* an angel? Will she love and accept you as Shane Maxton? Look at the life that Shane Maxton lived before you became him, how could anyone love that? He's not good enough for her, Shamsiel. You would give up everything for such a great risk? What if she wakes up from her coma and doesn't remember her past? What if she doesn't remember you?"

"I'll give it up, Michael, to be with her...she's been searching for me for centuries. I would rather take my chances on someone who had faith in my soul since the beginning of time, then those who would easily believe I would have turned my back on my brothers and bring evil to the world I was created to protect."

"And what if Gabriel continues to plague her on earth?"

"I guess that's my fight, Michael. And she's worth the fight."

Shaking his head slowly, Michael's body flickered in and out of focus, like an old silent movie running on a continuous wheel. The heavens faded around us into a dim light and shapes shifted and meshed together until the three of us stood before a narrow wooden doorway.

Jacob and I both stood at the opening of the room, but when he moved forward, I hesitated a moment behind him, unsure if my legs would hold me. I know I cried aloud, I know I sobbed her name, and I know I never felt such anguish as I did then. Grace lay before us beaten and bruised.

Jacob slowly pulled the chains that bound her broken mangled body to the small wooden chair she sat on. It was

244

toppled over, and knowing Grace, she had struggled her way there, bleeding on the cold hard floor, fighting *whoever* had chained her there. I collapsed to my knees in front of her and gently brushed her matted hair from her face. I heard my voice whimper her name. Her swollen battered eyes slowly blinked open to my voice. She tried to talk, she moved her lips, but only a small cry escaped. *If this is what Gabriel did to her soul in her subconscious, what has he been doing to her on earth for thousands of years? What lies has he told her? What horror has she seen while he tried to break her spirit?*

Hot tears fell from my eyes, blurring my vision of her. "Shh, baby, I'm here now. *Selah, it's me. I'm Shamsiel.*" I gently gathered her in my arms. Softly placing my lips to her forehead, I brushed my lips over her tender skin, "You're okay, Grace, this isn't really happening to your body, you're just in *perdition.* I'm so sorry." I lifted my eyes to hers to see if she understood where she was, that Gabriel had brought her to limbo, a state of purgatory in her own mind. Her body still lay safe, healing itself in her hospital bed, surrounded by people who loved her.

Her eyes spoke volumes to me, her body trembled and her lips tried desperately to move. "What was the gift you gave me?" she whispered.

My tears streaked faster down my cheeks, "Shh, Baby, it's okay..." *Shit, she doesn't think it's really me. Michael's right...Will she still want me, love me now that I'm not an angel any longer?*

"No...I need to know it's you...if after everything...it's you."

Michael's shadow fell over us, "Shamsiel, are you positive about your decision? Gabriel might still come after the girl here. We need to take her now."

I pulled her body closer and softly ran the tips of my fingers along her bruised face, as if I could wipe her hurt away. "Absolutely, Michael, she's worth it."

"So be it," Michael whispered. I knew he would never

understand. His angelic soul had never felt the freedom and love of being in a human shell.

Please, Grace...Selah...don't stop loving me because I am only human now. "No matter what happens from here, know that I have always, I will always love you and I will protect you always."

Her eyes grew wider and her breath came out in rough gasps. "What did you do?"

Would she ever forgive me for giving up my wings for her the minute I could have had them back? Was Selah like all the groupies Shane was used to, just in love with me for what I was? Being human came with such doubts and insecurities, they were nearly crippling to me. "If it weren't for me, you'd be where you're supposed to be. So this is my chance to let you start over. It's over, baby. Your punishment is over."

Lifting her body gently, I placed her into Michael's outstretched arms. "Will she remember this, Michael? Will she *remember me?*"

Michael cradled her tiny body in his great big arms and immediately her bruises disappeared and her cheeks filled with a beautiful splash of crimson. In this human form, I had lessened myself to, I envied Michael being able to heal her. That was supposed to be my job *and it should have been me.* But, I no longer could. "Have her love you as Shane and only Shane. For that, my dear lost brother, is all that you are, *for now.* You are not to tell her who you were, not until I have a final say in this. She may not remember any of this."

I weighed his words carefully. All I had to offer this beautiful creature was Shane and his pathetic selfish existence. And the hope that one day soon, we would be absolved for all our deeds and be given entrance back home to heaven one day. *For now, I would just be Shane.* And I couldn't tell her a damn thing. *I was screwed.* I just had to pray that she remembered all of this.

Turning my back, I walked away towards the unknown *mortal* human life that lay ahead of me. Then I heard Grace's voice scream out, "NO! No! It doesn't end this way! You can't leave me!" I turned back to run to her, but it was too late. She was no longer there. *Nobody was.* I was alone again, surrounded by a heavy darkness.

Out of the blackness, something pungent slowly crept past my senses and began burning my mouth and nose, traveling like lava through my nasal cavity and pooled into my lungs. Ammonia, *yeah that's the damn smell, ammonia.* Triggering my inhalation reflex to kick in, it felt as if someone grabbed my nose from the inside of my head and yanked on my brain. My eyes snapped open and I bolted upright. *Damn, that was really strong stuff, and why can't I move my arms.*

Where the hell am I now? White walls, hospital noises…lightheaded, dizzy, room spinning, my entire head was on fire and my eye socket throbbed like a bitch. A police officer sat in front of me with a small container of the offensive smell that woke me up. Smelling salts. *Oh right, now I remember, fondly I might add, Ethan knocking me out.* Well, my getaway seemed to be an epic fail because my wrists were pleasantly handcuffed behind my back. What a clusterfuck I woke up to. And it just got worse from there.

When I could get on my feet, the two officers dragged me through a small crowd of my friends. The only one able to look at me was Ethan and hatred filled his eyes. Lea clung to Conner and cried into his shoulder. *They all thought I did this to Grace?*

The officers hauled me through the exit and shoved me into the back of a patrol car. They didn't even tell me to watch my head like they do on television when I got in, so of course, my forehead slammed itself against the top of the open doorframe as they pushed me through. I sat silently in the back of the RMP, blood dripping down my forehead and into my fucking eye as the two officers joked about getting laid at some party the night before. It took twenty minutes for the cops to get to their precinct, and in that time, I could tell they were both lying about getting laid at that party the night before. *Doucheofficers.*

Next, they not so pleasantly dragged me out of the car and yanked me into a busy police station that smelled like piss and deeply fried Chinese food. Cops in dark blue uniforms walked around with papers flying out of their hands, radios blasting crimes and calls, yelling and throwing shit at each other. If I wasn't handcuffed it would've probably been fun to hang out with them.

Then they threw, *yes THREW,* me into a cell and locked me inside.

After two hours of getting to know the junkies in the jail cell I was kept in personally, a plain-clothes detective called my name and held the cage door open for me. As I was leaving, I bowed to my new junky friends and thanked them all for pissing and shitting right in front of me while asking me all about my music. Epic experience.

The detective, a tall muscular guy with a goatee, led me to a small interrogation room, offered me a cup of coffee with a sandwich and sat across from me. A small voice recorder lay on the table memorizing my words. The detective introduced himself as Detective Murrows and then *fist bumped me.*

"Listen, Shane. I get it. I understand." Murrows started running his hands over the blond peach fuzz that covered his head. "My girl pisses me off too. She just pushes me to the edge sometimes, so I get it."

Textbook interrogation technique - make the perpetrator *think* their crime was understandable so they would admit to it. The only damn problem was, I didn't commit any crime. "What is it that *you get,* Detective?" I asked sitting back against the cold metal chair, relaxing.

"I'm just saying, *I understand.* If I saw *my girl* dancing with some other guy, especially a loser like *Blake Bevli,* I'd want

248

to hurt her too. I'd want to hurt the both of them. I don't think that I'd be able to control *my anger* under *those circumstances.*" Murrows' caramel-crap colored eyes drew in a long blink and then looked slightly to the left and up; his lips tightened into a line and casually curled down. *This jackhat needed to work on learning how to make up better stories, he sucked at it.*

I offered him a small chuckle and nodded my head. "Looks to me like you're the one who should be behind bars then, because doing something to hurt *your girl, any girl* - I wouldn't understand *that.* And I sure as hell wouldn't have done anything like *that* to Grace no matter what happened between her and Blake." Giving him a wider smile, I continued. "However, I do agree with you on one thing – Blake Bevli is a loser."

Murrows stared at me through narrowed lids and blinked twice. *Maybe someone should get a professional to come in here and ask these questions, because I was kind of starting to feel sorry for this guy.*

"Maybe you don't understand, Shane. You are our prime, number one suspect. I can tell you're a man's man and don't like to be bullshitted, so let me lay it all out for you. Grace Taylor's blood was all over you. Shane, *it still is.* The EMTs and all your friends witnessed you holding Miss Taylor, explaining to everyone that it was *'all your fault.'* Shane, the EMTs saw the murder weapon in your hand when they got to the crime scene. If it wasn't for the snowstorm and one of our patrol cars had made it there to secure the scene prior to the EMTs moving the victim, you would have been arrested on the spot. So, why don't you just make this easy on everybody and tell me *the truth.*"

I looked him dead in the eyes. "That's all circumstantial evidence, Detective. I didn't do anything to Grace except try to get her to a hospital. Ask your EMTs who carried Grace's body through the snow to the ambulance, because it wasn't them. And the last I checked, this was America I believe, right? I'm innocent until *you prove I'm guilty*. Have fun doing that."

"Maybe you don't understand the weight of the charges they want to bring against you, Maxton. Attempted murder 2, Assault 1, Reckless Endangerment, Criminal Possession of a Weapon 2 and a slew of whatever else they could find to slap you with to put you away for a long time." Murrows started tracing circles on the top of the metal table with his index finger, "If you want me to help you with those charges, make them a bit *less* – you could lessen the *time* you get, all you have to do is come clean to me and I'll see what I can do."

I chuckled.

He leaned in closer and lowered his voice, "Come on, Shane, help yourself out here. If you don't, it's going to be a long time until you get to see her again. Hey, I mean, think about your band, man. Mad World isn't going to have their lead guy, think about what you're doing, Shane. Your band is hot right now. Don't you want to get back on stage as soon as you can?"

"I think you want my autograph. Maybe you want me to sing for you? Fuck you, Murrows. You know as well as I do that I didn't hurt Grace. So, go and find the person who really did. Yes, I found her there. Yes, I picked her up and carried her to the ambulance. Yes, I have her blood all over me. And yes, I gave the knife to the EMTs to bag up for the police. Check the prints on it, there will be more than just mine, I can promise you that."

Detective Murrows stood up abruptly, slammed his chair into the table, and stormed out of the room. Laughing, I looked towards the two-way mirror, shook my head and asked, "Does he have a lot of tantrums like this?"

I was then formally arraigned - charged for the attempted murder and attack on the girl I loved. The judge, being a hard-ass decided to remand me, deciding not to set bail and hold me until grand jury could indict me.

Every time I asked about Grace through the whole ordeal, every one told me she still hadn't woken up yet.

I asked about Grace every day, for seven days, while I waited in a cold cement jail cell. Each day, it was the same thing, she was still in a coma, and nothing had changed. I knew I made the right choice, I knew what I gave up to save her, *so why wasn't she coming back to me?*

With every passing day, I became more human than I ever was. Emotions ran raw through my body and clawed at my insides like a cancer. I barely ate the food they gave me and I couldn't tell how much time had passed, all I thought about was Grace and getting her back to me.

Grand jury came and went. I testified on my own behalf. Yes, I had said it was my fault, because I was supposed to protect her, *but I wasn't the one who tried to kill her.* However, given the circumstantial evidence against me that was presented, it was enough proof for a trial against me. So, I was transferred from a holding cell filled with the dregs of life to the majestic (read as shithole of the universe) location of Rikers Island, surrounded by the murky polluted waters of the East River, to await my trial; general population, housed in the dormitory cells of the Taylor House. Me, Shane Maxton, singer and lead guitarist of Mad World, once angelic being, surrounded by 14,000 prisoners who swore they were just as innocent as me.

Grace still hadn't woken up. *This shit wasn't going as I planned.*

Chapter 17

"Hey, Maxton. That girl of yours wake her pretty little ass up yet?" Luscious Carter, in for murdering his girlfriend *and her family (husband and kids)* - which he without a doubt committed, asked me. He seemed to try to take me under his wing. Said he loved music. Played a few instruments himself. Wanted to jam with Mad World. He was in for life.

"Nah, bro. Not yet."

"She'll come round, Rockstar, she'll come round soon."

"Hope so," I whispered.

"Then you could hire someone. Finish the job you fucked up on. Teach that bitch a lesson. 'Cuz, lemme tell you, Rockstar, when push comes to shove, you gots to start stabbing." Scratching at his chin he seemed deep in thought, "There's a trick to it. Gots to get them in the heart a few times, so no one can fix 'em."

"Holy fuck, Carter! Don't talk to me about it again. Shit, you are going right to fucking Hell."

He shrugged his shoulders and laughed, "Bet it ain't much different then here."

The small window in the prison library let a small amount of the brilliant sunlight in, lighting up the colorless prison walls. Every damn day since they locked me in, it was the same monotonous routine: get up from sleeping in a dorm filled with about a hundred prisoners, who smelled like piss and the worst body odor ever in existence. Get dressed in front of the prisoners, most of which called me *Rockstar*. Eat breakfast, and then back to the dorms until lunch, and then back to the dorms until dinner. There was a one-hour block of free time, either in a large gymnasium where we lifted weights, the prison library which housed about fifty books, or an outside courtyard each day at various different times.

There was a strict visitation schedule, which was based on

the first letter of each inmate's last name. Three visitors at a time, one time per visiting day, and all visitors needed to be registered before hand. Alex, Conner and Brayden came to see me every week. They told me all the bar gossip, anything going on that they thought might be interesting to me, but they always came with the same news about Grace. She hadn't woken from her coma.

Ethan visited me twice. The first time he visited all he did was grunt and yell, and then threatened to kill me if I got sentenced for her attempted murder. And if she didn't wake up, he'd kill me with his own bare hands.

The second visit was to give me the news that Blake overdosed and was dead. What could I possibly have said or felt about that? That's exactly how the real Shane Maxton's life ended. It was no surprise to me that Blake, Shane's old drug dealer went the same way.

It was five weeks, two days, six hours, fifty-six minutes and thirty-four seconds since I held a dying Grace in my arms, when a guard called my name over the crowd of inmates in the general pop recreational area. It was less than an hour before lights out and I was lifting weights with a bunch of bikers when they called for me. My heart almost burst from my chest thinking that someone had news for me about Grace.

There was no news about Grace.

The guards escorted me straight past the cells into the visitor's center and right to a young high maintenance looking district attorney who looked like she painted her business suit on and smelled of sex and vanilla body spray. She had her back to me and was busy talking on her cell phone. "...yeah, I have to 343 the case with that hot guitarist everyone is talking about...yeah he's so hot, you have to see how I dressed to meet him...so I'll be at the office in the morning with the papers since they're pushing this through so late...but I was thinking to offer to drive him home, *you know what I mean*..." She turned around, caught me smirking at her and ended her call immediately. Stumbling over her words, she basically informed me that I was free to go. I was being *'pulled and released since there was evidence that had come to light that excluded me without a doubt from being the perpetrator of the crime against Grace Avery Taylor.'* She wouldn't tell me what it was, but slipped me her card with her personal cell phone number on the back. *Yeah, you just wait by the phone there, sweetheart.*

"When do you think you'll call me?" She asked seductively.

I smiled at her, standing there in my fucking bright orange prisoner jumper wondering what psycho fucked up daddy issues or sexual dysfunction this chick might possibly have to give *me*, *prisoner #122773*, her damn number. "How about never? Is never good for you?"

"How about a ride home then? You're going to need someone to get you off this island, *Rockstar*. You don't strike me as someone who waits for a bus in the middle of the night."

"Nah, I'll swim if I have to. But thanks for the offer."

"You're not afraid of sharks, huh? You're that much of a *badass?*" She was slithering closer to me. *Ooookay, I'm still a prisoner. I still have the orange fucking jump suit on and all she sees is a badass rockstar. Nut.*

"Lady, how long have you lived in New York City? There's no way that sharks live in the East River. They all seem to work for the district attorney's office."

It took her a minute, but I think she understood my meaning.

I was handed back my personal effects in a sealed manila envelope and given my bloodied clothes back. Nice. My clothes covered in Grace's dried blood. I sat down heavily on the hard wooden benches they offer the wonderful prisoners and their visitors here for comfort, and clung to the bloodied clothing. All I wanted to do was get the hell out of this prison, off this damn island and head straight for Grace's hospital room. *I wasn't leaving her side until she woke up.* But showing up with clothes stained with her blood would probably get me lots of attention from the authorities.

As soon as the district attorney chick saw me hugging and breathing in my bloody clothes, she left in a hurry. I winked at her on the way out just to creep her out more.

The person I least expected to walk in through the prison doors came to get me.

Tucker and his father came with a new set of clothes for me, signed some papers as my lawyers and offered to drive me home. I nodded silently and followed them out to my freedom.

"I know it's past midnight, but instead of home, can you take me right to the hospital so I can see Grace?" I asked Tucker as soon as I sat in the backseat of his father's car.

Tucker spun his head around all exorcist style and popped his eyes open wide, "Are you shitting me? Grace woke up like a week and a half ago and she's been home locked in her room not talking to anyone but Lea. Nobody told you? I thought Alex and Conner were coming here like every day to visit you. What the hell, bro, shows you who your true friends are."

"She's okay?" I suddenly felt lightheaded and ready to pass out. *Why hadn't anybody told me? Why hadn't anybody put me out of my damn misery?* Tears stung my eyes and my heart felt a thousand times lighter; she was okay.

"Yeah, bro, she's fine. I haven't seen her yet though. Lea says she doesn't want to talk to anyone yet."

"Who do I thank for clearing me of the charges against me?" I whispered.

Tucker's smile tightened. "The detective's finally showed up at Grace's apartment earlier this afternoon to give her a formal interview and she told them it wasn't you. She said it was some stranger, an intruder who they happened to catch in the house."

We drove the rest of the way back to our apartment in silence. Everyone seemed to be sleeping when I got home so I just jumped in the shower to scrub the last five weeks of my life away, wondering the whole time what was going to happen when Grace and I laid eyes on each other again.

Chapter 18

When I heard a familiar giggle at the end of the hallway my heart just about stopped and my feet felt nailed to the floor. Sliding along the wall to help her stand, Grace, *my Grace*, was making her way out of Ethan's bedroom. She stumbled out, closing the door with a thud and fell, dropping the sexy as sin shoes she was holding in her drunk little hands. She slapped her hands over her mouth to stifle her giggles and *my* hands instantly balled into tight fists.

Seeing her for the first time in almost six weeks, I breathed in what felt like my first breath since I had last laid eyes on her. But as I inhaled, all I could smell was the bitterness of the whiskey and Ethan's nasty-ass cologne pouring off her skin. It didn't take much for me to realize what she must have been doing in Ethan's room with the way she was haphazardly dressed. A pair of loose fitting ripped up jeans that barely stayed up over her lower hips and the tightest little damn shirt I had ever seen adorned her body. The words *All I Need are Shoes, Booze and Bad boys with Tattoos* were spread tightly across those freaking gorgeous breasts I loved, and the shirt seriously ended just underneath them, showing off her entire tight creamy flat stomach. Her hair was disheveled and I swear she had that freshly fucked look to her that I'd been aching for weeks to put on her face myself.

Describing the feeling of my heart completely being torn to shreds in that moment, I don't think I will ever correctly express the utter torment that ripped through my body. There were no words for the despair. No way to describe how lost and hurt I felt standing there, watching *my world* leave another man's bedroom. I couldn't think a straight thought through the hurricane of human emotions that annihilated my heart.

When she saw me, she froze.

"What the hell?" I heard myself growl. *And oh, yes it was*

257

a fucking animalistic growl. I couldn't take it, I couldn't take the way those beautiful silver eyes looked at me. Wide-eyed and paled faced, Grace flinched away from the shock of me standing in the hallway catching her. *Sur-fucking-prize*. Thoughts of Ethan's arms wrapped around her, of his lips on her's, made me want to punch my fist through the drywall. Fucking pictures of them flashed in my mind as if I had caught them on a freaking Nikon instead of her just tiptoeing her drunk-ass walk of shame out of his room.

"What. The. Hell?" I repeated louder.

Then she had the damn audacity to bite that plump lower lip of hers and look at me like I was willing to take Ethan's sloppy seconds. *Oh hell, no.*

"Did you just *come out* of *Ethan's fucking bedroom*?" I screamed.

Grace's eyes widened even more and then she was gasping for air. A deep burst of crimson spread across her cheeks, and I fucking hated myself right then because it instantly became my favorite color. It killed me, it fucking killed me that this human could throw me away like I wasn't once a god and I still *loved* her soul. It. Killed. Me.

She shook her head and it wobbled her whole body. "Yeah, but nothing..." she started to deny what I knew had probably happened.

My vision blurred, my stomach churned and I seriously starting planning to scratch my own eyeballs out if I began crying in front of this girl. "Save it. It doesn't matter." I walked past her and my bare arm grazed the softness of hers and I heard a low gasp, barely above a breath. Disgusted with myself even more, because it was my lips it had slipped through. The anger of what she had done to *me*, to *us* made my blood boil hot in my veins. God forgive me, I wanted her to hurt inside just as much as I did. I stopped moving, our arms still just barely touching, and I leaned my head down leveling my eyes to hers. "Don't worry about locking the door behind you, we have easy ass like you coming in and out of here *all* the time."

A tear trickled down her cheek and she leaned away from me, slumping heavily against the wall. "We were talking..."

I laughed, "Right, was that before or after you fucked him? Save it, why the hell would I care? I don't want to listen to the blow by blow of your night."

Clenching her fists she tried to straighten up off the wall but failed. "Fuck you, Shane!"

After all the hell I just went through, after everything I had given up for her, *fuck me?* Uncontrollable rage pulsed through my body and I felt disgustingly human and weak with the power my emotions had over me. How every human could fight against blowing their own damn brains out to stop these intense, insane emotions, was a complete mystery to me. I wanted out. I wanted out of this body. Out of this world. I wanted my wings back.

Fuck me? I lunged at her and swung her body over my shoulder, caveman style. *I know, I'm a complete dick* but I swear every day being in this human body was making me more irrational. *No, I wasn't being irrational*, she slept with Ethan while I was getting out of jail, after giving up any chance I ever had to get back into heaven, all *for her!* I swear I felt the testosterone spike through my balls and spread out across the hallway. For a split second, I looked down to see if my skin was turning green and I'd be busting out of my shirt all Hulk-style. No dice. I seemed to be just temporarily fucking insane. I grabbed hold of the back of her thighs and carried her through the hallway toward the *Bone Room*. She didn't even scream.

Thrusting open the Bone Room door as hard as I could, it smashed up against the wall inside the room and echoed its crash like thunder through the apartment. I plopped her down next to the door and stood over her, my body wracked with the tremors of my anguish. "Fuck me? *Fuck me?* You want to go in the Bone Room with me?" I dropped, crouched down to her level and slammed both my palms against the wall on either side of her face. The drywall cracked beneath my palms. *Holy crap, rein it in, Shane, you're being borderline abusive here.* Yeah, I couldn't stop myself even if God stood before me, "Because I could really get off on some head right now, since I've been in *fucking jail* for over a month." I slid my hands down the wall slowly, never breaking eye contact with her. "I usually don't like my girls still wet from Ethan, but hey, if you're game...but if not, get the *fuck* out of my hallway."

Then Grace slapped me.

Her hand hit me so hard that my whole face moved, and I deserved it, I know I did. But I wanted her to hurt inside. I would never hit her, ever. But I wanted her to feel *this...this* emptiness that she left me with. Why the hell did she have to give herself to someone else? She was *mine.* Bile rose in the back of my throat as images of her legs wrapped around Ethan's waist danced like sugarplums in my head. I was losing it.

She slid herself up along the wall, never taking her steely gaze away from me. "Don't you ever lay your hands on me again, Shane. Get the hell out of my way," she whispered. The way she looked at me then, I don't know if I could ever handle seeing Grace look at me with that expression again; utter disgust. It killed me.

I stood up slowly, eyes still locked on hers. *God, let me walk the hell away from her, give me the strength because all I want to do is kiss her.*

She stormed past me slamming my shoulder with hers, and stalked down the hallway. I watched her pick up her shoes and head for the front door, and the way her outfit looked from behind caused a violent streak of heat to course through my insides. Grace's shredded pants gave the world an intimate view of her perfect curvy bottom, "*Sweet* fucking pants, I bet Ethan really enjoyed that hot little ass of yours. Sure you don't want to change your mind about the Bone Room?" My voice trembled.

She flipped me the bird. Then she left. *Just left.* No more fighting, no more denying any of it. Nothing. Not even a fucking *sorry. It didn't look like she remembered shit that happened when I rescued her from where Gabriel hid her while she was in a coma.* She had no clue who I had been and she moved on.

Storming into my room, I slammed the door hard behind me and sat on the floor clutching my chest, the ache was unbearable for any human and I wondered if the pain would actually kill me. I couldn't stand to breathe without her, so I stayed on the floor and waited to die.

I woke up swinging when an icy cold glass of something splashed across my face. Five guilty-ass-mother-fuckers stood over me. Conner, Lea, Alex, Brayden and Ethan. Alex, of course, was holding the glass, smiling.

"I'd start running, Alex, because as soon as I get up out of this bed..." I looked around me...*okay, I was on the floor...* "As soon as I get off the floor I'm going to kick your ass. Seriously? Why the hell am I on the floor?" *Oh, right that's where my heart broke last night.*

Alex's face reddened and he gave me a serious expression, "Look, Shane. We all came in here to say how sorry we were for not believing you and..."

"Forget it," I cut in as I got myself off the floor. "Doesn't matter. Someone has just got to tell me what the hell happened and who it was that actually did it. And why the hell nobody told me that Grace woke up and that she's okay."

Alex looked over to Conner and Lea and held his hands up in the air in surrender. "That's all on Conner and Lea, dude. I was all for telling you but...shit Shane, everybody thought you tried to hurt her, why would we tell you anything?"

I raked my hands through my hair. None of this mattered. And I wanted Ethan out of my room. "Lea, can I talk to you alone for a minute?"

261

Alex shook his head at me, "I'm not leaving this room until I know we're good. And you're okay."

I offered Alex a smile. "We're good. Now all you back stabbing losers leave. I have to talk to Lea," I said playfully.

They all filed out and I closed the door behind them. I didn't even turn to look at her. "I caught her coming out of Ethan's bedroom this morning. Tell me what the hell is going on, Lea."

"I don't know what's going on, Shane. She's broken. Shane, she locked herself in her bedroom until yesterday, when we forced her to talk to the detectives. Then Conner, Ethan and I talked her into going to the bar. I don't know what the hell happened with her and Ethan. The only thing I do know is that she knows the Shane you were before her coma was the angel that she'd been looking for, for over two thousand years and now you're not. *You* tell *me* what's going on. She thinks her angel left her, *did he, Shane?*"

I looked into her pleading eyes. "Get this straight right now, Lea. I am not an angel. *I'm Shane.* Whatever I once was, was given up, *for her.* And I would *never* leave her."

"Holy crap," she smiled. "What the hell are you waiting for then? Go get her and tell her."

"Yeah, sure, Lea. I'll get on the end of the line that starts in front of her bedroom door. Right behind Ethan. Besides, I can't tell her."

"Kind of like the line she's been thinking she was standing in for you. And why can't you tell her?"

"I'm not allowed to. End of story."

To hell with all of it. I gave up everything for her. And she handed it to Ethan. I bolted out of my room and ran straight to her apartment with Lea yelling at me the whole way.

Flying down her hallway, I kicked my foot at her door. Hard. And it freaking hurt. So what the fuck did I do? I did it three more times. Yeah.

"Open the door, Grace!" My yell scorched my throat like acid. My fist pounded on the door next. *This was it; I was fucking done with this girl, I...*

Her bedroom door swung open.

Ah. I was struggling for air.

I tried to take my eyes off of her. I swear to you *I tried.* They would have jumped out of my damn skull if I moved my sight away from her, I truly believed. She just took my fucking breath away. My hands gripped her doorframe, my knuckles turning white. I fought my entire body from lunging myself at her and slamming my lips against hers. She. Was. In. Her. Underwear.

My eyes traveled slowly over her creamy *bare* legs that went on *forever.* My heart rate just about tripled when a burst of goose bumps broke out along her skin. My gaze moved along the length of her inner thighs and gradually rose, then lingered on the tiny V-shaped black lace of her panties. My fingers itched to pull that lacy material to the side and taste her, dip my tongue deep inside her until she called out my name. My name; *no one else's.* I continued sweeping my eyes across her skin to her bare stomach and followed along the curves of her full breasts that were lying heavily against the lacy of her tiny bra. Rosy, perfect nipples peeked out through the lace. My jaw twitched painfully to nip at them and I clenched my teeth together tight. When my eyes finally found hers, my breath was heavy, my eyes wide and my arousal was throbbing against the inside of my jeans. "Ah," was all that came out of my damn mouth. There was no blood in my body; it was all pooled in my dick. I thought I would fall forward with the heaviness of it.

She placed her hands on her hips. "So, you're banging and kicking at my door so you can just tell me...*ah?*" Her. Smile. WAS. INTOXICATING.

She slept with Ethan. She slept with Ethan. She slept with ETHAN. DO NOT TOUCH HER! My body leaned into her room and I had to lock my arms in place to stop myself from going any further. "Band meeting tomorrow...at eleven...at the studio," I whispered hoarsely. I said nothing else; I just stared into her eyes and slid my hands through my hair wishing she could have been *mine*.

Lea stepping up next to us giggling, which stopped me from completely making an ass out of myself, because I was seriously about to reach my hands out to touch her. I glanced at Lea, who was smiling idiotically, and I stormed down the hallway away from Lea and that pure mind blowing jet black haired orgasm standing in the doorway next to her. I believe I might have growled as I left. Yep.

The rest of the afternoon and most of the night I spent drunk in my living room with Alex and Conner playing video games. Well, no not drunk. Completely and utterly trashed.

There are only five things I remember from those hours of my life that *I will never get back*:

1) I somehow ate a chocolate in the shape of a penis. *It was delicious.*

2) Beer shot out of Alex's nose. *Twice.*

3) I explained in detail to Alex how soft Grace's lips were. *Then I drew him a diagram to explain it further.*

4) I hid all of Tucker's underwear in my freezer. *I ran them under the faucet first to get them nice and wet.*

5) And at some point, I had a conversation with Alex and Conner that went something like this: "Okay, okay just shut the hell up for a minute, this is really-really important. We need to find someone to take us to *Taco Bell*. (Alex drunkenly raises his hand) Just, no—no way, you can't drive us. You're too drunk. So listen, I will buy whoever takes us to Taco Bell...I'll

264

buy them anything they want...I'll even buy them the car. (Alex drunkenly raised his hand again.) Alex, you want a burrito? A burrito? Buurrrrittttooooo, wow. That's just a fucking awesome word. I'll give gas money. (Conner says something incomprehensible) I just...shut up for a minute...if I don't get *Taco Bell*, you're going to see a side of me that you wished you hadn't seen. I know you think I'm joking, but I'm not. I'm not. I need...I need a fucking burrito. From *Taco Bell*."

I woke up the next morning on my couch with Alex slumped up against my shoulder surrounded by, I shit you not, fifty-four wrapped Taco Bell burritos and a slew of open half eaten ones.

I don't remember eating even one of them.

My head throbbed and my body ached, but I still threw on my running gear and forced myself to run with Conner through Central Park. We went back to Lea's apartment as we did every morning for coffee or water. I prayed that Grace was still asleep.

Sweaty as hell, I leaned against their kitchen cabinets and downed an entire bottle of water as fast as I could. I wanted to get out of there before either of the girls woke up.

As I swallowed the last gulp, my *kryptonite* walked in. She wore an old button up lumberjack shirt that fell off her shoulders and barely reached the curves of her bottom. Then, can you imagine what she did? She stood on her slippered tippy-toes and reached up for a coffee cup and that old button up lumberjack shirt slid up above her ass, giving me a view that made my damn knees go weak. *Damn, she was perfect*, and I could barely stop myself from grabbing that backside and burying myself inside...My thoughts stopped when I got an elbow in the gut from Conner, who was laughing his ass off at my expression. I probably looked like I was already having sex with her. Tossing my empty water bottle in the garbage, I stormed out growling. *Yeah, I've been doing a lot of growling lately around her, I know.* "Catch you later, Conner," I called out when I reached the front door.

I sulked all the way home. I locked myself in my bedroom, ignoring everyone who knocked on my door and listened to my iPod at an earsplitting volume. Every song reminded me of her. *Every song.*

I paced my room, panicking. My anger grew and grew until I felt like my forehead was going to explode from the pressure. How the hell was I supposed to get off this rock? There was nothing left for me here.

I stormed into the studio at a quarter to eleven and waited. The guys came in after me, watching me suspiciously, just waiting for me to blow.

At exactly eleven o'clock Grace opened the door to the studio. *She didn't have her guitar.* My gut twisted, *this was it.* I watched her walk in and shoot a small glance at Ethan, then smiled shyly at him. Of course, the douchebag gave her a *'I know what you look like naked because I banged you smile.'* They didn't kiss hello, which surprised me, because if I had just spent the night with her, everyone would know she was *mine.*

"There's our gorgeous girl!" Alex called out from behind his keyboard running out from behind it to grab her in a hug and swing her around like a little kid. It made my heart ache, that everybody was allowed to love her in their own way but *me.*

"Yea! Your casts are off," she cheered when he let her go. *God, she was so damn beautiful when she smiled.*

"Yeah, yesterday. Grace, my love, you look hotter than ever," he laughed. *Yeah, Alex, she does.*

"Fine. Let's get this shit over," I murmured as I stood up from the couch I was sitting on. I walked forward folding my arms across my chest. "Yeah, so Alex is back. We really don't

266

need another guitarist."

Silence and glares bitch-slapped me back in the face. But not from Grace, from Grace came a sad smile and a nod, as if she *agreed* with me.

"Whoa, what the hell?" Alex asked. "Dude, I'll be only on keyboard now, Grace does guitar, she blows me outta the water anyway." He gave her a wink, "Did you like when I said you *blow me*, that part?" *Great, now I'm picturing her blowing Alex AND Ethan.*

She winked back at him, smiled and gave him an eye roll. *She was going to be the death of me.*

Brayden walked over closer to Alex and they both glared at me, "Yeah, this is stupid. Let's just get to practice so we can set up a gig at Boozer's, it's been weeks, dude."

Screw this crap, I'm just going to say it. I hooked my guitar strap over my shoulders and hung my guitar in front of me. I locked my eyes onto hers. My stomach rolled, but I wanted to have my say anyway. I was angry, I was lost, and I was completed heartbroken. "Yeah, well we got rules in this band. Nobody can sleep with another band member, so Alex stays on guitar *and* keyboard." I held her stare, waiting for her to break, to shatter, to fall to pieces from my words. *Anything! Tell me you didn't sleep with him, tell me you're still Selah and I didn't lose everything for nothing, tell me you remember me, tell me love me even though I'm not an angel any more.* Tell me I'm enough as the damaged man I am.

Alex's eyebrows pulled together, "Dude, I haven't slept with any one of you motherfuckers. You're the pretty boy who was in jail for five fucking weeks, *Sir Fuckmebung.*"

"I didn't sleep with any one of you guys either," Brayden called out. "Now can we just play?"

Grace kept her silver eyes locked on mine. "Um, I think Shane is talking about me." The room stilled. Then all eyes were on her and mouths dropped to the floor, including mine. "Well, now that that's settled...I really did have a blast playing with you guys, and Alex," she snapped her eyes away from mine and looked to Alex. "Anytime you want to bring your guitar over to my place, I would love to play with you. I'll probably see you guys at the bar sometime." Then she turned on her heels and walked out of the studio and down the hall as if she didn't just stab me in the heart, twist the blade *and lick it fucking clean* in front of all my damn friends. I gagged back vomit.

The studio door wasn't even fully closed yet and Alex was yelling, "Which lucky son of a bitch got to tap that perfect ass?"

I grabbed at the microphone in front of me, switched my guitar on and started playing and singing. Bloodhound Gang's *Ballad of Chasey Lain*. I just changed the words and kept the same rhythm, but I knew she would know the song. I was no longer in control of myself. At all.

Hey Grace Taylor
I'm singing this for you
Before your next screw...
Oh, but the chorus, the chorus I screamed...
I bet you had a lot dick Gracie
But you ain't had mine...

"What the hell, Shane?" Ethan said as he ran out of the studio after her.

"Yeah, go run to her, Ethan! Go make her *feel* better!" I screamed. Yeah, then dumbass me tore my guitar strap off my body, tossed my guitar on the floor and went to run after them.

Alex and Brayden rushed me and tossed me to the floor before I could get to the door. Alex had me in a headlock, "Shane, what the hell is going on with you? Who lit the fuse on your tampon? Calm it down! You're acting like a crazy jealous girlfriend." I didn't stop though. I jumped up and continued walking towards the door with Alex swinging from my neck.

"Brayden, a little freaking *help* here!"

Brayden lunged at me and wrapped his arms around my legs causing the three of us to fall over each other and land heavily on the floor. Brayden kicked at my shin, "*Oh my God*, you are acting like Tucker right now, dude."

"Yeah, Shane I totally agree with Bray right now. What the hell is going on with you? Damn it, Shane, are you back on drugs? Because, I swear to God if you are, I will personally kick your ass out of this band, all the way to rehab. I'll call your freakin' *mother*, this time," Alex snapped.

"No!" I dismissed his stupid question rolling my eyes. "Are you kidding me? I haven't used anything in months. Want me to piss in a cup?"

Pushing them off, I stood up and wiped my hands on my pants. "Did you ever stop to think about what the hell it might be like to go to jail because all your friends think you're a piece of shit? And it doesn't help anything, that I'm fucking in love with her."

They both gasped out loud, jaws hitting the floor.

Ah crap. That wasn't supposed come out of my mouth.

Alex reached out to me theatrically then pulled his asinine hand back to touch his throat then his lips. Then he pointed to me, *with even greater theatrics*, eyes all wide, "You...you said the *L* word."

"Oh, shut up. It doesn't make a damn difference anyway. She doesn't even freakin' like *me*." I said stomping out of the studio.

I walked out of the building only to see Ethan and Grace smiling at each other and talking on the sidewalk. I walked past them without saying a word. There was nothing left to say. Yeah, I *was* a dick. But I also *was* an angel and I gave that up for *her*.

Chapter 19

I walked right to Central Park and tossed myself heavily on a bench. I sat there until I noticed jet-black hair pulled back tightly in a high ponytail and the scent of the sweetest wildflowers run right past me. She bolted down the runner's path without a glance my way and I watched her until she was a tiny spec along the path and the evergreens obscured my view.

Ten minutes later, I found myself locked in my bedroom with Lea knocking on my door threatening to unhinge my door if I didn't let her in. She was relentless.

I opened the door not even two inches wide and peeked at her through the small opening. "I'm not up for talking, Lea."

"Great, you sexy shithead, because all I want you to do is listen. I'll talk s-l-o-w," she snapped. Then she shoved her tiny little body through the door, which caused it to smack right into my head with a sickly thud. "You deserve that, maybe it will knock some sense into that gorgeous empty head of yours."

She dove right onto my bed and cuddled up in my blankets. "How many girls have you had in this bed, Shane?"

I gave her a sad smile and kicked at the foot of my bed. "It was only Grace until the second you threw yourself on there. What in the world would *Conner* think?" I teased her.

She giggled in the way that only Lea does and sat up. "Conner would think you skipped the vaccine they were handing out against *dumb-ass-ness*. Listen, Studley Maxton, I am definitely on your bed but don't let you mind wander, it's far too small to be out there *all* by itself," she quipped.

I forced out a laugh, "You're brilliant. Where do you get all this shit from?"

"Grace," she replied simply.

Collapsing on the end of my bed, I sighed heavily. "What are you doing here, Lea. I'm really not in the mood for your banter; I have too many problems to figure out right now. I don't want anymore."

"Okay, so let me guess. You are just going to ignore what's going on. Kick her out of the band and that's it? What, get drunk tonight, forget about her with some other skanky girl?"

"It's unbelievable how many problems go away by simply ignoring them and getting drunk. You should try it," I sighed.

"So, I have no choice but to follow along with both your issues and bullshit and watch the two of you destroy each other over and over again?" Lea asked.

"God, Lea. I'm so freaking in love with her it's going to literally kill me, I actually feel the pain of my broken heart. How do people live through this? She slept with my best friend after I gave up everything for her."

Lea nodded her head and slowly got off the bed. Walking to the door, she stopped just before she opened it. "You fucked half of Manhattan, Shane. Get over yourself. If you don't tell her who you are, everything that the both of you ever went through is worth nothing. And you'll be the one that's throwing it all away."

She slammed the door behind her.

So, straight to the bar I went.

Making myself comfortable at a table all by myself, I ordered a beer and a burger. I had five minutes of peace before one of the barfly's named Marie slithered next to me, and before even saying hello, rubbed her hands under the back of my shirt.

"I'm not in the mood."

"Since when is Shane Maxton not in the mood?"

"Since I first laid eyes on you."

"Don't be a dick, Shane."

"But that's what I am, Marie. That's exactly what I am."

Unfortunately, she stayed by my side and talked my ear off for I don't even know how long. She tried playing with my hair. She showed me how she performs oral sex with my bottle of beer. She took my phone and downloaded a bunch of stupid free apps. I ignored everything. I just focused on getting the hell out of this place and forgetting about Grace. She made her choice. I had to forget about Grace. Then it hit me how impossible that was because she was in every fiber of my being, she's tattooed on my soul. Always was and always will be.

I left Marie in mid-sentence and sauntered off to the bathroom. I didn't know how many drinks I had at that point, but I was really buzzed and I didn't think I could handle seeing anyone else. However, when I walked out of the bathroom, Conner, Lea and Alex were sitting at my table waving to me. Brayden and Ethan were at the bar talking to Ryan. Grace wasn't there yet. *Damn, now I had to stay.*

Okay, time for my game face. She was coming here, Lea is going to call her, and I knew it. Time to fucking pretend that this shit wasn't killing me. I couldn't start flipping tables and throwing people off her like I was her avenging angel.

I sat down hard on the wooden chair and gripped the table until my knuckles whitened and my fingertips ached. *God, get me through this.*

"You know, dude, I can drive you to the insane asylum before you throw yourself off a bridge," whispered a voice blowing hot in my ear.

I jumped at Alex's words and whirled around to face him, "What the hell? You scared the shit out of me, you dick. Why the hell are you all up in my ear whispering to me?"

"Well, I apologize, you miserable, whining, self-loathing pussy. I was sitting right next to you here, calling your name for a few minutes, but you looked like you were lost in Poor Me Land."

"Whatever, bro. I'm fine. I have no clue what you're talking about..."

And even though I warned her, Marie kept trying to change my mind about tonight's lack of *sex-capade* plans. She sat on my lap and softy pecked kisses all over my neck and chin.

I kept my hands off her by leaning one arm over the back of an empty chair and the other hand peeling the label off my beer, one long strip at a time; my new drinking pastime.

I was vaguely aware of the conversation that was spilling out around the table around me. Alex sat on one side of me crooking his finger down the front of one of the waitresses' shirts as she giggled. Brayden, Ethan, Conner, and Lea sat across from me and were talking in some heated conversation about another band, *Vixen4*, with their hands flailing about. Tucker, like the dog he was, was sitting drunkenly ogling Marie and poking her arm to get her attention. I tried four different times to get her to sit on his lap instead of mine, but she said she wanted to hear me sing later. *That wasn't happening.* The smell of her damn perfume was choking me.

Snapping me out of my funk, I felt a slight tingling feeling at the back of my neck and I knew. *I knew* Grace was there. With knee high black stiletto heeled boots, tight low rise hip hugging jeans, halter top, wild jet black waves and lipstick the color of deep red wine, she sauntered into the bar.

I started to hyperventilate. *Crap, just kill me now.*

"Wow, now that's a beautiful sight right there. Hel...lo, Grace," Tucker called out to her. Everybody turned their head to look at her.

She glanced at me quickly and looked away. The knife plunged in again. Which caused my mouth to vomit up bullshit, and so I found myself lifting my beer to her, "Hey look who it is, boys, the Holy fucking Grail of Pussies." Wow. I. Am. Drunk. But, I gave her my best smile.

Alex reached over and shoved me on the shoulder, "What the fuck is your problem today, jackhole? Sit down, Grace, and don't mind Shane, I think he's on the rag." He looked me straight in the eyes, "Here's another L word for you, Shane, *LOSER.* Oh, here's another, *LONELY.*"

Lea pulled over a chair for her and sat her right across

273

me, so I did what any mature man who once was an angel would do; I shoved my tongue down Marie's throat. The L word *sucked*.

Grace gasped, which made me stop because it confused me. I knew she couldn't have cared less who I kissed, *right?*

The waitress who was hanging all over Alex stood up, "Hey, Grace, what can I get you tonight?"

Marie tried to continue our kiss, but I spoke right into her mouth to the waitress. "Mind Erasers with straws, Mollie. And keep them coming, it's time to play a *game*." I drunkenly stood up, while the bar spun, and Marie fell to the floor and yelped. I looked down at her and laughed, "Whoops, *psf*. Better sit in your own seat, Marie, this shit is going to get wild." She had pink lipstick all over her face, which made me laugh harder until I locked eyes with Grace again.

"Marie, wow." Grace looked me dead in the eyes smiling. "Shane, I'm impressed, usually you don't ever get their first names. She *must* be *special*."

Okay, I way over thought my ability to speak correctly when all I could reply was, "Gah." Like it was a serious statement.

Tucker burst out laughing, "Yeah, for tonight at least. Right, Shane!" He slapped his hands against the table. "Hey, Grace, you need someone special for tonight?" *I might punch him in the nuts later. It was way too heavy to lift up my hands to him right now.*

Ethan stood up, walked behind Tucker laughing, and smacked him in the back of his head. "Shut the hell up, are you freaking twelve? Haven't you hit puberty yet, did anyone ever teach you how to speak to women?" he laughed.

Gah. Yes, that was my thought, again. Ethan is being all sweet and shrivelous...*shrivelous?* That's not the right word. Chivalrous? All knight-and-shining-armourish. *The fuck do I know.* Backstabbing best friend. "How freaking sweet, Ethan's protecting the Holy Grail," I snapped.

"Oookay!" Lea cut everybody off. "What drinking game are we playing?" She gave me that bugged eyed stare of hers that said, *'shut the eff up.'*

Perfectly timed, Mollie placed a Mind Eraser in front of me and I swiped it off the table. Okay, it was in front of Alex but she didn't give me mine fast enough and I needed it more. "We're going to play a little game called Answer This. Rules are, you get to ask anyone a question and they either have to answer TRUTHFULLY, or if you're a pussy and don't want to answer, you have to drink your Mind Eraser. Whole damn thing through the straw." I stared straight at Grace, "And no fucking lies." I sipped my drink, which somehow spilled all over my hands and Marie. *Whoops.*

Alex raised his hands, "Oh, me first, and this is to everyone at the table. Okay, answer this...Where is the craziest place you have ever had sex?"

That's a stupid question. I wanted to know why Grace didn't fucking want me anymore. I wanted to know why she banged Ethan while I was in jail, *for her!* I rolled my eyes (for a minute I thought I was going to actually pop them out of my head because they were so drunk. I mean I was so drunk; fuck it, I don't know what I mean. All I knew was that Grace was mean.) I sat back down while everyone went down the line giving their stupid answers.

"Bathroom," Brayden said.

"A fast food ball pit in the kid's play area," Alex laughed answering his own question. Everybody moaned. *"What?"* He said red in the face. *Oh God, yeah I remember that. It was so gross, balls were everywhere.*

Conner and Lea both giggled and said, "Ferris wheel." *Gah*, I remembered *that* too.

When it was my turn, Alex laughed and said, "Please do not say jail cell, because I'll piss myself right here, dude."

"Shut up," I laughed, took a deep breath, looked at Marie

and flat-out lied, "My answer is probably going to change later, but right now, fire escape."

"Boozer's bathroom," Marie giggled.

"Car," Tucker said.

"Park," Ethan whispered.

When it came to Grace's turn, I struggled to stay seated across from her. Nervous anxiety, raw and carnal, made my heart beat skip and stutter. Her eyes locked on mine, then she leaned forward, wrapped her perfect plump little lips around the straw, and drank her entire drink. *She didn't give an answer.*

The rosy blush that reddened her cheeks made it hard to try to look away from her. The strange thing was, she didn't try to look away from me either. The staring contest made my blood beat faster. My body shuddered, absolutely unable to look away from her gaze. Those silver eyes of hers were stunning. *Stunning.* Stun-NING.

"Hey, I got a question! When did you lose your virginity?" I heard Marie ask the table giggling.

Brayden started the round of answers again. "With these guys as my friends in high school, I was lucky if I got a girl even to look in my direction," he laughed. "I was seventeen, and deprived because of these idiots!"

"Yeah, seventeen here too! Prom night. It took like two seconds, that poor girl." Alex laughed.

Conner and Lea both took their shots.

"Sixteen," I answered.

"I would have done *all* of you if we went to the same high school. I was fourteen." Marie giggled.

"Twelve," Tucker bragged.

"Bullshit, you're probably still a virgin!" Ethan laughed. But he didn't offer an answer for himself and just drank his shot.

Grace's eyes still stared into mine. She drank her shot. Holy alcoholics anonymous! *Is she freaking trying to get plastered and why the hell is the bar spinning faster?*

About that time, Marie started to slide her hand along my leg under the table. I didn't want to break eye contact with Grace, so I just grabbed at Marie's hand and squeezed until she yelped. *Sorry, but my junk might seriously fall the eff off it I stuck it in her. Crap, now, I'm having inner dialogue in my head and I sounded like Lea.*

I had no idea what the next question was because I was drowning in the silver oceans across from me. I just answered with, "Silver." Everybody looked at me and laughed. *Idon'tcarethisisn'tatest.*

Grace drank another shot. Her eyes wobbled a bit. *She's just as tanked as me. I should stand up and tell her I love her. Show her my wings, oh yeah, they're gone.*

"Okay, okay...I got one for the beautiful Grace Taylor, who hasn't answered a thing here tonight and is getting so drunk that Tucker might start looking good to her," Alex teased. "How many people have you slept with, and is there *ANYONE AT THIS TABLE* you might *LIKE* with a capital *L*, AND have you and Lea ever licked kitties? Please tell me yes."

Grace slurped her drink up and Conner threw something across the table at Alex, but it went so fast I couldn't see what the hell it was. Looked like a duck. I swear it had freaking wings. *Not like me, I ain't got wings. Nope.*

When I focused my eyesight back to Grace, she was still looking at me but now she was biting that bottom lip of hers and I lost it. I didn't know what the hell took possession of my body but something did and I jumped out of my seat, slammed my hands down on the table (mostly because I could not stand up correctly) and had a damn tantrum. Yeah.

I believe what I tried to say was, "The point isn't to get fucking smashed, Grace! Be fucking HONEST!" The words all slurred together and I kind of sang it to the tune of *Twinkle, Twinkle Little Star.* So. What. We were all drunker than drunk. Me, reigning king of all drunkards.

Grace just sucked on the straw, with her eyes locked on mine, until it made that slurpy *nothing is left on the bottom* sound and smiled, "Is that what the point is, Shane?" Then she threw the straw at me.

Holy sweet mother of Mind Erasers. I jumped out of my seat again. *When the hell did I sit back down?* I dunno. Anyway, I jumped out of my seat again. "My turn for a question!" I yelled. My body shook, and swayed to the right, and left. I held onto the table for dear life. "Answer this, Grace, how was it to *fuck* Ethan? While you're at it, answer this, while you were *fucking* Ethan, did you think about that ex-boyfriend of yours that you *loved* so damn fucking much you couldn't be with me? Remember Grace? The night you told me about him while your hands were wrapped around *my* dick!" I slammed my palms against the table and spilled my drink across the top of it. Then I slumped back and Alex, great friend that he is, caught me and shoved me back up into a standing position. That was awesome of him. AWEsome.

Everybody fell silent. *Um, crap, I can't believe that just flew out of my mouth.* Lea dropped her head in one of her hands and grabbed for Grace under the table with another hand. Conner called me a drunken idiot, *like I didn't know this information about myself already.*

Grace sat up straighter and then leaned forward toward me. "I don't know how it is to fuck him, Shane, because I did not *fuck* Ethan. I have never slept with anyone, actually. I was saving myself for that ex-boyfriend...he was in...um...jail, but when he got out, he didn't want me anymore and he left me." Harsh vibrant streaks of crimson tore through her flawless ivory skin. I fell back into my seat as if she just slapped me across the face.

Ethan leaned across the table at me, "Seriously, bro? You think I would do that to you? I know how you feel about her. Stop screwing it up, Shane. You *love* her," he whispered.

I almost threw up, right there in front of everyone.

"Well, good evening there, *Bruce McHardon*, would you like to come out and meet the prettiest little virgin in the world? Grace, please, please, please, may I have your V-card. I will take such good care of it, I promise." Alex said, first addressing his lap then looking up towards Grace.

Grace smiled at him and laughed sarcastically, "Thanks, Alex, but I'm pretty sure I've just been royally fucked over, so I'm good for now. Thanks."

Yep. I almost threw up right in front of everyone. Again.

"There's no way you are a virgin! Like, you've never been with a guy before? What do you do?" Marie asked, laughing at Grace. *Oh damn, this is getting worse. Don't throw up, don't throw up.*

Grace locked her stare back on me again. *Oh my God, I am so in love with her.* "I've been with guys, just not full blown sex. And what do I do? Well, one of my best friends is a vibrator. It goes from *Oh Yeah,* to *Who the Hell Needs a Man* in ten seconds flat." She turned her gaze on Marie, "You should try it, *Marie.* In the long run, it'll be a lot less heartbreaking than Shane can be."

Can't. Open. My. Mouth. I will vomit.

Tucker jumped up, stumbled around the table and drunkenly threw an arm around Grace, "Grace, you're so beautiful. Please don't give Alex your V-card. I took you to Masa, Grace! We could go there again and get that champagne you love, and then we could get a room at any hotel in the city." She flung his arm off her and her eyes darkened with fury.

"Oh, wow. Hmm...um...I rather stick burning hot pokers in my eyes and eat crap, but thank you so much for the offer, Tucker. It was so kind of you, seriously," she said through clenched teeth. *So in love with her.*

Ethan smiled at Grace, "Well, I think it's pretty damn amazing."

Alex grabbed onto one of Ethan's shoulders, "Amazing?

Dude, that's the hottest thing ever. Oh my God, do you remember when she wore those little pink teddy bear pajamas?" He licked his lips looking at her, "Grace, my love, we need to create the most epic experience for you..."

With a roll of her eyes she stood up. She wobbled a bit; *I seriously thought she was drunker than I was.* She rested her hands down on the table trying to stand straight. "Well, thank you everyone. Why the fuck don't ya'll just...just continue the discussion of my vir..viginny...ginity, because in no way would that be, let's say, uncomfortable or embarrassing in any way to me. E...specially in front of Hot Pink Lips there," she slurred, pointing to Marie.

She pushed her chair in and moved backwards. "You guys can all take a vote on who I should hand my V-card to. There's no problem with that, right, Shane?" She shoved the table at me a bit. It didn't move much, but she tried. "Since I'm not in the fucking band anymore, right? I can fuck any one of these guys. Right? That's not a problem for you, right?"

Oh shit. I think she's mad at me. Now she knows how I felt when I thought she was giving it to Ethan. But, I couldn't say anything to her. For one, the opening of my mouth would cause me to puke and two, well, I had been a complete and utter douche to her and I deserved all her anger and more.

"Fuckasstard!" She screamed at me. *Yep, I deserved to be called that, whatever that is.*

Marie giggled drunkenly. "What's a fuckasstard, *Virgin*?"

Oh, I wish one of the girls would shut that chick up. *But seriously what is a fuckasstard?*

Grace leveled her eyes on Marie. *Holy Mind Erasers, this is the drunkest conversation I ever watched.* "It's a fucking asshole retard or a fucking ass in a leotard. Both you and Shane have fucking awesome lipstick." She shoved the table at me one more time for good measure. It didn't move, but I don't think she noticed.

Grace stumbled away to the bar and tried to climb over, but sort of crawled up on a stool, slipping off twice. "Ry...an," she sang.

Marie sucked in her teeth. "That's pathetic, really. Maybe she couldn't find anybody that would do her." She grabbed at my sleeve and tried to yank me up. "Come on, Shane. Take me home, so I can show you how much of a virgin I'm not."

Lea slapped her hands down against the table top, causing everybody to jump and look at her. "Why don't you have a nice big cup of *shut the fuck up?* Go home and lay by your *dish*. And the next thing that comes out of your mouth about Grace will be accompanied by your flying broken teeth. Do you understand the language I'm speaking, or do I have to translate to stupid slut for you? Run the fuck along now, go play a game of Hide and go fuck yourself."

Then Lea eyes snapped to mine, "And you. Shane, man the fuck up and cut this shit out. It's going to be a long hard lonely road to walk on waiting for her to forgive you if you keep this crap up." She leaned over the whole table and whispered loudly in my ear, "I think the worst hell you'd *ever* be in would be a life without her, knowing this was your *last* chance ever to be with her. Don't be a douche rocket!"

Lea slid back across the table and I grabbed my phone out of my pocket and typed a text to Grace. Lea was right but I was too damn drunk to talk to Grace. I'd only screw it up more.

Shane: I am so fucking sorry

Marie patted my shoulder and walked away. Thank God.

I need to get Lea flowers again.

The conversation in front of me continued. "Um...what the heck is a douche rocket?" Alex chuckled.

Lea huffed, stood up and crossed her arms. "Okay, I'm going to explain it fast and then I'm going to go over there to Grace and try to talk her out of a bell tower with a rifle. There are **five** levels of the *douche hierarchy*: douche, douche bag, douche canoe, douche nozzle and right at the top, the king of it all, when the douche is displaying *phenomenal* amounts of doucheness, is a *douche rocket.* It's when someone is such a douche, like the KING of douches, they can no longer be described as a douche nozzle, they are ALL the levels of douchery put together, and douche rocket is used. And right now, Shane Maxton is the biggest Douche Rocket on the planet!"

I had to agree with her. *I had to laugh too, because that shit was just funny.*

Behind Lea, I watched as Grace freaked out as her phone started vibrating in her back pocket. She fumbled for about one minute, almost falling off the bar stool, then finally managed to extract her phone from her pocket to read my message. "Ha! Sure!" She yelled.

Damn.

Grace gulped back a shot from off the bar and then Lea was beside her, wrapping her arms around her. My heart freaking broke. Again. I didn't realize I had any more of it left to break.

I stumbled my way across the room to Grace. It took a lot longer than I anticipated since I was still trying not to hurl. Or fall. Or just plain pass out. *Whose idea was it to play that dumbass game?* Mind Erasers, damn, that's the perfect name for them.

Grace swirled around on the barstool and I stumbled against her and leaned my hands on either side of her, trapping her. I breathed her in deeply and looked right in her eyes. A small gasp left her lips and her body shuddered. I moved in even closer to her and gently tapped my forehead to hers. Her body trembled more, so with one hand, I grabbed her around the waist to hold her up. I leaned my whole body against hers and she sank right into me. She freaking *melted.* I took another long deep breath and pulled her against me, bringing my lips to her ear and breathed the words, "Band practice tomorrow at ten.

Make sure you bring your guitar this time."

I let her go and stepped away, raking my hands through my hair. I walked backwards, still watching her, towards the door to leave. I had to walk out that door. *Why?* I puked as soon as I got to the curb. Yeah.

Everything went black after that. It was extremely hazy but I remembered someone, I think Alex, walking me through the front door of my apartment building. I remembered leaving voice messages on Grace's cell phone. But mostly, the night was blacked out and I woke up at nine o'clock with all my clothes still on, *in my closet wearing a sombrero*, and Alex and Ethan sprawled out on my bed.

Someone put lipstick and eye shadow on me. Oh, and across my forehead someone wrote the word LOSER.

With my head pounding and eyes blurry, I gulped down a few aspirin and jumped in the shower. After I dried and dressed, I grabbed a few ties from my closet and tied Alex and Ethan's ankles to my bedposts. Loading my *Super-soaker* was the next thing I did, and I sprayed their dumbass faces with icy cold water and watched as they fumbled and fell trying to get off my bed, but couldn't. EPIC.

We all stumbled grumbling into the studio at 9:45. Immediately, I grabbed my guitar and started playing the melody I had been working on and then sent Alex for coffee.

At exactly ten o'clock, the studio door thrust open and slammed itself up against the wall with a huge metallic bang. Alex and Grace came through the door laughing. Ethan and Brayden moaned in unison and grabbed their heads. Ethan sat behind his drum kit with his forehead on his snare drum and a pair of sunglasses on. "Bro, don't make another sound until I get my coffee."

I had been sitting on one of the couches with my guitar between my legs and my forehead resting on its neck nervously waiting for Grace. I anxiously chewed on a small black guitar pick. My heart stammered and pounded at the sight of her as she stepped in and when those intense gray eyes locked on mine, it stopped completely. I expelled a long deep breath that I didn't even realize I had been holding while waiting for her. I watched her body tremble and those gorgeous lips smile at me, like she was truly happy to see me. *She had to have listened to my voice messages. I wish I remembered what I said in them.* Her eyes lit up the room when they stared into mine and I knew that one day soon I would know her like no one else ever had.

Ethan's deep voice boomed, "Play that new rhythm again, Shane, let's all listen to it and improvise. Then we could sit around and think of some lyrics for it."

Grace unbuckled her guitar case and slid her guitar out. She looked down at it with a reverie and awe that made my insides ache. She carelessly tossed her case against the wall with her coat and sat down crossed legged on the floor in the middle of us and tuned up.

Without thinking, I answered Ethan, "It's got lyrics." The only thing I was concentrating on was Grace and how I needed to touch her. Somehow right then, I *needed* to touch her more than I needed to take my next breath. I walked slowly over and sat across from her, crossing my legs as she had done. Our knees brushed each other's and my body trembled when I felt her tremble against me. There was something alive and electric between us. There was no one and no way that it could be denied. You could see it and feel the crackling and thickness of it in the space around our bodies whenever we touched.

"What did you say, bro?" Ethan asked looking awkwardly from me to Grace. I wondered if he could see what I was feeling.

Grace's eyes looked from Ethan's into mine. *Beautiful.* "It has lyrics. I'm just not ready to sing them yet...it's called *Until You*," I told Ethan but I never looked away from Grace. I wanted to sing the words to her, but I couldn't, not yet. I was going to make this girl love me for who I was now, not what I had been.

And those words, they would tell her *everything*. It was killing me not being allowed to tell her everything.

A heavy silence lingered after the last of my words, and my fingers danced along my guitar strings, killing the quiet with the life of the song. A slow addictive melody languidly sang through the strings of my instrument as I watched Grace inhale and watch me wide-eyed. The notes started as tiny whispers; little echoes of murmurs; of secrets. They rose in volume and intensity and I smiled as I watched goose bumps travel all over her skin. I wanted to kiss each and every one of them.

I nodded my head at her, "Come on, girl, play with me," I whispered.

She moistened her lips and closed her eyes, listening to the melody I played for her. A stunning smile passed over her lips, lips I wanted to kiss more than I ever wanted anything in my life. Her fingers moved across her guitar, and I was lost, lost in the music that we were both creating. She thrust herself into the emotional passion of the riff and I could swear I saw something inside her break loose and knock down the wall of stone that she had built up around her. Our bodies swayed to the rhythm, forgetting who we were, just our raw souls singing through our guitars.

We played as one. Her elegant fingers pulsed along the strings with slow and steady notes telling of her longing and desire. I was completely mesmerized and captivated by her. She played the instrument in front of me as if it was an intimate part of her body. It made my skin tingle and burn to touch her.

I didn't.

The sharp tones of my melody are what I touched her back with; full of strength and power. Our harmony quickened together as if we needed a rush to our release, until an explosion of sound tore at our hearts, our souls. You couldn't tell our melodies apart, where my story began or her story ended. We reached inside ourselves and told each other our secrets through song, secrets that we couldn't say with words yet, like we wanted to linger in our anticipation of the beginning of our forever.

We twisted our notes together until we were breathless and there was nothing more to play. The silence deafened me.

Tears filled her eyes. I looked everywhere at her all at once. I wanted to devour her. Her pink wet lips, her tear filled eyes, her neck, her hands; all of her. I frantically searched her face, wanting...needing to let her know, my face heated and I swallowed hard, "I'm so sorry, Grace, I..."

"Please don't," she whispered, her eyes pleading. "Let's not try to hurt each other anymore with words. There's been enough damage. Let's just play," she said looking away. "And there are too many eyes on us, another time, Shane."

In between Alex's mad attempts to discuss the pros and cons of Grace's virginity, we practiced for three hours. "Hey, Grace. Do you know why men want to marry virgins?" Alex asked.

She rolled her eyes, "No, Alex. But I bet you're going to tell me."

"They can't stand criticism," he laughed.

Alex quickly walked out from behind his keyboard and sat in front of Grace, his expression completely innocent. "So, I've been thinking seriously about this. And I think I came up with an amazing idea, so just hear me out okay? The idea of a twenty-three year old virgin is thought by many to be an *endangered species*. So, I was hoping you would let us take you through the spiritual journey of this undiscovered land. I'd like to start a blog, a documentary of sorts, about the experience of *going where no penis has gone before*."

Grace's face increased in darker degrees of redness with each word from Alex. "Alex, I think..."

"No. Grace just...just hear it all out, okay?"

She nodded her head, laughing, and her eyes dancing

playfully.

Alex continued. "In our documentary blog, I will be portraying the role of head *virginarian*, strictly for the sake of research purposes," Alex giggled.

Grace laughed louder, "Alright, I'll bite, what is a virginarian?"

Alex's face reddened even darker than Grace's as he explained, "It's a person who only practices the fine art of having relations with those of the virgin persuasion. Now, let's shut off all the lights and play a game of who am I tasting."

Before I could punch him in the arm, Grace did. "Ugh, Alex don't even...Blah. Just stop," she laughed.

He looked back at her seriously, "You know, *Grace Taylor*, there are only two four letter words that are offensive to men. The words *don't* and *stop*. Well, unless they are used together."

Everyone burst out laughing.

Alex grabbed her by the back of the head and planted a friendly kiss on her forehead. "I'm glad you're back in the band, love. And I love that you let me tease the shit out of you. If I wasn't such a *LOSER*, I'd probably ask you to marry me; make me an honest man." He gave me a sideways glance and winked in my direction.

Chapter 20

Right after band practice, I met up with Conner at the park and went for a run. When we finished, we wordlessly walked to Grace and Lea's, the front door was unlocked so we walked right in and dropped our sweaty shirts on the floor by the front door.

Conner and I walked into the kitchen to hear Lea sigh, "Yeah, but he's just not Shane." We both leaned against the doorway of the kitchen, arms crossed over our bare chests smirking. Grace's eyes roamed all across the muscles of my chest, and slid down my skin over my stomach to my running pants. Her lips parted and her body leaned toward me. *Holy Eyeball Sex, I've never seen her eat me alive like that before.* "Who's not me?" I interrupted Lea.

Lea jumped and her hands flew to her chest and she yelped loudly, "You just scared the crap out of me!"

"Uh," was all Grace could manage as she blatantly gawked at me. I loved it. I freaking wanted more. I didn't want her to have any damn control, just like me, when I saw her. I wanted, *no, I fucking needed* her to run her hands up my chest and slam her fucking lips against mine.

I unfolded my arms and walked into the kitchen, tossing my cell phone on the table near her. Smiling at her, I grabbed a water bottle from the refrigerator and leaned against the counter, giving her a full view. Her eyes widened. I flexed and stretched muscles I didn't even know I freaking had as she watched me. I did freak out a little when Lea whispered under her breath, "*Hot damn.* That looks delicious."

Trying to ignore Lea, I twisted the cap off the bottle, held it to my lips and gulped the water down, *slow*. I let a long stream of it drop down my chin and onto my chest. A stunning blush spread across Grace's cheeks, down her neck, and I could tell she was struggling for air. Thousands of dirty thoughts raced through my mind as we watched each other; they all ended with her legs wrapped tightly around me, with me whispering her name over and over again. I was throbbing to be inside her, my hands tingled with the anticipation sliding them slowly over every inch of her skin. My lips burned to touch hers; my tongue craved to taste her. It took *all my fucking self-control* to stay on the other side of the room and just watch her, just touching her with my eyes, instead of throwing her on top of the table and claiming her as *mine* in front of everyone.

"Grace has a date tonight," Lea blurted out. Like a bucket of ice water to my face. What the *hell did she just say? What the fuck? Alex? Ethan? What the FUCK DID I MISS?*

I twisted my face in anger and crunched my empty water bottle with one squeeze of my fingers. "Letting Alex start his blog?" I asked through clenched teeth. I. Will. Kill. Him.

"Ah, that would be a no. But, thanks for making me feel like one of your easy skanks. *Again.*" Grace whispered.

She was acting hurt? She was hurt? She was holding my fucking heart in her hand and squeezing the life out of it every damn time I saw her, but she was acting hurt?

Lea craned her neck in front of Grace's face and pointed to me. "Do you effing see that chest?"

"Shut up," she whispered. Her eyes flitted from Lea back to me. I swear I saw tears in them.

Lea shoved Conner out of the kitchen, pushing him with both hands into the hallway. We were alone.

Fuck this.

I stalked toward her, eyes fixed on her. She bolted up and met me in the middle. She raised her chin and jabbed her hands onto her hips. "Think carefully about what you're about to say to me, Shane," she whispered.

Then the corners of her lips curled up.

Oh fuck me. I walked toward her until I backed her sweet ass up against the kitchen table. *Hard.* The air thickened around us, and I heard a soft intake of breath through her lips. I leaned down, pushing my body against hers, *damn* her nipples hardened through her shirt against the skin of my chest. The palms of my hands slid slowly onto the table on either side of her, trapping her between my arms. "Don't let him touch you," I whispered.

Her breath was ragged. "Give me a good reason not to," she said.

I couldn't stop myself. I didn't want to stop. I slid one hand to her waist and moved under her shirt, skimming my fingertips over her skin. I leaned down closer, breathing her in. Both of us panting and breathing heavily into each other, our lips moved closer.

And just as if someone, somewhere was sitting down orchestrating the shittiness of my life and messing with me, *cockblocking me to the ninth power,* my cell phone rang. A picture of a topless Marie taken in the bathroom of Boozer's popped up on my screen. *I am going to kill her. How the hell did she do that with my phone?* We both stared at the phone for a minute before I pressed ignore and stepped back, raking one hand through my hair, knowing the intense moment was over.

"Wow, Shane. Just wow. How has your dick not shriveled up and fallen off by now?"

"I didn't sleep with her."

"Ha. Every damn time your lips move, out pops a lie. The problem is, Shane, I don't care if you did. Get out of my way, I have to get ready."

"Don't let him put his hands on you, Grace. Just. Don't."

"Oh sure, good idea, no hands. Yeah, I like the thought of his tongue on me much better!" She pushed me off and stormed out of the room. Tears streamed down her face as I tried to run after her, but she slammed the bathroom door right in my face.

Thumping my forehead hard on the bathroom door, I could hear the click-click-click of Lea's shoes coming fast behind me. She slapped me on the arm before I could even turn around

290

to face her. *This chick is a beast.*

"What the hell is wrong with you, Shane? Tell her who you are! Stop playing games with her..."

I lunged at her, leveling my eyes to hers, nose to nose. "I. CAN'T. They told me not to. And, Lea? Look at me. WHO I AM is SHANE NOW! She has to love *him*. Not some angel that DOESN'T EXIST any longer.   What if SHE doesn't want ME anymore?   Lea, it's this obsessive thought in my head every minute since I found out who she was. That Shane Maxton isn't good enough for her. Fuck, *he isn't*. He was a lost piece of shit, Lea, but I'm here now and if she doesn't accept me in here, then I let her go, but I will love her every single minute for the rest of my existence. I have her name branded on my soul, tattooed on my heart. I will never love anyone else."

"Then tell her who you *were*, Shane. Please don't let her think he left her, don't let her think that she wasn't enough for him," Lea whispered.

"Who does she have a date with?" I snapped.

"Ryan, the bartender."

"What's going on with her and Ryan?" I growled.

She gave me the most evil smile I'd ever seen on her cute little pixie face. "I don't know. She saw him in the coffee shop after band practice today and he asked her out. And Shane, because you're hurting my best friend, I hope he kisses all your kisses away. I hope he erases every little sliver of her heart that belonged to you and writes his name on each one," she sneered.

She left me in the hallway, gagging, wanting to hurl.

I marched into the living room and paced back and forth mumbling. Conner watched me with interest from the couch. "Why do I feel like I've missed a few episodes of the soap opera you call a life."

Glaring at him, I cursed a lengthy monologue of harsh profanities and raked my hands through my hair.

Grace thundered into the living room, grabbing her coat

and fumbling with it to keep her hands from dropping it.

My eyes grazed over her legs, her hips, her arms, and dragging them slowly over the rest of her body, I cringed. *Why the hell was she wearing a dress like that? That's a dress you wear to get someone's hands on you.* "Oh God," I whispered.

As she heard my words, her eyes caught mine, a look of anguish washed over her face and her lips parted as if to say something, but they snapped shut like she decided against it.

The horrible sounds of the doorbell rang and she ran for the door. Charging forward, irrational thought saying to stop her from leaving, but Conner grabbed my waist and pulled me back.

"Let me fucking go!"

"Are you losing it, Shane? What the hell are you going to do, hit him until she likes you? That's not going to work! What the fuck are you on?"

I shrugged out of his arms and dragged my hands over my face. "I'm not high, Conner, I swear. I'm just fucking in love with her."

"Oh crap."

"Yeah."

"Shane, it's not Ryan's fault. Grace made her choice."

"Conner, she never even knew I was a serious option. I have to get the hell out of here." I searched through my wallet and pulled out a condom. I knew it was a bad idea. I knew it was crude, filthy and disgusting. But I needed to have the last word before I left her to someone else. I rushed down the hallway to the front door.

Ryan was leaning against the doorjamb with a dumbass, *'I'm getting laid tonight'* smile almost splitting his face open. Yes, I thought about punching him in his bright shiny minty fresh mouth. But I refrained from violence.

"Excuse me," I murmured in her ear as I pushed through the doorway, she leaned away to give me room to pass. *Yeah, thanks.*

As I stepped by, I slowly reached my arm out, brushing it past her waist and I thrust the wrapped condom into one of her closed hands. I grazed my hands lightly over her hip, leaned in close, and looked right in her eyes. Time seemed to slow down at that moment as if we were locked eye to eye forever. Slowly, I brought my lips to her ear, "Just pull the fucking trigger on me now, *please*." I pulled back and watched her shiver against my words. She searched my face, tears filling her eyes.

"Hey, Shane," Ryan said.

I said nothing else, but shoved my hands in my pockets and stormed off down the street. Conner was right next to me. *Good friend.*

Straight to Boozer's. Within an hour, I was buzzed to high heaven with Conner sitting next to me. "So, your plan is to stay drunk for the rest of your life and not deal with the fact that the girl you're in love with is out on a date with someone else? How is this *any different* than you using drugs again?"

"I'm a little busy trying to reach black out status. You don't mind if I ignore your love pep talk, right?" I said as I downed another shot.

"Just answer one question for me then."

I circled my hands in the air for him to continue disturbing my drinking progress.

"Isn't she worth fighting for?"

"Yes. I'm just not worth being the winner. Shane Maxton is a piece of shit."

Conner shook his head drunkenly up and down. "Yep. He was. But then he cleaned himself up about nine months ago and became one of the best guys I know. Shane, don't waste the rest of your life wondering if you're good enough for her, let her decide for herself if you are."

Sometime after that, I vaguely remember crawling up the steps to Grace and Lea's apartment. I was so going to wait in Grace's bed for her. *I was not letting that bartender mix her drinks.*

Laughing and shushing each other, Conner and I fell into the girls' apartment. "Dude, do you have a key to the apartment? *Areyouserious?* You are so married already!" I slurred.

"Shh...Shush up. You're gonna wake 'em up!" Conner yelled.

"Yeah, well it's too late for that, you idiots," Lea laughed, standing over us with a bat. "With all the damn noise you guys were just making you are so lucky I didn't call the cops!"

"So you gonna make us play baseball?" I giggled.

Lea hung the bat over her shoulder, turned around and walked down the hallway. "I'm going to get a little help," she laughed.

Conner and I untangled from each other and tried to stand. I didn't know about him, but the earth was moving way too fast for me, so I kept low to the ground. "Con, I think my world is fucking spinn' outta control. You feel that?"

"Screw you, Shane. This is all your fault. You made me drink. Do you think I could stand on my head?"

"I dunno. Why you wanna step on your own head? That's stupid. I'm gonna hide from Lea and Grace. Help cover me with these pillows. Wow, they are *so* soft," I giggled drunkenly. I was beyond drunk. And I really needed a flashlight. Taking every cushion off the couch, I built the best damn pillow fort ever created. By a twenty-three year old drunk guy. Best. *Ever.*

Conner slumped against the wall, fell on his head and giggled, "There's my beautiful girlfriend. Shane. Shane? Sha...ne? Where the frig is Shane?"

I popped my head out of the couch cushions and waved to him. Well actually, I tried doing those Navy Seals hand signals, but I don't think he understood. "I'm in my fort."

Conner crawled towards me and looked up at Lea who

had just walked back in the room, "Uh oh, Shane. Look who's here. It's *her*, Grace. Shane? Shane?" he whispered. "Dude, ask her to get in the fort with you!"

Grace stood in the doorway. I died a little. She had nothing on except a tiny little tank top and those little boy shorts that I loved on her. But, that wasn't what hit me. It was the way the moonlight spilled in through the window and gently fell against the softness of her skin. The way it made her glow; I have never seen someone wear the moonlight more perfectly.

"Okay, that's enough. Come on, Conner, let's go to bed," Lea said, pulling him up off the floor. He stumbled drunkenly against the wall giggling. "Grace, Shane really, really, really likes you...you make him happy when skies are gray," he drunkenly sang, I believe to the melody of *You Are My Sunshine*. I forgot that he could sing pretty well when he was drunk.

Lea looked back at Grace with a small smile and a giggle. "You got Shane?"

Oh God, did she have me. She's had me for thousands of years.

Grace smiled back at Lea, "Yeah, sure." My heart leapt and the pillows all crumbled around me.

I looked up at her, staring blankly, and slurred, "God, Grace, you're so fucking exquisite." There's a medical term for that, what I just did, it's called diarrhea of the mouth, when you just have no control of your bodily functions and shit just starts flying out of your lips. Yeah, because I was supposed to be pissed off at her for going on a date with Ryan, and I was well aware that he might be in the room down the hall waiting for her to come back to bed. *Crap, I think I'm going to be sick.*

Then she smiled at me. Grace Taylor *smiled* at me with those stunning lips and tears in her eyes. I will never forget the way she looked at me that night. Okay, I probably would forget because I was juiced to the high heavens, but I hoped I didn't forget, because it was a look filled with forgiveness and love.

And it was mine.

She walked over to me and fixed all the pillows back on the couch. She kept glancing at me as I watched her. She walked to one of the closets where they kept extra pillows and sheets and fixed the couch for me to sleep on. I staggered to my feet and collapsed on the couch as I wrapped my hands around her waist and pulled her down to sit next to me. With one hand, I yanked my tee shirt off and threw it on the coffee table. I leaned back against the pillows of the couch and brushed the back of my hand against her leg, feeling the warmth of her skin.

I turned my head towards her and leaned in closer, "How was your date?"

She looked down at her hands, my fingers softly stroking circles along her skin, and then our fingers entwined themselves into each other. "I didn't go," she whispered.

My heart raced. That wasn't what I had expected to hear. The room spun even faster and I felt light headed. I lay down along the couch and pulled her gently into my arms, laying her against my body. "I know I'm drunk as hell, Grace, but, just stay with me. I need you like I fucking need to breathe."

"Shane..." she breathed. Then she nestled into me and I remembered what it felt like in heaven.

Softly, I placed my lips on the nape of her neck, just below her ear, inhaled deeply, breathing her in, and kissed her. "Shut up and go to sleep, Grace."

This is where we belonged.

Chapter 21

Why would someone be trying to drill a hole into my skull? Holy crap, someone was trying to give me a lobotomy. I had to peel my eyes open with both my hands to get up. Sitting up, I had no clue where I was or how I had gotten there. The only thing that my eyes could focus on was a wooden baseball bat in the corner of the room and I wondered if I somehow had used it to play baseball without remembering. Do you know what the trouble with real life is? It lacks special effects movie music to clue you in on what the fuck is happening around you. Because at that moment, I would have bet someone should have been playing horror-danger music. I completely thought that this life I was stuck in was quickly becoming a very complicated drinking game. And I was losing horribly. *I wondered if my liver jumped ship last night, I would completely understand if it did, I had been totally abusive to it.*

I met up with Conner at the bathroom as he stumbled out holding his head. "Bro, you might want to wait before you go in there," he warned. The warning was way too late, I gagged in the doorway.

"Holy sweet mother of bathrooms, what the hell crawled up your ass and died?" I held my nose as I looked through the cabinets for aspirin. "Con, you need to contact the military, because that is a potent freaking chemical weapon, my eyes are tearing!"

Laughing, we made it to the kitchen where Lea, *the most wonderful female friend ever*, had coffee waiting for us. Conner and I both slumped down onto the kitchen seats and laid our heads down on the cool table.

Sweet loving Lea handed both of us coffee. Then she leaned her palms on the table and stood over us. *Uh oh.* "Whoever it was who got up in the middle of the night and drunk pissed all over my once clean toilet seat better hope they never do that again, but it's okay, don't either one of you worry your little hung over heads a bit about it. I cleaned it all up with one of your toothbrushes, thing is, you won't know whose I used…" I peeked over my arms at her. She grabbed her coffee cup, walked a few steps away and leaned against the counter. "And, why the hell does Shane have a toothbrush here?" She was smiling. I dropped my head back down against the table hard.

"GOOD MORNING, BOYS!" Grace yelled from the doorway. I cringed and lifted my head, shaking it. "You're pure evil," I whispered before my head collapsed back onto my arms.

"Why the hell are you girls up so early on a Sunday making a racket waking us up?" Conner asked. *Yeah, great question. Didn't Grace have a hot date last night? I hoped that Ryan didn't walk out of her bedroom right then, because I would kill him. I didn't remember seeing her home at all last night. Okay, truthfully, I didn't even remember coming here last night, but still.*

Lea placed her hands on her hips, shaking her head, "Con, I told you. Grace and I are going to my parents. We'll be back tomorrow. Grace is going to pick up her bike *and* maybe we'll go out dancing tonight." She winked at Grace, "What do you say, Gray? You up for dancing at one of the beach clubs?"

Oh, hell no.

"Now that sounds like a good idea. I'm going to need to pack a little skirt and some heels then," she said as she poured herself a cup of coffee and stirred in some sweetener.

I leaned back on the kitchen chair to look at her and folded my hands behind my head. I was trying to stay as calm as I possibly could, since I hadn't seen any sign of Ryan yet. It wasn't too hard, but I had a sinking feeling that he was just sleeping late from being up *all night*. "So how was your date with the bartender last night, finally get laid?"

Grace's eyes widened and her coffee cup froze midway to her lips. "Are you serious right now?" Lea gave Conner a sideways glance and a shove, which made his coffee slosh all over his hands. Then both of them started to leave.

Grace jumped up. *Yeah, I flinched,* so what, and she slammed her cup of coffee down on the table. The dark liquid splashed over the top and spattered all over the table. She stood right in front of me leaning down, leveled her eyes to mine, and I didn't make a move to lean away. She was so close I could smell her shampoo and soap on her skin. "He damn near wrecked my ass he was *so big.* Thanks for the condom, one just wasn't enough though. So, yes, Shane, I am one well-fucked girl right now!" Then she moved even closer, like she was about to kiss me, or I was about to kiss her. *Damn, I couldn't think straight!* "I didn't know how much I needed to be with him. It's like I needed him like I needed to breathe. Ever felt like that, Shane?"

I took a long, deep breath, blowing it back out through clenched teeth. Slowly, I pulled myself out of the chair, not breaking eye contact with, she stood up moving her body in tandem with mine. "What did you just say?" She didn't have to answer me, the memories from last night came flooding back, pouring over my head, pulling me under; drowning me.

She didn't go.

Grace backed away from me and looked over to Lea. "I'm going to pack some more stuff. Let me know when you're ready to leave." She walked around me, giving plenty of room so she wouldn't accidently brush into me.

My body went rigid, muscles all stiff and tight, and knuckles white. I hated it when I planned out a whole conversation in my head and the other people don't follow my script! I always ended up looking like the *King of All That Is Douchebaggery.*

"My God, Shane, you are the biggest asshat in the whole world!" Lea screamed in my face. "You ran out of the house like a God damn five year old yesterday and she told Ryan she couldn't go out with him! She stayed here the whole night. Alone!" She stomped into the hallway and continued her tirade at me, "And maybe you were too damn drunk to remember, but when I woke up this morning, she was wrapped in your arms on the couch, Shane. She stayed with you the whole night. She's right about you. You don't deserve someone like her."

I dropped to my knees hard. Pain shot up through my legs, rocking my bones. Lea was right; I didn't deserve her. I didn't deserve someone who stood by the memory of us for thousands of years, who believed in our love for so long, when I couldn't even get though a conversation without irrationally accusing her of things that only I have done.

"Do you like, take classes to be *that* freaking stupid, Shane? If you don't stop, you are never going to be with her. It can't actually be this hard for you to like just one girl, can it?" Conner asked.

"I *am worse* than Tucker," I said hanging my head in my hands. Yeah, I cried. Fuck it; I'm a mush when it comes to her. *Grace is my everything.*

Lea's clicking heels walked back into the kitchen. Then they kicked me, hard. "Get up off my damn floor and go in there and spend the rest of your fucking existence making that girl forget you are an *asshat* and make her love you, *asshat!*"

I wiped at my tears before she could see them. It didn't matter, I knew she could see me wiping the tears away so she knew I was crying, but yeah, whatever.

"And go put a damn shirt on and cover up your eighteen pack or whatever you got going on under that skin, you are making me drool."

"Lea, stop saying crap like that to me and stop the gawking, awkward."

Lea smiled down at me, "You, sir, are a bit easy on the eye, so therefore I shall stare at you. If you feel at all uncomfortable, I could always knock you over the head with something until you're unconscious and take pictures. Now go get Grace!"

Scrambling off the floor, I ran down the hallway and banged the side of my closed fists against Grace's bedroom door. *Nothing.* Well, actually I thought I heard someone whispering; maybe she had a radio on or something. I pounded my fists on the door again. "Grace, please open the door," I whispered.

Red-eyed and trembling, she opened her door. My legs almost gave out from beneath me; *I was the cause of her sadness. I have been the cause of her sadness and suffering for so long.*

It was time to change that.

I slowly stepped up to her, brought my hands to her chin and touched each side of her face. I ran my thumbs along the underside of her eyes. My breath came out labored and my voice thickened with sorrow, "I don't know how to do this, tell me how to fix us."

Grace leaned her face into my hands and sighed heavily. "Just be my friend, Shane, start there. Anything else might kill us both."

I pulled her into my arms and crushed her against my chest. She melted right into me and put her head against my heart. "Damn, girl. I'm so sorry I've been such a *Tucker* to you."

She pulled her head off my chest and laughed, "Yeah, like what are you doing, taking lessons from him or something? I was thinking of kicking your ass out of the band and getting him to come back!"

Our bodies parted slightly, and I kept my arm around her shoulder and walked her out into the living room with her bag. "Difference is, I'm so much better looking than him that you just accept it from me, right?"

She laughed and hip checked me, "Lea," she yelled over my shoulder. "I'm pulling the Jeep around!" Grace walked out the door but I still held onto the bottom of her shirt and kept the soft material clenched in my fingers. Slowly walking backwards, she smiled and the material slipped through my fingertips.

Lea and Conner walked up behind me and I got elbowed in the gut by one of them, most likely Lea. "So, I don't see any bruises or cuts on you, so it doesn't look like she kicked your sorry ass like I would have," Lea teased. "What happened?"

Pressing my lips tight to keep from smiling, I couldn't fight the chuckle from bubbling in my chest. "I'm coming with you to your parents. It's been a few months since I've seen Mr. and Mrs. Rossi." I gave her a wink.

Lea bounced on the balls of her feet and she held her hand over her smiling mouth, "Holy Discovery Channel Sex, Conner, we are going to get caught in a porn storm between these two. Conner you better be coming with us too, because if I have to watch them making googley-steamy-nasty-dirty-sex-eyes at each other, there won't be a vibrator in the world big enough to satisfy me!"

Conner's eyebrows shot straight up his forehead, "Where the hell did I find someone like you? That's so hot, and I would like to see you use this vibrator that you speak of."

I wrinkled my nose at the both of them and leaned back, "Ookay. I'm going to get my running bag; I have some clothes in there that I could take." Then they started sucking on each other's face as if I were invisible. *Yeah.* I definitely needed to get the hell out of the hallway.

Within ten minutes, Grace was in front of the apartment honking her horn and adrenaline was bursting in little pinpricks of heat all over my skin. I hoped Grace wasn't going to be mad that I was coming, but I decided when I was on the floor in her kitchen, on my knees, I was never letting her go. Never. She deserved a man that would fight for her, a man that would be the best man he could be, and I was taking the job.

The three of us ran to Grace's double parked Jeep and Lea opened the passenger side door and yanked the front seat forward. Conner and I climbed into the backseat silently, shoving our bags in the small space behind the seats. Lea pulled the door closed after she climbed in and gave Grace a small sideways smile. "They wouldn't let us go without them."

Through the rearview mirror, I watched as Grace's lips curled up into a stunning smile and then her eyes met mine. For a small moment, we stared at each other, in the chaos of the city, before she pulled the Jeep into the street and drove, I knew that *starting as friends was bullshit*, we were way past that. But I'd give it to her anyway, for about a week, *then* she was mine. And to send that point home, on the Jeep's audio system played *So Far Away* by *Avenged Sevenfold*. God, I'd love to do a show with those guys. "Love this band," I said to Grace in the mirror. She raised the volume, *hell yeah*.

Grace drove south down Second Avenue and we sat in traffic, moving only a centimeter at a time across the Queens Midtown Tunnel. Lea moaned and complained about how many people lived in the city, while Conner and I continuously kicked at her seat. After two hours of traffic, Lea had all the windows open and was singing horribly to *Limp Bizkit's* rendition of *The Who's Behind Blue Eyes*. I pleaded with Conner to get her to shut up, but he just laughed at me.

I didn't pay any attention to any other music or anyone singing after that, I just looked forward and focused on Grace's face in the rearview mirror. Every once in a while, she would glance there to change lanes and I caught her smiling at me watching her. Before I knew it, she was parking the Jeep in front of Lea's parent's house in Belle Harbor, the smell of the beach and salty water filling the air.

The four of us shuffled out of the car stretching, yawning and smacking each other. Caroline Rossi, Lea's mom, burst through the front door and ran at us screaming, apron flapping in the wind. "Anthony! They're finally home!" She grabbed Lea and Grace up in her arms and swung them around.

Caroline let go of Lea, but held Grace by the shoulders

and looked her up and down, beaming. "You look healthy enough, but you need to put on more weight. You're all skin and bones, dear."

Lea laughed loudly and slapped Grace on the bottom, "Don't worry, Ma, at the rate she's been devouring ice cream and alcohol, she'll pack on the weight within the next week. Her ass is gonna be so big she'll have moons orbiting it." *Was it wrong that for some reason that turned me on?*

Rolling her eyes at her daughter, Caroline giggled, "You need help, dear. Let's go in and say hello to your father." She then turned to Conner and me, kissing us both on the cheek. "Hello, boys, come on inside. Anthony has a game on and I'll have lunch ready in a minute. We'll see if we can fatten Grace up a bit today." She grabbed Lea and Conner by the shoulders and walked with them into the house.

Grace stood frozen on the sidewalk, with her mouth hanging open. Me, I was watching her ass. Moons orbiting or it not, it would always be perfect to me. When she stepped forward, I gently grabbed her by the waist and pulled her back. She fell back onto me, laughing, with her back pressed tightly up against the front of me. One of my hands held onto her wrists, and the other was around the front of her waist, restraining her from moving. I skimmed my hand up from her waist, along her sides, until I brushed aside the hair that fell in waves down her neck. Then I brought my mouth to her ear. I breathed in deeply and whispered, "I'm kind of in love with your ass just the way it is."

She leaned her head closer to mine and my whispering lips touched her soft cheeks, "Shane, shut up. I really hate you right now."

I chuckled, dipping my lips into the crook of her neck and kissed her. Hot spikes of heat shot deeply into my belly and she moaned softly. "No, you don't, Gray." *And then? Then, I kissed her neck again and ran my tongue along her skin. She. Was.*

Shaking.

"Dear God, now I need a change of panties. Mine are soaking wet," she whispered.

No thoughts in brain. Me want girl.

I was seriously having trouble breathing air normally.

Grace spun around in my arms easily, her whole body still trembling in my arms. "You know, Shane, if you could stop all your insane outbursts against me for five minutes, I would really love to see what that warm tongue of yours could do to the rest of my body."

Her eyes locked on mine and I could feel mine widen, as I felt her heart beat drumming against my chest as fast as a hummingbirds. Then the realization of her words slid right over me and I held her closer. I tightened my grip on her wrists, my whole body stiffened and I sucked in a slow deep breath. She looked at my lips and I knew she wanted me to kiss her, so I leaned in slow and laced one of my hands through her hair; pulling her towards me.

"Are you two coming in? Lunch is almost on the table!" Caroline yelled from the doorway. *You have got to be freaking kidding me!*

I let out a low moan, slid my hands back down to her waist and turned her towards the front door. "Ah…yep. We're um…coming, Mrs. R.," I said breathlessly. I slid my hand to the small of her back and gently pushed her to walk alongside me into the house. We glanced at each other and I brushed a strand of dark hair that fell across her cheek behind her ear. She bit her lip and I wanted so badly to know what she was thinking.

Please do not let anyone notice me walking strange. I felt like I have a third leg, and that wasn't my ego talking either, *that's just how damn hard I was.*

We walked in (okay, I was limping) to Lea's father, Anthony, yelling, "There's the comatose kid! How are you feeling, Gracie?" His arms opened wide and he grabbed Grace in a giant hug. "Ah, Jesus, Caroline! You're right, she's all skin and bones." He shoved her comically in front of one of the plastic covered dining room chairs and pushed her shoulders down until she sat. He kept one hand on her shoulder and the other grabbed mine, giving me a hearty handshake. "Hey, and the *rock star* is here too! How you doing, son?"

"Hey, Mr. Rossi. Thanks for having me today. I'm doing great. How have you been?" I answered.

He lowered his gaze and stepped closer to me. "Good, good, son. I'm sure glad that everything was settled and you didn't have anything to do with hurting our Gracie. Lea told me that you were the one to help her when that son of a bitch got his hands on her. We're forever in your debt, Shane. I knew you couldn't have hurt her." He slid in front of the dining room chair at the head of the table, and sat down, leaning back with his arms folded across his chest. A serious expression crossed his features, "So did anybody get the son of a bitch, yet? Or am I going to have to make some calls..." Holy shit, it's like the *Godfather*.

"Shut up, dear," Caroline cut him off, while placing an enormous platter full of spaghetti and meatballs on the table. She waved her hands at him to settle him down. "Let's have a nice delicious Sunday lunch and not talk about all this horror, please." She fanned her hands over her face dramatically, "You men can talk about all this *Law and Order, CSI* crime stuff after eating. Grace has been through enough already. She doesn't want to hear anymore." She walked back into the kitchen, only to come back with more food, salad, Italian bread, garlic knots and a huge pitcher of water with slices of fruit floating in it.

Then lunch/dinner began. I had never seen so much food in my entire life, and everything was delicious. And the conversation was very entertaining to say the least; it started with the most insane giggling from Grace and Lea.

"Gracie, dear. When was the last time you ate any food?"

Caroline asked.

"Um, I had a handful of Tic-tacs on Thursday," Grace answered. Lea looked over at her, while shoving an enormous spoonful of spaghetti in her mouth and laughed. Grace slurped up a long strand of spaghetti, smacking sauce all over her face.

"I can tell, dear. Don't you girls ever cook for yourselves? You do know how to make nutritious foods, don't you?" She glared at Lea.

Lea looked thoughtful while she chewed on her food. She took her time swallowing and then answered. "Well, we did make some Spam with Oreo Cookie glaze last Wednesday. That was yummy, right guys?"

What the? Spam with Oreo Cookie glaze?

"I see," Caroline grumbled. "Well, does anyone have any good news or surprises to tell us?"

"I won a whole dollar in a scratch off game!" Grace giggled madly.

"Have you been drinking, dear?" Caroline reprimanded her.

"No more than usual," Grace smiled back.

It was like watching a sitcom. This shit was hilarious!

Caroline smirked at Lea then glanced at Conner, "Well, Lea, I just can't understand why you're not married yet." Conner sunk lower into his chair. *Wuss, if it was me I would have gotten down on one knee right there.*

"I'm just lucky, I guess. No really, I mean, I love Conner and all but I'm holding out for Johnny Depp," Lea answered batting her eyes.

Johnny Depp? Like, Captain Jack Sparrow?

"And you, Grace? What's your excuse?"

I smiled to myself. *Give me two weeks, lady. Then I'm on one knee.*

"I'm waiting for the zombie apocalypse, because that's the theme of the wedding I want. I figured all the guests could just eat each other and I could really save a few bucks on food, you know?"

I completely snorted my water through my nose with that. I hoped nobody noticed. It got all over my shirt and the worst part were those tiny bits of fruit in the water. Did I mention it shot out my nose? Bits of fruit? Yeah.

"No, no, Caroline. Why should these girls buy the cow when you could get all the milk for free?" Anthony laughed along with the girls.

"Oh my. Well, I just want to know if either of you will be giving me grandchildren anytime soon?"

This is when Conner started to choke on a meatball. He was grabbing at his throat and coughing; me, I laughed.

"I'm allergic," Grace laughed.

"Conner's family eats their young, so that's a no go for us," Lea smiled.

"Oh dear," Caroline mumbled and covered her mouth with her hand.

Lea's hands flew up in the air, "I win! Biotch!"

Grace threw her napkin into her plate. "You, my friend, are the undefeated champion! We shall have a parade in your honor and a statue built in your likeness."

Lea held up her finger and giggled, "Umm, build it in chocolate and erect it outside in the front yard, then everyone can eat me!"

These two were bat-shit crazy, and I would thank God every day of the rest of this life for leading me to them.

Chapter 22

We sat around the living room after dinner. Conner, Lea and both her parents argued and debated about what they should name grandchildren or some nonsense like that.

Grace sat on one of the old couches with slumped shoulders, and watched the discussion, without expression. Her eyes moved from the loud laughter and yelling to her folded hands on her lap. A heavy sadness seemed to blanket her features and my breath stalled; I recognized her loneliness. I knew it all too well. The need to touch her was overwhelming to me, so I sat next to her, her beautiful face turned to mine. Our lonely eyes met each other. No words were spoken between us, nothing needed saying. Our eyes and souls were connected in a room full of life, and we had been the two loneliest people in the world, I understood her; and we didn't have to be alone any longer.

In front of us, the laughing and teasing went on. My heart ached as if it were a real pain, for her. These were the only people she had left; Lea was like family to her.

I slowly reached my hand out to her and I could see her breath quicken a notch at the anticipation of my touch. Both of us looked down at our hands side by side in between us waiting for the collision of our bodies. When I slid my pinky along the side of her hand and up to the tip of her elbow, her breath caught and our eyes locked together once again.

I leaned in close to her. "Want to take a walk?" I asked in a low whisper that blew the loose strands of the hair against her neck.

Grace's head tilted back as if I had caressed her and a mischievous twinkle danced wildly in her eyes. "I have a better idea. Want to go for a bike ride?"

My stomach clenched. Why in the world would she want to go bike riding on a cold March day? "Yeah, sure, but I was kind of hoping I could hold your hand while we *walk." I also want to kiss you until you're a puddle of sexy sauce on the floor, and then I want to lick you up,* slowly.

She laughed and snorted, giving me a playful shove off the couch. "Come on, the garage is out back, and I'll let you hold my hand." She glanced over to Lea and smiled at her, giving her a wink. "Shane and I are going for a ride. We won't be too long."

Why did I have the feeling those two were laughing at me and she was going to put me on a bicycle with a giant banana seat with glittery pink fringe sticking out of the handlebars? Hell, I would slap some bright pink lipstick on and paint my damn nails if it meant I could spend time with Grace again.

Lea smiled wide, eyes twinkling, "Sure, when you guys get back, we can get ready to go somewhere on the beach to dance tonight." She gave me a wink. "Have fun." *Oh, yeah. Something was definitely going on.* Freaking bike probably had a little bell and a basket. *Screw it, I was ready to ring the bell, so bring it on.*

We grabbed our jackets and threw them on. She led me through the kitchen and out the side door into the backyard, all the while, holding my hand and tugging me forward, "You might want to zip up; it gets pretty cold by the ocean if we ride fast."

Ride fast? Yeah, my mind went completely to sex right there.

We walked through the empty yard and she opened the garage door letting out a low sigh. Yeah, my mind went completely to sex right there too. Well, until I looked into the open garage.

"Oh, fuck me. Grace, I thought you said bike! That's a..."

Blushing, she handed me a helmet from off one of the shelves and strapped one on herself. I knew my mouth was hanging open.

"A Harley Davidson Super Low 883?" She laughed. It was taking my breath away. "You still up for a ride, Shane?"

"Crap, Grace! Every single day I spend with you...you

310

have managed to shock me and turn my world upside down..." *Yeah, I started babbling. Next, I probably would be slapping on lipstick and doing my nails.*

Then, she did the sexiest fucking thing I ever saw a woman do. It wasn't a lap dance or a strip tease; she raised her leg, slung it over the bike, and pushed it out of the garage, through the backyard into the front of the house, *effortlessly.* I could barely walk alongside her; I was so damn turned on. It took a great deal of self-control not to bend her over that bike and own her right there. It was primal and animalistic; my body ached so badly for her it was bordering on fucking *pain.*

"Grace, there's no freaking way I'm riding bitch behind you." I wanted her body wrapped around me.

She slid herself over the gas tank and patted the seat behind her. "Then you drive," she said throwing me the keys.

"God, you're so damn beautiful," I whispered.

I slid up behind her and she settled her body into my lap. My helmet automatically collided with hers as my head slumped forward when the warmth of her body nestled perfectly in between my thighs. Muscles along my legs stiffened and twisted; my entire body was in flames. I placed the key in the ignition, turning it and when the engine roared to life, the vibrations of her body against mine almost sent me over the edge. *I needed to get a handle on my arousal or else I was going to embarrass myself up against the back of her ass on this bike.* I eased off the clutch, kicked my feet up and pulled out into the street. I wrapped one hand tightly around her waist while the other steered and Grace leaned back into me and smiled. We cruised down the streets alongside the sandy beaches of the Atlantic Ocean, cold wind whipping on our faces, burning our eyes and stinging our uncovered hands. The waves along the shoreline lapped against the beach and I could swear I heard it over the rumble of the engine.

Wanting to get closer to the ocean, I drove up onto the

boardwalk and rode above the old wooden slats for a few miles. Then I just needed to stop and sit with her in the sand, so I parked the bike and helped her off. Wordlessly, I took her hand and pulled her onto the beach, over the sand and right to the cold waves that crashed themselves against the shore.

I sat down on the sand and gently tugged her to sit down beside me. Our hands lingered in each other's and neither of us said anything. We just quietly stared out over the shimmering waters of the Atlantic, savoring the warmth that had sparked an inferno in our hands.

Softly, I pulled her closer to me and sat her in my lap with her legs draped over mine. A distant look fell like a shadow over her face and she busied herself by staring at her hands. I wondered what her thoughts had turned to, making her look so sad. Softly cupping her chin in one of my hands, I pulled her face to look at me. There was a fluttering feeling in my stomach and my heart hammered *un*rhythmically in my chest. I studied her face, trying to gauge if kissing her now would be too soon for this *friendship* she wanted to have.

Her chest rose and fell faster under my stare. Softly, I skimmed my fingertips from her chin across her jaw, down her neck and into her hair. My fingers were icy cold and I knew the feel of them on her skin was like fire. I pulled her head towards me, my lips gently pressed against hers, both of us panting and struggling for air. Then, I slowly pulled away. Pain darkened her features, and I knew I made the right decision on the kind of kiss. A small tender kiss like that had us both panting and wanting more. I wanted to take this *friendship* slowly, because by the time we got to more than friendship, we'd be fast, hard and explosive. I wanted to savor every moment of Grace.

I leaned back on my arms and smirked at her, "So what the heck was all that crazy talk with Lea's parents?"

Grace pinched her lips together, and sighed heavily shaking her head. *Frustrated, love? I feel your pain.* She shifted herself on my lap and I pretended not to notice; it almost killed me. Cursing under her breath at me, she lay down on her side in front of me, leaning her head against her hand. "It's just a funny game we play when her mother asks us inappropriate questions. Caroline knows we were just teasing her. We call it, *Oh Dear*. When someone asks us questions that are too personal, we try to come up with the craziest answers. The first person to make her mom say *oh dear* wins. Lea usually wins. You know Lea, she's got *a way* about her, sometimes you have to wonder where she comes up with some of the things that fly out of her mouth," she laughed.

"They've been like parents to you, huh?" I asked.

Her eyes turned glassy and looked out across the ocean. "Yea, they took Jacob and me in after my parent's accident and after my release from the hospital. I was fourteen and Jake was eighteen, but he left for college soon after my parents died."

I watched her carefully, wondering if I should say something more. I wanted to see what she had to say about her *ex-boyfriend* and if she had any clue if I was still *Shamsiel*. Clearing my throat, I took a deep breath and just went for it. "So what *did* happen with that ex-boyfriend of yours?"

Her eyes slowly moved back to look into mine. They probably tried to measure my sincerity for few moments, lingering on thoughts before her words emerged. "I was an idiot," she whispered, looking away. "I just loved him so completely that everything and everyone dulled in comparison to him. But it wasn't in his nature to love *me* the same way. When he had the chance to take me with him, or stay with me, he just left."

She thinks I left her here?

I was in complete shock. *What would cause her to think I left her, when it was me who gave up everything?* "It's kind of hard to believe that someone would leave you, Grace. Do you still love him?"

A strong winter wind blew her hair tossing it wildly across her face, dramatically, "Always and forever, and then an eternity after. A girl will never forget her first perfect innocent kiss." She breathed in deeply, "We were in really different places in our lives, Shane. I don't blame him one bit for his decision. He was someone very awe-inspiring and I know I didn't deserve his love...I just...I just *physically hurt* knowing that for so long, I held onto him when I had no chance to be with him, ever. He made the choice just to leave. I know it was supposed to be to make me happy, but it sure as hell didn't."

"The man was a bigger jackoff than I thought," I cringed. I needed to make her forget about angels and just fall in love with the *human me. That's all I had to offer her now.*

She smiled at me and shook her head slightly, "No, we just *really* weren't supposed to be together. It was a real Romeo and Juliet type of relationship. We were completely forbidden to be together."

I leaned my face closer to hers and whispered low into her ear, *"There is a charm about the forbidden that makes it unspeakably desirable."*

"Mark Twain? Shane, how do you know all those quotes that pop out of your mouth?"

My lips tingled from the wideness of my smile. "How do you know all the people the words belong too?"

"Touché," she said laughing.

I shifted even closer to her, so that my lips were now touching the warm skin of her cheeks. *"Hear my soul speak. Of the very instant that I saw you, did my heart fly at your service,"* I whispered.

"Shakespeare. The Tempest." She teasingly pushed my face away. *"Words have no power to impress the mind without the exquisite horror of their reality.* Edgar Allen Poe."

"You know, Grace, you are the only girl that can go toe to toe with me without batting an eye."

She batted those stunning eyes at me. *Fuck, I wanted to pounce on her. If I stayed on this beach any longer, I was going to lose myself inside her. Take it slow; don't let her know who you were!*

I almost punched myself in the nuts for ending our talk, but I had to. I couldn't stay there alone with her, without touching her in the way I really wanted to, or telling her the stuff I really wanted to say. "Want to head back now? I heard something about taking a little hottie out dancing tonight..." Taking her hand, I helped her up and we walked through the sand back to her bike, holding hands.

"So you're taking out a little hottie, huh? *Lucky girl,*" she laughed as we climbed back on the bike.

"Yea, well, it's pretty much a lost cause. Last time I made a play for her and talked to her, she just wanted me to treat her like one of the guys. It's a damn shame, because I think she's freaking amazing."

She blushed about ten shades of *sexy as sin* red across her cheeks. "Wow. So what are you going to do about that?" She challenged me.

Lowering my face to just an inch above hers, I brought my eyes right to hers, "I'm going to do *everything* I can fucking think of to change her mind."

A small gasp fell past her lips and with it, I turned around, started the bike and drove us towards Lea's parent's house. She grasped onto my waist, slid her cold hands under my jacket and shirt, and laid them against my skin. I thought she was trying to kill me. *Was there a more perfect way to die?*

Chapter 23

We really tried to wait for the girls to get ready, we really did. Conner couldn't take being in the house with Lea's parents any longer, while they planned out how many children Conner should father and what to name all six of them. So, instead of waiting in the middle of the battlefield they called a living room, we waited for the girls at a bar called *Sunsets*, right off the beach.

Conner slouched himself against the bar and hung his head in his hands, groaning.

After ordering two beers from a bartender with bright orange hair, I turned to Conner and nudged him with his beer. "You okay, bro?"

Raising his head only slightly, he groaned even louder, "Six kids, Shane! They expect six kids and they have named them ALL for us!" He straightened up and raked his hands over his face. "I am twenty-four years old. I've been with Lea for eight months and they are talking about us having six children. I feel sick. I don't even think I could take care of a fish."

Sipping my beer, I gave him a nod. "Do you love her?"

Conner sighed. "Yeah. I do. But *marriage?* Dude, how they hell do you know if you've found the right girl, I mean how...?" He froze in mid sentence and started laughing. "I'm an ass, look who I'm asking this question to."

"Number one, shut up and fuck you," I said, holding my fingers in the air counting at him. "Number two, I...uh..." I completely lost my train of thought.

Grace had walked in.

Um.

Ah.

Yeah, having trouble breathing.

The tiny little denim skirt she was *barely* wearing made those perfect legs that ended in a sexy pair of black stiletto heels look endless. The fringed waist of the skirt hung low on her hips,

316

showing off the flat smoothness of her belly and the sexy as sin curves of her hips. A deep burgundy low-cut shirt draped across her chest accentuated the plump full curves of her breasts, and Conner and his problems, and the rest of the damn bar just disappeared. Damn, she was *perfect*.

My heart was pounding hard in my ears as my eyes slowly crawled over her body and devoured every inch of her I saw. She smiled at me and flipped her dark hair over her shoulder, making me just about blow a load in my pants.

"Oh, my God, Grace. Shane is completely eye fucking you and I'm creaming in my panties right now. How does that not affect you?" Lea laughed.

Seriously, does she think I can't hear her?

"Uh..." Was all Grace answered her with, and then she ran her tongue along her bottom lip.

Lea's eyes widened as she gawked at Grace and yelled, "Holy fellatio! You are standing there licking him up with your eyes! Do you freaking hear the old seventies porn music playing in your head?"

Grace turned her attention to Lea and swayed a bit, "I freaking feel drunk already. Come on; let's go get me some liquid courage to deal with him."

"Yeah, well, don't let your thighs rub to close together, because you look like you're about to have a walking orgasm," Lea laughed.

"If only," Grace laughed, as she walked up next to me, laying her hands down on the bar.

I stepped up close behind her, leaned my hands out on both sides of her and put them flat on the bar. Slowly, I shifted myself closer to her body until I was flush up against her back. She was breathing hard. I was well aware that she could feel just how happy I was to see her as I pressed myself up against the soft curves of her bottom. I brought my head down to her ear, and I felt her shiver beneath me. My whisper bristled against her ear, "What do you want, Grace?"

"My breath back," she whispered.

I nuzzled my face into her hair and nipped my teeth along her ear, "You think you're breathless now? Just wait, Grace."

Her breath puffed out faster and she stretched her neck for me to have better access. To which I indulged, and ran my lips down. "So, for now, what would you like...to drink?" I asked.

She snapped her face to mine and turned her body to face me. "Sex on the Beach? A Screaming Orgasm? A Slippery Nipple? A Leg Spreader? A Bend Over Shirley?" Her hands had grabbed my shirt to pull me in closer.

Laughing, I dropped my hands to the warm skin of her hips and laid my forehead against hers. "What the hell is a Bend Over Shirley?"

Her hands unclenched and flattened across my chest, and then she slid them down slowly, hooking her fingers into the front pockets of my jeans. "Maybe I'll show you later..."

"You two are making me feel like I need to wear a condom over my head so I can't get pregnant from just listening to the both of you. Shane, it's Raspberry vodka, lemon/lime soda, grenadine syrup and Maraschino Cherries," Lea chimed in.

I looked at Lea, hating her at that moment *for fucking up the moment*, but I had no idea what the hell she was talking about. "Huh?"

Lea laughed, filled with raunchiness, "Holy sexual tension! Do you even know that we are here with you? We want Margaritas! Let's go, Shane, snap out of heat! Conner, man up and dance with me!"

Conner laughed and shook his head, "Why don't you and Grace start and let us men watch? I need a few beers after spending the afternoon with your father telling me what I should name our six children even though I apparently will end up eating them." He saluted her with his beer and frowned. *Shit, he was pretty upset about what was said by her parents.*

318

"Okay, boys. Enjoy the show then," she winked at Conner and pulled Grace right onto the dance floor. Grace yelped, and offered me a little goodbye wave and a smile. Lea quickly spoke to the DJ and immediately the track turned into *Tonight I'm Loving You*. Grace and Lea whispered to each other, laughed, and gave us a shy glance. *What the?*

As the music started thumping through the speakers, Grace's hands brushed the curves of Lea's hips. She opened her hands sensually and spread her fingers, slowly sliding them up the sides of Lea's body to just under the curve of her breasts.

"Oh my God," Conner whispered.

The two girls kept their eyes locked on ours, and continued to dance. *For us.* Lea slid her hands up Grace's neck and ran her fingers through her long hair, twisting it all into her fists. She arched Grace's head back slowly and brought her face to the bare skin of her neck, and with open lips, slid them against her soft flesh.

"They…" he stammered.

"Ahhh…" I answered.

Grace bit her bottom lip between her teeth, eyes still fixed on mine, sparkling with silver streaked mischief. She brought her hands gently to Lea's face and brushed the back of them over her cheek and lightly slid her thumb over her lower lip, dipping it in Lea's mouth. Lea gave her finger a small bite.

"I…" Conner stumbled.

"Oh," I answered.

Grace pushed Lea's head gently down and Lea's body slid and ground against hers. Both of them were sweaty and breathing heavily against each other.

I had to shift my weight to relieve the increasing pressure of myself against my pants. Blood rushed through my body and all I could see was her.

"That's just," I started.

"Shut up, Shane. Your voice is messing with my fantasy

right now," he murmured.

When the song ended, those sexy girls ran back to the bar next to us, panting for their Margaritas. We stood there frozen, tongues hanging out and stared at them. Lea grabbed both their drinks off the bar and pulled Grace to the side giggling. "Looks like they enjoyed the show, huh?" Lea walked her further away from us, winking.

Conner turned his head in my direction, but actually kept his eyes on his girl, "Yep. She's the one. Definitely."

Slapping him on the back, I laughed then looked back at Grace. She and Lea were sipping at their drinks as two guys sauntered up to them blocking my view of my sunshine. *Oh hell no.*

"Wow. You guys looked hot dancing out there. Can we buy you two your next drinks?" Douche number one asked Grace. Then he reached out and touched her elbow.

"Thanks, but we are both here with..." Before Lea could finish her Double Douche rejection, I stepped in between them and without saying a word, I put my hands on Grace's waist and led her to the other end of the bar. I spun her around facing me and backed her up against the bar, "Finish your drink. You're dancing with me."

She slurped the Margarita dry and her lips lifted up into a sexy grin.

"Damn, Grace. The way you wrap those beautiful lips around that straw and look at me with those breathtaking eyes, it makes it real hard to focus on anything else." I stepped back, grabbing her around the waist, and pulled her to the dance floor, real slow, swaying her hips against mine. Her eyes never left mine; she fucking intoxicated me. Pink's song *Try* came over the speakers. That song was sexy as all fuck, but dancing to it with Grace made it *sinful*, and I couldn't get enough of her.

I slid my hands down to hers, grabbing both her wrists and slowly lifted her hands up over my shoulders and around my neck. When her fingers laced together behind my head, I sighed *out-fucking-loud* and ran my fingertips back down along the bare skin of her arms, tracing little hearts and circles across her shoulders, continuing down over her sides. I skimmed across the bare skin of her waist and gently held my hands against the small of her back. Her skin was damp from dancing, which made my fingertips press themselves against her skin even harder; she held me closer.

I brought one hand up and ran my fingers along her jaw, stopping under her chin and I tilted her head back. Her midnight colored hair reflected deep blue highlights from the lights above us, and when her silver eyes flecked with lavender kisses looked up into mine, she shuddered and gave me a heart-stopping smile. Song after song, we danced against each other; sliding, slipping, floating. Touching. Teasing. *Tempting each other.*

But I didn't kiss her once. *No, I was saving her lips for later.*

"Hey, PORN STARS!" Lea interrupted up. "I need a bathroom break and I need my bitch with me. Shane, go keep Conner company, while I borrow your um...*girl*," she giggled, dragging Grace out of my arms.

My limbs felt stark and lifeless without her in them and my stare trailed after her, wondering if she felt the same emptiness as I did.

Conner met me at the bar and handed me an icy cold beer. I gulped it down, trying to cool my body with it.

"Looks like you two are playing nice now," Conner teased.

"You have no idea how hard it is for me not to fucking devour that girl in front of everybody."

"Wow. *Seriously?* Because it looked to me like you two were completely devouring each other on that dance floor." He shook his head at me laughing, "Lea is right; watching you guys is like watching porn and eating candy."

I laughed while I watched the crowds of people blocking

my view of the bathrooms, still lightheaded from Grace's touch. My entire body hummed with need to feel her again, touch her smooth skin, slip myself inside her, and all reason and rational thought abandoned me. "I'm going in that fucking bathroom after her," I said propelling myself through the crowd.

"Seriously? Holy crap!" he called after me.

Weaving through the dancing bodies, my world seemed to move in slow motion. Almost in arm's reach of me, I saw Lea and Grace run through the crowd laughing with each other. Lea ran a few steps ahead, then instantly, Grace was gone from my view. Chills flushed through my body and my shoulders tightened. Sharp spikes of adrenaline ripped through my human flesh.

Gabriel stood before her, blocking her path to me, bearing down toward her with fists shaking. He lunged closer to her with a fevered glare. "How about a dance, *Grace?*"

Grace went rigid and lifted her chin to him in pure sweet defiance, "No. Get out of my way."

I was almost there.

His head flew back in laughter, his massive shoulders shaking. He lunged towards her again with flaring nostrils, "Why not just one little dance? I can't stop thinking of that kiss yesterday."

Kiss yesterday? Oh, hell no.

My body tensed as I reached out and grabbed hold of his shoulder, "She said no. Now get the fuck away from her," I growled.

Gabriel slowly turned his icy blue eyes on me and one tight corner of his lips pulled up, smirking. "I will have my turn to dance with you, Grace, mark my words," he said.

Yeah. I was going to pummel him right there in front of everybody. What would he possibly do, yank out his wings in front of every human in the place? "Turn and leave now, before you aren't able to leave without a fucking medical examiner to haul your dead ass out."

Gabriel's mouth curled into a sinister smile, "Big words, pretty boy." Then he turned his back on me and stalked off, disappearing into the dancing crowd.

I noticed him again watching us, as he lingered by the front door.

Whirling around, I cupped her face in my hands and searched her beautiful face for the truth I knew she would never tell me, "Are you okay? Did he touch you?"

Shaking her head, she broke eye contact with me, "No he didn't. Thank you." Her voice was thick and her hands grabbed me, pulling me closer. "Come on, let's just get another drink and forget that psycho."

I led her to Conner and Lea who were by the bar watching us. Lea put her arms around Grace and I patted Conner on the back and smiled as if I wasn't planning to go kill someone. "Hey, order this gorgeous girl another Margarita. I'll be right back; I have to use the restroom."

I tore out of the bar and stood alone on an unnaturally silent city street. Tremors of pure white rage ruptured uncontrollably throughout my body when I heard his gravelly voice behind me. "She's my toy now, Shane. Not. Yours. You can't win the war with her."

I could feel my muscles and veins strain against the skin of this body, aching to fight him. "I'm not fighting in any make-believe war you think you've started, Gabriel. News-fucking-flash, *I'm human*. I don't have to deal with any of this crap. I'm just a regular human in love with another regular human girl."

"Such a stupid choice you've made. Humans die so easily; don't you remember that? With a silly little snap of my fingers, I could break your pretty boy neck as we speak."

I touched my fingertips together in front of my lips and gave him my best playful grin. "*Please* do. It's been a long time since I've been let into paradise, *brother*. And how beautiful

323

would it be, Gabriel? To enter heaven as the soul of a human and not an angel? To have *free will in heaven*. Isn't that what the war in heaven was supposed to be fought over? You've handed me everything that you're lusting after, asshole."

Instantly, he closed the distance between us, manically clenching his jaw and his fists, "You know nothing of what we fight for! You've been tucked away safely for thousands of years, dishonored, humiliated, FALLEN!"

Yeah, so I pulled back my arm and punched him square in the face with all my weight. He fell back onto the ground and I stumbled after him. I lowered myself to level my gaze at him. "That's where you're wrong, *Gabe*. I never FELL. I was PUSHED, and now I'm a HUMAN, not a fallen angel. I'm not dishonored, I was betrayed. I wasn't humiliated, I was humbled. I'm not fallen, because I was forgiven."

I stood up over him. "Your stupid war is between angels. Thanks to you, I'm no longer one. So if you want a war with me, it won't be one you can win. Leave Grace alone. She's innocent and I love her."

Leaving him on the street, eyes wide, I strolled back into the bar.

Grace was sitting on a barstool with some guy talking to her. Her eyes were set on the bathroom doors waiting for me and as soon as she saw me, she shook her head, sagged against the bar, closed her eyes tight and smiled. I walked right up to her, slid my hands around her waist, and nestled my face in her hair.

"Excuse me, but this pretty little lady is taken for the rest of the night," the guy standing next to her said.

Keeping my hands on her waist, I leaned back to look at her. Smiling at each other, we both turned to stare at the guy. "What the hell did you just say?" we both growled simultaneously.

The guy repeated his outrageous statement and Grace

blatantly laughed in his face. She ignored the strange look he gave her and she went to walk away towards Lea.

Then he grabbed her. He grabbed her by the elbow and spun her around. And before I could kill the guy, Grace's fist spun with the momentum and she cold-cocked him right in the nose. Blood spurted out of his nose and dripped down his face. "Touch me again and the next thing you'll feel is six feet of dirt over you."

She turned, looking at me, and my God, she gave me the sexiest smile, which made my knees weak. Behind her, the jerk moved forward again, but I held out my hand, smushed him in the face, and shoved him back hard. The guy went flying into a crowd of dancing bodies and got lost in their movements.

I grabbed her by the waist and pulled her body flush against mine. She melted right into me. "You have some messed up friends around here."

"None of them are friends," she whispered through lips close enough to kiss. "Come on, let's get out of here," she said pulling us all to the door.

Holding hands, we walked back to the Rossi's house in silence with only the swooshing sounds of the waves lapping against the sand filling our ears.

Mrs. Rossi had the two couches in the living room made up with pillows and blankets for Conner and me to sleep on. She came out of the kitchen when we walked in, explaining to us that *premarital sex will send you straight to hell if it happens under her roof without at least a ring and wedding date set.* Lea rolled her eyes and stomped up the stairs. Conner huffed and puffed the same way. Grace just glanced at me, smiled and nodded her head goodnight as she bounced her perfect bottom up the stairs. *Yeah. I was sneaking up there later.*

The girls thumped and giggled loudly above us as Conner and I tried to get comfortable on our makeshift beds.

"Crap, I feel like I'm fifteen. I'm a grown-ass man, so I

should be able to sleep with my woman," Conner grumbled. I listened to him whine and complain until his voice was only low mumbles, his breathing grew into light snores and sleep overtook him.

I stayed on the couch for a while, just listening to the silence as I watched the dance of car headlights through the window and across the ceiling, each time someone drove down the street.

My thoughts were on Gabriel and what needed to be done to protect Grace, when I heard a small movement at the top of the staircase. Soft padded footsteps landed on each stair and tiptoed slowly behind the couch I was on, stopping right above me. I could hear her breath and feel her eyes on me in the darkness of the room.

With only a small chuckle escaping from the back of my throat, I sprang up from the couch, grabbed her around the waist and dragged her over the back of the couch and into my arms. Grace let out a small yelp and I pressed the palm of my hand gently over her lips. Our eyes focused on each other's in the dim light, each waiting to see the other's next move.

I could feel her breath quicken beneath my hand and slowly, I slid my fingertips away from her lips and brushed them softly down her chin and neck. Her lips parted, waiting, hands gripping the front of my shirt tightly. In one quick move, I flipped her under me, onto her back, and reached my hand up to brush my thumb along her bottom lip. I pressed my body tightly against hers, while she ran her fingers along my jaw, over my cheeks and through my hair. I just about died when she pulled her knees up to my hips and wrapped her long smooth legs around me.

"Grace Taylor, I am going to kiss you right now and you are not going to run away from me, because you have no excuse now. Then you are going to go back upstairs to bed and all you are going to think about are my fucking lips on yours and nothing else. Not strange men that want to hurt you, or buy you drinks, not Ryan, not Tucker, not even Ethan. I swear to you, Grace, I will not let you think of anything or anyone else until I put my lips back there again. *Only mine."*

Brushing my mouth across hers, her breath quickened and her lips smiled wide before she wrapped her hands around the back of my neck and I crushed my lips against hers. Our lips moved against each other, slow and needy. A soft low whimper escaped from between her lips as we deepened the kiss.

She clawed at the bottom of my shirt, frantically pulling it up over my head. Our lips broke contact for a second, a low growl tore from my chest, and I slammed my lips against her when I was free of my shirt. *God, I wanted her.* I ground my hips into hers and a sweet as hell moan purred out of her lips. I wanted to hear her moan my name. My hands burned to rip her little pajama bottoms off so I could bury myself deeply inside her. I wanted to spend the rest of the night worshipping her body with my tongue, to taste every single inch of her silky soft flesh.

I lost myself between her lips, wrapped in her legs, in the soft whimpers that slipped from her swollen wet lips, in the tremors that hummed through her body. God, I loved feeling her shiver beneath me; I craved making her quake more.

Now I could. I could love her and worship her. I could kiss her and taste her. I could have her completely, because I was human now. There would be no punishment this time.

My fingers moved in slow circles over her. Her lips glided smoothly against mine, with each small flicker of my tongue, her body rocking against mine. I licked and kissed across her jaw and down her neck. She whimpered when I lifted her shirt and took one of her rock hard nipples into my mouth.

She softly trailed her fingertips down my chest, over my stomach and under the waistband of my pants. Her warm hand wrapped around me and slid up and down my swollen skin. "God, Grace," my voice croaked. I knew I had to stop this from going any further. But, damn her hands pumping up and down on my cock felt good. Fuck, I didn't want to stop. I wanted to feel what it was like inside her. I bit down softly on her nipple, and the sexy as sin moan that escaped her lips made me rock harder against her hand. *What the hell was wrong with me?* I squeezed my eyes shut tight and cursed myself under my breath. *Where the hell was my self-control?*

I placed my hand over hers and tugged it reluctantly out of my pants. We looked at each other panting, breathless, her eyes questioning and beautiful.

"Go back upstairs, Gray, and go to sleep," I rasped.

She smiled up at me and bit down on her bottom lip, "I sure as hell don't want to, Shane."

I softly ground my hips into hers one last time and placed both my forearms on either side of her head. I leaned down and nipped her lips, then pulled her over me and sat us both up, her legs straddling mine. "Grace," I whispered skimming my fingers over her moist lips. "I want to be inside you so damn bad right now. But when I do that, I want to hear you scream my fucking name as you claw your nails down my back. You can't do that here."

"I'm never getting to sleep now," she giggled.

"Baby, I'm going to be taking a cold shower for weeks after this," I teased.

"You know, I've noticed since I've met you, that doesn't really work too well," she said as she stood up and fixed her shirt.

"Remember tonight...for it is the beginning of always," I whispered as I watched the pale moonlight stream through the window and fall against her skin.

"Dante Alighieri, Shane?" she giggled as she made her way to the stairs.

"Shut up and go to sleep, Grace."

As she reached the first step, she turned towards me

once more. God, she was the most beautiful thing I'd ever seen. She touched her fingers to her lips, smiled and walked up the stairs.

"I found whom my soul loveth: I held her, and would not let her go...Song of Solomon, Grace," I whispered into the darkness.

Chapter 24

Pure chaos is what the Rossi's house was like in the morning. Conner and I sat cringing at the breakfast table as music blasted, neighbors stopped by and food was thrown. The closer it got to lunch, the crazier it got and right after lunch the four of us were desperately trying to get the hell out of that house and away from the madness. However, the only thing I could really focus on were Grace's lips.

I cornered her against Lea's bedroom door and whispered hotly into her ear, "Got plans for the rest of the day?"

"No plans," she whispered sliding her hands up my arms.

"Good. I want to spend the rest of the day with you. Want to go for dinner?" I asked.

"I'd love to," she squeaked. "I, um, was going to ride the bike back and leave the Jeep here. Do you feel up to riding or do you want to take the train back to the city with Lea and Conner?"

I touched my hand to her cheek and brushed away a loose strand of hair tucking it gently behind her ear. "There's no way I'm missing out on a ride between your legs all the way back to Manhattan."

Her eyes dilated. "Um, yeah. I'm ready to go right now, then."

I pressed myself against her warm body and kissed her deeply. I pulled roughly at her hips, hoisting her legs to wrap around me as I pushed her up against the door. The heavy ache to be inside her was building into an obsession. I slipped my fingers under the material of her sweatpants and plunged my hands beneath, cupping her bottom so she wouldn't fall.

She gave me a deep groan, "Oh, Shane."

The way her voice whimpered my name caused a low noise deep in my throat and I slid my fingertips under the fabric of her lacy panties. I skimmed them against her skin. Beads of sweat burst across my forehead when she pulled her head back and bit her bottom lip, trying to silence her soft whimpers.

"Fuck. Grace. You. Are. So. Wet." I growled into her lips. I pulled the thin lace, holding it tightly, desperately wanting to rip it from her skin. "We have to get the hell out of here or we're going to end up having the whole Rossi clan and the neighbors watching me have my way with you."

Dropping her legs from my waist, she grabbed the collar of my shirt and pulled her mouth roughly to meet mine. "That's not making me want to stop anything."

I ran my hands over her bottom, slid them up her sides and up to her breasts, moving my thumb in soft circles over her nipples. "We need an entire night to start exploring each other like I want to, not five intense minutes against Lea's door."

"An, entire night, huh?" She teased. "You've given this a lot of thought?"

I leaned my forehead against hers, our breathing evening out, slowing. "Since I first laid my eyes on your silver ones."

We left as soon as we could, waving our goodbyes to Lea and Conner at the entrance to the subway, as we roared past them on the bike.

With her arms wrapped tightly around my waist, the ride was simply intoxicating. Smelling the air, feeling the rapid shift of temperatures, and the sensation of her body wrapped around me was overwhelming. Our bodies moved together while the engine roared and vibrated under us. Back and forth, leaning, swaying, accelerating, and braking. Everything was in harmony, the ground, the bike, us. *Us*. The way it was always supposed to be. My mind went quiet and it was easy to lose myself to the moment. I ran my hands up and down her legs to keep her warm and just to keep reminding myself *that she was real*.

We coasted along the East River to Long Island City's *Water's Edge Restaurant*. The restaurant was home to huge open bay windows along the entire side of the wall that faced the city; the view was breathtaking. The Manhattan skyline was almost as stunning as Grace's wind swept hair and flushed cheeks when she took off her helmet.

Holding hands, we were seated right in front of the huge windows. I ordered a bottle of wine and we sat across from each other staring, lost in each other's eyes. Neither of us let go of the other's hands, even when the wine arrived.

"I'm glad you cancelled on Ryan," I whispered to her.

"Yeah, why is that?" she asked, teasing.

"I told you before, Grace. I want to kill any man that looks at you."

"You remember saying that to me?"

"I remember everything, Grace."

I watched the turmoil in her expression. I watched fear wash over her features. In that moment, I wanted to tell her who I had been, I wanted her to know the real me, but I knew I couldn't. Michael told me not to. Michael told me to have her love me for what's left of me; not for the part of me that's gone.

"*Everything?*" She whispered back.

"Yeah, Grace. Especially the part when I asked you to try to find *whatever it was you were looking for in me.*"

She gulped down the entire glass of wine. "Shane," she breathed. "You are all I can see right now." Shaking her head, she blinked her eyes as if she was trying to shake herself awake from a dream. Then she plunged the knife in, "Crap, it's like I'm one of your groupies, right? I understand it now though, all the girls and what they were thinking, I mean, damn, Shane. You treat a girl like this and she'll definitely get the idea that it's okay to give herself to you for a night."

"You still don't get how I feel about you, do you?" I whispered.

Grace offered me a small shrug and gulped down more wine.

"Is that what you think I want, just one night?" I asked her.

"Isn't it?" She whispered.

"No, Grace. Not with you," I answered. "And I'm sure going to have fun proving that to you," I winked at her.

Grace's body stilled, and then a shiver seemed to pass over her. Those silver eyes grew large and her cheeks flushed five shades of crimson. The rest of our dinner was full of us holding hands, touching each other, and jumping on her bike to rush home to be alone.

I drove up and backed into a small space between two cars in front of her building. Just as I was about to get off the bike, Grace unstrapped her helmet, threw it on the ground and slid her entire body against mine. I fumbled and tore at my helmet strap as she slammed her lips hard against my lips. Letting my helmet fall, it bounced and rolled along the edge of the sidewalk. Its echo danced against the buildings and silenced the city around us.

My hands slipped under the sides of her jacket and under her shirt; the heat from her body burned against my fingers setting me on fire. I slid them slowly down, settling on the sweet curves of her ass, my heart pounding hard in my chest. She squeezed her thighs tighter around me and grabbed fistfuls of my hair. Whimpering my name, she unzipped my jacket and glided her hands under my shirt and up over my chest. Our mouths were hard and raw against each other's. Falling together and pulling apart, tongues sliding roughly, as if we couldn't taste enough of one another. Cupping her bottom, I stood up, her legs still wrapped around my waist, digging her heels into my back. My cell phone vibrated in my front pocket and she rocked her hips against it. *Damn, that was hot.*

I growled, gripping my fingers tighter. "I need to be inside you," I breathed into her mouth. I climbed off the bike carrying her, kissing her lips, her neck, her jaw, clutching her tight against the front of my body. My mind was insane with lust. I needed to take her into the damn building before I slid

333

myself inside her on the seat of the bike on a New York City street. I never needed someone that much, ever. I couldn't think straight, all I could feel was the smooth hot skin under my hands and all I could hear were the low whimpers and moans of my name. That was my world.

Carrying her up the steps, I fumbled and slammed her back against the front door; she moaned deeply into my mouth. I pulled my head away and stared at her closed eyes. Her lips were parted, and she was *panting*.

I leaned forward, pressing her harder against the door and nipped her earlobe between my lips, giving her a sharp little bite. I nipped down her neck, scraped my teeth against her jaw and raked them up again to her ear. "Keys. Now." I growled.

She reached around into her pocket, all the while giggling. Pulling out her keys, she wiggled them in front of me and brushed her lips against mine. "Take me in, Shane. *Please*," she whispered against my lips.

Holding her up against the door with my hips, I grabbed the keys, slammed my lips back onto hers. I jammed the key into the door, missing the keyhole a few times, until I finally opened it and we stumbled through the doorway. I kicked the door closed behind us, leaned her up against the wall in the entryway and slid the zipper of her jacket down. *I needed her clothes off, now.*

"Um. Hey guys!" Lea's **IRRATING** voice cut in.

Grace froze. *Screw that*, I kept kissing her lips. She turned her head towards Lea and I kissed her cheeks and her neck, sliding her coat off her shoulders. I wasn't going to stop, oh hell no. *I needed in. Screw it, Lea could watch for all I cared.*

Lea cleared her throat, *you know, the one I wanted to strangle at this point*, "Wow. I do hate to stop this beautiful thing that's about to happen, but Conner and Ethan have been trying to call you, Shane, for like an hour already."

Barely able to breath, I fixed my glare on Lea. "Get to the point, Lea. Is someone either dead or in jail?" I asked, pulling out my phone and reading through the text messages.

Lea brows lifted. She took a deep breath, shook her head and blew it out loudly, "No, worse. Vixen4 just showed up at your apartment and they needed a place to crash. And crash your place is exactly what they seem to be doing right now. I'm sorry, Shane."

This shit doesn't make sense. The guys could handle the girls of Vixen4. I gritted my teeth together, I did not want to leave Grace at all.

All the messages were from Alex pleading for me to come home. All but *one*. One was from an unknown number.

Unknown: You can't have what's mine. Meet me outside, or I kill off your band one by one. G.

"Damn, I forgot Ethan told them they could stay with us." I looked at Grace trying to explain, sliding my hands down her arms, "They're a handful." *I'm going to kill Gabriel, then come right back here.* I raked my hands through my hair. "Grace, I…"

Biting her bottom lip, she leaned forward and whispered deep into my ear, "Will you try your best to come back tonight? You have to finish what you started, Shane. I'll try to wait for you…"

I'm going to kill Gabriel.

Kill. Him.

As calmly as I could, I cupped my hands around the back of Grace's neck and pulled her lips up to mine. I nipped her bottom lip between my teeth and tugged gently, "God, baby. You are delicious. I'll try my best. If not, nine o'clock practice tomorrow. Vixen4 will be doing studio time after us." I didn't want her to feel the anger shaking off my body or the intense hatred I had for the one being who had managed to hurt us for so long. I needed to put an end to the game he was playing. "I'm going to need to throw a bucket of ice down my pants," I lied as I slipped out the front door. I didn't need a cold shower, Gabriel's words had already done the job.

Chapter 25

The anger in my body boiled as I ran down the front steps of her apartment. Then a dark form moved quickly out of the shadows and quickly intensified into the solid figure of Gabriel. Passing through the fence, cars and motorcycle, moving toward me expressionless, as if he hadn't a care in the world. Not yet realizing his death by my hand was moments away.

"Tsk, tsk. Shane, I can feel your anger and fury like the weather. I always loved how humans demonstrated their weaknesses so publicly. Are you really planning to try to take my life? My existence? And as a human, how would you accomplish that feat?"

"Fuck you, Gabriel."

"Yes. Perhaps *that* might leave a scar."

Gabriel was in front of me instantly, hands grasping the collar of my jacket and dragging me into a small alleyway a few yards away from Grace's apartment building. He shoved me into the shadows of the buildings and I tumbled nosily into a couple of metal garbage cans that lined the alleyway.

I struggled to get up, my hands flexing and clinching at my sides. "You really think I won't fight you for her? You think I'm going to give up so easily?"

Spreading his ancient wings across the dark walkway, he stood before me and glared down at me. His eyes were wild, dark, tormented and so fucking *haunted*. "She'll never love a dreg of life junkie womanizer like you, Shane. And I'm going to make sure she sees you for what you truly are. You're not the angel that she wants, you're nothing." Slowly, he removed something from one of his pockets, and angled his hand, hiding whatever it was from my view.

Anger seized me, my fists shook with rage and I wanted to throttle him like an animal. I shoved my hands against his chest, pushing him back, "I will fight for her. And I *will* win."

His hand, like a steel grip, claimed my throat and panic swept through me. Lifting me with one hand and holding me above the ground, he rammed a syringe into my jugular, shoving filth into my veins. Yanking the empty needle out of my neck, he dropped me to the ground and smiled down at me. Euphoric heat surged through my veins.

"Gabe, you're not fighting fair..." I lazily smiled up at him as the high gushed through my body.

"That should be enough heroin to kill that pretty-boy shell you call a body. Twice over. Grace will only know you as the has-been drug addict you were. They won't find your body until morning, little brother. By that time, I'll have Grace wrapped around my fingers, Pretty-boy."

"Aw, Gabriel, you keep calling me a pretty boy and I might start thinking you find me attractive," I murmured as I fought with my body to stay in control.

"Even in your last breaths, you joke. Just think about how your little Grace will feel when she sees you're nothing more than a junkie. Maybe, I'll even add to her heartbreak by wrapping your dead body around one of your repulsive whores. Then she'll see Shane Maxton for who he really was. Don't worry, I'll be the ANGEL who comforts her."

His laughter echoed between the walls of the brick buildings that towered over my body. My limbs started shaking violently and my mouth filled with foaming salvia. My thoughts were warm and fuzzy, all I could do is scream out for Michael, and beg for some sort of help.

Then the heroin hit. Warmth enveloped my body, it was one of those *warmths* that separated your mind from your body, and I could feel nothing of how my body was shutting down, convulsing and snarling on the cold street. Everything felt perfect and I would have sworn that we lived in a world where everyone rode on pink unicorns and nothing could ever go wrong. There was no danger, Grace was a lost thought and my veins almost burst with the high.

I know in my haze that I heard my voice calling for Michael, and somewhere deep inside my brain, I sensed that this feeling wasn't supposed to be this good.

My heart rate escalated to a wild drumming rhythm and my heart almost burst from the pressure. My body was overdosing, but my high let me feel nothing but pure pleasure. Somewhere inside the sublime euphoria, panic took hold, and my heart sped up even faster. I felt my breaths coming out in struggling gasps and my brain pounded against my skull. I wanted to die. *Please Michael, take this poison out of me.*

Crawling out of the alley, I stumbled into the dark street and collapsed in front of a yellow taxi barreling towards me. Brakes screeched, but then strong, feathered arms pulled me up, lifting me over the vehicle and into the night.

Michael carried me; the heat and burn of the heroin tore out of my body, leaving me twisted and tortured, but utterly sober. I blacked out, spiraled into nothingness, the earth falling from beneath my feet; I fell. And I landed hard.

When I opened the door to my apartment with trembling hands, it was 7:30 in the morning. Cringing, I stepped into what looked like a frat party exploded all over my once clean walls. *What the hell could make such a disaster?*

My answer walked in on red stiletto heels, with wild and messy shoulder length dark hair, and wearing nothing but a pair of little red lacy panties. Ignoring Bliss, heroin poster child, one of *original* Shane's lifelong friends, I bolted to my bedroom (which one of the guys had the decency to lock for me). My heart was hammering erratically in my chest and my hands shook violently from the quick withdrawal of the drugs in my system. *How the hell was I going to get through a band practice like this?* I knew from experience, this was just the beginning.

I needed a run. I needed to go for a run and work off this... this... uncontrollable... feeling. My legs shook. I bounced on the balls of my feet. My skin crawled. *Fuck. It was 7:40! An hour and twenty minutes. I have an hour and twenty minutes before Grace will see me. She couldn't see me like this.*

I tore off my shirt and pants and ran into the bathroom. Bliss was right behind me, yapping her high-pitched scratchy voice off at me, "Where the hell have you been all night? Alex was telling me about your new little guitarist. Says you got some serious feelings for her. Shane Maxton don't do serious. What's your story?"

I slammed the bathroom door in her face and turned the shower on. I needed the shakes to stop. I needed my muscles to calm down. Scalding hot water slid over my body, sending searing pain through my skin, into my pores and veins. Falling to my knees, my body convulsed against the absence of the drugs. I fumbled halfway out of the bathtub and grasped hold of the damp porcelain of the toilet bowl. Nausea knotted and cramped at my stomach muscles until I purged what toxins were left inside me; my naked body twisting and fighting against itself across the cold tiled floor. My temperature soared and my muscles ached savagely.

Crawling back into the tub, with whatever little energy I had left, I scrubbed my skin raw with soap. My flesh itched and craved its high. *I can't do this. I can't let Grace see me like this. I needed to cancel practice.* This body couldn't fight this need, not in front of everyone.

The blazing stream of the shower rinsed the soap away. I watched the tiny bubbles whirl in circles as they were flushed down the metal drain and I wished I could liquefy and follow; flow into the running water and eventually evaporate into the world.

My hands pawed blindly at the spout of the faucet, but my hands were too heavy and weak to turn the water off. My whimpers echoed against the tiled walls and mocked me.

I didn't know how many minutes passed before someone

reached over me and turned the water off. I was falling in and out of consciousness when cool hands wrapped a soft towel around my shoulders.

"Forgive me, Shane, I forget how easily breakable human bodies are," Michael's voice whispered against my cumbersome body as he wrapped his wings around me and lifted me up.

Instantly, I felt the pull; the slow pull of all the filth disappearing from all the cells of my body. Draining me. Draining me until my eyes focused, until my breathing became steady and my heart beat strong.

"Is she truly worth this, Shane?"

"You've never felt how soft her lips are," I whispered to him as I struggled to stand. Quickly, my body felt lighter, healthier, and stronger. *Relief*.

"Is lust all that this is about?"

Lifting my gaze to meet his, I held his icy blue stare. "Michael, I've spent thousands of years in a prison in Hell and every single moment my thoughts were of her and not the suffering. I've spent months here in this twisted drug addicted body trying to forget her through lust with other women and I can't. I've been broken and she's my missing pieces, *all of them*. My heart wants what it wants. She is the other half of my soul. I will never feel whole until she's mine."

A slight smile played against his lips as he nodded his head and disappeared. The air around where he stood shifted and shimmered until I was standing naked, completely alone.

Even though I was completely dry, I wrapped the towel around my waist and walked back into my room to get dressed. Bliss jumped out of the kitchen and followed me through the hallway, unaware that my human body almost died on the other side of the bathroom wall moments ago, or that an archangel had been an arm's length away from her.

She trailed me to my room and whined while I searched my drawers for clothes. Turning my back to her, I dropped the towel and quickly slid up a pair of boxers and jeans.

She leaned against the frame of my door and crossed her arms over her still bare chest. "You know, Shane, both of us half dressed in your room could be lots of fun. I haven't seen you in over ten months, how about a little playtime?" She pulled a vial of some sort of drug out of her damn panties, closed my door and slithered up next to me like a slutty snake. She was even hissing some bullshit about something.

I ignored her little bottle of addiction. "Damn, Bliss, doesn't your left leg miss your right leg?" I quipped, grabbing my tee shirt and headed for the door.

She moved in front of me, thrusting her chest in my direction. "Whoa. Shane, are you saying I can't keep my legs closed *like it's a bad thing*?"

I walked around her, not even looking at her chest. "All I'm saying, Bliss, is that you have climbed to the top of the skank tree, then fell," I turned around and looked her deadpan in her bloodshot eyes. "And you banged every guy on the way down. I don't want to touch *that*. And yeah, I have some serious feelings for Grace. So serious that my interest in sticking my dick in any willing girl ceased to exist."

"I don't believe it. You're fucking lying. You're too much of a whore, Shane, one girl will never keep you entertained for long."

"Think whatever you want, Bliss," I murmured.

A nasty smirk creased her lips, "Tell me, Shane, is she okay with all your other girls? Is she accepting of how much of a whore you really are? How about the drugs, Shane? Does she even know? Remember the last time we got high together?"

"I've changed. I grew up. I've been clean for nine months and the last time we got high, I went on such a bender I ended up almost dying in the bathroom of Boozer's with that little red head friend of yours you introduced me to. I'm not going back to that *darkness*."

Opening my bedroom door, I stormed down the hallway yanking my shirt over my head. Bliss followed behind me, still whining. Still wearing nothing but those little red panties.

I walked out of the hallway to Grace standing at my front door talking to Ethan. Her eyes snapped straight to Bliss and the sheer look of horror that crossed her face was like a bat to my knees. Her face flushed bright red, and I knew she immediately thought the worst of me. The worst part was that I couldn't even blame her for it; I had never proven myself different from what she saw then.

From where I stood, I could see the tears well in her beautiful eyes and my heart ached to reach out and grab a hold of her. She raised her chin and met my gaze. Time froze. I could see hatred and disgust in those eyes; and then nothing. Her stare turned stoic and she blankly turned her head, devoid of all emotion, as if she just switched herself off. *No, she switched me off.*

"I got coffee for everyone downstairs if practice is still on," she said innocently.

When the word coffee slipped from her lips, Alex climbed out from behind the couch wearing a pair of black boxers with a giant yellow smiley face on the front. "Ah, Grace, my love, you always have the most perfect things coming from your lips. Lead me to the coffee."

Alex stumbled over the couch and walked past Grace through the front door and down the hall humming idiotically about coffee. Ethan followed him.

Grace looked at me once more with lips trembling, and turned to leave. I lunged for her shoulders, pulling her gently back inside, desperate to set her straight. But as soon as my hands reached her she flinched and my heart sank.

Jumping at the opportunity she saw, Bliss strutted past us slowly and bit her lower lip looking from Grace back to me. "Let me know if you find my bra, sweetie. I'll round up the girls and

343

we'll meet you in the studio in a bit," she purred.

What the hell would possess Bliss to do that? Fuck, Grace was never going to believe anything I said now.

Bliss sashayed her nasty ass back down the hallway, giggling. Grace's eyes were glued to Bliss as she walked away. "Damn, Shane, did you choose the wrong girl last night," she whispered.

"Grace, don't. Don't even think any of your stupid shit about me. The only person I wanted to be with last night was you. It's always you." I deadpanned.

Slowly, Grace's eyes traveled back to mine. "Sure, Shane. Whatever you say. It's not like I don't know how you are, Shane, so please don't mistake me for stupid." She yanked her body from my grasp and smiled sweetly. "I'm going into the studio to practice. I'll see you whenever you get there. Remember I brought you boys coffee," she said without a care.

I stormed down the hallway in search of Bliss, who of course I found sprawled out, still wearing only her undies, across my bed. "Get your filthy ass off my bed. I'm not fucking playing games with you," I seethed.

Bliss's eyes widened for a second, and then a slow smile lit up her face, "She must have one hell of a golden pussy, huh, Shane?" She lifted herself onto her knees and crawled across my bed seductively. "You know, even gold tarnishes and loses its shine, sweetie. And when hers does, I'll be here to play with you."

Screw this. I couldn't take it anymore. I grabbed her by the shoulders, shoved her out of my room, and locked the door behind us. "Gold doesn't tarnish, you're thinking of silver, which is nothing compared to the worth of gold, *kind of like you.* And believe me, that girl will never lose her shine. Now, fuck off."

I ran into the living room where Brayden and the rest of Vixen4 were getting ready to head to the studio.

Brayden nodded his head at me, "Hey, bro."

Not making any eye contact with him, I just nodded in his approximate direction, and we all walked to the studio. Well, not me, I ran. My heart thumped wildly in my chest as I wondered what I could say to make Grace understand that I wasn't messing around with Bliss. I thrust open the studio door, slamming it against the wall as Brayden and I walked in.

"Oh man, make them go away," Ethan whispered under his breath when Vixen4 came in behind us. He gave a tight glance to Alex who nodded in agreement. "It's going to be a long sleepless week."

Immediately stalking in from behind me, Bliss and the rest of the members of Vixen4 moved forward and circled Grace, closing in on her fast. From behind his drum kit, Ethan bolted upright, rigid and ready for a fight. The skin on my arms prickled with a burning intensity to protect Grace, so I leaned forward to march in between them, but Alex's arm reached for both Ethan and me. "Dude, it's Grace. She'll be fine. Let her piss on her turf," Alex laughed. And he was right. This awe-inspiring creature had handled a hell of a lot worse in all her years on earth than Vixen4.

"Hey there. *Grace.* We're the Vixen4," Bliss sneered, flipping her dark hair behind her shoulder. "They call me *Bliss,*" she hissed. They surrounded Grace like predators to prey.

Grace casually slung her guitar strap over her head and smiled wide. "Oh, is that what they call you? I wonder what they call you when you're not around," she said sweetly as if it were sugar from her lips.

Bliss stepped even closer to Grace and grimaced, hissing like a pissed off cat. "This here is Scratch," she said pointing to her pink haired bassist. "You might want to ask Shane why we call her that, unless you've already seen the scars on his back?" she lied.

Grace's eyes snapped to mine and they danced with laughter as giggles shook her shoulders. "Wow, *Bliss.* The color jealous bitch doesn't suit you, so why do you bother wearing it?"

Oh, thank God she doesn't believe any of this shit. My shoulders relaxed with relief.

Bliss snapped her mouth closed, and then she laughed sarcastically. "Wow, the little shit has a mouth on her pretty little face. How fucking sweet is that," she laughed again and gave Grace a snide look. "This is Cream," she said pointing her finger to the blonde hair guitarist. "And this here is Essex," she jabbed her thumb at her drummer who stood there with arms crossed and dressed from head to toe in military fatigues.

Bliss charged at Grace, stopping an inch in front of her face. My fists tightened and my body fought itself to surge forward, but I didn't move. Neither did Grace, she didn't even flinch, not even a tiny bit of eye widening or a gasp.

"She don't look like very much to me, gentlemen," Bliss turned to face me sneering. Brayden must have seen my fists and my stance, because he was immediately on me, holding me back from ripping Bliss's head clean off her body. Then, Grace laughed. She freaking laughed out loud right in her face, and as always, I was amazed by her resolve and her strength.

"Wow, *Bliss*, how long did it take you to come up with that one? Did it keep you up all night?" Grace giggled turning her eyes to meet mine. My breath faltered.

"No, Shane kept me up all night," Bliss snared.

I shook my head no and tried to struggle out of Brayden's hold. Ethan jumped up and helped hold me back. The spark went out in her silver depths as she watched me. Then Grace turned her stare at Bliss and looked dead in her eyes, smiling another sweet smile. "So, *Bliss*, tell me how much semen do you swallow to become that stupid? Why would I care who kept your creepy looking ass up all night? And Shane, well, we all know **you could slap a wig and stilettos on a fucking three legged chair and Shane would try to fuck it.** I wouldn't be bragging about getting a piece of Shane, anybody could do it."

Grace stepped closer to her, bumping into her, as if she was a badass gang member about to pop a cap in her ass. It kind of scared me a little, and it turned me on a lot.

"Ah man," Alex murmured from behind me. "I love that girl. You guys are so lucky I broke my arms to get her."

I struggled against Ethan and Brayden, groaning. Alex caught my line of vision, leaned in really close to me and whispered, "Hey, LOSER, I'm thinking, now I could be wrong, but maybe...just maybe, fighting with Bliss right now is NOT going to get Grace to L-word you back. I'm just saying, though. Calm yourself down, man."

Grace gave me a tight smile, walked right past us and bumped shoulders with Bliss causing her to spin around like a rag doll. "You guys ready to play?" Grace asked, plugging her guitar into one of the amps. "Or you guys going to bring in the mud and watch Bliss and me go at it for your viewing pleasure."

Alex looked at me and bit down on his lip, moaning, "Grace covered in mud, *yummy edible dirt*." He ran over to Grace, picked her up and twirled her around. He nestled his face near her ear, "You're my most favorite girl ever."

I clenched my teeth painfully as rage roared through my body. I croaked a small, EM-Fucking-BARRASSING, protest when his hands touched Grace. And before I could think about what I was doing, my hands wrenched Alex off of her, shoving him away.

Alex held up his hands laughing. "Relax, bro. She's all of ours, not just yours." Then he stuck his tongue at me and winked. Ass.

"Just keep your hands off her, Alex," I said as I yanked Grace out of the studio and into the hallway. With my hands around her shoulders, I leaned her against the wall and took a step back, leveling my eyes to hers. Raking my hands through my hair, I whispered to her, "Say something to me, Grace. Tell me that you know me better than that."

She leaned her back against the wall, and strummed a few chords on her guitar that was haphazardly hanging off her shoulder. "Lie to me, Shane. Tell me that you didn't leave me and spend the night with her."

I staggered back as if she slapped me.

She shook her head and laughed, pulling herself off the wall, "You know what? Don't bother, Shane. We were just friends, so there's no bad crap between us, it's none of my business what and who you do. Let it go, I know we didn't have anything more between us. Let's just do what we do best together, okay?"

I swallowed back bile and squeezed my eyes shut, shaking my head. Before my arms could grab her in an embrace, before the phrase, 'I was Shamsiel' passed my lips, she walked past me, leaving me alone in the hallway.

Grace plugged her guitar back in and without any warning started playing the first song to our set. Slamming violently on her strings, her voice exploded through the studio, anger visibly ripping through her. With her eyes locked on my mine, she tore through riffs with a fury.

Heat swept over my skin as I savagely grabbed my guitar and responded to her angry music with mine. My fists pounded against my instrument, my fingers clawed at its strings. I twisted myself into her melody backing her against one of the studio walls. I might as well have been trying to fight against a mountain, she maintained her rhythm and fiercely powered through my advance. Piercing each other with our voices and our harmony. It wrecked me; it tore my heart, her anger, her passion.

I just had to stand there and take it. I had to stand there and watch her hurt. I had to watch her destroy me. All because I couldn't tell her shit.

Chapter 26

"Shane, if you were anymore stupid, I would have to water you twice a week!" Lea's voice screeched through my phone.

"Wow. Lea, thanks. That just made my shitty day better. What the..."

"Shut up, Shane. Just tell me if your dumb angel ass slept with any one of those skanks from Viven4 last night!" she snapped.

"No," I answered.

She growled through the phone. I seriously held it away from my ear for a minute and looked at it. *I could still hear her growling.*

"NO, you won't tell me or NO, YOU DIDN'T PLAY PIN THE PRICK ON A SKANK LAST NIGHT?" Lea screamed. My phone wasn't even to my ear and I heard her crystal clear.

"Pin the Prick on a skank? Seriously, Lea, give me a break. I wasn't even with them last night. Grace caught me walking in and changing my shirt with Bliss behind me, nothing more," I explained.

"Well, my best friend just called me extremely upset, Shane. She called for a BOYS HATER CLUB NIGHT! That hasn't happened since we were fourteen! Go talk to her and tell her everything, right now!"

I squeezed my eyes tight, and I swear, for a few moments I thought I might be having a heart attack from the sharp pain that slammed through my chest, into my lungs and right up my throat. "I can't," I whispered into the phone. "Besides, she won't want me as Shane Maxton, until I prove to her Shane's a good guy."

"Hey, douche? You're a man now, start acting like one." Then she hung up on me. *Burn. That stung.* That woman's mouth was lethal with words.

I looked up at the ceiling of my bedroom, cringing inside. I came straight home from band practice; right after Grace tore out of the studio like she'd self destruct if she stayed any longer. She shot daggers at me when she left, and the sick part was that it felt like those dagger actually *cut me*.

Screw this. If she were upset, she'd be going for a run. I changed quickly into my sweats and raced to her apartment.

Grace was barreling through her front door with her little white hoodie on, sneering at me. God, I wanted to kiss the hate off her lips.

"Yeah, I thought you'd be ready for a run," I said, offering her a smile.

"And you thought this because..." she prompted slamming and locking the door behind her.

"Because you're pissed off at me and when you get angry you run. It's what helps you think, clears your head," I whispered, moving closer to her.

"You are very arrogant, Shane Maxton, to think that I'd be thinking of you or feeling angry with you." She bent down and began stretching, never taking her eyes off mine.

I shifted myself even closer to her, until my face was hovering just above hers. Her lips parted and her eyes held firm to mine. My fingers ached to touch her lips and my body flooded with heat. "No, babe. You do think of me, you are angry with me, and Grace, you want me every damn bit as much as I want you."

Her skin flushed bright pink and she swallowed hard. "Well crap, Shane, now I really need to run," she whispered back.

So we did. For two hours, I kept her pace and we ran around Central Park, stomping our anger and issues beneath our sneakers.

When we cooled down and ended back in front of her apartment, I couldn't help but smile when she asked me, "Want to come in for some water?" She held the door open and her eyes challenged mine, as if she wasn't taking no for an answer.

Like I was going to say no to her, *ever*. I pushed myself through her door impatiently. I needed more than just water to quench the thirst I had for her.

Just like she could hear my thoughts, she walked down the hallway in front of me, grabbed at the bottom of her hoodie and pulled it over her head really slow. She wore a tiny tank top underneath that barely covered her smooth back that glistened with a damp layer of sweat. When she shimmied out of her bottoms and stood in front of me with just her tiny boy shorts on, every single nerve ending in my body stood up rigid.

She looked back over her shoulder toward me, biting down on her bottom lip.

I yanked my shirt over my head and threw it behind me on the floor. "Come here," I whispered as I closed the distance between us. Wrapping my arms around her, I pulled her against my bare chest. Lowering my face into her neck, my breath hot against her damp skin, I tasted her salty sweetness. My tongue caressed her skin and my hands slid up her slippery stomach cupping themselves around her breasts. I pressed my hips into her and a small whimper slipped past her lips.

Slowly, she turned around to face me, sliding her index finger seductively along the lines of my tattoo. "I'd love to hear the story behind this one day," she whispered, kissing and gliding her tongue over the inked lines. She looked up at me through her long dark lashes and my breath caught. I wanted to drown myself in her skin.

"God, Grace," a moan vibrated deep within my chest. Bending my head down, I rested my forehead against hers and fixed my eyes on her. I ran my fingers gently through her hair grasping handfuls and knotted them in my fists. Holding onto her head firmly, I pulled her face to mine and covered her lips. I took the smallest nip of her bottom lip and tugged, pulling back. Backing her against the wall, I slipped my tongue inside her mouth, pure lust pounding through my veins.

Her hot sweaty palms against my chest pushed me away. It shocked me. Seriously, it almost killed me. A whimper tore from my chest, as if I was a wounded animal. Her distance felt like an amputation.

"Ahhh no, no. I can't…I can't do this," she moaned and pulled away. "I'm done, Shane," she whispered.

I jerked away, pulse racing. I focused my eyes on hers and stood up straight and tensed, "What's that mean, Grace?" I asked through clenched teeth.

Tears rimmed her eyes, as she looked away, "I'm. Done. Shane."

I slid my hands back up along her scalp and gripped her hair tighter between my fingers, tilting her head so she would look back into my eyes. Searching her face, I growled, "Grace, what are you done with?"

"You."

The wind knocked out of my chest and I inhaled unevenly, trying to catch my breath. Instinctively, I pushed away the sharp pain of her words. My hands flew off her, yet I still spoke my heart. "Don't give up on me, Grace. I'm here with *you* now."

She backed up, laughing at me with tears streaming down her face. *Fucking laughing and crying.* "Shane," she shook her head slowly. "You have this special way of making any girl feel…completely insignificant, and I couldn't care less what you say or do, I won't agree to be insignificant, inconsequential, or easy replaceable for anyone."

Then I gathered every ounce of strength I ever had to stand my ground, and watched her walk the fuck away from me.

Within the hour, Lea was calling my cell phone again, ranting and raving at me. Alex and I were at a diner, eating and well, truthfully hiding out from the girls from Vixen4 who were at the moment, performing one of their shows at a small venue on the West Side. We didn't feel up to hearing Bliss screech about itchy track marks or cheating boyfriends.

She huffed into the phone, whispering. "I'm hiding in the bathroom of Boozer's so I can talk to you! Where the heck are you? You better not be at Vixen4's show or I will punch you in the nuts so hard your future children will feel it!"

The thought caused me to laugh out loud, "You're freaking insane, Lea. Alex and I are at a diner. I thought you girls were having a Boys Hater Night, you know burn a bunch of my pictures and talk about all the crap *I've never done behind Grace's back.*"

"Shane," she whispered. "Get your sexy ass down to Boozer's now. Ryan is making lovey dovey goo-goo eyes at Grace and she's staring at his lip ring like it's a life preserver and she's effing drowning!"

I coughed my soda up all over Alex, who sat across from me cursing and trying to wipe himself clean with wads of crumpled napkins.

"What am I supposed to do about it, Lea? Go all caveman on her? Storm down there and grab her by the hair and drag her all the way to bed?"

"Oh, that sounds...nice..."

"Lea!" I screamed. By that time everyone in the diner was listening to the conversation and Alex had soda and ketchup smeared all over his shirt and face.

"Listen, Shane. Marie just told her that nothing happened between the both of you that night we all got drunk at Boozer's." *Which night is that? Because we seem to get drunk at Boozer's every night. Focus, Shane.* Lea continued, "Not that I thought you did anything with Marie, you wouldn't stick your dick in a shark's mouth..."

"Lea, I didn't do anything with Bliss either. Shit, Lea, I haven't slept with anyone since I saw Grace that first night. I've told her, but she doesn't believe me. She doesn't trust me."

"You're both, like, on fire when you're together, Shane,

and she's fucking terrified you will consume her and she's going to get burned. She doesn't know it's you, she thinks you are only Shane Maxton, you have to tell her!"

Of course, since that's all she had to say on the subject, she hung up on me. Again. *How the hell does Conner deal with her?*

Of course, when Alex and I walked into the Boozer's, Grace was sitting at the bar with Ryan drooling at her like a dog in heat. A dog that needed to be put down. When she turned her head in my direction and finally noticed me, a guilty look crossed over her face. *What the hell?* I could feel the color just drain out of my face as white-hot anger ripped through my body. *Was telling her I was once an angel going to make her love somebody like Shane? How could you fall in love with someone because of what they once were?*

Ryan followed Grace's stare and frowned in my direction. Nice friend. A sudden thought of Boozer's needing a new bartender filled my mind, *and yeah, I know how petty I sounded, but I hated him that moment.* As if Ryan could hear my thoughts, he dragged his body back across the bar away from Grace, leaving her sitting alone, watching me.

I raked my hands through my hair and walked out the front door, Alex trailing behind me.

"Hey, you okay?"

"Just awesome," I answered him.

Clapping a hand on my shoulder, he pulled me back against the side of Boozer's. "So tell me how it feels," he murmured.

I lifted my head to look at him, his green eyes wide with wonder. "How does what feel?" I asked him.

Alex shrugged his shoulders and leaned against the cold brick of the building, "Being in love with her." He tilted his head to the side, raised his eyebrows at me and waited.

I rubbed at the back of my neck and tried to avoid his

stare, "Dude, shut up."

Alex crossed his arms, watching me, a slow smile burning across his face. His voice turned soft, "I'm kind of serious, Shane. I never felt what you look like when you look at her."

I covered my face with my hands and raked them across the sides of my neck, looking at him. "There is nothing in this world I have ever wanted more than to bury myself inside that girl. I...I have no fucking common sense when she's near me, all I can think of is *her*." I rubbed my face again with my hands, "It's like I've turned back to being a junkie, trying to score my next fix *of her*. It's sick, Alex. And all she thinks is that I'm this fucking asshole who will sleep with anyone and she's just the next notch on my belt. Ever since I saw her in the audience that night, the first time I laid eyes on her; there was no one else worth thinking about. "

"So, I don't get it, then why did you just leave the bar?"

"Because maybe someone like Ryan is better for her than a piece of shit like me," I mumbled.

His smile slipped and his eyes rolled. "Okay, Shane. What the fuck did you eat for lunch, a narcissist burger with a side of self-esteem issue fries and a whiny ass frilly beer? You sound like a freaking girl."

My eyes almost bugged out of my damn head I laughed so hard.

"Dude, the next thing you'll be asking me is how fat your ass looks in a dress and if the highlights in your hair make your eyes sparkle. Don't let Grace slip through your fingers because you're a chicken shit cry-baby, that's not the Shane Maxton I know. And if you start wearing glitter and lip gloss, you're out of the band." Then he slapped me in the head and walked back into the bar. Dumbass. *But a dumbass with a good point.*

I stalked into the bar after Alex. He was right, or course. I was being a whiny girl. Grace was mine, and all I had to do was tell her.

Lea, Conner and Tucker sat around a table covered with milkshakes and half-eaten burgers, talking. I collapsed heavily into a chair, while Alex ran after some girl, pinching her ass all the way to the bar. I looked at Lea, "Where's Grace?"

"She left. I think she went to go look for some idiot who I *thought* was as sweet as an *angel*, but is just a stupid DOUCHE," Lea snapped. She finger-tapped her annoyance on the table and waited for my reply. When I didn't give her one, she propped her head up with her hands and leaned across the table with a tight smile. "My mistake, I completely read the dude wrong. I *thought* he really cared about her. Turns out he has this secret identity that he doesn't want anyone to know about called Super Douche."

Conner whistled and gently placed his hand across Lea's scowl to stop her from further lashing out at me. "Babe, you can't change Shane. I don't know why you get so hell bent on changing the world one couple at a time. You live in some romance novel. Just leave them alone, they'll figure it all out."

Lea's nostrils flared. It scared the shit out of me, so I can't even pretend to know how scared Conner might have been. She turned her stony brown gaze at Conner and bared her teeth. *Holy Mother of All Evil Girlfriends!* "I'm going to choose to ignore your asinine statement, because I happen to like it when you put your *BEEP* on my *BEEP*, twirl it around and then you add your *BEEP* to my other *BEEP* and give me the best damn *BEEPS* of my life." Taking a huge breath, she continued jabbing a finger at his shoulder, "AND, I'm not trying to change the world, Conner! Oh, and for your information, this crappy world will NOT change the least bit until..." This would be the part when she directed her narrowed eyes at me and rolled up her sleeves. "Until people tell THE TRUTH!"

"The truth," Conner, Tucker and I whispered, all nodding our heads in rapt attention, waiting for her hysterical words of wisdom. Not one of us wanted to be the first guy to laugh and lose a nut.

"Yes, the truth..." Lea calmly sat back in her seat and fixed her shirt and pants. "Let's just say this world won't change until there's a truthful... ah...advertisement...about tampons...um...where the women are all curled up on their beds, angrily drinking wine and eating graham crackers smothered in marshmallows and chocolate, while crossing out all the pictures of the cheerleader's faces they hated in their high school yearbook."

Tucker was the first to laugh, "He twirls what around your beep?" He was also the first to get whacked upside the head by her, which made the rest of us crack up.

"Hey, Tucker?" Lea asked starting to laugh herself. "You know what a satisfied woman sounds like?"

"No...what?" Tucker asked.

"Yeah, I didn't think you did," she answered laughing harder.

Tucker laughed and wiggled his eyebrows, "Oh, Lea. We all know you find me extremely attractive and want me to beep you in the beep."

"Tucker, have you ever heard of eye candy?" Lea asked sweetly.

"Hell yeah," Tucker winked at her.

"Well, you're more like eye broccoli to me." Lea laughed. She swung her arm around Conner and nodded to me, "Come on, let's get out of here and wait for Grace at home. She really did go looking for you, Shane."

My thoughts scattered and all I could think of was seeing her face again. I jumped out of my seat, spilling one of the beers on the table and laughed. "As long as I don't have to witness any of his beeping your beep while we wait."

Chapter 27

When we got back to Lea's apartment, Grace was standing in the kitchen with the refrigerator wide open, empty water bottles littering the floor and a dozen eggs smashed at her feet. She looked pale green and sick; she couldn't even focus her eyes on us.

"Grace, are you okay?" Lea asked concerned.

Her dilated eyes squinted desperately towards me, "I'm really thirsty," she mumbled. Her knees looked about to buckle under her and I rushed over to her and placed the back of my hand against her forehead. She fell limply into my arms; her skin was on fire. "Grace, you're burning up." I looked at Lea, "Get some aspirin and juice."

I lifted her gently into my arms, and I swear it was like touching fire. Carrying her through the hallway, she tried to wrap her arms around my neck, but she seemed too weak to lift them. As I opened the door to her room, I gasped and my entire body stiffened with annoyed anger. Even though the walls of her room had been re-sheet rocked and painted since the fire, she had no furniture, except a large mattress lying across her bare floor. Her laptop and guitar were leaning against the far wall.

"God, Grace, you don't have a bed?" I asked, lowering her softly onto the mattress and brushed a stray hair from off my face.

Lea was next to me handing me a small glass of juice and a handful of aspirin.

"Grace, baby. Please open your eyes and take these aspirin." I whispered.

She looked up at me through narrow lids and tried to smile. *"God, he is so beautiful, he looks like an angel,"* she murmured. Then she swallowed the pills and closed her eyes. A cold sweat broke out all over my body and a sharp painful chill surged through my spine. I looked at Lea for help, but she just

358

offered me a tight smile and walked towards the door.

"Lea, wait. We can't leave her in these clothes, she's soaking wet from sweating. Find something that she can wear to bed. I'll leave, so you can change her," I whispered.

I stood in the hallway while Lea changed her and when she told me to come back in, I was shocked by what Lea dressed her in. A small sexy tank top and a pair of lacy boy shorts was all she wore. Leave it to Lea. I knelt next to her, pulled the covers up to her chin and kissed her scorching forehead. "Get, some sleep, babe," I whispered. *I'm sleeping on the couch until she feels better, and if that fever doesn't break tonight, I'm taking her to the hospital.*

She opened her eyes halfway and lifted a hand to my face. I leaned into her palm, worshipping the softness of her skin. "Don't go, Shane. Stay with me."

Forever Grace.

I smiled down at her, "Okay." Getting up quickly, I pulled off my shirt and jeans, and threw them into her hamper. With only my boxers on, I slid under the covers next to her and wrapped my arms around her waist, pulling her tight against me. "Are you okay, does anything hurt?" I asked, nuzzling my face into her neck.

Her words were slurred and slow but I had no problem figuring out what she said, *"Just stay with me, Shane. The devil says he loves me, and he's coming to get me. Crap, I hope I didn't say that out loud."*

"Shut up and go to sleep, Grace," I whispered softly before I placed my lips on the nape of her warm neck, just below her ear, and kissed her.

She slept restlessly for a few hours, and at some point in the early hours of the morning, she woke up screaming and sweating. "Shh," I murmured, brushing my hands over her cheek. "You're safe, Grace; I won't let anyone ever hurt you again." My lips pressed a soft kiss over hers.

She slept straight through the next day without moving, just a few whimpers here and there. I only left her room to run to the bathroom or grab a sandwich from Lea. The rest of the time, I spent holding Grace or using her computer to buy her some bedroom furniture. I constantly kept her iTunes on, letting her playlists fill her room with soft calming background music.

On the second day of us tangled in her sheets together, with her legs wrapped tightly around my thighs, her eyes fluttered open, lips smiling. As a soft glow filtered through her curtains, I sang along to the song *Hallelujah* by *Rufus Wainwright* with warm whispers into her ear. My hand drew small circles along the exposed skin of her lower back, traveling over the lacy material of her shorts until my aching fingertips met with the bare skin of the back of her legs.

As I touched her, she took her bottom lip between her teeth, bit down tightly and moaned softly in contentment.

I shifted my body, and as my fingers danced delicately down her legs to the back of her knees, I pressed my thighs harder between her legs, feeling her warmth seep through my skin. Her body trembled and her breath caught.

I hovered my face over hers and our eyes locked in the soft low light from the window that teasingly fell over our bodies. I searched those eyes for answers, for emotions and an exquisite crimson blush slowly spread across her cheeks, and quickly reached over the flesh of her neck and across her chest.

Slowly, as our eyes were fixed on each other's, our bodies began rocking against each other. Her eyes fluttered closed and she groaned, pressing herself harder against me, her soft hands skid trails of fire across my bare chest. My body throbbed; ached with anticipation of being inside her, any part of me; my tongue, my fingers, *all of me.*

"God, Grace," I murmured into her open lips, hovering over them breathing her in, "I never needed someone the way I need you." Then our lips touched softly, gently savoring, nipping and kissing each other with a growing hunger. I could feel her pounding heart slamming itself up against her chest, her breasts heaving with panting breath against my skin. She wound me up so tight, twisted my insides into hard granite, I swear if she just grazed me with her hand, I would have fucking exploded from my pure unadulterated need for her.

My needful fingers slid up the back of her thighs again, reaching the lacy trim of her panties. I pressed my thigh harder against her hot core and cupped the curves of her bottom spreading her legs open. I slowly skated my fingers along the lace trim, slipping every once in a while beneath them into her wet heat.

"Baby, I need to taste you," I growled with jagged breaths. I trailed my tongue along her jaw, nipping and sucking at her skin, down her neck and licked hungrily at the top curve of her perfect breasts. My tongue burned to plunge itself deep inside the heat that was scorching and drenching my fingers.

She yanked down the material of her top so I could taste more of those perfect tits, her nipples hard and sweet like fucking candy. She whimpered and rocked harder against my hand. "Yes, please. Shane, please..." she begged softly.

Then? Then could you guess what happened?

Fucking Lea.

I told you her mouth was lethal. Because when her voice broke through the stunning erotic sounds of Grace begging me to taste her, I almost dropped dead. My fucking balls were so blue that if I looked in the mirror a damn Smurf would be looking back at me.

"Hey!" Lea banged on Grace's bedroom door. Grace's body trembled as I groaned from putting a few inches of distance between us. "Pizza's here," she said as she burst into the room. "Let's go, Grace, you need to eat something," she sang idiotically.

There is something so wrong with that girl. HOW could she NOT smell the ALMOST SEX in here? I was so lightheaded that I swear black and blue dots danced in front of my eyes.

Grace lifted the sheets over her head and straightened her shirt, "No, go away," she moaned. I felt her squeeze her knees together, giving me a frustrated moan. I could tell the ache in between her thighs was as maddening as mine. A slow smile crept across my face knowing I still had her ass cupped in my hand under the covers.

"I got one of the pies with *spinach and black olives*," Lea sang, bouncing on the balls of her feet. All I could think of was what things I could possibly throw at the woman to make her leave. There was nothing. I wish I had a brick.

I chuckled when Tucker and Conner appeared in the doorway behind Lea. Chanting some dumbass pizza song. Yeah, there went my erection. I plucked the covers from Grace's eyes, but still kept both our bodies covered. Alex, Brayden and Ethan filled the doorway behind Tucker and Conner joining in the pizza chant alongside the others. Laughing, I leaned my face into Grace's neck and with my voice still shaky and full of desire I growled, "I'm locking the damn door next time."

She bit down on her lip, "Next time?"

"Yeah, Grace. *Next time*," I whispered, pulling my head back to look at her. Her heather eyes seemed in as much pain as I felt. I slowly skimmed one of my hands across the front of her panties, dragging it teasingly over the wetness, applying pressure in all the right spots. Her lips parted slightly, and then she bit down hard as she clutched at my hand and pressed it hard against her. Her eyes silently begged me for more. Damn, my girl was hot. *Hot and fucking dirty, with all of our friends watching.* I lifted her ass with the one hand that still cupped it and pressed my other against the dampness the front of her undies, rubbing my fingers in quick hard thrusts. She rocked against my hand, the moisture of her sliding over my fingers, until her insides tensed and her body trembled in pleasure, "PIZZA, YES, PIZZA!" Shattering against my skin, she came undone right in the palm of my hand. Her eyes locked on mine the entire time.

All of our friends still stood at the door chanting about pizza along with her.

The most stunning shade of blush spread across her cheeks and I had trouble breathing from her beauty. "That was the most exquisite thing I have ever seen," I whispered into her ear. Sliding my cheek against hers, I apologized, "And I'm so damn sorry."

She tilted her head back a bit to look into my eyes. Her bottom lip trembled and her shoulders fell forward, "Sorry that happened?"

How could she ever think that? "No, Grace," I moved closer, whispering into her hair and kissing her neck. "I'm sorry I had to stop."

Chapter 28

Lea immediately dragged Grace into the bathroom to shower while the rest of us started demolishing the pizza. After ten minutes of waiting for her to shower and change, I walked myself into Grace's room without knocking. No one noticed me standing there.

Grace had her hands on Lea's shoulders, a serious expression covering her face. "Shh. Lea, stop. Of course, I keep telling Gabriel no. I don't want to be with him, I want to be here. This is my last chance to live a normal human existence and I want it. Please believe me, okay? I know I've drilled it in your head that I wanted something and someone else, but he's gone. Shamsiel is gone. Maybe he left to save me, maybe he just didn't love me, I don't know. But I get it now."

Lea's eyes caught mine, but she continued the conversation without letting Grace know I was listening. "What do you get now?" she asked.

"I've spent my entire existence trying to create this perfect fairytale happily ever after future; bending fate to the way I thought it should be, or living in a past that I was never supposed to have. I've never lived in the present, and cherished the moments I'm in," Grace explained.

My heart almost flew out of my chest and fell before her feet. I stepped through the door interrupting her, "That sounds like a pretty enlightened view of life." Her eyes widened when she saw me and I offered her an innocent smile, "Sorry, I didn't mean to cut in, but I wanted to see if you were okay. And, I, uh, seem to remember you *screaming* you, uh, wanted pizza." I gave her a little wink.

Laughing, "Shut up," she whispered. "I'm not enlightened, more like grounded now."

Lea threw her arms over her head, and her face reddened with anger. "Grace is being harassed and WE think that this is the same guy who has been trying to hurt her!" she blurted out. "His name is GABRIEL, Shane, and he just shows up HERE and threatens her!"

I laughed so fucking hard at the thought of Gabriel trying to threaten her in front of me, I snorted. "Well, then I guess that it's a good thing that I'm stuck staying here tonight, huh?" I shoved my hands in the pockets of my jeans, wincing a bit when I accidently nudged my dick that was still cursing at Lea behind my zipper. "So, Gabriel, huh? Why's he harassing you?"

Lea sighed dramatically and walked for the door, "You two really need to tell each other *everything*. You two stubborn asshats are perfect for each other," she mumbled on her way out.

I watched Grace's eyes turn to saucers and she swallowed hard, "He's nobody. Just someone I thought was a friend, but he isn't. It's nothing to worry about," she said.

I stepped closer to her, and rubbed my thumb along the smoothness of her cheek. "Well, let's see, Grace. About six weeks ago, someone attacked you in a bar and I was stabbed. Then there was the fire in your apartment that someone set on purpose. Oh, yeah, and don't forget the part where some guy stabbed you and tore your insides up and you were in a coma for four weeks. And your best friend thinks *Gabriel* has something to do with it, and you think it's nothing?" I gently tugged her closer to me and sighed, "I really wish you could believe in me enough to let me know what's really going on so I could protect you."

She leaned into my hands and her knees seemed to liquefy and melt into me. It was intoxicating thinking that I could make her react like that with the touch of my hands.

"He was my ex's best friend and he thinks he's in love with me. And well, to make a long story short, he thinks if he can't have me, no one else should either."

My heart stopped. Seriously, it did. It stopped and I

gasped for air for about a minute before my lungs could fill again. *Gabriel was in love with my Grace. That's what this was all about? He wanted what was mine from the beginning, as simple as that.* I could feel the strain of my muscles against my skin and I clenched my hands tightly into white knuckled fists. "That's what this is all about? He *loves you?*" I hissed through clenched teeth.

Grace's gaze on me faltered and she looked down to the floor. "This has nothing to do with you anyway, so you don't have to bother yourself with it. Anyway, why did you say you're stuck here tonight?"

I cupped her cheeks in my hands. "I'm not letting anyone hurt you, got it?" I moved closer and slowly covered her lips with mine, "But, I do understand him loving you so much that he doesn't want anyone else to have you."

She whimpered into my lips and slid her tongue longingly against mine. I backed her against the wall, and twisted my hands through her damp hair. Gabriel had no idea what love was. Love wasn't forcing someone to feel the same thing you do for your own benefit. Love is patiently waiting for centuries to touch someone's lips again; love was giving up everything of yourself to let someone else be safe. Love is that breathless feeling when you want someone. It's the need to be a part of someone or you won't feel whole. My love, my Grace was my gravity, what kept my feet stuck on this earth.

My lips continued to sweep across hers fiercely, tongues twisting and dancing. We didn't come up for air. She clawed her hands up my chest and I tugged at the waist of her pant bottoms. I was five seconds away from slamming myself into her against the fucking wall until she forgot what Gabriel looked like.

A presence slid up next to us. It giggled. It quietly sang the words, '*It's getting hawt in here, let's take off all our clothes.*' Then it slid up real close to us and screamed, "Hey! Pizza! Let's go! She's needs to eat, Shane!"

Cupping her face with both my hands, I brought my forehead against hers and laughed, "You know, with Lea around, I can understand why there hasn't been many guys in your life," I said teasingly.

Laughter bubbled out of her mouth as she playfully smacked me in the arm. "Shut up! *Although*, you're probably right!"

"Come on, you really do need to eat," I said, tugging her gently by her waist into the hallway. I nuzzled my face into her neck as I walked behind her; my arms still wrapped around her tightly. "By the way, *everyone* is stuck staying here tonight. Our entire apartment building is having a cleaning service, uh, *disinfect* what Vixen4 did while they stayed there. Then it will be decorated for Vixen4's after show party tomorrow so they can mess it up, *all over again*," I sighed.

When I mentioned Vixen4, Grace's lips tightened and her head jerked up, her eyes narrowing. *She still thinks I'm screwing around with one of them? Has she seen those girls up close? They're like the Walking Dead lathered with body glitter and sequins to help them sparkle. Ick.*

We walked into the living room, where everybody was crowded around the television watching some old horror movie, eating pizza right out of the boxes that were stacked high on top of the coffee table. I grabbed a bowl of popcorn and sat across from Grace as she tucked her feet under her on one of the chairs.

Lea shoved a paper plate of pizza at her and snarled at her until she took a bite. After she ate half the slice, Lea backed off and sat on Conner's lap snuggling into him.

Alex sat next to Grace with a wide smile on his face, directing it right at me. He gave me a wink and leaned over onto Grace's chair. "I can't stop myself from thinking about where I might get to sleep tonight. Any chance that you may need some company later?" he whispered loud enough for me to hear. Then the assface turned to look at me again. "Or, is there someone else you would LOVE to spend the night with?" He finished his question by blowing me a kiss. *Yeah. I need to rethink my best friends.*

Her eyes widened and she leaned towards him giggling. "No thank you, Alex, you slut," she said rolling her eyes.

"I'll just let you think about it for a while," he laughed back.

Then her eyes met and held mine.

I almost threw myself on her when I watched her suck in her bottom lip. I seriously held onto the seat of the chair so my body wouldn't fling itself at her; *cock first.*

A bright flush of crimson ignited along her cheeks, and all across her chest her skin puckered into tiny goose bumps. *Freaking hell, she was thinking the same dirty thoughts as I was.*

She shifted to stretch her legs out in front of her, squeezing her knees together, biting down harder on that little lip. *Freaking hell, she was thinking even dirtier thoughts than me.*

Hell yeah.

Chapter 29

When the first movie ended and before the next one was popped in the DVD player, Grace hopped out of her seat and grabbed the empty bowls of popcorn that were in front of me. She gave me a little smirk, "You ate all the popcorn."

I devoured every inch of her with my stare, from top to bottom, and smiled back at her. "I was...hungry."

She stepped closer to me, skimming her knee against mine, "Yeah, you look like you're starving."

I moved forward, leaned my elbows on my knees, gently wrapped my hands around the back of her legs and slowly ran my fingers over her calves. Standing above me, she shivered. "Yes, Grace, I am a starving man."

I could swear she nudged my knees open and stood between my legs, or maybe I pulled her closer with my hands, I didn't know. All I knew is that it took all of my strength NOT to yank her onto my lap so she would be straddling me with my hands fisted in her hair while I licked every bare part of her skin that I could see.

She glanced at the pizza boxes on the table and said, "You don't see anything that looks tasty to you?"

Is she thinking about pizza? Because in my head she's bent over the coffee table screaming my name...

I slid my hands up over the back of her knee to her thigh, "Oh, I see something very tasty, Grace. As a matter of fact, my mouth has been watering for a fucking taste of it."

A handful of wadded up napkins bounced off my face and I turned towards the direction they flew from. I was seriously in a daze.

Alex and Tucker were making stupid faces at me. "Hey, there, Shane. How about you let go of Grace so she can make some more popcorn, before I throw up from all the sexual innuendos you two are smacking each other with? How about that, hmm?"

I let go of her leg.

Grace giggled and walked into the kitchen with the empty bowls.

Tucker reached out and punched me in the shoulder. "There is no way that Grace Taylor is going to let you *taste her*, you stupid whore. I'm going to be the one to cash in that V-card. I have everything to offer her, like a future. You, just have a stupid guitar and a *bone room*." He stood up and started walking for the kitchen.

Alex and Ethan burst out with heavy laughter. Ethan threw a crumbled paper plate at him. "Tuck, you don't have a chance!"

"Yeah, bro. She already has a pussy in her pants, she don't need another one trying to climb in there to cash in her V-card. Besides, the amount of alcohol Grace would have to drink to sleep with you would probably kill her, then you'd have to do a corpse," Alex teased him.

"Shut up! Fuck you guys, I'm tapping that ass no matter what, *live or dead*. That's what a curling iron is really for anyway." Tucker yelled as he entered the kitchen.

Alex gagged, *"That's what a curling iron is for?* Dude, that's messed up, he's thought about this scenario before, eww. Don't let him talk to her. Just don't."

Everybody looked at me. *Everybody.*

"What?" I asked confused.

Alex pointed to the kitchen, "You're going to let him corner her in the kitchen? The idiot is probably in there with his junk out, a resume, and all his stock portfolios, trying to talk her into marrying him. Curling iron in hand; just in case."

Everybody was still looking at me.

I stood up and stretched. "I'm not worried about Tucker. She wouldn't touch him with a ten foot pole." But, I walked into the kitchen after him anyway. I am such a caveman.

Alex chuckled low, "Now he's got me imagining Grace grinding herself around a ten foot pole."

I heard Lea smack him then ask, "What's the curling iron for?"

"To warm up the corpse," Alex chuckled back. I heard the sounds of Lea smacking him again as he yelled, "Tucker said it, not me!"

In the kitchen, Tucker was leaning up against the countertop holding two bottles of soda while Grace's back was facing him as she watched the microwave popcorn pop. She was tapping her foot restlessly on the floor.

Before I could make myself seen, Tucker started with his bullshit, "So, have you done anything about that little problem of yours?"

"What problem would that be, Tucker?" she asked, not even bothering to turn around and look at him.

"You being a *virgin*," he whispered moving closer to her.

"See, Tucker, that's where you and I have a difference of opinion. I don't see that as a problem. My problem is that I have arrogant assholes who think they are good enough for me to hand it to them in exchange for a stupid dinner of disgusting sushi and expensive champagne," she snapped back at him.

He inched even closer to her, "If you're looking for Mr. Right, Grace, I'm *right* here."

"Are your parents siblings?" I asked. *I have, in the past, asked Tucker that same question.*

"You're so adorable when you act all tough like that. Have you given any thought to working for me? I know your medical bills must be crazy with you not working, let me help you out and come work for me as my personal assistant. We can have lunch breaks together, *alone*, in my office every day." He slithered closer. "I know how to *please* a woman, Grace." *If he gets any closer, I'm breaking off his dick, and* then shove a curling iron down his throat.

"Then *please* leave me alone," she answered.

"Okay, okay. No naked times during lunch breaks, but seriously, come work for me, get to know me better. You won't regret it."

"Were you dropped on your head as a baby or did your mother just throw you against a wall?"

"Grace, you're so beautiful I just want to kiss you right now." He stalked closer to her and she balled her hands into fists ready to punch him.

But I couldn't let him touch her. "That's enough, Tucker, leave her alone," I cut in between them. "You just don't know when to quit while you're ahead, do you?"

Tucker's eyes widened, "Dude, I'm trying to help her," he jabbed his index finger at Grace. "She's the most unemployed person I know and I was trying to help her out by offering her a job."

I stepped right in front of him and folded my arms over my chest. "And don't forget offering naked lunch breaks in your office." I leaned so close to him our noses almost touched and whispered, "Leave her alone. She's mine."

Tucker's face turned bright red and he stormed out of the kitchen. "You can't have all the beautiful girls, Shane, it's not fair. I'm going out to the bar to hang out with Bliss; you guys are boring the shit out of me!"

I looked at Grace and chuckled, "Oh, and to answer your question, I think his mother definitely threw him against the wall. I fucking love that your hands are balled into fists about to bash his face in." I grabbed the soda that Tucker left and helped her take the rest of the crap back into the living room.

After the next horror movie, which I didn't even watch because I was too enthralled with staring at Grace, completely zoned out in a fantasy about her being handcuffed to my headboard during the whole movie, she ran to the bathroom. The movies must have been getting to her, because she came back immediately and asked if Lea could go in with her. *How freaking adorable was that?*

Even more adorable was when she fell asleep curled up like a little lost kitten on the chair. I got teased mercilessly by everyone when I placed a blanket over her and gently kissed her forehead. *Screw it*, they all knew I was in love with her.

The teasing continued the whole next day too, especially after her surprise delivery of brand new bedroom furniture, but I didn't pay any attention to it. I just spent my time watching her. Everything she did amazed me; from the way she ate to her reaction to guys picking her up at Boozer's that night. Yeah, I watched her. Watched, and waited. Waited until she realized she was mine.

She stood against the bar next to Lea with some spiky haired fucknut pacing in front of her like she was his next snack. He stared at her tits as he tried to talk to her. I laughed loudly, because all she did was fix her eyes on me through the crowd and smiled. *Maybe she was getting to the point where she was realizing how I really felt and how she really felt about me. But just in case she hadn't figured her feelings out yet*, I made my way over to them to tell him to fuck off. *Nicely.*

I slid in between Grace and Mr. Fucknut. *Nicely.* I even smiled at him. It was even genuine. Then I politely pushed him away from her with my index finger. "Move away. Now," I said. Grace gave a little gasp, but I didn't look at her to see whether or not it was from anger or astonishment.

Mr. Fucknut's eyes widened as he looked up at me. He was so damn drunk that he might have pissed himself. I wasn't sure, so let's just say he did because I'm that awesome. "I...I...was just trying to..." he stammered.

Just in case Grace hadn't figured her shit out yet, I looked at Fucknut and said, "MINE. Now move away." *Yeah, I flicked him with my thumb and middle finger, so?*

The drunken idiot raised both his hands into the air in

surrender and squeezed his eyes shut. "Sorry, dude. I didn't mean any disrespect but your girl's really hot." He stumbled away and introduced his face to the cold hard floor a few feet away. His friends gathered around him hooting and hollering. Jackhats.

I felt a light tug on my tee shirt and I turned towards Grace. Her long dark lashes lifted, revealing those heart-stopping eyes to me, her cheeks flushed pink and her smile almost took my fucking legs out from underneath me. *Hell yeah, she was beginning to figure out she belonged with me.*

I leaned my head down to take her lips, when the most horrible screeching sound violated my ears. "Shane!" Bliss shrieked, shoving her body between us, grabbing both my arms in her claws. "Babe, I need you right now," she said trying to tug me away. I shook my head, and then looked behind her. Ethan was standing near the back hallway waving to me frantically. *Damn, what the hell happened now?*

Leaning back towards Grace, as Bliss pulled me forward, I brushed my lips against her ear, "I'll be right back."

Bliss dragged me across the floor towards Ethan, who took me into one of the back rooms, where Bliss's guitar lay on the floor, smashed into pieces. She stood next to me, giggling.

Damn, I wanted to be any place but back there with them. Shaking my head, I leaned back and crossed my arms. "Did you do this shit on purpose?"

Bliss giggled.

I moved closer to her and noticed small clumps of white shit around her nose, and the outsides of her nostrils were red and raw. "Are you fucking KIDDING ME?"

Bliss continued to giggle. "Guess you gotta play with me now, Shane," she cooed grabbing for my hand.

Hell no! I jerked my hands away from her and stepped back.

Ethan picked up the pieces of the shattered guitar in his

hands and threw it against the wall. "I don't know about you, Shane, but I've just about had it with all this shit. After this weekend, Vixen4 is no longer welcome here. Not until they clean themselves up."

Bliss stopped giggling and looked back and forth at the both of us. "You're not going to do that to us." She turned her gaze on Ethan, "Don't you remember how close we all used to be? Ethan! Don't you remember how close ME AND YOU were? We had a serious relationship!"

"I was nineteen and drunk the entire time, Bliss, and you dumped my sorry ass for one of your roadies. Three days is not a relationship. Get over it. And get some help." Ethan stormed towards the door and held it open for me.

"Shane!" Bliss stomped her feet as I walked towards Ethan. "Shane, come on. All I want is to play with you and spend the weekend with you. You used to be fun!"

I nodded my head toward the lockers along the back wall. "There's a few bar guitars in the lockers, Bliss. You're more than welcomed to play one of them tonight, but Ethan's right. Don't come back here unless you're clean. Finish the weekend, and then don't bother us anymore."

We left her there with her mouth wide open.

Walking back into the crowded noisy bar, Ethan nudged my elbow. "Sorry I bothered you with that shit, but she doesn't listen to anyone but you. And I didn't mean to take you away from Grace."

"No worries, bro, I just hope Grace doesn't think I took Bliss into the back room to mess with her."

Ethan chuckled, "I'll set her straight when I see her. Hey, do you think Bliss and the girls are gonna be okay?"

I looked back at him and smiled, "Ethan, Bliss is so high she probably forgot the whole conversation already. She'll be trying to do body shots off Alex later and give Tucker a lap dance. Just like always."

He clapped me on the back when we reached the bar. Grace was facing away from the crowd throwing back a shot and slamming it down hard against the counter. *Oh, she's pissed off.*

"Damn, what did that shot glass ever do to you?" I asked as I walked up next to her, placing my hand on her lower back.

My hand was yanked away by a screaming Bliss. "No one walks away from me, Shane! You know you want this as much as I do!"

"Ew, Shane," Grace said pointing at Bliss's snarling mouth. "Was your dick just in that?"

I laughed. "Definitely not."

Bliss slid her hands up my chest and a disgusting wave of nausea churned in my stomach, burned at my throat and threatened to pour itself out. "Don't lie, Shane. Let's go back there and finish what you started," the words exploded like acid from her mouth.

I yanked her hands off my chest and threw them down. "Why don't you stop lying and go get ready for your show. And stop the junk you're shoving up your nose too. You're driving us all crazy."

Bliss's bloodshot eyes bore into mine and she shoved me with both her hands. I laughed, and she stomped away when she didn't get the reaction she was looking for.

Grace gently bumped me with her shoulder and slid me a shot glass full of whiskey. "Wow, what did you do to her that got her so angry with you?"

Shaking my head, I rolled my eyes at her and drank my shot, "It's not what I did, Grace, it's what I wouldn't do with her."

Gulping back her drink, her eyes locked onto mine, "Shane Maxton saying no to a girl, isn't that unheard of? She's pretty *hot*, Shane, what gives?" She stood up, never breaking eye contact with me. Her hands clenched at her sides, ready to start a fight with me.

"She's not you," I whispered, looking right into her eyes. I leaned my body against hers and slid my arms around her tiny waist. "Grace, I still have the taste of you on my tongue and the feel of your body in my arms. You're not easy to get off my mind. As a matter of fact, I haven't thought about anything else since I first laid my eyes on you."

She wriggled out of my arms and stepped away, shaking her head at me.

"No matter what I say, Grace, you'll never believe in me. You'll never know the real me." I dropped my hands heavily against my sides and walked away backwards. "Grace, open your fucking eyes and *see who I really am*. Damn it, Grace." I was a few feet away from her now, still moving back. "I *need* you to see me for who I really am...I need you to take me *as is*, accept me, with all my flaws and all my fucking sins."

I lost myself in the sea of people surrounding the stage and smiled when Vixen4 started playing their first song. Bliss was up on stage. Of course, she chose my fucking guitar to play, probably her way of saying fuck you to me. *Whatever.* I really could not have cared any less.

Alex swung his arm around me and pulled me to a table with two pretty blonde haired girls impatiently sitting there waiting for him, tapping their long pink dragon claws on the table. *Gah.*

"Shane, you have to hear what these two beautiful ladies are saying about us." When we returned to the table, Alex's arm still around my neck, both girls gave us pouty faces and left without a word. Just walked away, shaking their heads and mumbling about perfect couples.

I gave Alex a questioning look as I sat down, "Want to let me in on the joke?"

He sat down across from me arms folded. "Dude, I don't know whether to be angry or awed right now." Then the dumb ass stared at the table not saying anything.

"Alex, just tell me what's going on. I don't have time for

this."

Alex nodded his head up and down, still staring at the tabletop.

I huffed out a huge breath. "Dude, you just got here, you can't be drunk already."

He held up his index finger and then lifted his head to look at me. "Did you see those two hot blondes?"

"Yeah," I said rolling my eyes.

Alex pursed his lips. "They just had a conversation with Grace, Lea and that hot waitress Mollie." He placed his hands flat on the tabletop. "It seems that those three lovely ladies told the two blondes that they shouldn't bother trying to get with you and me tonight because we," he looked at me seriously and pointed back and forth between us, to make his point clear. "We, meaning you and I, are in a serious relationship." He folded his arms and exhaled loudly. "Now my question to you is why would this be said of us?"

Leaning in, my heart seemed to freeze. Grace was chasing off other girls. "Alex," I smiled so damn wide it felt like my face would crack in half, I couldn't help it. "Alex, they were chasing the girls away."

"Interesting," he smirked. "Why would I be involved in that scenario unless one of them was interested in me? Hmmm. Think I got a shot with Grace?" he teased.

I kicked him under the table. "I think you got a better shot in a relationship with me," I laughed. "Dude, you have to see how Mollie looks at you, you'd be blind not to."

"Very interesting," he chuckled.

Ethan collapsed into the chair next to me and patted my back. "What's up, gentleman?" He turned his eyes to me and leaned forward. "You need to kiss my big white ass, Shane. I just talked to Grace about you. Poor thing thought you had left her to go back stage to hook up with Bliss." He shook my shoulder with his hand, "Don't worry, bro, I set her straight. You know,

Shane, she's fucking crazy about you. Just saying. Whatever you do with that information is up to you. But, you know, if you hurt her, it's a slow death."

"Ahhh. That's so hot," Alex murmured looking past us into the crowd. Grace, Lea and Mollie were dancing with Ryan. The fuck had his hands on Grace.

"I'm going to kill that bartender," I said.

"Yeah, let me know if that gets you the girl, douche rocket. I'm going try it this way." Alex chuckled as he jumped on top of the table, crawled across it, jumped off it, walked into the dancing crowd and grabbed hold of Mollie's waist. Dumbass.

Ethan and I walked past the dancing crowd, ordered two beers at the bar and watched Alex make a fool out of himself with Mollie. For a guy who was as musically talented as Alex was, he sure as shit couldn't dance. He just stood behind Mollie, arms raised out to the side and did the airplane. *With duck lips.*

Vixen4's set ended and the girls ran off the stage screaming to the bartenders for tequila shots.

Ethan walked away from me as soon as Bliss slithered up next to me with her shot glass in hand. "Blah," was all he said as he walked past her shaking his head.

"You still pissed at me, Shane?" she purred as she leaned on the bar next to me. Holding up her glass to the lights above her, she looked into it and bumped her shoulders against mine. "Thanks for letting me use your guitar, sweetie."

I shifted my weight to stand farther away from her, "Whatever, Bliss. I'm not up for one of your games, so you can go play by yourself."

She grabbed one of little saltshakers off the bar, yanked my hand towards her and sprinkled salt over the back of it. It spilled all over the floor, but she didn't even seem to notice; her eyes bloodshot and unfocused as she looked at me. "I never thought you'd say no to me, Shane. I've always crushed on you, you know that, right? I can make you feel so good, sweetie.

379

Better than that little pop tart that sings for you," she slurred as she tried desperately to lick the salt off my hands.

"Get your tongue off me. I don't know where it's been," I gave her a warning. I wouldn't have to think twice about siccing Lea on her ass if that diseased tongue actually touched me.

Bliss leaned back looking at me as if for the first time. Then she shook her head slowly and let out a low sigh, "Damn, Shane. I never thought I would see the day. You really *like* that pop tart, huh?" She tilted her head back, drank her shot, squeezed the lemon over her mouth, and licked her fingers. But I only saw it in my peripheral vision, because I was looking at heaven across the room.

My attention had been suddenly drawn to the hallway doors at the back of bar as Grace sauntered through them, Lea by her side. Her eyes collided with mine from across the bar and then they glanced quickly at Bliss. *Damn it, she was going to run! She was going to take me standing next to Bliss all freaking wrong.* Her head tilted to one side, towards Lea, and words passed between them. Her silver gaze fixed on me again and then a slow sexy smile spread over her face and she licked her lips. "Oh," I croaked out loud to absolutely no one, *like an idiot*.

Grace strutted, *oh my God*, she freaking strutted across the bar towards me like I was a finish line. My damn brain went fuzzy and I leaned forward anticipating her lips on me. *I must have looked like a damn fool. I couldn't keep my eyes off of her.* All of a sudden, my palms went sweaty. Perfect.

When she stood in front of me, I nodded at her, holding myself back from grabbing her face in both my hands and kissing her wet lips. Next to me, still standing there, Bliss crossed her arms. "Get lost, Grace, Shane and I want to be alone," she snapped.

I opened my mouth to shout at Bliss, but before I could, Grace cut me right off with her presence.

Grace stepped right up to me, so fucking close that I

could almost taste her, so fucking close that I could feel the heat of her body on mine. She tilted her head back to look up into my eyes, and raked her tongue slowly across her teeth. Oh. My. God*I'mgoingtofuckingexplodeinmypants*.

"Well, I was just going to tell you that you're doing your shots all wrong." Grace said darkly, as she leaned her gorgeous-perfect chest against mine and reached her arm past me for one of the lemons on the bar. Her nipples tightened and hardened as they slid over me. My lungs suddenly forgot how to correctly breathe oxygen in. My breath faltered, my heart stuttered and it tried desperately to break through my chest. With her other hand, she reached behind me on the opposite side, sliding her tits across me the other way, and poured some tequila into my shot glass, leaving it on the edge of the bar. I leaned forward to take her lips.

"Yeah, is that so? Believe me, little girl, I know how to do shots, and I could probably drink your little ass under the table any night!" Bliss taunted, causing me to stop moving forward. But I couldn't stop myself from licking my lips and sliding my hands up Grace's thighs and hips to pull her tighter against me.

Grace leaned her face closer to mine and gently brought her hands to the waist of my jeans, unbuttoned them and pulled the zipper all the way down. She slid a lemon slice in the waistband of my boxers, laying it against the head of my cock. A low moan tore past my lips and my body vibrated, waiting for her next move, desperate for her touch. She slowly slid her hands up my chest, lifting the bottom of my shirt all the way up to my neck. She grabbed my shirt in one of her hands against my neck and whispered, "You want me to show her, Shane?"

"Hell yes, Gray," I croaked.

With her free hand, she dipped a finger slowly into her mouth to get it wet, then skimmed the moisture all along my skin, from my neck, over my chest and down the tensed muscles of my stomach. Small tremors continued to vibrate my body under her hands. *Fuck, I could only imagine how my body would react to being inside her.* Sprinkling the salt along the wet trail, she leaned down and licked all the salt away, starting on my stomach, lightly pressing her tongue along the salty trail and slowly working her way up. The second her tongue touched my skin, I was struggling for air. When she reached my neck, she grabbed the shot glass, slammed it back, and bent down to take the lemon wedge from the inside of my boxers, sliding her hands up the front of my thighs and rubbing them against each side of my painfully throbbing cock. She slammed the glass down and stood up with the lemon between her lips. Her eyes locked on mine, and she gently placed the lemon in between my wide-open mouth and pressed her lips hard against mine. I raked my hands up her side, over her breasts and around her neck, as I kissed her hard with the damn sour lemon between us.

Her lips smiled against mine and she stepped away. Both of us were breathing rough and shallow, and I had a lemon smashed tight between my teeth, lemon juice dripping past the corners of my mouth.

I grabbed the shot glass from the bar and spit out the lemon. I grabbed her hips, pulling her body back against mine, and in between breaths, I whispered, "Let's get out of here."

Grabbing our coats, we ran out of the bar into the pouring rain.

Chapter 30

Stumbling out of the crowded bar, we ran with our hands locked, and the cold rain and wind whipping through our bodies. Within seconds, we were drenched while the echoes of thunder rumbled through the skies. By the time we reached the corner, we could hear Ethan, Alex and the rest of the gang calling to catch up with us. The plan was originally for us to all go to the after show party for Vixen4 in my building, *but fuck if I didn't want to change those plans now.*

Grace and I turned back and watched our friends, all of them, a half a city block behind us, covering themselves with giant black umbrellas. Alex was jumping in a huge puddle and Lea was screeching and cursing at him.

"Craptastic," Grace murmured, shoulders slumping forward.

I felt the rumble build up in my chest before it escaped as a loud growl past my lips. Grace locked eyes on me and heat just tore through my body, burning my skin. All I could think about was her lips on mine and her legs wrapped tightly around me. I threw myself on her, pressing her backwards and pushing her against the wet brick wall of the apartment building. I took a deep breath in, her scent filling me. Leaning hard against her, I slammed my lips on her, digging my fingers into her wet hair and pinning her body against the wall. With my dick throbbing against her body and huge droplets of rain dripping down our faces, she gripped my hair with both hands roughly, and rocked against me. Pressing her body hard against me, I raked my lips along her wet jaw and trailed my tongue along her neck, licking at the cold raindrops that streamed down it. We groaned into each other's mouth until we could hear the voices of our friends catching up to us.

We broke apart panting, grasping at each other's clothes.

Jumping out of the shadows, just a few feet in front of

them, we dashed across the avenue against the light, as they yelled at us from the corner. It made no difference how fast we ran, though, because they all caught up with us in the lobby of my building. Grace let out a low whimper and leaned against the wall, her clothes soaked and caked against her body. Taking a deep breath, she sighed loudly and looked in my eyes, "Can I borrow some dry clothes?"

What? No damn way. I stalked toward her, still breathing heavily from our kiss. My hands found her waist and I brushed my fingertips against her warm wet skin. I clenched my fingers tightly and pressed my body into hers. Her breath caught and my eyes frantically searched her face. "Is that what you want right now, Grace? Dry clothes?"

Pushing her body against mine, she moaned. "No. Not what I want at all. What do you want?" she whispered, her breath ragged.

I leaned in closer, burying my face in her neck and sliding my hands up the front of her body under her coat, "I'll tell you what I damn well want right now, Grace. I want to smother those beautiful nipples of yours in fucking honey and then lick and suck them until you beg me you take you."

Fuck, her body trembled when I said it.

"Then I want to slowly pull those little lacy boy shorts you wear to the side and *really* taste you. I want to bury myself inside you so deeply that I make you forget what your fucking name is. I want to completely smother and consume you, so all you see is me." I nipped softly at her neck and ran my tongue up to her jaw. "I want to watch your face when I sink deep inside you. I can just fucking imagine it, the way your hair will spill across the pillow, the way your silky skin will feel under my chest. I want to lose my mind in you." Her breathing came faster and heavier.

"Damn, girl," a voice purred next to us, making me realize for the first time that we weren't alone. *Son of a...*

We both shifted our eyes towards the voice, and standing

beside us was Lea, red-faced and smiling, nodding her head up and down. *Obviously enjoying our show.* "Holy crap, Grace! Shane, if she says no, fuck Conner, you can have your way with me," she laughed.

Grace gaped at Lea, her expression fiery and cloudy. Her head fell back against the wall with a soft thud and her eyes met mine.

Grace shook her head, pushed her hands back through her hair, exhaling harshly and heaved herself from my grasp. My fingers closed down hard into fists in her absence. "I'll meet you guys upstairs," she snapped, looking at Lea. Then her eyes collided with mine again and she launched herself down the stairwell towards the studio. *That was the opposite direction of the party, the opposite direction of where everybody was.*

Lea looked at me and giggled. "Wow. Go get her, Shane!" she said, shoving me onto the stairs.

I flew down the steps after her, my heart dancing in my chest, "Grace, wait!"

She slammed open the studio door with open palms, and I was right behind her, grabbing her waist, spinning her and pulling her against me. I kicked the door closed behind us. The temperature in the studio rose instantly.

We tore our wet coats off and they splattered onto the floor. Reaching for her, she shivered under my fingertips when I grasped my hands on her hips. Her eyes lifted to mine and we stood staring at one another. Beads of rain still dripped from our hair onto our skin, our blood pulsing hot and fast through our bodies.

Her hands reached up through my hair as I bent forward, licking her lips and covering her mouth with mine. I pulled her against me tighter, and a deep groan rumbled in my throat as I pressed my body onto hers.

On instinct, my body pushed against hers until I walked her backwards, through the dark studio, until her back met with one of the huge speakers. I couldn't be bothered with the lights, because the only thing I could think of was the feel of her warm smooth skin. Our mouths moved hungrily together and a burst of hardened goose bumps spread across her skin just under my fingertips.

"We're on the speaker," she mumbled against my lips. *Fuck, that was the perfect place to be.*

"Uh huh," I murmured and reached my arm behind her to click the power switch on. The speaker came to life with a low hum and I could feel the deep vibrations of it tremble through her body. She exhaled a warm shaking breath against my neck, and whispered, "Shane." My name whispered through her lips was almost my undoing.

I ran my hands along her rain soaked skin to the bottom of her short little denim skirt, pulling it up over her thighs and hips, as I brushed my tongue over her lips. Cupping my hand over the back of her bare thigh, I slowly lifted her leg to wrap it around my body. She bit and tugged at my lips when my fingertips gently skimmed over the warm wet material of her panties. *Damn, her fucking panties were soaked.* I kissed her harder, deeper. My body tense and straining against my clothes.

"Please, Shane. Don't..." she whimpered rocking herself against me.

I slid my finger under the wet fabric and took the thin lace of her panties in my hand and stilled. The back of my hand lay just against her warm wetness, and I pulled away from her lips to look in her eyes, searching for what she wanted.

"Please...don't stop, Shane," she softly whimpered. She rocked herself against my fisted hand, "Shane, if you stop, I swear I will *kill* you."

"Grace, I'm going to touch you until you scream my name. Then I'm taking you to the party with your scent still on my fingers and your thighs still trembling," I chuckled, then slid my tongue between her lips into her mouth. She gasped as I grazed my fingers over her folds. "I'm going to make you so damn crazy right now that I'll be sure that every single moment you're not with me like this, you'll be thinking of what it might be like when I'm deep inside you." I brushed my lips along hers, and down over the wet skin of her neck and across her collarbone. I yanked the material of her shirt away, and lowered my mouth over her breasts. Taking one of her nipples into my mouth, I licked and sucked, still teasing her warmth with my other hand. She whimpered my name. *Damn, it sounded so sweet from her lips.*

Biting down softly on her nipple, I looked up into her eyes. "Say my name again," I whispered.

"*Shane,*" she exhaled.

She moaned my name as I thrust two fingers inside her, my thumb dancing small circles over her clit. Her body just melted over my fingers and I could barely hold back from pulling myself out of my pants and taking her right here. She rocked herself against my pumping fingers as I tugged at her nipple with my teeth. Her head thudded against the speaker, the vibrations of the bass humming over every inch of our bodies making every movement amplify in intensity. Pushing, pulling and curling my fingers inside her, I reached up with my free hand to raise the volume of the speakers. She moaned deeply in my throat as the vibrations rocked us faster.

She raked her hands over down the front of my shirt, unbuttoned my jeans, clawed desperately at my zipper and pulled me out. A small moan escaped from my mouth when she grasped my swollen flesh with both her hands and slowly pumped my throbbing cock.

My pants fell past my hips to the floor, loose change and keys crashing against the speaker and rolling away. She arched her body and rolled her hips over me, rubbing my hardness against the slick tender parts of her flesh where my fingers were. *She was perfect, so fucking perfect. The head of my cock gliding along her drenched skin was so fucking perfect.* "Oh, God, Grace," I growled. "I want to be inside you so damn bad right now, it hurts."

"Don't stop, Shane, please," she begged.

I have to honestly admit that I thought about it. I wanted it. I wanted to be inside her so damn much. She slid my cock through her folds even deeper and the fucking pleasure was so intense that I had to still her movements with my hands to stop myself from burying myself deep inside her. *Fuck, it hurt.* But I couldn't let her first time with me be up against a damn speaker like she was one of band's groupies; she'd fucking hate me for it after. My mind could barely focus on stopping. "Grace, I'm not *taking* you here, baby. Your first time ain't going to be on a speaker in the studio," I hissed. My dick was throbbing against my words as she continued to slide her hands up and down it.

Tilting her head, she licked her tongue across my lips, and increased the grip and speed of her hands, "You want to be my first, Shane?"

My head fogged up. I was floating on a cloud of need. I had never wanted to be inside a woman so badly. Blinking my eyes to help me focus, I smiled against her mouth and breathed, "No, baby, I'm going to be your last." *Because I was sure as shit going to be.* There would be no one after me.

With my words, the roll of her hips became frenzied and her grip on my cock tightened as she clenched and convulsed around my fingers. Her body shook as she said my name over and over, until I kissed her deeply to muffle her moans.

Her body slowly stilled, but her hands continued to slide over me until we heard the door to the studio slam open against the wall. Her hands stopped for a moment and her eyes widened.

"Hey! Shane, are you in here?" Bliss shrieked through the studio. Only the low hum of the speaker echoed an answer, vibrating along the walls. She flicked on the light and I watched in awe as Grace's eyes lowered down to me in her hands. She made a small gasp, which made me feel like a fucking superhero. She slowly and quietly slid my cock once again along her wetness. Holy fuck. Seeing the way we looked together, seeing the way my dick was at the entrance to her, made me bite down hard on my fucking lips to stop myself from begging her to forget what I had said before and let me in.

Plunging us back into darkness, Bliss clicked the light switch back off, but she stayed just inside the door, listening carefully and waiting to see if I was hiding from her somewhere. Grace continued to stroke me against her and it just became too intense. She had too much power over my body; she had control of everything. I pulled her closer, nuzzling my face in her neck, biting down gently on the skin of her shoulder to stop myself from coming. I took a long deep shaky breath, "Grace. Don't. Move." I begged deeply into her ear.

She slowly slid her hands up and down my body, not stopping for a second and I bit down into her shoulder harder. I slid my hands up over her body to her hair, grabbing fistfuls of it, as my body trembled from the intensity of holding myself back, hovering and sliding against her.

Somewhere in the background, Bliss puffed out an annoyed breath. Then her heels stomped down the hallway. The door click closed and I whimpered Grace's name out loud.

Leaning my head back, and looking into her eyes, I pleaded with her, "Don't move, babe. Please."

Grace shifted back and slowly lowered her leg from my hip. Her eyes were locked on mine, heavily lidded and beautiful; a sexy smile spread across her lips. She slid down my body, her tits gliding past my cock, nipples grazing it, making it jump and pulse with intensity. Before I knew what was happening her lips were around me, and her tongue swirled itself over the head of my cock. *I couldn't think past the sensations. I couldn't think past her lips. The pressure was immediately building into something I couldn't hold back.* I twisted her hair in my hands as she slid her mouth perfectly up and down my shaft, taking me so fucking deep that my hips just flexed into her from the sheer mounting pleasure. I was so close to exploding, I tightened my fist in her hair to pull her mouth away, but she thrust me back inside her. Over and over again. I'm fucking breathless and panting loudly, moaning deep in my throat. She slid and sucked hard and it was just too fucking much. It was too fucking perfect. Each plunge into her mouth was more intense than the last. I looked down at her, and in the dimness of the studio, I saw her eyes as they looked into mine. The moment was too intense. I was in complete rapture; no one had ever made me feel like that. No one. She cupped my tightened balls in her hand and slowly kneaded them and I'm done. She took me in deeply and I exploded. My body rocked with spasms and I cried out, rolling my hips against her.

When she pulled me out of her mouth, my knees buckled and I slumped down to the floor. Both of us were done, half-naked, completely sated and still panting. Our bodies were trembling and shuddering against each other's. I pulled her into my arms and held her close.

Chapter 31

My body felt tense and coiled tightly in some sort of an agitated ball of muscle. Leaning my back against the wall in my completely redecorated living room, I stood guard, waiting for shit to go down. Shit always goes down at one of Vixen4's parties. *I mean, just looking around my once awesome apartment to see fucking stripper glitter, pink neon streamers and glow in the dark paint splattered all over my walls made me want to kill someone.*

When Grace and I went up from the studio, I managed to dry her clothes and lock my bedroom door before the majority of the people came. As soon as strangers started pouring in, everything felt too intense for me. The music sounded too loud. The colors and people in the room were too vivid and all I could do was keep my eyes on Grace to stay grounded.

She was sitting in the middle of my crowded living room on the couch next to Lea. The frayed fringe of her little denim skirt brushed over her thighs, hugging her curves and her jet black hair hanging in waves over one shoulder. Soft ivory skin begged me to touch it. Pink plump lips begged me to kiss them. No matter how many girls I had hooked up with trying to forget her, no one had ever come close to making me feel the way Grace did. Not one of them. That girl could stop my heart with her words, she could send my blood pulsing with a single glance and she could inspire a song with the sound of her sighs.

She sat whispering quietly to Lea, softly worrying her bottom lips between her teeth, her silver and lavender laced eyes pinning me against the wall. I could still feel her body against mine, the warmth of her lips, the silky wetness of her, the smell of her desire. I watched her eyes move up my body and she wiggled in her seat. *She had to be thinking about what we just did in the studio, same as me.* My heart pounded faster. Her breathing became even faster. I could tell by the rise and fall of her chest, her mouth parting.

She leaned closer towards Lea, breaking eye contact with me for the first time since we got there and they both stood up and walked towards the bathroom. I watched her go, the sway of her hips mesmerized me and I followed them through the crowd. Somebody stopped me to say hello and I couldn't even remember our conversation or whom it was with. My eyes were plastered to the door of the bathroom as Lea and Grace came out, then the room turned; spun out of control.

The length of the hallway that was between Grace and me seemed to shift and move. The partygoers dancing around us turned into ghostly shadows of themselves. The music morbidly changed into harsh unharmonious sounds that sounded strange and painful.

Then Gabriel was there, grabbing Grace around her waist. His hands were sliding all over her skin, the soft flawless skin that was only for me to touch. He was whispering things to her I couldn't hear. He was breathing his lies into her and I couldn't get to her quickly enough. His expression was hungry and the anger coiled like tight bullets that surged through my veins. The rage coursed through my body so strongly that the shadows of people parted for me without even acknowledging my presence, until I could reach her.

"LEAVE ME ALONE, GABRIEL!" she screamed, thrusting her body from him and stumbling hard against the wall.

I was in between them, instantly fixing my eyes on hers. I could see the pure terror cloud her eyes, her body shaking. I swear I fucking think she growled at Gabriel, like she was trying to protect *me* from *him*.

Turning my gaze on Gabriel, I smiled at the piece of shit and blew him a kiss. "Grace," I whispered into her hair. "Grace, get behind me." I gently shifted her away from trying to maul Gabriel. Adding to our little gang, Lea, Conner and Ethan were next to Grace before I could turn on Gabriel.

"How sweet, Grace, the *rock star* is here." Gabriel bumped his body against mine and leaned into her face. "There are *so many ways* to torture a person, Grace." *What the fuck?*

"Get the fuck away from her," I growled, shoving Gabriel from her. Ethan lunged toward Gabriel, following my lead, but Gabriel just turned around and bolted through the crowd. In a rush of dancing people, we lost sight of him. I found myself glaring in the direction that he ran. *He was going to pay for scaring her.* But, as I moved forward to chase after him, Grace flung her arms around my waist and held me back. I twisted against her and looked into her terrified eyes.

"Don't go after him, Shane, just forget him. He's all talk." Tears welled in her eyes.

Smiling down at her, I swung my arm over her shoulder and pulled her into my arms. I kissed her forehead and laughed, "Oh, Grace, I've seen you pummel guys a hell of a lot scarier than him. Come on, you need a drink, you're trembling." I shifted her forward, towards the kitchen and over the rising volume of the music, I whispered in her ear, while my lips skated softly along her neck, "I'll never let him take you from me. *Never.*"

We made our way through a sea of sweaty dancing people into the kitchen. I elbowed an angry red-faced Ethan and pointed to the cabinet with our hidden stash of our finest whiskeys, "Control your anger, bro, that piece of shit is mine. Get the girls a safe drink to calm them down."

Like a dumbass secret spy, Ethan tried nonchalantly to open the high cabinet. Without anyone seeing, he took down a bottle, twisted off the cap and gulped a shit load down.

"Nice recon, dude. I don't think anyone saw you get the hooch down, but they did hear you slurp the shit up," I laughed, grabbing at the bottle. I eyed everyone in our little circle and made a twirling action with my fingers, "Around in a circle, just us, everybody take three big swigs until we feel invincible." Grace watched me carefully and I gave her a wink, her shoulders seeming to relax a little.

After the first round, everyone coughed and wheezed. After the second round, everyone coughed, wheezed and giggled. After the third round, everyone giggled and grabbed onto each other. Lea snorted and yelped, "Holy germ swapping backsplash, Ethan! No cups?"

"Sorry, Lea, but this is one of Vixen4's parties. There is no way any of us should drink anything unless it's from a bottle we have opened ourselves."

"Oh, my shit. That is terrifying," Lea gasped wide eyed.

Ethan eyed me and couldn't control his shit anymore, "So, who was that back there? And what did he say to you?" The venom in his voice was thick. *Damn, he even scared me a bit.*

I elbowed him hard in the side. Yeah, the big ogre just looked at me like I was an irritating mosquito. "What the hell, dude?" he hissed under his breath.

Grace's mouth opened and then closed, then opened and closed again, struggling to come up with something.

"That *was* her ex's best friend. He's been harassing Grace into going out with him and she doesn't want to have anything to do with him." *More like he was my ex best friend and he's been coveting my shit for thousands of years and now he wants to...*I scanned Grace's face. He had been her confidant for so long, what if she had developed some sort of feelings for him. "You don't want anything to do with him, *do you?*" I asked.

A brilliant blush spread across her cheeks, "Shane, I thought I made it perfectly clear in the studio today what I want." *Hell yeah, that's my girl.*

Holding the bottle to my lips for the fourth round, I choked around her words and my lips burst into a huge smile. "Damn, Grace. I completely forgot what you said in the studio. You'll have to repeat the conversation to me again sometime, if you want." I handed her the bottle and brushed my finger gently over the back of her hand, wishing it were my lips over hers.

Smiling, she slowly brought the bottle to her mouth, licked her sexy as hell lips and took a drink without taking her eyes off mine. *Yeah, I wish I were that lucky bottle right now.* "That's not a problem at all. I remember everything I said to you, and everything you said back. I would definitely love to have another discussion on the subject, because I've really been thinking about it and there's so much more I'd like to *add*." *Damn, in my head, she's sitting on the counter she's leaning against with her long legs wrapped around me and I'm so deep inside her...*

I shook my head trying to clear the dirty thoughts and chuckled, "I'm going to hold you to it." *Nope, dirty thoughts still there. Now, I'm a kitchen chair and she's straddled over me, riding me real hard...then real fucking slow.*

She bit down on her lip as if she could read my mind and liked what was written. Her cheeks darkened, "Yes, please do. Hold me to it." *Oh, I'll hold her to it, I'm tying her feet and wrists to the damn chair, ass in the air going to hold her to it.*

"Bam-chicka-waa-waa," Lea slurred. "Watch out, Conner, the porn's about to fly!" She leaned against Grace giggling and snorting, "Does anyone think it would be a fuck of a lot safer for Grace if we all went back home? Seriously, ex-boyfriend's friends, Vixen4, I've had enough for one night."

Hell no. I knew Gabriel was gone. He was probably at her apartment waiting to get her alone. She was safe here with me. I laughed and slid my hands to her waist, tugging her against me. "Let's forget about ex-boyfriend's and their douchebag best friends. We're not letting anything happen to her, so why don't we dance or something? This is a party isn't it?"

Lea jumped up and down clapping her hands, "Karaoke?"

"Let's go!" Ethan yelled and turned around to face the crowds of people. "Everybody, out of my way," he barked as the party goers parted in front of him with their eyes wide.

Making our way into the living room, I could hear the harsh tone deaf howling of some poor girl singing some sappy pop song. Fuck that, she sucked, I was drunk and I wanted to sing. Fuck everybody, it was my apartment, my karaoke machine. I grabbed the microphone out of the chick's hands and winked at her. Pushing her gently to the side, I handed Grace the book of songs and wrapped my arms around her waist hugging her back to me. "Pick something that means something to you, forget what happened before. Just live and have fun. I promise nothing will happen to you. I won't let *anything* hurt you," I lightly peppered her neck with kisses as she looked through the songs.

"Oooohhhhh," Lea said, her eyes lighting up. "Conner, let's do *You're the One That I Want!*"

Laughing, Conner smacked her ass, "No way; do they have *Paradise by the Dashboard Light*?" They all huddled together and scanned the songs with Ethan alongside them.

Then someone tugged me, trying to pull me away from Grace. "Hey, Shane. Long time no...see. Why don't we find somewhere a little more private? You know...to catch up."

Hmmm. Jenny? Traci? Calli? Jessica? Beats the crap out of me. Whatever-the-hell-her-name-was pushed her way in between us smiling and winking. "I have a girlfriend who would love to join us." Oh, yeah Rachel. She and one of her friends took turns on the *original* Shane in the Bone Room once upon a time.

Grace gasped next to her, balled up her hands and started punching numbers into the Karaoke machine. *Shit, she picked a song without me.*

I turned the best stink eyed glare I could on the chick. I probably looked like a freaking animal, but I was really buzzed. I looked the girl up and down, shook my head hell no, and sneered. "Sweetheart," I called her *that* because I wasn't sure if she was Rachel, or *Rockell? Rochell?* "You're about two six packs of beer too soon for me. Come back in about thirty minutes after I get myself totally trashed, then maybe you'd be half as beautiful as the woman standing next to me." I locked my eyes on Grace's and fuck if she was wasn't struggling to breathe from my words. "Better yet, don't bother coming back in thirty. I have everything I've ever needed right here."

Grace handed me the microphone with tears in her eyes. "Sing this with me," she whispered.

The intro guitar rhythm to *Broken by Seether featuring Amy Lee* filled the room and slowly quieted the voices of the crowd. Lifting my head to the ceiling, tears stung at my eyes threatening to fall like the notes of the song. Then Grace's hand tugged on mine, and my emptiness; my complete and utter loneliness disappeared; unshackling its fierce bindings from my soul. Realization dawned. As long as Grace was standing next to me, I would never be lonely again.

Intensity, live and breathing, filled the room. As soon as I sang the first words, the room completely silenced, but when she joined me, damn if our voices together didn't bring the crowds closer to us. Raw and savage, we were more than singing, we were telling each other everything. I couldn't look anywhere but in her eyes and we started slowly dancing around each other, microphones almost touching, in a tight circle, focusing just on each other. There was no one else in the room. There wasn't an obsessed angel after her, there weren't demon's knocking on our doors, and there wasn't two thousand years between us. Just us, just Grace and me, and we were broken. Broken from the other part of us so long ago.

Our voices melted harmoniously together as we exploded in chorus and I reached out for her, hooking my finger around one of the loops of her skirt. I slowly pulled her against me, both of us feeling each other's pulse race and our hearts hammering against our chest, beating in time to the music.

As the last note played, screams erupted, echoing

throughout the apartment and pulling us back from each other. I leaned forward, kissing the top of her head and I held her arms up high. The crowd roared louder. I waved my hands towards Grace, "The stunning Grace Taylor of Mad World!"

The catcalls were ridiculous. Alex, the douche, made them the loudest. Laughing, Grace jumped up onto the coffee table and swept her arms in my direction, "The sexy Shane Maxton of Mad World!" Jumping off the table, she flew right into my arms, and I caught her, just as I always would.

Nuzzling my face into her hair I whispered, *"She poured out the liquid music of her voice to quench the thirst of his spirit."*

"Nathaniel Hawthorne, Shane? You kind of amaze me," she giggled.

"Yeah, well you kind of amaze me too."

Leaning into my chest, her hands slowly ran up my chest and fisted her hands in my shirt, just over my heart. "God, Shane...you make it all hurt less...and let me forget for a few moments..." her voice murmured softer than I'd ever heard her speak. Tightening her grip, she clung to me closer, trembling. *Fuuuuccck.*

I gripped onto her hips, digging into her skin, raking my fingers up her body into the silky veil of her hair. Her heavy shaking breaths touched down along my neck. Stepping forward, I pressed against her body until she was leaning back against my bookshelves, next to the karaoke speakers. Resting my forehead on hers, I clenched her hair tightly between my fingers, twisting and pulling back to force her to look up at me. "Then lose yourself in me, Grace, just like I've lost myself in you."

The next thing I knew, we were being yanked apart by Ethan and Alex who were drunkenly singing about *having chills that were multiplying, and that we'd better shape up, because we're the ones they want.* Yep, their rendition of *You're the one that I Want,* dance steps and all.

After their serenade to us, I slapped both Alex and Ethan

398

in the back of the head, "Did you not see the intense moment I was having with her? What the hell is wrong with the both of you?"

We were stumbling through an ocean of sweaty dancing bodies trying to make our way into my empty room to get the hell away from all the people. Ethan turned on me laughing, "Shut it, it's not like you were going to throw her a hump on the bookcase, at least not while everybody is here to watch."

Alex stopped in his tracks at Ethan's words, "Oh. That. Would. Be..." His red unfocused eyes looked at me teasing, "I will pay you to watch that. Name your price."

I smacked him upside the head again. "Shut up," I whined. *Yeah, I whined.* "You both ruined my moment."

Laughing loudly, Alex threw his arm over my shoulder as we tried to catch up to Grace and the others in the crowd. "You know, bro, I have a special cream for that whining of yours, it's called Shut the Hell up Cream. You rub it all over your junk so you can grow a pair of balls and tell the girl you love her already."

Reaching my bedroom door, I elbowed Alex off me, "Yeah, thanks for the pep talk," I chuckled and unlocked my door. We all piled into my room and locked the door behind us. Ethan held up another bottle of whiskey and we sat in a circle, taking turns drinking, as the sounds of the party surrounded us from the other sides of the walls.

I leaned my back against my bed. Grace sat across from me, long legs stretched out, crossed at the ankles, her eyes never leaving mine.

Everyone talked around us, moving in fast motion. Everything moved and shifted into my peripheral vision. Lea sitting on Conner's lap laughing, Alex trying to sit on Ethan's lap, Ethan wrestling him away cursing, and Brayden was juggling. In the middle of it all, the chaos outside, and the chaos in, Grace sat peacefully. All I could do was stare at her, watch the way she flung her head back in laughter, the way her legs rubbed against each other, or the way her skin slowly turned ivory to pink because my eyes could not look away. I was in awe of the goose bumps that puckered along her arms and the rise and fall of her chest. This wasn't love that I felt. This was beyond love; this was something *more*. Whatever it was, it ached in my bones.

"Earth to Shane! I asked you a question!" Lea laughed, while pinching the skin on the inside of my thigh. Tears stung my eyes, it hurt so bad. Son of a monkey's uncle. Fuuuccck, she pinched with her nails and I thought I must be bleeding out all over the floor. It hurts worse than being stabbed in the shoulder. The burning sting traveled down my leg, shaking me free of my Grace Taylor tunnel vision. I just wanted to yelp in pain, but I squeezed my lips together so no one could call me a pussy. *What damn question had she asked me? How hard I'd like to choke her?* "Huh?" is what I managed to say, finally seeing everyone else around me.

Alex was leaning up against Grace and he was giggling.

"We were talking about believing in soul mates. I. Just. Asked. You. If. You. Believe. *In soul mates*," she spoke slowly as if I was a foreign preschooler trying to understand English for the very first time.

My gaze leveled on Grace again and I could see her piercing silver orbs peeking out at me through long thick lashes, waiting. I opened my mouth to speak, but she made me breathless, made my mind empty and my body shiver.

Alex chuckled low. "Soulmate," he said in a deep rumbling commercial-guy voice. "What Satan himself puts in his morning coffee. It's good to the last drop. Start your day in an apocalyptic way. Get Soulmate at your local grocer, today."

Lea pinched him in the exact same place as she pinched me. He howled like a little kitten. I smiled at Grace, "Hell yeah, I believe in them."

Grace's eyes fluttered closed and she tilted her head back

against the wall and slid herself up. "Let's get out of here, I'm hungry."

Jumping up, I unlocked the door and stepped out into the insanity of hallway. Bright red lips were on me instantly, "There you are!" Bliss's voice screamed as her arms wrapped around me.

Grace swore and gasped beside me, stepping herself away from us.

I shoved Bliss away scowling and reached for Grace, "What the hell is wrong with you?" I asked Bliss when my fingers found Grace's.

Bliss smiled sweetly and tried to step in between Grace and I, "You sounded great singing. We should do some work in the studio together, just you and me." She rubbed her hands up my chest, and Grace tried to let go of my hand, but I held on tight.

I tugged gently on Grace's hand until she stood in front of me, "No thanks, Mad World is absolutely perfect the way it is right now," I snapped.

The rest of Vixen4 slinked up behind Bliss, arms crossed like they had shit to say. "Shane, you guys aren't much fun anymore," Cream snapped.

"Yeah. You guys haven't partied with us too much while we were here, what gives?" Essex pouted. They were moving closer.

"Maybe it's their new guitarist," Scratch said. She stood on her tiptoes to see around me to Grace and sneered, "What was your name again?"

Grace squeezed my hand and stepped out from behind me. Locking eyes with Lea, that mischievous smile once again dancing over her lips, "I'm sorry, what did you say? I'm not fluent in stupid drunk slut." Crossing her arms, she laughed, "I don't remember. Lea, did they offer that class in our high school?"

That's *my* girl.

Lea giggled nodding her head seriously, "Skank 101. No we definitely didn't take *that* nasty class."

"Bitch," Bliss snapped crossing her arms in front of her chest. *That was all she could think to say?*

Okay, this is stupid and knowing Bliss, it was going to escalate into blows and then I'd have to hit a girl. I opened my mouth but Lea shoved me back. Hard. Alex's heavy arm landed on my shoulder and he pulled me back a step. "Relax, Shane. Grace isn't breakable," he whispered.

Lea laughed loudly, "Oh, one syllable word war. You don't even need a brain to play that game! Okay, my turn! CUNT!" She was jumping up and down all excited.

Grace was shaking her head and waving her hands at Lea, "No, no no. You can't call her a cunt, she lacks the warmth and depth of one. Slut is much better; it really fits her, *well, all* of them better."

Bliss stomped her foot, "Fuck off, you stupid bitch!"

Lea growled, "That's not one syllable. Skank!"

"Ass," Grace called making a funny face at Bliss.

"Whore," Lea added.

"Ho!" Grace yelled, laughing.

"Cow," Lea continued. Alex mooed loudly next to me.

Bliss's face burned a deep shade of red, *holy crap I think her head might explode!*

Lea tilted her head, I think in wonderment of Bliss's new skin tone, "Should we move to two syllables or phrases now? It doesn't look like they understand the game." Her cheeks puffed out, she was trying desperately not to laugh.

"Should we talk slower?" Grace asked annunciating every syllable slowly.

My body tensed when I heard Bliss's throaty growl. She pitched herself forward, launching her body at Grace, spitting and screaming. Alex held me back tightly.

Like slow moving frames in a movie, Grace smiled like the sun had just come out of hiding on a cloudy day, stepped forward into Bliss's lunge and smashed her fist right into Bliss's mouth. She didn't even cringe when her fist hit, she didn't even stumble back from the motion.

Bliss's body slammed back against the wall and crumpled to the floor. My eyes were on Grace instantly, shoving Alex out of the way to grab her around the waist. She immediately threw her arms up ready to block the other members of Vixen4, but none of them moved. They just looked down at Bliss and laughed. Ethan jumped in front of Grace, ready to defend her, and I swirled her around to face me.

"Well, hello there Mr. Rockstar," she smiled up at me.

Pulling her closer, I slid my arms up her spine, "Hello yourself, Miss Ultimate Fighting Champ."

Bringing her hands up around my neck, she pulled me forward and whispered over my lips, "Take me home, Shane."

Chapter 32

When we got to the door, we were greeted by police officers, who were ending Vixen4's little get together. Ethan, Grace and I stayed for a few minutes making sure everyone left the apartment while Lea and Conner helped Brayden and Alex carry a passed out Tucker back to Grace's apartment.

As the police escorted the last of the partygoers out, Ethan, Grace and I stood in my destroyed apartment and cringed. Grace's eyes were wide as she took in the mess, "How the hell are we going to clean this up?"

Ethan laughed and walked to the door, shaking hands with the officers, who thank God we knew, so we didn't get any summons *this time. Or arrested. Again. Fucking Vixen4.*

Grabbing Grace by the waist, I lifted her over my shoulder as she giggled. "Bliss's problem. She'll call a cleaning service." I carried her, ass to the ceiling; one arm wrapped around the back of her thighs, out the door and locked it behind us. "I seem to remember someone telling me in the sexiest voice I've ever heard to take them home. And that's the only thing on my mind right now, Gray."

She smacked me on my ass and told me to walk faster.

However, since I have the shittiest friends in the world, when we got there, Tucker and Alex were sound asleep on the floor in sleeping bags in Grace's bedroom. Brayden was snoring loudly on the couch and Lea was attempting to make hot chocolate for everyone. Ethan plopped his ass on one of the chairs in the living room and laughed at us.

Fuck that. I grabbed a huge metal frying pan and a metal spoon and clanged it loudly over Alex's head while screaming. The douche snored louder. Tucker didn't even move. I wondered if he was still even breathing, but then I didn't really care, so I left the room. I walked back into the living room, burdened with a pair of giant blue balls and watched a horror movie with the rest of the cockblocking idiots.

Grace sat on the floor with her back against the couch, leaning her shoulder up against my leg. In the middle of the first movie, she tilted her head on my knee and I played with her hair, twirling the silky strands between my fingers. She turned her head to look up at me and I twisted her hair in my fingers tighter. I leaned my face down to hers, pulling her hair back. "Come to bed with me," I said.

Letting her hair fall free from my hands, I grabbed her by the waist and pulled her up gently. Holding her hand, I led her through the hallway into her bedroom. She turned to face me in her room, gave me a cute little pout and nodded toward our two sleeping friends. I just shrugged and pulled her against my body, "I'm just dying to put my arms around you," I whispered. With our body's touching, I walked her towards her bed, my lips hovering over hers, reaching past her to pull down the cover on her bed.

She crawled into bed and I slid in after her, molding my body with hers. She turned her body towards me so our faces were almost touching. Pale moonlight fell gently across her bed through the open curtains.

I brushed a loose hair from her face, tucking it behind her ear and skimmed my fingertips over her neck. She shivered. "Tell me more about Gabriel," I whispered.

"I really don't want to talk about him, Shane. I don't want you anywhere near him either. He's a monster," she murmured.

I leaned my head on my arm and stared deeply into her eyes wishing she would tell me everything, wishing she would just ask me who I was, so I could just smile and without really telling her, *tell her*. "I promise Grace, I won't let him hurt you. I'll stay here with you every night if I have to."

"I believe you. And I think you staying here every night might make me feel a little itsy bitty bit better," she giggled and showed me how little by bringing her index finger to her thumb.

I brushed my thumb over her lips, "The way you sang to me tonight, was...you just completely took my breath away, Grace," I whispered. My body inched closer to her, we were completely touching, everywhere along our bodies.

"We've sung like that since my audition, haven't we?"

"Yeah, we have." *Since the dawn of time, my love.*

Still touching my thumb lightly against her bottom lip, I slowly dipped my finger in, "All I thought about was what it was like to be buried between the lips of a woman who could sing like that." *It's me, Selah. Take me all, I'm yours to have forever.*

Her heart raced in her chest. I could *feel* it flutter like a butterfly's wings against me, and mine matched its speed instantaneously. Running my finger slowly along her jaw and down her neck, I brushed my lips against her cheek to her ear, "Why did you choose that song for us to sing?"

"I wanted to tell you how I felt. Why I was always so mean to you, Shane," she whispered.

Pulling my face back, I searched her eyes, hoping she'd really see me. "Because you feel broken?"

Tears pooled in her eyes, "Completely shattered," her voice whispered, cracking. It tore at my heart. *How will I ever make it up to her? How could I ever make this better?* Thousands of years of hurt and pain, of never knowing, of lies. Alone.

I softly brushed away the tears that fell from her eyes. She inhaled deeply as I slid my hands from the wet tears on her cheeks to take hold of her waist. I gently rolled her over, sliding myself on top of her, my knee slipping between her thighs, opening them. She trembled beneath me as I slowly leaned down, and then *she wrapped those gorgeous legs around me, holding me tight.*

I brought one hand back to her face, trailing my fingertips across her lips. "Then let me in, because I promise you, I will pick

406

up every little broken piece of you, *every single fucking piece, Grace.* For the rest of my fucking life, I will put you back together...I'll make you whole again," I whispered.

Both of us stopped breathing. Time stopped, the world went on spinning, yet we were its only two inhabitants.

I brought my lips to hers, and traced the outline of them; skimming so softly over them, touching and dragging so lightly over them, the warmth of her breathe mingling with mine. While lacing my fingers through her hair, I parted her lips with mine and dipped my tongue in. My body shuddered as her tongue met with mine and she moaned into my mouth. Her hands raked up my arms, dug into the skin of my back, and we deepened our kiss. We devoured each other's lips, drowning completely, intensely in each other's kisses. Desperate, needy kisses.

Leaning up on one arm, I clawed at the bottom of her shirt, yanking it up over her breasts. Our lips parted just long enough to drag it over her head. Grasping the back of her neck, I slammed her lips back against mine with a low growl. My hands skimmed all over her bare skin, grasping, kneading. I couldn't get close enough to her. "I can get lost in your lips forever, Grace," I whispered against her lips. "So beautiful. Perfect."

Our lips were soft and teasing, then rough and wild. My hands fisted in her hair, tongues dancing, grinding our bodies against each other. Exhaling heavily into my mouth with shaking hands, she roughly tore at the waistband of my pants, pulling them down along my hips. Sliding her hands over me, she gripped her warm hand around me. I bit down on her lip and moaned aloud at the intense sensation. *Only she, only Grace could make me feel like this.* I was lost to her; she had me so fucking completely.

"Hey!"

It was Tucker's voice. *Tucker's voice? What the hell?* Then the reality hit me. Alex and Tucker were still in the room with us. *Fuuucck, I moaned too damn loud.* Both of us lay there, silent and not moving. Her hand was still tightly around me and God forgive me, but I fucking slowly thrust myself against her. It may have been even more than once. Honestly, I only stopped because she was shaking with laughter next to me, which kind of felt really fucking good too.

"Hey, Alex! Get up! Get up! Shane's about to bag Grace!" A load smack and a cursing Alex were heard next. Rolling away from Grace, I grabbed her tee shirt and yanked it back over her head.

"Wait! Hold on! I need to get my camera phone!" Alex drunkenly screamed from the floor, and then fell. "You're not thinking about OUR BLOG, Grace!"

I could barely make out Grace struggling to put her arms into her shirt, and Alex and Tucker falling over each other on the floor to be the first one to the light switch. I tucked the covers over us, kissed her forehead quickly and leaned the back of my head on my arms on her headboard waiting for the light.

Tucker got to the switch first and flicked it on. Grace was innocently sitting up on the other side of the bed from me cross-legged with her hands folded in her lap over the tucked up blankets. *God, she was beautiful.*

Tucker looked like a rabid dog, all foaming at the mouth, red-faced and baring his teeth. "Alex. *I'mnotfuckingkidding* I heard them *kissingandshit!*" he slurred. Pointing his finger at me and spitting, "What the fuck were you guys just doing? I know those sounds," he yelled.

I looked over at Grace innocently and she shrugged then yawned, "We were sleeping until some drunk asshole sleeping on my floor woke us up with his screaming." Tucker punched his pillow a few times.

But Alex? Alex, sat back and looked back and forth between Grace and me, then he drunkenly smirked at me. Then he winked. *And blew kisses at me.*

"Fine!" Tucker screamed. "I'm going to take a fucking piss." He stumbled over his sleeping bag and fell, and then crawled to the door. Before he tumbled through it, he turned back and faced me, "Remember you robbing-fucking-backstabber, she was with me first! The fucking minute you toss her for something new, I'm all over that ass." *Yeah. Definitely not happening. Yeah, I'm going to go beat the shit of that prick right now.* I flung the blankets off my legs to go after the dick, but Grace's hand grabbed for mine and she entwined her fingers to mine, holding me back.

Tucker flicked the light off and he fell against the wall in the hallway giggling and cursing, then slammed the bathroom door. He started singing immediately after.

Alex's deep chuckles filled the room. "Whoa, Tucker has serious issues. Everybody knows Shane wouldn't sleep with someone in his band, that's against the rules, right, bro?" Silence. Grace squeezed my hand tight. "Oh, and hey, Grace? You might want to turn your shirt right side out again," Alex said bursting out in laughter. "I'll never be so drunk that I can't tell if a chick is dressed wrong, that's for damn sure."

Son of a...*Ah, it was pretty funny.* I laughed back, "Dude, why don't you find another room to sleep in?"

Alex's dark figure moved around on the floor getting more comfortable in his sleeping bag, "Nuh, uh. But, if you're changing the rules of the band, I'm all for watching." *Then he made kissing noises.*

"You're disgusting," Grace laughed next to me.

I grabbed one of the pillows behind my head and pegged it where I thought Alex was lying on the floor. "Hey, thanks, bro. I need a little somethin' to hold down here."

I slid my arms around Grace and pulled her across the empty space between us into my arms. "Don't worry, Grace. I'm sure you've heard all those rumors about Alex and me having a torrid affair that we don't want our fans to know about. Well, it's true, and he really just wants to watch me, not you." I teased her about what she and Lea told those two blondes at the bar about Alex and me, so they'd stay away from us.

She laughed loudly and burrowed her face in my neck, "Oh God, you heard what we said to those girls, huh?"

I held her tighter and said, "It was brilliant. I don't want any of them, they're not you," I whispered. Her body stilled but she didn't say anything back to me.

I brought my lips to her neck and peppered light kisses along her skin, "Hey, Alex?" I called.

"Yeah, dude?" he answered.

"Desperately want to change the band rules," I whispered.

"I don't blame you one damn bit. But, Shane, if you hurt her, we'll kill you."

I ran my lips over her shoulder and pressed a kiss right over the tattoo of her broken angel's wing, *my wings*. The part of her body she marked with my story, with my fall; how she loved so fiercely the angel I was. I wished I could be that perfect being for her still; she deserves a god for what she lived through. "Then I'll be living forever."

"Um, you guys know I'm still right here, right? All this bromantic talk is making me think I should leave the room and let the both of you sleep on the bed."

I squeezed her tighter, tucking my hands around her belly and laughed, "Shut up and go to sleep, Grace."

A few moments after, Tucker stumbled back into the room, fell over Alex and then fell back asleep. Alex cursed at him for the full five minutes it took for Alex to get out from underneath him, until his words lulled into soft snores. Grace and I laughed quietly into each other.

When I knew they were both asleep, I softly tucked her hair behind her ear and whispered, "Grace?"

"Yeah?" she asked lifting her head a bit.

"What *did* you do with Tucker when you went out with him?"

She rolled over and looked directly into my eyes in the dark. "He just kissed me in his car. He tried to do more, but I didn't want to. I don't like him like that."

I squeezed my eyes shut tight and clenched my teeth. His lips on hers, *I want to kill him*. "No more," I whispered.

"No more what?"

"No more kissing anyone but me," I said.

Her breath quickened and her lips were on mine, consuming me. "No more," she whispered when she broke free, then cuddled closer to me and we drifted off to sleep.

Chapter 33

I woke slowly, at first, not realizing where I was, brighter and brighter the light shined behind my closed eyelids. Stealing my darkness. The bed underneath me felt like the softest most exquisite place to lie and the silky strands of hair that fanned out, that my head lay softly against, smelled of wildflowers and heaven. Delicately, the slow slide of my hand beneath the covers met with smooth bare skin tangled with mine.

My eyes fluttered open to the afternoon sun streaming through the open curtains of the window. I lay on my back and Grace, *my Grace*, was tucked tightly into my side, half her body draped across my bare chest, our legs tangled with each other's under the sheets.

Skimming my fingertips under her shirt and down her spine, a raw heat spread across my body, a desperate need to have her.

Then Grace shifted in her sleep, her sweet lips brushing against the bare skin of my chest, one hand spreading itself over my flesh, sliding down the muscles of my stomach. *Fuuccck, my body was on fire, burning to be inside her*.

Her body was so damn warm and soft against me. Then she cuddled closer against me, shifting her body with a deliciously erotic slowness over mine, so that our bodies were perfectly aligned together. My rigid hardness was throbbing like a caged animal against her hot center. *Please, please, please let us be alone in this room right now*.

Letting out a deep groan against her silky skin, I slid my body completely over hers, the tense muscles of my thigh gliding teasingly against the V-shape of her pajama bottoms. Torturously slow, I traced my lips along her neck and jaw, moving my tongue softly along her flesh to her mouth. Lightly pressing my fingertips along all the bare skin I could feel, I hovered my lips just above hers, "I can wake up to this perfection every morning for the rest of my life, Grace." *Those two douchebags better not be still sleeping on the floor, because I'm not going to be able to stop this.*

Leaning my palms down on the bed on either side of her face, I brushed my tongue along her lower lip, then took it gently in between my teeth and nipped at it, savoring her exquisite taste. *Who in this world doesn't wake up with morning breath? I never woke up with anybody next to me like this, ever, but seriously, she fucking tasted like honey, and I wanted to devour every fucking part of her.*

She moved her body under me, a small rocking rhythm, which achingly rubbed her heat against my cock. All I could do was nip at her skin harder and tightly fist the sheets into my hands. "With a few exceptions," she whispered against my lips.

"Like?" I asked in a low whisper.

"A hell of a lot less clothing," she exhaled.

The fuck if I cared who the hell was in this room with us. I had to fucking have her. "Grace..." I growled low, shifting myself on one elbow and pulling her knee up to wrap her leg around me. Sliding my hands beneath the material of her pants, slowly to her silken thighs, pressing my fingers into her skin, I kissed her long, deep and hard. It wasn't slow and tender. It was hot and frenzied and when she opened her mouth to me, I completely lost myself in her lips.

"God, it tastes like someone shit in my mouth last night," Tucker moaned from the floor. *I. Want. To. Cry.* Tears stung at my eyes, my balls ached so damn bad, and my poor dick, it was never going to forgive me, never.

Reluctantly, I dragged my lips off her skin, both of us breathing heavily against each other. "Oh God," I moaned. "Why are they still in here?" I had to wipe away the stinging from my eyes.

Laughing, Grace pulled back the covers and sat up, moving away from me. Shaking her head, she sat on the edge of

413

the bed, swinging her feet. I tried to grab at her hand, but the bottom half of my body refused to move. If it didn't get relief soon it was going to cause a riot.

Then Alex's dumbass head popped up from where he slept on the floor. "If I don't get coffee in me soon, I might kill someone," he croaked. "And Tuck, you taste like that because you're such a fucking asshole." They were both looking at each other and didn't seem to see Grace and me.

I sat up slowly, but man, it hurt like hell.

Tucker sat up next to Alex, "Where the fuck am I?" He scanned the room and his eyes widened when he saw Grace, then almost popped fully out of their sockets when he noticed me. "I slept on the fucking floor in Grace's room? And that douchebag slept in her bed?"

I was so not in the mood to hear his shit. I practically growled and moved to slam my fists into his face, but Grace held her hand out to stop me. "Whoa. Stop. Alex? Shane? Please go make coffee. I need to speak to Tucker alone. Again," she sighed.

Tucker gave me a smug look, and then he mouthed to me, "She wants me." I narrowed my eyes at him then laughed. Jackhat. Alex laughed at Tucker too, walked over to me, and pulled me off the bed, patting him me on the back, "Let's go, dude," he said.

I had trouble walking. Yep.

Alex pulled me into the hallway and shot me a serious look. His eyebrows pulled together, hands planted heavily across his chest and his eyes scanned me up and down. *What the hell?*

He scratched at his chin, "Dude, you haven't gotten laid in a long ass time, have you?"

"No," I croaked. "Haven't wanted anybody else since I met Grace."

Alex grabbed me, laughed and yanked me into the bathroom, shoving me in. "Dude, you're having trouble walking.

414

Go take care of yourself before you poke someone's eye out!" Then he slammed the bathroom door in my face. "I am impressed though," he yelled on the other side of the door. "But, don't come out until you feed the monster!"

I actually stood there, staring at the door for a moment, not believing any of the shit that just happened. Then I locked the damn door and went to it. No, I'm not going to tell you exactly the way I jerked myself off in Grace's bathroom. *Twice*. Why? Because both times, it lasted not even two full seconds and it barely took the edge off. I needed Grace. I craved Grace. And I was going to have her tonight, *no matter what*. Besides that, I was going to find a way to tell her **everything**. Fuck everything, I had to have faith in her that she'd accept me for who I was now. That had to be good enough for her, because that's all I had to give her.

Chapter 34

Leaving from Grace's around three in the afternoon just about tore my heart in half. I could tell by the way she stared down at her hands, and her dull monotone voice that she didn't want me to leave, *but I needed to.* I needed to see Michael before I told Grace anything, because the last thing I needed to do was throw myself off the great bridge of sin again and get myself punished for crap I didn't do.

So with a dull ache in my chest, I waved goodbye to her and walked out the door. The guys were right behind me. We really needed to make sure a cleaning service had been called for our place and Vixen4 was gone. But with one look from me, Ethan and Alex both shoved me away. "Go do whatever it is you need to do, bro. We got this," Ethan said.

I stood in the middle of the sidewalk and watched them walk away, wondering where I could possibly go to get Michael's attention. Immediately, I turned on my heels and started for the subway, because I needed to get to lower Manhattan.

Twenty minutes later, I stood in front St. Paul's Chapel in lower Manhattan. Built back in 1764, it is the oldest church on the island, but that's not the reason I went there.

St. Paul's Chapel sits directly across the street from where the World Trade Center used to be. On that horrid September day back in 2001, the little church remained undamaged, despite the destruction and sheer terror that occurred just behind it. It stood tall and defiant on that day, with its spire standing out in the dust, smoke and debris. The epitome of hope in the middle of hell.

In all of Shane Maxton's memories on this earth that I held, of all the places he'd ever visited, I had never been anywhere more moving than standing in front of that church. Sorrow and grief was still evident in that place, and more than once, I had to wipe away silent tears that fell down my cheek.

Michael stood in the small graveyard, overlooking the cold stones that spiked out of the hard earth beneath his feet. He glanced at me once, but didn't smile. He held his breath for a few moments, and then puffed out a heavy sigh. "This place is where you thought I would be?"

I shrugged and walked closer to him, standing shoulder to shoulder. "Maybe it's because I'm fully human..." I waved my arms around us. "Tell me you can't feel the hope in this place, the humanity, Michael. I need you to see why I need to be with her, and why I'm choosing this."

Michael stood still in expectation. He swallowed quickly squeezing his eyes closed, and lowering himself to his knees on the ground.

I stood over him, "No matter how much hate was brought here, hope was born. *That's what humans do.* For all that's horrible and wrong here, Michael, they will always bring with them hope. It fills me with awe, this feeling. That's what Grace holds, all this time. All this time, Michael, hope is what kept her going. Hope is what I have, that when I tell her I'm no longer an angel, she'll settle for an ex-junkie with a heart full of scars, who has loved her since the beginning of time. I'm telling her who I was. I can't be punished for the truth. God is not hateful."

I walked away slowly, leaving Michael leaning forward on his knees in the middle of a graveyard, while hundreds of New Yorkers busily went about their day around us. "No not hateful, Shane. Just gone," he called after me.

Chuckling, I turned around to look at the angel. Holding my hands out around me, I spun in a slow circle, "No, Michael, think more like a human. He's everywhere. *You just don't have faith in him anymore.*"

Michael's posture suddenly stiffened, his muscles rigid and taunt, mouth falling open in an audible gasp.

"That's right, Mikey, I just went *there*." Shoving my hands in my pockets and bouncing on my toes, I smiled at him, "And now, I'm going to go buy the biggest freaking diamond I can find in Manhattan, so everybody can see how much I love the girl who only wanted *me* for thousands of years."

That's exactly what I did. Another subway ride to 57th Street and 5th Avenue; Tiffany's.

It only took me fifteen minutes to find the perfect ring to slide onto the hand of the only girl I'd ever loved. For those of you that get off on that crap, it was *beyond fucking beautiful*. A perfect brilliant center antique cushion cut 2.5-carat diamond wrapped in a delicate platinum design of smaller diamonds that sparkled like Grace's eyes. And yeah, I walked right out of the damn store with it, tucked deep in the pocket of my jacket. Now all I had to do was think of a way to ask her that would hold a special meaning to her. Write it in roses? A hot air balloon ride? Sky writers? Crap, I never thought I would have to think about this. This was going to be the hard part.

Chapter 35

The first show that Mad World was going to perform with Grace and Alex together, *and with me out of the slammer*, was at seven o'clock that night. I was at Boozer's by six, relaxing with a beer in my hand, ring in my pocket, and my heart crashing against my chest.

At ten minutes to seven, Grace walked through the front doors, flanked on both sides by Conner and Lea, who both wore worried expressions. And Grace? Grace was unnaturally pale, clutching her arms around herself tightly; body tense and rigid. *What the hell was going on with her?* I combed my fingers through my hair, my scalp prickling with an uneasy chill. When her eyes met mine, an unshakeable sense of terror poured over me and I ran right to her. Grabbing at her shoulders roughly, I lowered my eyes to hers frantically, "Grace, what's wrong? What happened?"

Her bottom lip quivered and her eyes pleaded with mine. "After the show, I'm going to have to leave for a while, Shane." She opened her mouth to say more but the words didn't come.

What? No. No fucking way.

"Is this about Gabriel? Did something happen? Or is this about me, Grace?" I squeezed her shoulders, while searching her face for answers.

She gave me none.

Then Ethan was behind her, lightly drumming his sticks on her shoulders, *and my freaking hands*. His eyebrows pulled together when he saw the terrified expression that lay across her face, "Hey, you okay? We have five minutes to get to the stage, why you so late?"

Alex and Brayden jumped next to us then and excitedly pulled us to the stage. They hadn't noticed Grace's unease or my worry. She gave me a fake smile before climbing up onto the stage, "I'm fine, I just need a drink," she blatantly lied.

Ethan shoved two drinks at us, and she grabbed for hers as she yanked off her jacket. I automatically sucked in a breath when I noticed the low cut shirt that clung to her body like pale pink paint, so damn fucking tight that her nipples pierced through the thin silky material. She gulped back her shot, and I had to shake my head free of the desire to run my lips around her breasts so that I could dampen that silky material until her nipples could be seen through the wetness.

I quickly pressed her body behind one of the speakers, and lifted her chin to me. "Babe, you need to tell me right now what's going on." I could feel the tremble of her chin beneath my fingertips and my stomach felt like it bottomed out somewhere. "Are you in trouble? Is this about Gabriel?" My chest ached and an angry heat flushed through my body. I moved closer to her, touching my body to hers. "What the fuck is going on," I growled.

She cringed with each word, then raised the palm of her hand against my cheek, "Shane, just sing with me, okay? Just play that guitar of yours by my side tonight, the way that only you can." Her eyes were pleading with mine.

I couldn't end the discussion like this. What the hell? I grabbed at her waist but she slid out from behind the speakers and instantly captured the audience's attention. *"Grace, please,"* I called after her but the sounds of the crowd chanting our name drowned out my voice. She pulled my guitar strap until I was out in front of the audience and the sound was deafening; it thundered and vibrated the stage under our feet. She turned towards me and stared into my eyes and the tears that rimmed her lashes just about killed me. Then after a deep breath, she gave me a slow sexy smile and leaned in closer to me, "Come on, Shane. Play with me," she whispered.

Somehow, my fingers found my strings and I played just for her. My ghostly melody drifted slowly from my guitar. Alex joined me by twisting his fingers over his piano keys, creating the intro to one of our ballads. The crowd quieted down, but it completely silenced with the first sounds of Grace's haunting voice. I looked out over the crowd of people, then back to her. I watched her on stage next to me and I was completely captivated by her more than ever. More than when we were in her father's garden and I was just a blind faithless immortal.

Grace fingers danced through the melody playing with a passion, telling her story and laying all her secrets in front of everyone. Her body melted into her guitar; letting it know her intimately, becoming a part of her body and her soul. I couldn't take my eyes off her, and then she fucking sang my words and looked in my eyes. And I was on my damn knees with my eyes locked on hers, listening to her haunting vocals. Raw and powerful, stirring a reaction deep inside my heart where the darkness once ruled and hope seemed like a really bad joke.

My heart was pounding in time with Ethan's beat, every inch of my skin tingled and I had no idea how I had ever thought I could be here without her. My soul belonged to her, it always had.

The pain from you gone, is just too real
Burning so hot, it becomes numb
It's a lie when they say time could heal
Am I too lost to be saved?
I've become as cold and hard stone
My eyes are opened to everything
Please help me find my way home
Listen to the sounds my tears make
Filling up my heart, filling up the world
Save me from myself, take my hand
Say my name, breathe your warmth into my cold
Will I be lost forever?
I have nothing left inside, after all these years
Hope was just a thing to laugh at

The last beats of your heart still pounding in my ears
And when darkness comes back for me
Laying under the brick and stone
Will I hear your haunting whispers
And know I'm not alone?
Please save me from myself
This prison in my mind
Where all I could do is remember
All that was left behind
Am I too lost to be saved?
I've become as cold and hard stone
My eyes were opened to everything
Please help me find my way home
Find my way home
My way home

Needing to touch her, feel her heat, her warmth against me, I moved across the stage and slid my back against hers. With our backs touching one another, the intense and electric charges between us took over and spiraled into something tangible. Her voice still rising alone with mine, she slid her body around mine, as if she was a hot breeze on my skin. For a few minutes, I wondered if we would actually burst into a brilliant ball of flames and consume everything around us.

When our last song was finished, as both our voices held their harmonious notes, I watched a lone tear fall down her cheek. Whatever was making her cry, I had to fix it and I needed her to know. To know everything, without wasting any more time. Too much time had been wasted already. Turning to face her, I gently tipped her chin up, making her look into my eyes. The gesture was so intense that the crowd watching us held their breath in silence, waiting with heavy anticipation of what I was going to do.

I dropped my guitar, letting it swing behind me and I

cupped her face with both of my hands. "I love you, Grace Taylor," I said through the microphone before I yanked it from around my head. Then I brought my lips to hers and kissed her in front of everyone. A slow, deep kiss causing her hands to twist my shirt into fisted clumps as she pulled me closer. Her hair tumbled around me, I slid my fingers through the hot strands, entwining my fingers within the locks, and I lost myself completing against her lips.

Within moments, the crowd erupted into an outpouring of screams and cheers. Then Ethan's deep laughter detonated through the speakers, "God, Grace, were you the only one who *didn't* know?"

Laughing at Ethan, I reluctantly pulled my lips from Grace's. A stunning blush colored her cheeks, her lips were still parted and her breathing was heavy like mine. Then she opened her eyes and they were clouded with terror and tears. My stomach churned, almost rolling right out of me. *What the hell was she thinking right now that made her look so terrified of me?*

She ripped the microphone off her head and gave me a panicked tight-lipped smile. "I, um, need a drink," she said through her clenched teeth. She looked down at her hands, and then placed one softly against my cheek. She looked up into my eyes as tears streamed from hers, "Shane Maxton, I love you more than I ever loved another human being." Dropping her fingers from my skin, she turned her back to me and jumped off the edge of the stage, walked to the bar right to that fucking fuckwad Ryan. The crowd still cheered and clapped, as they watched her gulp back her shot. I held my hands up, high above my head, stretching my fingers wide so the audience would quiet down. Seeing me, Alex brought his fingers to his mouth and whistled into his microphone and the crowd immediately silenced.

I bent down, picked up my wireless mic, and put it close to my lips, "I'm not done, Grace." I watched her pick up her second drink and freeze.   "Look at me. Really *look at me*, Grace," I said.

Slowly, she turned her body and faced the stage with her drink squeezed tightly in her fingers, with her eyes locked on the floor. Lea and Conner walked up next to her. Lea lifted Grace's chin until her eyes fixed onto mine.

I could still see the tears glistening, but I couldn't stop, not now. "I've waited for what feels like *two thousand years* to tell you how much I love you and *to touch your lips again*," I called to her. The crowd exploded in screams again and I swung my guitar around and started to play feverishly, the words and music pouring out from my heart.

I didn't know I was lost
Until you found me
I never knew what love was
Until you touched my hand

I lost myself long ago
In between your lips
And now here you are
You steal my breath away

Until you I never really knew heaven
Cause until you it was only ever hell
I didn't know I was so far gone
Until you brought me home

I promise you, girl
I know you're shattered
I'll pick up your pieces
And make you whole again

Cause until you girl

I've been shattered too
Since my very first kiss
It's only been you

Before I even ended the song, I jumped off the stage and ran to her. I gently took her face in my hands, wiping away her tears softly with my thumbs and pressed my body against hers. Bringing my face slowly down to hers, I gently kissed her lips.

She squeezed her eyes tight, grabbed onto my arms, and dug her fingernails into my skin. Pain shot through my arms. "Please don't be Gabriel. Please don't be Gabriel. *Shane, please just be Shane. I can't take this anymore.*"

"No, no, baby. Grace, it's me," I whispered against her lips. I couldn't stop the tears that stung at my eyes and streamed down my face for my poor Grace. "A feather, Selah. I gave you a feather. That was my gift to you. You asked me when I saved you from Gabriel in your coma. A feather from an angel's wing."

Her knees buckled as she threw her arms around my neck and her body shook with sobs. I held her upright and slammed my lips against hers, tasting the salt of our tears. "I love you. I love you. I love you," she whimpered against my lips.

I swept her feet off the floor and cradled her in my arms; our lips locked together. I carried her through the bar like that, out the front door and around the corner to her apartment building. Lea and Conner walked alongside us, trying to sing the song I wrote for her, but epically failing at it. Conner drunkenly messed up the words and Lea's voice cracked so horribly I was afraid for my ears.

None of it mattered. Nothing mattered before we stood in front of each other in the warm hazy light of her bedroom. Nothing mattered until then, standing and facing each other for the first time in centuries, knowing the truth of who we really were. I could see the questions in the silver orbs of her eyes, but I just shook my head and reached my hands out to cup her perfect face. Words were not what we needed then, everything could be said later, what we needed was raw and primal. Something to lessen the tense electricity that coiled tightly and hummed like it had breath between us; we *needed the fire*.

We stared at each other, each nerve ending in our bodies buzzing with anticipation, pulsating with a feverish need to touch. My chest tightened when my fingertips touch her skin, and the tilt of her head into my hand made me know she was all mine. It was overwhelming. Then she sighed my name, *"Shane,"* she whispered, and I was *ravenous*.

"Grace," I sighed against her mouth as I slowly brushed my lips over hers. "You, Grace, you're my heaven." Oh my God, she was my heaven, she was my everything. Everything.

Her chest was heaving, her breath warm against my mouth, and her hands clenched tightly around my neck, pulling me in deeper. Growling into her mouth, I deepened the kiss, our tongues licking and dancing, needing and wanting. She slid her hands under my shirt and up my chest; our kisses became rougher and harder.

This would be her first time in this body, and I knew I had to be gentle. I knew I needed to hold back and it was going to kill me. "Gray, I promise I'll be as gentle as I can," I whispered, raking my lips along her jaw up to her ear. My hands trembled with their slow gentle movements, and my body shuddered from holding back.

She tore her lips away from me and leaned back. Yanking my shirt off, she threw it on the floor, and looked deeper into my eyes than ever before. Taking my lower lip roughly between her teeth and tugging me forward, "Please don't. Don't hold back, Shane. I've waited too damn long; I need every ounce of you right now."

Oh God, yes.

My body slammed against hers, pushing her forcefully against the door. "Thank God, because I have no fucking desire whatsoever to hold back on you," I breathed heavily, then slipped my tongue deep between her wet lips, devouring her.

My hands tangled in her hair, our tongues roughly slid against each other, and her hands were clawing down my skin. Uncontrollable and so fucking delicious. Lifting her arms above her head, I ripped her shirt off, letting it fall wherethefuckever, and I crashed my lips back against hers. I ran my fingertips along her skin until I reached the lace cups of her full bra and wrenched them down. *Fuucckk, I needed this off now. I needed everything off.* I spun her around, pressing the front of her body against the door and unhooked her bra, removing it from her body with my teeth. Her skin was so soft and smooth against my lips. I was never going to get enough of her, *never*. Slowly, I trailed my fingertips over the creamy skin of her shoulders and pressed my body against hers, burying my face in her hair.

Wrapping the long dark strands of her hair around my fingers, I tugged her head to one side and traced my tongue and lips along her soft flesh.

When I pressed my erection against her bottom, a small whimper escaped her lips. Her tight little ass pressed itself back, grinding against me, making me throb and vibrate almost painfully. Taking her shoulders in my hands, I twisted her body around to face me again.

Of all that is freaking holy...she was perfect. My eyes ravaged her, drinking in her beauty. Her skin was like cream, her nipples the color of pale pink roses. Cupping her breasts gently, I sucked a breath in, trying to savor every single feeling. Lowering my head, I took one nipple into my mouth and sucked hard, Grace's head fell back hard against the door and she moaned loudly. With each tug and lick from my mouth, she arched her body into mine. "Your skin's like sugar," I whispered.

Breathing heavily, she pulled me to her lips with one hand clenched tightly around my chin. With the other hand, she tore at the button of her jeans and pulled down the zipper. She yanked at the button on my pants next and they dropped heavily around my feet.

Her pants hung open, baring the tight skin and curves of her body. I skimmed my hands against the material, guiding it all the way down her silky legs, trailing kisses down as my head lowered with them. "So beautiful, Grace," I murmured against her trembling skin.

Her little lacy panties were darkened with her dampness, and I almost fully lost it, right there. I tried breathing slowly as I gently lick and nipped her inner thighs. I was breathless and dizzy, just her smell alone was intoxicating, making me feverish beyond anything I could ever imagine.

Kneeling before her, I lifted the back of her knee, slowly sliding my tongue over her bare skin and then I raised it over my shoulder. Her breath quickened and she tangled her hands through my hair when I ran my fingers under the wet lace of her panties and lightly brushed my fingertips over her warmth. "You feel like heaven," I said. "God, Grace, I want to slide my tongue over every inch of your skin. I can't help myself when I'm this fucking close to you."

Lifting my eyes to look into hers, I stared up at her and watched her expression as I slowly slid a finger deep inside her. "So wet," I murmured.

Her breath caught and she whispered the sexiest fucking sound I had ever heard. She slid along my fingers, I tore the lace right from her body and my mouth was on her instantly. "Oh God," she cried and rocked against my lips. My fingers pumped slowly in and out of her as my tongue licked and sucked hard against her. *I never knew a woman could taste so damn good.*

"Please, Shane," she whimpered and pulled me up by my hair. I stood up and gazed down into her bright eyes. There were tears in them, breathless happy beautiful tears. Gently, I cupped her face in my hands, "You have had my heart with you for thousands of years, and I have been so *empty* until now."

"I'm completely yours, Shane, forever," she whispered. Slowly, she slid my boxers down and we stood before each other bare and hungry. *So fucking hungry.*

Leaning back, I ran my eyes over every inch of her body, worshipping each part of her. Her soft skin, the curves of her hips, the swell of her breasts, the pink of her lips...

My eyes locked on hers, as I slid my hands around her waist, cupping her bottom and lifting her into my arms. She wrapped her long legs around my waist and I slowly eased into her, burying myself deeply inside her, *finally.* I groaned and pressed my forehead to hers. "Ah, Grace," I cried out and slid back with the most delicious slowness. "I love you so much," I growled. I slid deeply into her again, hoping the pain wasn't too bad, but with the way she bit down on her bottom lip and squeezed her eyes tight, I knew it did.

Pulling myself all the way out of her, I carried her to the bed, still wrapped around me. We tumbled against her sheets and she pulled me deep inside her again, and we stilled, looking at each other. Then she smiled and rocked her hips against mine.

"Fuck, Grace. You feel so good," I whimpered, thrusting into her. I was lost to her; there was nothing but her. The feel of her slick skin against mine, the sounds of her murmurs and the sensation of my cock plunging over and over deep inside her. Our lips moved across each other's skin, fingertips clawed, hands grasping at flesh tight, her hips matching my thrusts. It was so fucking intense that it was almost too overwhelming; too fucking good. I never wanted it to end. My body trembled and strained with the effort of not finishing.

Grace screamed my name and dug her nails into my back as she clenched around me so tightly I exploded, spilling myself deep inside here. No woman ever made me come so hard, no woman ever made me feel like that before. I couldn't fucking stop. After the first time, I just kept ravaging her body, taking everything she would give me. Grace gave me all and each time was more intense than the time before.

An hour before dawn, as I tried to consume her again, she laughed and shoved me away playfully. "Oh my God, Shane. I can't effing move; I think you broke me," she laughed.

Exhausted and muscles shaking, I wrapped her in my arms and covered us with her blankets. She snuggled her body into me. Our bodies fit perfectly together, as if we were made for each other. I pressed my lips against her shoulder and skimmed them over the back of her neck. I rested my face against her warm skin and smiled. Gently stroking her hair back, I whispered softly into her ear, "You're mine forever now."

Instantly, she spun around to face me. "But…how in the world are you here with me? You left, I watched you leave," she asked.

I couldn't tell her what I gave up; I was too damn scared of her reaction. *Yeah, now I'm just a pussy whipped chicken shit.* Hell, I turned into Conner. *I kind of liked it.* I pecked tiny kisses across her face hoping she'd drop the subject. "What's the point on living in the past? This is where I am right now. Right here in front of you."

Immediately, I could feel her heart rate speed up and the panic rising off her. "Why won't you tell me? What did you do? What happened?" She lifted her head and leaned it on her elbow, waiting for my answers. "Please tell me, Shane. Please. You had Michael do something. He asked you to make your decision. What did you do?" My stomach dropped when her beautiful pale skin turned into a greenish hue.

Son of a…"I gave it all up," I coughed out. "I'm completely human. Mortal. Both of us are."

Her eyes widened and she stopped breathing. "What? Why?" she exhaled.

"You were the best part of me, and when they took you away…" Tears stung at my eyes when I looked at her. *God, if I wasn't good enough for her now, if all she wanted was an angel, if being Shane wasn't enough...*"Truth is, a soul of an angel is only capable of one pure true love, and you are mine. It didn't make a difference that you were human. The kiss, the first time my lips were on yours...the hell...I wouldn't take one moment of it back..."

She sucked in a harsh breath.

"When I saw you, and you looked so much like you did as Selah, I couldn't think of anything but being with you again. Don't push me away now, Grace. I can't live without you. For the rest of my life, I want to spend every moment showing you how much I have loved you. I learned long ago to savor every moment, not to waste a second of it. I once found the other half of my soul and I've spent the last 2000 years in hell, and here, just wasting my time until I could be with her again. Did you think that I wouldn't give up everything I could, anything I could to be with you again?" *Please let me be enough for you, please.*

Tears streamed down her cheeks in silent sobs.

"Don't cry, babe. Every damn tear I have seen that fell from those silver eyes broke my heart. This, right here with you is the closest that I'll ever come to heaven. That's all right by me, because you are my heaven, Grace." I wiped away her tears, "Unless you don't want me like this," I whispered.

She wiped at her tears, "I was going to leave tonight...Gabriel threatened me..."

"Shh...Grace. Gabriel works on fear and lies."

"Shane, I'll take you anyway I can get you. But Gabriel, he's shown me so many things," she whispered. "I trusted him for so long."

Shown her things? The only way an angel could show someone their thoughts and manipulate them is by *kissing...them.* My body tensed, muscles hardening into a granite kind of tense. I locked my jaw tight and spoke through clench teeth, "He showed you things? You mean he...he touched you?"

431

"Yes," she whispered.

"He put his fucking lips on you?"

With wide frightened eyes, she nodded slowly, "Yes."

"I'm going to fucking kill him."

She let out a long deep breath, and then gave me an evil smile. "Good. May I help?" That just turned me on again, so I pulled her over me and without warning, I thrust myself deep inside her. The way she looked down at me and moaned made me almost come right then, but I held back and took my time as she rode me. I pulled her face down to mine, making damn fucking sure I erased any lingering traces or thoughts of Gabriel from her mind.

Chapter 36

Peeling my eyes open slowly, a heavy feeling agitated and churned in the pit of my stomach. Cautiously, I lifted my head from where it lay against the warm beautiful body besides me. Grace was tucked tightly in my arms, our legs tangled together under mountains of blankets, her bare skin hot against mine.

The heavy feeling seemed to spill through my conscious into the room, pressing firmly down on my shoulders. A slow slide of my hand from beneath her exquisitely smooth skin caused her body to shift and slide; a sweet purr escaped her lips as she slept. I slowly traced my fingertips down her naked skin, wrestling against the troubling emotions that had awakened me.

Something thudded sharply against the door and I narrowed my eyes in that direction and pushed myself off the bed. The clock on her dresser said it was nine o'clock in the morning. No one else should be in the house with us, because Conner and Lea would already both be at work. That heavy feeling became thicker, more weighted against my chest, and sparks of adrenalin flamed all over my skin.

Grabbing my jeans off the floor, I stepped into them quickly and pulled them up. Yanking last night's tee shirt over my head, I tensed my hands and opened her bedroom door.

I could see Gabriel pacing back in forth in the living room as I stood in the hallway. As I stalked towards him, he stopped pacing and leveled his glare at me. "It's time for you to go now, *Shane.*"

I moved closer to him, my chest bumping his hard. "There's no way I am ever leaving her with you. She's mine," I growled.

Gabriel laughed, took a small sidestep and turned his back to me. Placing his hands on his hips, he chuckled again. "I was thinking of making Grace some breakfast. I know French toast is her favorite." *Delusional bi-fucking-polar-angel.*

My hands clenched as my entire body shook with rage. Blood pounded in my ears and clouded my vision as I lunged forward. All I could visualize was beating him senseless. It was foolish of me to forget he was an angel and I was just a man.

His hand was around my throat instantly, my feet raised up off the floor. My hands clawed at my throat, desperate to alleviate the choking pressure of his fingertips. His sharp steel feathers emerged from behind him. A raw energy hummed from his entire body and his pupils blazed with the fires of Hell.

The sound of my slowing heartbeat thrashed in my ears, and I could feel my human body shutting down from the lack of oxygen. My lungs burned and my chest convulsed against the emptiness. "I'll make sure to tell her you said goodbye. Maybe, I'll even leave a few singles on her nightstand so she knows what she was worth to you last night," he snarled. My vision blurred and darkened, but not until I saw Gabriel extract one steel feather from over his shoulder and then I watched him plunge it into my chest. A rippling fire tore through my skin and surged around my convulsing heart. My veins trembled deep beneath my skin, desperate for the flow of blood that was ripped from them violently. I never felt physical pain like that before, *ever*. My world went black as the warmth of my human blood seeped through my shirt and spread itself down my chest.

I'm going to come back and kill this motherfucker until he's beyond dead.

Even in the darkness of my mind, in the complete emptiness of my soul, a vengeance twisted; breathing itself into a frenzy and snaked through my core. I could no longer feel my body; I could only hear my slow raspy breaths and the gurgling blood that filled my throat and spilled from my lips.

Falling in and out of consciousness, I could hear Grace's screams from somewhere above me. Her cries. Desperate. And calling for *me*. My eyes burned with tears, my body burned with numbness; paralyzed and broken, once again, not able to save her.

I struggled to breathe, stay aware, and fight against the oblivion trying to pull me under. I had no idea where I was or how long I was there.

Muted daylight streamed in through a thin rectangular window at the base of the low ceiling. *Basement* was the single thought in my mind as I choked and vomited up the metallic taste of blood.

Then a bright light shone down from the top of the stairs and Gabriel's laughter echoed harshly along the stone walls that surrounded me. I could hear Grace's fight and then the terror of the wet sounds of her body slamming against the concrete and the steps, landing heavily, crumpled on the floor in front of me.

The tears poured out of me, blurring my vision of her. I wanted to scream out for her, reach out and hold her in my arms, but all that came was the raspy spit of blood from my lips. My mind spun out of control, maddening, rage, pure fury; I could not get to her. Terror. Real, tangible, alive and raw. I could do nothing but see her dying in front of my eyes and hear her breath within my ears. I wanted to claw out of this skin. I begged for release. Let me go, let her live. *God, take me...do what you will...but spare my Grace.*

Then in the dim light of our prison, she opened her beautiful eyes.

I wished he had killed me. The horror in those eyes when she saw me...the absence of my movements, there was nothing I could do to take the pain from her...the complete and utter despair was crushing. Crushing and squeezing the life from me faster.

"NO! SHANE!" She threw herself over my mangled body and cradled my head in her bloody hands, pulling me up against her chest. She gripped at my chest and my neck trying to find a pulse. She was screaming my name over and over, begging me to get up, begging me to move, and begging me to live. All I could do was look at her through my tears and scream on the inside.

Gabriel's laughter broke through her screams. He stood large and imposing behind her. *And how did my beautiful Grace react to him?* She fucking ignored him. "Stay with me, Shane," she pleaded repeatedly. "Please don't leave me." Tears poured from her silver eyes, landing against the skin of my face; yet I could not feel them and that pierced me deeper and hurt way beyond anything Gabriel could ever do to me. The inability to feel her, not able to save her, not able to fight for her...the thoughts swam together and faded in and out of the darkness and the emptiness that was trying to consume me.

With a sudden whoosh of air, Gabriel swung his arms around her, yanking her back violently, locking her in his arms. His lips bent down to her ears, but his eyes were locked on mine. "Grace, my love. You *can* still save him," He slid his tongue along the edge of her ear and she cringed against him. "Come with me and I will let him live." She squeezed her eyes shut and struggled against his arms and mouth.

Inside me, the fury boiled over, bursting into flames.

Opening her eyes, she focused right on mine, as if she was trying to tell me something. With all the strength I had left in my body, I blinked and whispered through my throat that was quickly filling with blood again, "Don't, Grace, don't listen to him."

"Time is running out, Grace," Gabriel snarled, pulling her further from me.

My body convulsed as my mouth flooded with so much blood that it began to pour out from my lips, spilling thickly to the floor. I took one last shallow breath through my nose and exhaled a whisper, "Your heart belongs to me."

Gabriel raked his lips along her neck embraced her tighter. "Then, watch him die, Grace." She heaved, her body spilling its contents onto the floor.

My vision blackened and a low hum began to fill my ears.

Echoing like a far away dream, I could hear Grace screaming, "I WILL ALWAYS BELONG TO HIM, GABRIEL, NEVER YOU!"

That was a fucking sucky way to die.

Chapter 37

I've heard it said that when you meet your death that the life that you have lived flashes before your eyes. All your memories, your deeds, your sins are weighed and measured, seen before you like your own personal movie. I would think most humans would compare their lives to a made for TV movie, with all plot devices nicely put in their correct places. Or maybe if you were lucky in life, you could compare it to a beautiful Hollywood epic romance. *Mine, not so much.* It was like watching a horrible B-rated movie with low-budget special effects. And, my movie screen blows up to shit and everybody in the theater is screaming and running for their lives. Grace's beautiful face was all over the screen, hunted by Gabriel. Gabriel was forever waiting and hiding in the background, trying desperately to cause mayhem and war.

I could clearly see what had happened to everyone and why through the flickers of each scene. Gabriel was at the heart of it all. Since the beginning, he loved Selah and was jealous of our love for one another. He betrayed me and took Selah, hiding her in the bodies of humans who had died, allowing her to live out the rest of their lives, keeping her soul from heaven. Every time she died, she would be hidden in another body, and she never knew it was Gabriel who did it. She thought it was her punishment for falling in love with me. An awful existence. An incomprehensible existence. A harsh, ugly, deplorable existence. However, it only made Grace stronger, and only made her love me more.

Gabriel tried to break her from loving me. He tried to sever the bonds she clung to, the only good she had ever seen in her existence, and tried to make her love him. Simply because, if she loved him and created a child with his evil-angel-ass, a Nephilim would be born. Then the world and all its humans would be destroyed once more. Not by floods, but by the chaos and evil that the Nephilim would bring; the humans would slaughter themselves. Gabriel would win the war and there would only be heaven left. Only angels left.

However, Grace could never love him. Never let him touch her, because she loved only me. The movie of my life that flashed before my eyes sucked, and I wanted my damn money back.

Then everything just disappeared, and I ended up just standing in complete darkness. Alone.

Waiting.

Well, that just wasn't going to work for me. There was no way, in any existence that I was going to stay in darkness while Gabriel hurt Grace. No damn way.

The blackness that had engulfed me started to become lighter and a bright light shone off in the distance. *Are you shitting me? What is that, the clichéd light at the end of the tunnel?*

Dark figures walked through the bright light, creating strange shadows that danced across the radiance. Michael and Raphael.

Everything seemed to slow down; time, movements, even my thoughts. Pure white-hot adrenaline surged through my body. I lost all rational thought, and I could hear nothing from Michael when he spoke to me.

Every part of my body shook with violence and rage consumed me. Storming to within an inch of Michael's face, I growled, "Take me back to finish him. I need to help Grace, she's been through enough."

My arms were locked in their hands and I was being pulled backwards. From their hands, a strange calmness tried to enter my body, but I refused it. Then I was in Grace's living room with Michael and Raphael holding me tightly.

In front of us, Gabriel in all his demonic glory, wings spread out wide, stood over Grace laughing manically. His eyes

439

were cold and remorseless, his fingers twisted tightly in fists ready to hurt her.

Grace slowly stood up in front of him, her face reddening with every calculated movement she made. "You and your merry men can tear me to shreds, Gabriel, but I *will* go down fighting. You can have my body after it's cold and dead, but you will *never* have my soul." Her voice was dark and full of pure raw hatred.

My muscles stretched against my skin trying to fight my way through the angels to save her. I didn't care how many times I had to come back from the dead, or what I had to give up for her, *I would always come back for her.* Gabriel would NEVER have her.

As soon as the thought ran through my head, Gabriel's eyes looked past Grace and locked on mine. He snarled loudly at me and his eyes flamed bright red.

I heard Grace's gasp when she turned her head and saw me, but I couldn't take my eyes from Gabriel's. I tried to lunge forward, tried to twist out of their grasp, "You lay one finger on her, Gabriel, and I WILL FUCKING DESTROY YOU!"

"Oh come now, *Shane*. We both know I've laid more than one finger on her already," his voice clawed at my skin like sharp glass. He walked past Grace taunting me.

Screaming and struggling to get free, my body rocked with tremors. With every ounce of strength I could gather, I lunged forward, trying violently to get my hands on Gabriel. Michael and Raphael grunted, trying to restrain me, but they lost their grip and stumbled backwards.

I charged toward Gabriel with violent glee, slamming him into the wall with such brute force that it cracked the drywall and it crumbled over us. Gabriel shoved me off and dark shadows surrounded me, Gabriel's little demons. I hadn't noticed them before, but now they scurried around us, sniffing and growling like rabid dogs.

440

"NO!" Grace jumped in front of Michael and her screams tore through me, "Michael, *do* something!"

When Grace distracted Gabriel with her scream, I clenched up my fists and pounded him in the face. I continued hammering my fists into his head until I was yanked off him and thrown against the wall by his little band of monsters.

Fucking hob-goblin-fucknuts. Pain sliced through my shoulders and down my arms, my spinal cord burned as if it had been set on fire. Stumbling from the wall, I leaned against whatever I could to help steady me.

Seeing my weakened state, Gabriel rushed towards me, but Grace threw her body in front of me and held her arms out to stop his advance.

Tingling bites of horror sparked across my chest. "No, Grace! Get behind me!" I tried to yank her behind me, but when my hands touched her skin, she fell into my arms and wrapped herself around me sobbing. My hands were around her instantly, holding her close to me. Bringing my lips quickly to her, I kissed her forehead and said, "I am in fucking complete awe of your strength and your reverence. But you *have* to get behind me, babe." Then I looked at Michael and his eyes met with mine. "See *what's right,* Michael. Stand up and fight with us," I whispered.

Gabriel charged at us, with his steel claws grasping and reaching out, trying to get us. Grace's body stiffened in my arms and she tried to pull me away. Then suddenly, without any movement or sound, Michael stood in front of us, blocking Gabriel from his attack. The archangel's wings spread the span of the room, towering over everyone, and Gabriel stumbled back with fear in his eyes.

Gabriel's little monsters swarmed around him in fear, backing themselves against the opposite side of the room from us.

Michael turned toward Grace and me, and he gently

cupped her cheeks between his giant hands. Lowering his gaze to her, his eyes widened and his lips parted.

Grace lifted her chin up higher to him and she touched both her hands to his hands, holding them against her face. "Yes, Michael. Take a good look at my soul and at what I have been through because of Gabriel for the last two thousand years or so. Weigh and judge it well, Michael. Shamsiel and I had never done anything wrong."

Michael straightened his posture as if he was going to move away. But Grace held onto his hands tightly, stepping closer to him and leaning in, "The darkest places in hell are reserved for those who maintain their neutrality in times of moral crisis."

Now my girl was quoting Dante Alighieri. What chick could freaking do that?

Michael's lips curved up into a slight smile. "You *are* so much like *Job*, Grace. You never faltered in your search for him, you never lost your faith, and you never questioned it." Then his eyes smiled at me, "And you. You gave up your heavenly place to be with her. I stand in awe of the both of you."

Turning his face toward Gabriel, his lips pulled back baring his teeth. "Gabriel, your envy, lust, greed and all the trouble you've caused in between, are far worse crimes than that of a simple kiss. A simple kiss that I might add was forgiven and sanctioned long ago. If I remember correctly, and I assure you I do, Selah was supposed to be escorted by you into heaven, forgiven for her slight transgression. And Shamsiel was to be given a SHORT sentence in prison, then be reunited with her."

"NO!" Gabriel's voiced boomed. Its sound vibrated below our feet and made Grace clasp her hands over her ears. "I will not let him have her. SHE IS MINE!"

As Gabriel's face contorted and reddened with his rage, a calming warm breeze drifted slowly through the room. It quickly tangled itself into a sublime sensation that crept along my skin.

Looking at the other expressions of everyone around me, it was evident that I wasn't the only one who felt it. Everyone, except Gabriel, who still had his face twisted in rage and his monsters, felt it. I knew in my heart and with all of my soul, who the presence was.

"Enough," a small voice whispered musically in our minds. It jingled lightly like a breeze blowing through wind chimes. Warmth spread throughout my body, filling it with the deepest feeling of love that I had ever known and I squeezed Grace's hand to let her know that everything was going to be okay.

When he realized that we were hearing and feeling something he could not, Gabriel's mouth fell slack. His face blanched, making him as pale as the wings I once wore. Shaking his head, he backed up closer to the wall away from us, cocking his head to listen for the voice of God. By the well of tears in his eyes and his clenched jaw, I knew all he could hear was silence. The messenger of God, Gabriel, the mighty archangel, shunned by his creator. *Priceless. The bastard deserved it.*

Beside me, Grace puffed out a faltering breath, and she slid to the floor on her knees. I crumbled down next to her, landing on my knees, and I gathered her closer to me.

"It is a pure soul who can hold true the innocence and timelessness of passion in another soul. Each unveiling of the greatest pieces of the other, locked together at the heart for eternity," the voice sang to us. When it silenced, the quietness was so painful and empty that you craved to hear it again. I squeezed my eyes tight when the voice spoke directly into my thoughts, *"Shamsiel, how exquisite this love is. My child, you were once one of my faithful loyal angels, and now a faithful loyal human. Live a beautiful life together and then both of you come home to me. There is a high place in heaven for you both when you get here. Cherish her; no one will ever love another like she has loved you."*

Gabriel slithered back even further, his nasty mutant

friends clawing their way to hide behind him.

Michael stepped towards him and rumbled, "Go back where you came from, Gabriel. Your evil cannot darken this tale, it was written from the heavens."

Gabriel's army of fallen angels slowly dissolved into dim shadows, twisting and crawling to get away. As Gabriel's form faded along with them, his eyes lingered on Grace. His voice whispered softly, "I did truly love you, that was never a lie." His eyes met with mine and a small smile danced evilly along his lips, "We will meet again, *Human*." Then he lowered to his knees, unclenched his fists, and let them fall loosely to the floor. His chest heaved with shallow breaths and his body gradually lost color, finally vanishing from the room.

I pulled Grace onto my lap and held her tightly until her breathing evened out. Both of us were bloodied and beaten, struggling to breathe with the pain that surged through our bodies. Her hands gripped my arms and she sobbed, "I watched you die."

Grunting in anguish, I softly ran my fingers through her tangled bloody hair and leaned my forehead against hers. Bringing my mouth to hers, I kissed her through the pain, "Not even death could keep me from you."

Raising my head, I glanced at Michael and Raphael. They both stood over us, smiling. Clearing his throat, Michael asked, "Do you still want time here, brother?"

I looked back to Grace, her silver eyes watching and waiting. My heart tightened in my chest, all its shattered pieces coming back together, hammering blood through my body, "No, Michael. I *need* more time here. As long as we possibly can have here, *and then an eternity after that.*"

Raphael knelt down beside us, laying his hands on our shoulders. "Gabriel will be cast back to the abyss he clawed himself out of, and you both will have weeks of healing to do." Leaning forward, he touched his lips to my forehead, as Michael bent over Grace to touch his lips to hers.

The images were harsh, they were painful, but I knew in the end that the angels did whatever they needed to do to keep our human bodies there.

How do angels leave half-dead humans on earth after promising them a full life and a high place in heaven? They had to create a scenario to cover up our little fight with the demons. They couldn't leave us in Grace's living room with the amount of damage to our bodies and say it was an intruder or a fall down the stairs. Oh, no. Not my *wonderful* brothers. They put us on Grace's motorcycle. There was way too much damage to our bodies. The angels had to make it look horrific.

Chapter 38

I gripped at the handlebars tightly as the Harley's engine vibrated and roared beneath us. Grace's thighs were clutched firmly around my hips; her arms wrapped snuggly around my waist. The sun was warm on our backs, the first warm day of an early spring. We zipped down Fifth Avenue, both of us wondering how the hell we got from the living room with Gabriel to the seat of the bike. But, I kind of guessed, and I knew it was going to be bad. So damn bad.

It was nothing more than a dark blur that slammed into the side of us. There was no sound of tires screeching. There was nothing but a loud metal crunch and the pounding of my heartbeat hammering in my ears. My body tore itself over the steel handlebars and I was airborne, hitting the ground with a wet slap and sickening roll. It skidded alongside the blacktop of the street, my leather jacket shredding and dissolving into nothing as it scraped along the ground.

There was no feeling at first, and then the agony thundered through every cell of my body with a vengeance. My limbs shook violently, and I couldn't get enough air into my lungs to breathe. I looked around wildly for Grace, trying to lift my head, but my helmet felt so heavy, I couldn't hold up its weight. Looking up, the sky and buildings above me spun and blurred. Warm thick liquid spread on the pavement under my body, soaking my clothes.

I could hear screams and sirens as if they were on a muted television. Then Michael's form stood above me. Kneeling down next to my shoulder, he laid his hands against my face and turned my head to the side. His touch soothed the fire burning from the pain like a drug. Thick metallic tasting blood poured past my lips, helping to clear my airways and making it easier to breathe. With my head tilted on its side, I could see Raphael in the distance, cradling a limp and broken Grace in his

446

arms as the ambulance arrived and people crowded around. Voices were everywhere, but my heartbeat pounding in my ears drowned them out. "Grace," I tried to call. It came out garbled and wet. "Grace, not even death could keep me from you," I choked out as my world faded to black.

The good thing about the blackness was that when it arrived, taking over and devouring me completely, it also took away the pain. I felt nothing. I just wandered in the darkness waiting until I would see Grace again. There was no sound, no feeling or sense of time. There was nothing, not even a string of thoughts completed; the only thing I could remember of it was just waiting for Grace.

Then the blackness shifted and every so often, I heard a sound or felt a slight pull or tug somewhere on my body. After some time, the sounds and the feelings became more frequent until my body drew itself from its hiding spot and I opened my eyes.

People dressed in scrubs ran to me, their voices monotone and barely understandable. Behind them, through the sea of scrubs across the large expanse of stale hospital air laid Grace. Her eyes were closed, skin battered and bruised; her dark hair matted in clumps against the white of her pillows. My insides rolled and the vomit spurted dark, acidic and pungent from my throat. There were so many damn tubes attached to her, so many tangled and weaving over her body, it made the bile rise again, scorching my esophagus. Thick tubes plunging down her throat to breathe for her, through the veins of her bruised and bandaged arms to hydrate her, tubes that were shoved up her nose and dozens more sneaking and twisting under her blankets. Every one of them straining to keep her alive.

Reaching up, I gripped my hands tightly on the safety rail of my hospital bed and tried to haul myself up. The nurses were frantic, shushing me and shoving me back, but all I wanted to do was hold Grace. I slapped back at the nurses hands. I just wanted to touch Grace, because I needed to know that she was okay. My chest was heaving with the strain of my movements and a low wail passed through my lips. One of the nurses gently ran her hands over my hair, and sighed, "Miss Taylor will be just fine, Mr. Maxton, but you both need to stop trying to kill yourselves by getting out of your beds to be near each other." I looked up into the nurse's golden brown eyes. Her skin was thin and crinkled together with deep wrinkles, but her expression was soft and kind, so I stopped trying to pull myself up, trusting her words. Then the old cow shoved a needle in my arm and the world turned dark once again. *I hate hospitals.* All I wanted to do was whisper in Grace's ear, just to tell her how much I loved her. *Dumb old nurse.*

Road rash shredded the layers of skin off my legs, and almost every bone on the entire right side of my body was broken. My ribs were fractured, splintered and my internal organs punctured. In addition to all of that, my jaw needed to be wired shut while I spent time in and out of consciousness.

Days passed. Weeks went by, and when the tubes and machines were taken from our bodies, our bones were still bruised and aching. But we didn't care. The instant all the tubes were removed, and all that was attached to her was one lonely IV in her hand, Grace crawled out of her bed and into mine. We spent days wrapped around each other, still healing, while our friends visited and the scent of get-well flowers decayed in our noses.

I had no idea how much time had passed when I woke one morning to Grace quietly staring out the window next to our bed, a lone tear streaking down her beautiful face. "Hey, beautiful," I whispered, running one of my bandaged hands along her arm. "What are you thinking about?"

She gently shifted her body and looked up at me, smiling and smoothing her fingers through my hair. "I just keep thinking about everything that was said and how happy I am lying in this horrible hospital bed with you. Makes me wonder where we go from here. I mean, our lives are open unwritten books, so we could do anything together from here, it's just..."

My throat tightened and I had trouble swallowing. I loved this girl so much I had difficulty breathing when around her. I lifted my hand to her face and softly ran my thumb along the bottom of her lips. "I know where I want to go from here," I whispered quietly to her.

Her eyes narrowed and she bit at my thumb, "I swear if you say Boozer's I will break whatever is left not broken on your body right now." The hospital bed shook with our laughter, which kind of freaking hurt like hell, but like everything else with Grace, it was worth all the pain.

I leaned forward and kissed her lips gently, then leaned my forehead to hers. "I want to wake up every day I have left to the warmth of your lips on mine, the sound of your voice singing next to me, the feel of your fingers on my skin and your heart beating music with mine. How about becoming my wife?"

Not even a heartbeat passed before she gave me a breathy, "Oh, hell, yes!" Then her lips were on mine and my hands were slipping under the bed sheets to feel the warmth of her skin. Running my fingertips up her inner thighs, I hooked a finger into her undies and started yanking them down. I didn't given a damn where we were. I hadn't been inside her for weeks and my dick was planning to hold a protest to get back into his favorite place. She even scooted her plump little ass to help me pull them down. That is until throats were cleared and my whole damn family stood in front of us, arms crossed and laughing.

We never get a break. However, a few days after I asked her to marry me, we were released from the hospital and we were finally free to be together. Still bruised and scarred, we locked ourselves in her bedroom with our guitars and didn't come out for days. There were centuries of things we needed to catch up on, and damn, did we.

She found her engagement ring entwined in the strings of her guitar and cried when she realized that I had bought it before everything came to a head with Gabriel. I felt like a dick, not being able to ask her in some epic glorious romantic way, but Grace didn't care. All that mattered to her was that we would be spending the rest of our lives together. As I said before, she's perfect.

Chapter 39

I'm a man, so I don't really think about weddings and crap like that. I was more excited about the marriage than the wedding, but I think our wedding turned out to be pretty freaking awesome. We waited until that Fall, because Grace refused to limp down the aisle. We rented out a small bed and breakfast in the small town of New Hope, Pennsylvania. It was October 18, the leaves on the trees were bright red and orange, and the air was crisp and cool.

I stood outside on the old stone patio in my black monkey suit next to my best men Conner, Ethan and Alex (since I couldn't decide on one) framed in the bright hues of Autumn surrounded by the Delaware Water Gap. Tucker, the douche rocket sat in the first row of seats, arms crossed and looking down at his shoes. *Loser.* Ethan elbowed me in the ribs and nodded in Tuck's direction, "You're breaking his poor heart," he chuckled.

I smiled, laughing back, "Yeah, I guess I am. Since I'm marrying the girl who was supposed to be his first wife, huh?"

Conner almost choked while laughing and Alex gave me a serious grimace, "Are you sure you're ready for this?"

With lightness in my chest, I gave Alex a wink, "I've never been more ready for anything in my life."

Alex shook his head, "You know we could still run, dude. There's time," he whispered with a smile on his face. We all burst out laughing, knowing how untrue his statement was, because I wouldn't run from her for anything. Even the minister who was there to marry us laughed and shook his head.

Then the music started playing, my palms started sweating, and I felt like a little boy in the biggest freaking toy store in the world. Mollie and Lea slowly made their way down the aisle and smiling at me, they stood on the other side of the minister. Gradually, the music changed into a song that made my damn eyes want to tear and I held in my breath so they wouldn't show. Grace wanted walk down the aisle to *Hallelujah* by Rufus Wainwright, the song I had played for her when she was sick. I completely understood, because she was my Hallelujah, after everything, and with every breath I ever took, she was my salvation. She was my fall and she was my saving grace.

Then Grace stepped onto the white carpet sprinkled with red and violet rose petals rolled out before her. My heartbeat raced, drumming wildly in my chest and I bit down hard on my bottom lip. She was beautiful, stunning, exquisite...she just...completely took my breath away. Michael wrapped his arm in hers and they began their walk towards me, and the world around me just melted away and all I saw was Grace. My gaze ran slowly up her flawless body sheathed in her elegant lace dress and then we locked eyes, and I couldn't stop the tears for the life of me. I didn't even want to, so yeah, I cried big wimpy tears on my wedding day; screw it, *she was* my Hallelujah.

Then with a giant smile, Michael kissed her on the head and Grace let go of him. *Next, she surprised me when she literally ran down the aisle to me.* Breathless and smiling, with tears in her eyes that matched mine, *she ran to me.*
Then I married her.

Epilogue

Two Years Later

I have no idea how the two of them planned it so perfectly. They both denied having anything to do with any planning, plotting or scheming of anything remotely to do with the situation we were in, but as I ran through the doors of the emergency room with Conner next to me, both our wives gave each other a knowing smile. *How would it even be possible?*

Grace and Lea waddled in behind us, both exactly forty-one weeks pregnant, in labor, on the same day. It was curiously insane is what it was. However, as curious as I was about how they managed to find themselves in the same exact situation, I couldn't help but be the happiest man ever to walk this earth. I was about to be a dad.

Okay, so my stomach rolled a little bit at that thought and I might have lost all the color in my face. I might even have choked back some vomit at that thought, because I was so damn nervous, but I was so damn happy too.

Grace was having my baby.

Today.

As in right now. This second...I was going to be someone's father. Wow!

I grabbed Conner's arms and shoved him faster through to the maternity floor, both of us nervously giggling like two dumbass schoolboys.

"Hey, Tweedle Dumb and Tweedle Dumber, did you forget something," Lea called out from behind us.

Conner and I froze, and then slowly turned around. The girls were all the way down the hall, grasping onto each other in pain. *Shit.*

We ran back to them and helped them the rest of the way in, while Lea cursed at us and promised to feed us 'a healthy serving of our own penis and peppers when she popped her little blob out.' Whatever the hell that meant.

Then the next thing I knew, Grace was being pulled away from me, dressed in one of those sexy (yes, I'm freaking kidding) hospital gowns and hooked up to those annoying monitors that beep like crazy. Then the sound of my baby's heartbeat filled the room, *slow and weak*, over the small device set to measure the stress of the baby's heart. At that point, all hell broke loose.

Nurses poured in and a doctor rushed up to the side of Grace's bed and explained that an emergency cesarean section was needed, because our unborn child was in distress.

Grace's eyes filled with tears as she looked at me; I had never ever seen her so frightened. "Whatever you need to do to help my baby, do it."

Then I was frantically pushed into a smaller room and had scrubs shoved in my hands, "You're the father, right? If you want to be in the operating room for the birth, you need to wear these..." I couldn't focus on what else the nurse was telling me. My body had broken out in a cold sweat and all I could do was blink my eyes like a fucking idiot. At some point, after the nurse stared at me for a few moments, then proceeded to smack my cheeks lightly, I nodded my head and quickly dressed.

Grabbing me by my arm, the nurse yanked me back through the hallway and propelled me through two doors into a sterile operating room. "Do not touch a thing, Mr. Maxton. Everything in here is sterilized for the safety of your wife and unborn child." I felt a little lightheaded. Okay, a lot lightheaded. I thought I was going to be sick...

With my leg muscles tightening, and my breath bursting strangely from my lungs, I looked all around the room, swallowing back bile. Where was my wife? Did something happen to my wife while I was getting dressed? Where is she? Where. Was. My. Wife?

Then I heard her beautiful nervous laughter as they rolled

her in on a gurney.

"There's the daddy-to-be," one of the nurses chirped. "Your wife here was just laughing and saying that you might be passed out somewhere..."

Rushing over to the gurney, I smoothed my fingers along her cheek, "Everything will be fine, Gray. I'm right here. You know I'll always be right next to you."

"Okay, Daddy-to-be. Move on over to that side so we can put Mommy-to-be up on the table."

They helped Grace to stand and then sit down on the operating table. In my head, everything seemed to get blurry and move in slow motion, then toggle between fast forward, and warp fucking speed. Behind Grace, the nurses were untying her gown, the anesthesiologist inserted a needle right into her spine that made her lips pinch together, and her eyes squeeze shut. My body went numb; *I was going to kill him for hurting her.* Irrational thoughts flooded my brain.

An enormous blue sheet was lifted over her head, blocking our view of the bottom half of her body and she just smiled up at me. *What if something bad happened? I wouldn't live here without her. I wouldn't do this without her.* Fuck me. Do they not realize I'm taller than the damn sheet? The surgeon is slicing her open on my favorite place to lick her skin and my knees began to buckle.

"Look at me, Shane," she whispered.

I tore my eyes from all the blood and found calmness in her silver irises. Grabbing her hand, I held onto her tightly with both my hands. I never wanted to let her go, not now, not ever. We just stared at each other, both of us beyond terrified, until the miraculous sounds of our baby's cries filled the room.

With tears in my eyes, I was handed a perfect little life, wrapped tightly in a pink blanket, with the brightest bluish-gray eyes I had ever seen. "Happy Birthday, Baby Girl!" The nurses yelled.

I held on to her with trembling hands, kissed her wrinkled little forehead, and gently placed her into Grace's arms.

I was in complete awe.

I dropped to my knees. *Thank you God for letting me live this.*

"Hi, little Emma Grace. I'm your mommy, and your big goofy daddy is somewhere on the floor," I heard my wife coo softly. Everything was perfect, so perfect.

They took Emma into the nursery, finished stitching up Grace, and moved her into the recovery room while the nurse escorted me out into the hallway. She told me a whole bunch of crap I didn't listen to, because I just wanted to run through the hospital telling everyone what just happened. I dashed away from the nurse and ran, just ran up to anyone and everyone I saw, and told them my wife just gave me a baby girl. A healthy baby girl. When I rounded the last corner, my feet fumbled underneath me when I thought I saw a familiar face offering me a small smile and a wink, but it couldn't be. *It just couldn't be. It was not going to happen.* The face melted in with the other people in the crowded hallway, but I stood there tense and angry.

Moving forward, I searched more closely into the faces as they stepped onto an open elevator, but I didn't see anyone I was looking for. Restlessness falls over my muscles, and I quickly walked back to the nursery where my daughter was. Behind the huge glass window that kept the newborns safe, the nurses cleaned my daughter and wrapped her sleeping form. I laid my hand on the cool glass, in awe.

"I hear congratulations are in order, Shane." A deep voice came up from behind me. When I turned, I was face to face with a smiling Michael.

"Thank you, Michael. Look at her, she's perfect," I pointed to Emma sleeping in her little plastic hospital bassinet with the giant sign on the front of it that read: EMMA MAXTON.

Sleeping in the bassinet next to her was Conner's daughter, LILY HART. *I still couldn't believe this happened on the same day.*

"Perfect," Michael agreed.

I tilted my head back towards Michael, "I think I just saw our old friend, Michael."

He leaned his back against the wall and slowly placed his bronze hands in his front pockets. He kept his stare straight ahead on my sleeping daughter. There was a long pause before the angel responded with a stoic blank stare. "Evil can never hide itself for too long, Shane. Its ego is too big not to be heard or seen for so long."

We stood in front of the nursery window for a long time, watching Emma and Lily peacefully sleeping. We stood together silently, until the sun shifted itself across the sky outside, until more little bundles were carried in and other families celebrated new life. We stood there, until we felt that we could truly look at one another again, with the knowledge that this story may or may not end here. That this, *that we*, could be touched by evil again.

"I will never let him hurt my family," I said.

Michael slowly leaned forward and pushed himself off the wall. Down the hallway, I could hear the voices of my friends running to meet the babies. Alex and Mollie ran around the corner first, holding hands and about five dozen pink and white balloons. Ethan, Brayden and Tucker followed behind with giant smiles plastered on their faces, each holding two enormous teddy bears each.

Michael clapped his hand on my shoulder and squeezed me gently. "Gabriel may never show his face again. We won't know until he makes his next move." His hand fell to his side and he walked past me towards the exit sign, "Until then, just love them fiercely."

The End

At least until Shane sings to me again...

Come visit my blog at
http://christinezolendz.blogspot.com
Friend me on Facebook or drop an email at
ChristineZolendz@aol.com
Or you can visit me on Goodreads.

Thank you so much for reading!

Made in the USA
Lexington, KY
20 October 2017